EMILY

&

HILDA

JT Hine

To my mother, who bought my first three bicycles
and never asked where I was going.

Acknowledgements

Countless people supported me in writing this book. I am grateful to the readers of my blog, *The Freewheeling Freelancer*, who reacted and commented on the serial version as it came out. I would especially like to thank John Frazee, Vicky Lee, Gary Porter, and Julia Shields for reading the manuscript and providing comments. Kerry Genova of Writers Resource Inc. edited the book, and Kim Olson proofread it.

CONTENTS

Pay It Forward

EMILY SCREAMED. Her eardrums exploded as intense white light surrounded her. She felt herself falling to the left as the bicycle flew out from under her. She tucked and landed on her hip and shoulder.

Blinded and hearing nothing but ringing in her ears, she smelled ozone. The earth felt damp beneath her, cooling the road rash on her side and shoulder. A buzzing sensation on the back of her neck and over her head seemed to push against her helmet.

She felt the pain build in her shoulder and left arm. The darkness after the white light resolved into swirling colors and shapes as her vision returned. Out here in the middle of nowhere, there was nothing to hear, but she thought the ringing was less.

After a few minutes, she blinked and looked around. Her bicycle lay against the bottom of a blackened and smoking oak tree, planted by a farming family long gone. Steam mingled with the smoke from the wet stump. Bits of branches, bark, and wood lay on the ground downwind from the tree.

She got up carefully. Trying to hug herself hurt her arm even worse. The rain that had soaked her had stopped, but the wind was picking up. That rain had also soaked the oak leaves littering the road and caused her crash.

She regretted going out on this training ride alone. Mary and Joanna had both backed out at the last minute. Emily was at least twenty miles from town, and it would be dark in another hour and a half.

She worried about her arm, but she was sure that it was only scraped badly and not broken. Still, her favorite Shebeest bicycle jersey was bloodstained and torn, and her spandex shorts had big holes on the left side. The road rash on her arm and side and the cut on her cheek were clotting.

She was more worried about her bicycle, a three-thousand-dollar Colnago that her stepfather had bought for her birthday four months ago. She had been winning amateur racing events all season and was hoping to win two more races before winter consigned her to the spinning studio at the gym until spring. She shivered and walked over to the bike.

The front wheel looked like a pretzel after hitting the tree when she flew off the pavement on her left side. Lifting it up, she tried to roll it, but the front wheel ran into the fork, and the bike stopped. Her mood shifted from tears to frustration.

It occurred to her that not having a little tool kit under her saddle was probably a bigger oversight than taking the risk of riding alone. She shrugged; she didn't know how to fix anything anyway.

She reached for her cell phone and found the whole pocket missing from her jersey. The cell phone was lying in two pieces on the pavement where she had fallen. She pocketed the pieces and picked up the bike.

At least the Colnago was light. She hefted it on her good shoulder and started walking along the highway. She was hardly an elegant sight, wobbling awkwardly in her cleated, hard plastic racing shoes. She considered going in her socks, but the gravel on the edge of the road was sharp and nasty looking.

With something to do – even if unpleasant – she felt her scrapes less, except maybe for the bruise on her left hip, which was her main shock absorber hitting the pavement. She figured that, at worst, she could make it back to town in three hours, if she could not hitch a ride.

Hitchhiking. Her mother would have a bigger fit over that idea than her riding alone. The lack of any traffic was the main reason that she trained on this highway, which ran to an abandoned army post fifty miles west of town. Her parents would be at the Durstens' party until after midnight, so no one would miss her as she hiked along the deserted road.

After a half hour, she had stopped shivering. She took off her shoes, tied them to the saddle post, and started walking on the pavement. It was not comfortable, but she was moving at a better clip. The bicycle, light as it was, had begun to dig into her shoulder, so the smoother gait helped with that.

Cornfields extended in all directions as the asphalt ribbon seemed to disappear into a yellow tunnel of corn in the distance. She had never really looked at the scenery – or lack of it – before. As the shadows from the stalks spread across the road, she noticed how the fields went from yellow to golden to purple. As the sun began to sink out of sight behind her, the purple fields slowly turned dark. There were still maybe forty-five minutes of light left.

Emily noticed the Evening Star (Venus, she remembered) appear up ahead while there was still plenty of light. Beyond the rustle of the wind, she heard a sound behind her. She shifted as she walked and saw what looked like a small bear with a flashlight in its mouth, weaving back and forth on the road, maybe a quarter mile back. She stopped and squinted.

A bicycle. With panniers. And a dark form sitting almost erect on it.

Emily stared as the bicycle came closer. Bicycle tourists belonged to a different universe, especially the bike-packing variety who often rode through town. Generally unkempt, looking unwashed, with assorted collections of gear lashed to their bicycles and panniers, more like peasants fleeing an invading army than regular people. "As likely to steal supper as buy it," her mother would say as she crossed the street to avoid meeting them. The men never shaved, and the women never had their hair combed. Still, Emily wondered why they always seemed so cheerful, why they always waved when her racing team blew past them.

The sound she heard took form. The bicyclist was singing loudly. She weaved happily as if waltzing to the music, which indeed she was. It wasn't a familiar song, and Emily thought that she had all the hits on her playlists.

It *was* a waltz! The rider was not wearing earbuds but was singing from memory—in German. As the rider approached, Emily could see that she was a strong, black woman. Certainly not a kid, she could be any age from twenty-five to sixty. She was riding a fifty-nine-centimeter frame, which could take a six-foot man. Under her helmet, a smile spread across her face. As she reached the final line of the waltz, the rider leaned back erect and belted out the coda with her arms spread out. Emily guessed that she was rolling at fifteen miles per hour with no hands and four panniers! She grabbed her handlebars and coasted to a stop alongside the stunned Emily. The muscles in her forearms rippled as she braked.

"You know, you got it backwards, girl. It's supposed to carry you, not the other way around." The way she grinned, Emily felt comforted, not put down.

"I crashed, and I'm walking home."

"The next town, I take it."

"Yes. About fifteen miles, I guess."

"Hoo-ey. That's a long hike." She dismounted the bicycle and parked it, supported by a kickstand that would hold up a truck. She smoothly unbuckled and removed her helmet, which she pulled off a long ponytail of shiny black hair. With her angular cheekbones and tall, spare frame, she made Emily think of something awe-inspiring. An Amazon, perhaps.

"Your parents probably don't want you talking to strangers." She put out her hand. "I'm Hilda."

"Emily." She took Hilda's hand and felt her strong, confident grip. She also noticed her crisp, clear accent like the British actors on BBC mysteries. "What brings you here? There's nothing but an abandoned base on that road."

"I know. Which makes it perfect for unmolested camping. The parade ground made a beautiful campsite.

The grills in the picnic areas beat campfires any day, and the water still runs in the toilets. Someone forgot to turn that off, I guess."

"Are you crossing the country like the other bicycle tourists I've seen?"

"Probably. If I am, I'm only halfway there, and who knows what will happen tomorrow?"

"But you're alone!"

"So it would seem. And it would seem that so are you."

"But I live here –up there a ways, anyway." Emily looked to the distant end of the road.

"I assume you aren't walking because you like to carry expensive bicycles in the dark."

"Front wheel hit a tree when I slid off the road. Did you see the leaves back where the oak tree is?"

"I did. Went through there shortly after the rain stopped. I hate leaves. They're worse than snow." Hilda pointed to the bike on Emily's shoulder. "What have you got there? May I look?"

Emily swung the bike off her shoulder. Hilda grabbed it easily, flipped it upside down with one hand, and set it gently on its handlebars and seat.

"Very nice bike. You wouldn't have a spoke wrench, would you?"

"I don't have any tools," Emily said apologetically. "If I did, I wouldn't know what to do with them."

"Probably on one of those sponsored teams with a pro wrench to fix everything."

Emily nodded.

"Long-haul touring bikes usually don't break down *except* in places like this. Maybe I can help."

Hilda considered the front wheel. She went to her bicycle, rooted in the right pannier, and came back with a camping lantern, a flashlight, and a zippered bag.

"Got what you need right here. That wheel may look like a pretzel, but it's perfectly formed for the kind of twist the spokes will give the rim if it's hit just right. The rim isn't broken or cracked." She turned on the lantern. "What the hell, girl. You're a mess!"

"It almost doesn't hurt already."

"But that road rash could get infected. Here, you hold the lantern, so we can see this. I'll be right back."

Hilda went back to her pannier and extracted a first aid kit and a pack of disposable wipes, the large kind that hospitals use to bathe patients.

"Ouch!"

"Sorry, but we need to clean this off. Did you see the bits of asphalt and gravel in your wounds?"

"Is that what it was? I was going to clean up when I got home."

"Too much torn flesh to wait for that. Hold still."

Emily winced a few more times as Hilda cleaned out the wounds and applied second skin to the worst of them. "Your face looks okay, now that it's cleaned off. Just let it heal as is."

With her wounds dressed, Emily felt much better already. Hilda put away her first aid kit and came back.

"Let's look at your steed. Hold that lantern up, and I'll show you what to do."

"Thanks." Emily raised the lantern and watched as Hilda loosened the brake and quick-release lever and removed the wheel.

"This is all we need." Hilda held out a steel ring with square cuts in it. "Spoke wrench. They come in different sizes and only weigh a few grams. This one can handle the three most common spoke nipples. Watch."

She set the wheel on the ground and let some air out of the tire. Then she inserted a square cut around a spoke nipple near the valve and twisted it a quarter turn.

"The spoke nipple is a nut on the threaded end of the spoke, right?"

Emily nodded, although this was news to her.

"Think 'righty-tighty, lefty-loosey.' Can you remember that?"

"Righty-tighty, lefty-loosey. Got it."

"That applies to all right-handed screw threads. On your bicycle, that means every thread *except* your left pedal."

Emily nodded again.

"Here's the catch. Think of where the nut goes on the bolt or, in this case, the threaded end of the spoke. We're looking at the wheel from inside the rim, but the spoke nipple is screwed on the *end* of the spoke, so you look at it from the tire side, not the inside. Make sense?"

"Yes." *This is interesting*, Emily thought.

"So, we loosen the spoke this way. See?"

"It looks backwards from here, but not if I imagine looking through the tire."

"Good. Only loosen a quarter or a half turn at a time, so the pressure comes off the wheel evenly as we work our way around. I like to go to the opposite side of the wheel for each next spoke, but some mechanics just work all the way around. I'm playing it safe here. I got the first six. You try some."

Emily gave Hilda the lantern, then worked her way back and forth around the wheel, loosening spokes a little at a time. Suddenly the wheel jumped out of her hands with a twang.

"Omigod! What was that?"

"The wheel righting itself. Are you okay?"

"Just surprised. What about the wheel?"

"It's probably fine. We managed to loosen it all the way without setting anything wrong permanently. Now we just need to tighten and true it."

"You mean, I can ride it?"

"Not now, but you won't walk home."

Hilda showed Emily how to start tightening the spokes carefully so that they exerted their pressure on the rim evenly. Eventually, the wheel felt hand tight.

"Let's put it in the wheel truing jig," said Hilda.

"You have one of those?" Emily asked, looking at the loaded panniers.

"No. You do. It's called a fork. Here, slip the wheel back onto the bike."

Hilda had Emily check the rolling direction of the tire and tighten the quick-release levers after the wheel was in its fork.

"Now, spin the wheel and see where it rubs or wobbles out of line. Then tighten the opposite spokes to pull it over, a quarter turn of the spoke nipple each time." The two of them took turns until the wheel was not wobbling. Then Hilda checked the roundness by holding a screwdriver near the rim as it spun to see if it bulged out of a circular path. It was almost perfect.

Emily tightened the opposing pairs of spokes needed to pull the rim into round. Hilda pumped up the tire with the long frame pump from her bike.

"I think you can ride home," Hilda said at last. "It's dark. Do you have a light?"

"No." Emily's elation sagged as she considered the empty, dark road. They could not even see the loom of the lights of town from here.

"Here. Let's lash this flashlight to your handlebars. I'll ride on the centerline side in the unlikely event we meet any other vehicles. Besides, that's an emergency roadside job on the wheel. You should get a new wheel before you go out again."

They put their helmets on and set out together. Hilda's 850W Night Rider headlight lit the road comfortably for both of them, riding side by side. Emily told Hilda about her family, her school, and her racing team. She loved riding more than anything. Hilda turned out to be an army brat whose parents met in Germany, where she was born. Her father retired there, and Hilda grew up bilingual as well as bicultural and biracial. "All-American girl, that's me!" she said. She was only riding as far as town to catch the train to Chicago, where a friend would join her for the eastern half of her trek.

An hour later, they coasted to a stop outside Emily's home. Emily untied the flashlight and gave it to Hilda.

"I don't know how to thank you, Hilda. Why don't you stay the night here? I know my folks won't mind."

"I'd love to, Emily, but I already have an e-ticket for the train tonight, and I don't want to miss it."

"But–"

Hilda put her hand on Emily's shoulder and squeezed gently. The hand was warm, strong, and firm.

"It's okay. Just pay it forward. You know what that means?"

"I think. Do someone else a favor?"

"You got it. Give me a hug and go help someone else someday."

After Hilda's brightly flashing taillight disappeared around the corner, Emily realized that she had never gotten her last name or any contact information. She parked her bike in the garage and went upstairs, snagging a protein bar and a carton of orange juice from the kitchen on the way. She took a shower and put her clothes in the trash. She donned a fresh pair of pajamas. Then she fired up her computer and looked up the winter maintenance class schedule at the K-Bikes bicycle shop.

PART ONE

HILDA

1

CHICAGO

H ILDA STEPPED OUT OF THE BLOWING COLD and into the bar. The neon sign in the window boasted Deschutes beer on tap. She had fond memories of Bend, Oregon, a couple of months back, when she toured the brewery before crossing the High Desert. Chicago was a long way from Bend, but she was glad to visit the Windy City again. She paused at the door.

A long bar stretched in an *L* out the wall to the left and across the wall opposite the door. Tables in the space before her, mostly couples. Some looked like dates. Two looked like business meetings. Eight men at the bar, three women. The women were all unattached. That is, one gold digger at the end of the bar, and two probably married to the guys ignoring them to watch the game on the big screen TV. Four free stools, three tables. Back exit to the right by the restroom sign.

Two bartenders; a white woman, late twenties, on the left, and a burly black man with salt-and-pepper hair opposite the door. He gave Hilda a steady appraisal, then suggested the stools to his left by raising an eyebrow and cocking his head slightly. Hilda was already walking toward that spot.

Hilda scanned the room in the mirror behind the bar while the barman drew her pint of Jubelale. The man seated nearest the back exit to her right was checking her out in the mirror. Standing six feet tall, with high, angular cheekbones, a long black ponytail, and a slim, muscular frame from living on her bicycle, Hilda was used to men staring. Her only dress, a black acrylic number that went to bars as easily as the opera, seemed as dark as her skin. She did not need high heels at her height, which was good because the lightweight black shoes she carried in her pannier could go anywhere the dress could.

Hilda finished checking out the other customers at the bar. A large man with a florid face and a massive beer belly two stools to her left. Beyond him, four of his buddies were drinking cans of Budweiser. The rest of the customers were engrossed in each other or the game.

She returned her gaze to the man staring at her. His head was the same distance from the stool as hers, with long black hair combed back and touching his shirt collar. Dark skin, but Moorish rather than African or Indian. She had seen those features everywhere in Spain and among the old Spanish families of California. A small, aquiline nose, more like a hawk than an eagle, sat attractively under eyes that smiled when he grinned at her in the mirror. She smiled back briefly.

"He's new too," the barman said, breaking the mirror contact to place her beer on the bar. "Don't know a thing about him, but he only arrived fifteen minutes ago."

"Thanks."

"No problem, sister." He took out a cloth from his apron and moved away, wiping the bar as he went. Hilda felt safe in this place. It was a rare pleasure simply to walk around the corner from the hostel and find a place to enjoy a quiet beer, knowing that the staff had her back.

She had slept almost the entire way on the Southwest Chief from Kansas. Taking the train was a welcome break from riding US-50 from Sacramento. Hilda liked her own company, but riding "the Loneliest Road in America" had taken solitude to a whole new level. She had seen enough cornfields and prairies. Except for the teenager with a twisted front wheel outside Newton, Kansas, she did not have a conversation from the Nevada-California line to the Amtrak Station last night.

In the mirror, she saw the large man to her left heave himself off his chair and start toward the restrooms, which took him past her stool. Instinctively, she brought her elbows back to her side just before the big hand squeezed her left buttock.

Pushing with her foot, Hilda shoved the barstool around on its bearings. Her left hand, bent in a karate chop, drove into his solar plexus as she slid off the stool, landing squarely on his right foot. With the man pinned by her foot, she planted her right foot next to him, head-butted his nose, and then kneed him in the groin with her right leg. He went down in a heap.

Hilda looked at the four men still sitting, stunned, at the bar.

"Any other would-be Weinsteins here tonight?" They looked away. She reached down and pulled the dazed assailant up. "Go to the john. Your pants are wet."

She could feel the stares as she turned back to the mirror and sat on her stool.

The man to her right had left his stool and was halfway to her place. The barman moved to the end near the restroom, holding a long Louisville Slugger with the ease of a conductor's baton. The large man stopped to turn around, saw the bat, and continued to the exit.

"Very impressive, madam." His accent was Spanish but clear. "I saw him touch you, and left my seat, but you dispatched him so quickly that my help was useless."

"I'm glad that you were so slow. You might have been collateral damage."

"This happens often?"

"No, but I have to treat all moving males as targets until the swinging stops."

"I see. Like I said, very impressive. May I present myself? Diego Cortéz y Goméz."

"Hilda Paisley. *Encantada.*"

"*¡Habla español!*"

"Just enough to order supper or get in trouble, *lo siento.*" Sorry.

"In any case, I already wanted an excuse to approach you before the encounter with that boor."

"I had not planned on being the entertainment tonight." She caught the eye of the barman, who signaled his approval with a tip of the head. "Just happened to recognize the Deschutes label and felt like having a beer."

"Then let me buy you another."

"I haven't finished this one. Let's discuss it if I do. What brings you in here?"

"Almost the same. I wanted to sit in a corner with a beer and observe the people. You brew great beers in America, and people-watching is our national pastime."

"With your name, please don't be from California."

Diego laughed. "No, Spain, but we were from California and Mexico also. My great-great-grandfather returned to Medellin after we lost California to the US. We have relatives throughout the Southwest."

"So why Chicago?"

"To meet a friend tomorrow. We are planning to ride US-66 to Los Angeles."

"Ride? Bicycle or motorcycle?"

"Bicycle."

"What a coincidence. I rode that route last year. I hope you like riding on the shoulder of Interstate 40 because much of US Bicycle Route 66 is on the interstate. It's like riding around Los Angeles."

"I'm sorry to hear that but amazed and pleased that you have ridden it. We have read so much about the new US Bicycle Route, that we thought it would be fun."

"It might be more fun with someone to share the trip, but I usually ride alone. And on that road, even I was wishing I had someone to complain to."

Diego chuckled. "Please have lunch with us tomorrow. I will call Cristina and let her know. She will want to meet you."

"I'm free tomorrow. When and where?"

"Give me a moment." Diego pulled out his cell phone and speed-dialed. Hilda could follow enough of the elegant Castilian to know that Cristina would be pleased and that he suggested the restaurant at their hotel.

"She's delighted. So, tomorrow at noon?"

"Which hotel is yours?"

Diego winked. "You understand more Spanish than you let on. The Sheraton."

"That's not far. They let me park my bike in the luggage room."

"Are you from Chicago?"

"No, but I've been here often enough to have stayed in several places downtown."

"I have never met someone else who rides a bicycle on long tours but stays in hotels."

"Believe me, I usually camp, and I prefer HI Hostels in big cities. That keeps the cash in the bank for the times when I feel like being pampered."

"This is our first bicycle tour in America. We studied the accommodations situation, so we know that we will have to camp. We have been doing that on short tours in Europe, but I know it will be different here."

"It will be. Let's chat about that too. I've camped in Europe, so maybe I can point out some important differences. In fact, I can show you my route and tell you what I think of the places where I stopped. It might suit your track in reverse."

"That would be wonderful. Thank you so much." Diego looked at his watch. "I need to go back and get ready. Cristina will arrive at O'Hare from Boston in the morning, and I want to be there early."

"Remember, it'll take her almost an hour to get out after the scheduled landing time."

"Oh, yes. Thank you." He waved to the barman for his bill and pointed to Hilda's glass.

"Diego, you're buying lunch tomorrow, right?"

"Of course."

"Then don't buy my beer tonight. See you at noon." She extended her hand. Diego took it to his lips, then put a large tip on the counter before he left. Hilda could swear he was either skipping or dancing. The man was seriously delighted. It made her feel good.

CR CR CR

The next day brought bright sun, moderate temperatures, and a gentle breeze. Hilda had breakfast in the cafeteria of the hostel, sharing a table with a couple who had come to the city for a conference of emergency medical technicians and a scholar researching immigrant histories. Her mind invigorated by the interesting conversation, she took her bike out for a fast ride on the Lake Front Trail. The south wind blew her back in plenty of time to shower and change into a blouse and skirt. She decided to walk to the Sheraton. Along the way, she noted that the Fine Arts Museum had a special exhibit on Native American artists. She might try to catch that after Jack arrived tomorrow afternoon.

Entering the restaurant, she paused out of habit to scan the crowd and note the exits. She spotted Diego by the window with a poster model for Scandinavian

Airlines—tall, slim, blonde, blue eyes. She wore a blue skirt and white blouse, with a blue scarf that brought out her eyes.

Diego rose as Hilda approached the table. He kissed her hand again and turned to introduce his friend.

Cristina Halvorsen's handshake was stronger than Hilda expected. Her smiling eyes were at a height with Hilda's own. Her English carried that clean, clear enunciation of a Continental European who spends more time speaking English than her native language. As they sat and took up their menus, Hilda learned that Cristina's father was Danish, her mother Spanish. She worked in Boston and Frankfurt as a financial analyst. She met Diego while riding the *Camino de Santiago* last summer.

"So how do you keep up your bicycling during the year?" Hilda asked after the waiter took their orders.

"Besides commuting to the office," said Diego, "I ride with a club on the weekends." He looked at Cristina.

"I keep a bike in Boston and in Frankfurt, so I don't need a car when I am in either place. I take short tours on the weekends, like along the Main and the Rhine. On a long weekend, I might take a train to Trier and ride down the Mosel River."

"And I go up to Santander when she comes home to see her parents."

"There's good cycling in Europe, I know," said Hilda. "Has either of you ridden in the US much?"

"Just around Boston," said Cristina, "and as far as Kittery, Maine, using the MTA to Newburyport."

"Nothing yet," said Diego.

"Anything hillier than the *Camino*?" Hilda asked. Cristina shook her head.

"The Estremadura around Medellin is more challenging than the *Camino*," said Diego, "but none of the climbs are as high as the mountains here."

"Well, going west from here, you'll cross the Rockies and the Sierras, but you will find that the gradients are easy compared to the *Camino*. Never more than seven percent. Just uphill all day."

Just then, Hilda heard a familiar popping sound outside the restaurant, coming from the hotel entrance lobby. She rose to her feet and pulled the table away from Cristina and Diego just as the glass doors of the restaurant shattered in. As the first screams reached her ears, she reached for Diego's right shoulder; Cristina caught her eye and reached for his left. Before the glass finished hitting the floor, both women were down on top of him.

Hilda rolled away to free the couple.

"That way." She indicated the kitchen, which was the closest door to them. "Now!"

They ran crouching to the doors, pushing them open as they heard shots coming from the lobby and zinging into the restaurant. With Hilda in the lead, they raced to the back of the kitchen, past the stunned staff to the back doors. These led to the service passageway, which Hilda recognized as connecting with the emergency exits from the stairwells. She stopped at the emergency exit and opened it carefully. An alarm began to sound, but by then, there were alarms pealing everywhere. The driveway to the parking garage seemed clear. Diego and Cristina followed her toward the street.

At the corner, she looked left and saw smoke coming from the hotel entrance. Several people were lying immobile on the street outside, and one car was a melted hunk. The sound of sirens reached them from Columbus Drive.

"This way." She pointed to the right. "Let's go where it's safe." They ran down Water, past New Street, and turned the corner at McClurg. There, they stopped to catch their breath.

"Shouldn't we go back to help?" asked Cristina.

"Not now. You heard the sirens. With an active shooter, the first thing to do is to flee."

"That doesn't seem right, running away," said Diego.

"We're not running. We're surviving the shooting phase. We'll have more than we can handle after that stops."

By the time the first police cars arrived, the smoke had blown away, but there were still occasional pops of gunfire. A SWAT team arrived and ran into the building. Suddenly, it was quiet, except for the moans of the wounded.

"Now we can help. How's your first aid?"

Diego said, "Some training in the army, but I never had to use it."

"I can help get things," said Cristina. "What about you?"

"Army nurse. Not my first combat scene. Let's go."

They jogged over to the hotel entrance. The police cordon immediately closed ranks, but when Hilda explained that she was a triage nurse and that her companions could help, they let her in.

The rest of the day unfolded in a familiar fog, which was recorded on the world media. The lobby was a melted, twisted mess from the car bomb, which had been detonated just before a band of four men ran into the hotel with automatic assault weapons. By the time the SWAT team had gunned down all four, they had killed about three dozen people and wounded maybe fifty more. Being lunchtime, the restaurant and the coffee shop were full, and a tour from Germany and France was assembling to board the blackened bus sitting next to the bombed car.

Hilda and her little team made their way through the lobby, checking for survivors among the bodies. They found six, but two were too badly hurt to be moved.

By the time the paramedics arrived, Hilda and a doctor who had come down from his hotel room had organized a makeshift triage station in the coffee shop. They pointed out the wounded to the ambulance crews in order. Diego and Cristina found themselves in the strange position of calming irate hotel guests who could not understand why they were not being transported first. Half of the wounded were not English-speaking; it was good that they could handle most European languages between them.

Suddenly, they found themselves sitting on a blackened bench in the coffee shop, watching the crime scene technicians work. All the wounded were gone, and the dead were being photographed, outlined in chalk, and bagged to be carried out. Hilda checked her watch. It was four o'clock. Had they really been there that long?

The familiar exhaustion after the adrenaline rush overtook them just as a pair of Chicago Police Department detectives approached. Hilda rose and met them. After introductions, they answered questions and promised to come by the precinct at ten o'clock the next day for detailed witness statements.

The two detectives were interrupted by a team of FBI agents. The law enforcement types huddled in a discussion, ignoring Hilda and her friends.

"I think we can go," said Hilda. "Let's see if your room is habitable. I want to go back to the hostel, but not until I'm sure you're okay."

"Why so fast?" asked Diego.

"Because when they stop chatting about who's in charge, one of them will remember that they have not taken your passports. But by tomorrow, you will have proven that you're not flight risks."

Diego nodded his understanding and led them up to his room. The elevators were not working, but the lights came on as they climbed to the fifth floor. The key worked, and the door opened. Inside, they turned their attention to their cell phones, which they had turned off when the constant dinging started. Each had hundreds of messages, so they used Facebook to let most of their contacts know that they were safe, and they sent emails to their respective parents. That done, Hilda suggested that Cristina and Diego wait until most of the police cars, which they could see from the balcony, departed before venturing out for supper. Obviously, the hotel would not be serving meals that night.

They made a date for nine the next morning, and Hilda took her leave. She made her way down the stairs, unsure if the elevators would be reliable, and used a side entrance to Columbus Drive.

As she fixed her supper in the hostel kitchen, she realized that they had never had a chance to talk about their bicycle touring. She had no idea when the police (and maybe the FBI and ATF) would finish with them. She pulled out her cell phone and hit speed dial.

"Jack, are you still planning on arriving tomorrow?"

"Yes, but it will be evening, I think. This south wind slowed me down, and I'm only in Milwaukee. I plan to leave before dawn tomorrow. There are some monster hills south of Milwaukee."

"Tell you what. Take it easy. Stop in Kenosha or Waukegan and come in the next day. I'll be busy all day tomorrow."

"You okay?"

"Yes, but I'm a witness to the Sheraton attack, so the police want to interview me. I'm staying at the HI Hostel, and I'll keep you informed." She heard the silence as Jack digested the news.

"How close a witness?"

"Close enough. I'll tell you all about it when I see you the day after tomorrow."

"All right. Be safe."

"You too. It's dangerous out there." She ended the call and turned her attention to the pasta sauce.

2

INDIANA

"C'MON, EAT UP. I want to get out of town this morning." Hilda looked down at Jack as he wolfed his oatmeal, and she cleared her place.

"Jeez, Hilda. What's the rush?"

"I want to be deep in Indiana before Detective Hanson or his sidekick wishes they could ask me something else."

"They said you could go, didn't they?"

"Says the MP investigator who never needed additional information to clarify something that came up."

"Oh, I see what you mean."

"Besides, it's a Federal case, and the FBI and ATF can talk to me anywhere along the route they want to. They have my phone number and email address."

Jack rose and cleared his place. They did the dishes in silence, then took the elevator up to their mixed dorm room. Twenty minutes later, they turned in their keys and went to the bicycle and luggage room. Ten minutes after that, they were speeding down Lake Shore Drive. The wind had come around to the north and pushed them toward US Bicycle Route 36 at a brisk twenty miles per hour. The air was cooler. Fall was on its way. Hilda was glad that they were headed generally southeast; two years before, she had ridden directly into a blizzard here on Halloween.

At nine thirty, they crossed the Indiana line in Calumet City. They stopped for lunch in Crown Point, at a picnic bench in Sauerman Woods Park.

Jack speared an olive from its plastic container. "You never told me how it went at police headquarters. How were your new friends, Diego and Cristina?"

"Okay, I guess." Hilda took a bite of her sandwich, prosciutto and gruyère on a baguette, and chewed slowly. Jack was a patient listener, by disposition, and by training. "Cristina had never been to a police station before, and they were both more than a little apprehensive. I'm glad I went over early and escorted them."

"All they know is the Spanish police. No one wants to have a conversation with the *Guardia Civil.*"

"You have the picture. Anyway, the two Chicago detectives were very gentle with them and backed up my reassurance that they weren't suspects. Frankly, Hanson and the other guy—"

"You said Schmidt yesterday."

"Right, Schmidt. Anyway, by the time we arrived, the media had made heroes of them both for coming back to help after getting away safely. As far as I know, no one else got out of the restaurant unharmed. We recounted all the information we could, and they let us go."

"But the Feds—"

"Were waiting for us. They wanted their own interview, but after having Diego and Cristina repeat everything, they were satisfied that they couldn't add anything to the investigation. An agent took them back to the hotel in one of their black sedans."

"Why'd they keep you all day?"

"Why do you think? Combat army. Triage nurse. The ATF guys almost peed their pants when I could confirm the order in which the gunfire and the explosion occurred and the distinctive sound of the bomb. They could not have made sense of the unfolding of the attack so quickly otherwise. The car bomb was the most powerful any of them had ever seen, but it was about like the IED's you and I saw in Baghdad. That gave them a lead that they went off on."

"Brava. I'm surprised you were let go at all."

"I was almost late for my meeting with Diego and Cristina in the afternoon. The police didn't have any reason to hold me. I made Hanson and the FBI guy—Norman—test my cell number right there in the office. They can reach me if anything comes up."

"You'll have to go back if they ever catch anyone to try."

"Yeah, but by then, I'll be retired. Again."

Jack chuckled. "So, what's this gig in Virginia?"

"A hospital in Charlottesville likes my résumé. They have a pending maternity leave in the ER. Right down my alley. The city has two top-100 hospitals, so I can stay as long as I want."

"I've been there. Nice place. Have you?"

"I passed through when I rode the TransAmerica Trail. Very pretty. It seems like a peaceful place too."

"When do you start?"

"Not till after the New Year, so there's plenty of time for us to ride there. If you want to come along, that is."

"Of course. Any plans for Thanksgiving or Christmas?"

"Not yet. You?"

"Well, since we're heading that way, I was thinking of dropping in on my brother Joe near Baltimore. They have a big place on the Chesapeake Bay, with a guesthouse. They've been bugging me forever to come stay for a while. Interested?"

"Are they cool with me?"

"Absolutely. Joe's quite taken with you, actually. He's wanted to meet you ever since I told him about meeting you in Iraq."

"And his wife. Linda, is it? I remember you're saying she's British."

"Yes, but the family is originally from Egypt. She's a dual citizen and grew up in Kenya of all places."

"Sounds interesting. If they still want to see us, let's do it. We can get there by Thanksgiving, even stopping in Indianapolis and Columbus."

"And Pittsburgh. You said you wanted to ride the Great Allegheny Passage."

"Absolutely."

Jack composed an email to his brother while Hilda collected their trash and put it in the recycle bins.

ଔ ଔ ଔ

If ever there was a place for smooth roads and tailwinds, it was Indiana with a northwesterly breeze (if you were heading southeast). Long, straight, lightly traveled roads saw them speeding through the cornfields and soybeans. Although the autumn air was cool, they both were sweating by the time they stopped at a farmhouse on the Kankakee River near Wilders. Hilda had arranged to stay with a Warmshowers host, who, luckily, was flexible about arrival changes when she was detained in Chicago. They had a shower and joined their host, Frederick, in the kitchen to prepare supper. Fred was in his fifties, lean, wiry, and tanned. A pair of reading glasses stuck out of the pocket of his flannel shirt.

As often is the case with Warmshowers, it was a simple meal. They could smell a multitude of spices in the humid air. Fred motioned to a cutting board with a knife, and a bowl with a grater on the kitchen counter.

"We're having what I was planning to make for myself," he said. "Today is chili day. I make it up in the Crock-Pot and freeze containers for future meals, so having guests tonight is no problem. All you have to do is grate the cheese and chop some parsley while I set the table."

Fred called himself a "retired Federal worker," but it was clear from the conversation over dinner that he had worked all over the world. Jack had to ask them to slow down when Hilda and Fred got into an excited exchange in German.

"He lived two blocks from our house in Kaiserslautern!" Hilda told him.

"Yeah, but about ten years earlier," said Fred. "That was before the posting to Bahrain."

"Then you probably speak Arabic too," said Jack.

"It's a little rusty, considering where I live now." Then he switched to Arabic to tell them where he lived in Manama.

"This is so cool, to stay with someone who knows places I've been," said Hilda. "What brought you here?"

"My wife was from Wilders, so when I retired, we came here. Her parents were getting on—mine were gone already—and, after all, she had followed me all over the world for thirty years, so it seemed fair. After they died, Margie and I did a lot of traveling, so living here did not drive us nuts. And we enjoyed being Warmshowers hosts. The company is always different and interesting."

"And now?"

"Well, she died only last year, so it's too early for me to make any major changes. I really enjoy having bicyclists like you coming through, so I'm inclined to stay here, but I'm still trying to discern what I should do."

There was a pause, which Jack ended. "Sorry about your wife."

"Thanks. We had time to grieve together before she died, and it was very peaceful at the end. Considering that we all have to go someday, we should pray to be so lucky as to go the way she did." He smiled and reached for the chili pot. "Seconds? I know you burned off more than one bowl riding all the way from Chicago."

They all dug into another helping of the spicy chili.

Fred had Wi-Fi throughout the house and a private guest room upstairs. It was as cozy and luxurious as either of them had ever seen.

"How'd you luck into this?" Jack asked.

"Random draw. I remember one couple in Gary, who were renovating their house, and everything was stored in the second bedroom. I slept on the floor with scrap lumber and boxes of belongings teetering over me."

"I mostly camp in people's backyards with Warmshowers. I think I've been indoors twice."

"Yeah, this is nice." Hilda pulled her small tablet computer from her pannier.

Jack had one too. "Let's check on the world while we have a connection."

Both devices began dinging furiously when they booted up. Mostly news feeds about the events in Chicago.

"Omigod!" Hilda exclaimed. "The FBI has arrested a half-dozen people already. No one had even claimed responsibility before the first two were caught."

"That's very fast work. But it figures. Only a handful of groups could've assembled a bomb like that and coordinated it with an assault. Any names yet?"

"No—wait! Here's an article about Abu Namr and the Forebears of the Mahdi."

"Uh-oh. We ran across them in Iraq. Nasty bunch."

"They must have been working on this for years. It's not easy for a radical group to organize in the US like that. One-off converts, yes, but to plan, recruit and train a team, and assemble materials for that kind of operation?"

"I'm glad we're past that." Jack opened his email, deleted most of them, and went back to the *Chicago Tribune* website. "Looks like you're famous, Hilda." His face was serious. He swung the screen around to show her a full picture of her coming out of FBI headquarters. "An anonymous source credits you with the information that led to the speedy arrests."

"Oh, shit. That's just what I *don't* need! I might as well ride with a target on my back."

"No good deed goes unpunished. On one hand, we know that the Forebears will certainly be looking for you. On the other hand, there's no mention of where you are, or how you get around. It'll take them a while to find us. You can drop off the internet and set up a new identity while we ride east. I'll do all the bookings and other contacts because it seems that they don't know about me yet."

Hilda's shoulders slumped. "This is a nightmare. I spent years looking over my shoulder in Afghanistan and Iraq. I shouldn't have to live like this here."

Jack took her hand and held it silently for a while.

"For starters, let me see what they can find out easily." He started by Googling her name, checking on Facebook, LinkedIn, and other social media. He searched in military and public databases. "You keep a pretty low profile. Only a Facebook account, and nothing in Google. I see that you don't post anything either. It's all stuff from friends on your timeline."

"It's been like that for years. I got tired of the weirdos."

"You don't have much of a profile, either. No hometown, no relatives, no photos. Just a dozen friends. That's good."

"I'll unfriend them and hope that the bad guys have not made the connections to them already." She began tapping on her keyboard, surfing through her contacts. "Done."

"Deleted the account?"

"Yes."

"I'd email each of them right away about the situation and tell them to be wary of anyone trying to ask about your whereabouts, even people you both know. Ask them not to give out that you ride a bicycle, or where you've been. I'd tell anyone who knows that you're going to Charlottesville that the job fell through and that you'll let them know where you end up next."

An hour later, Hilda and Jack had done all they reasonably could to erase Hilda's presence on the internet. They knew it was only a matter of time before the Forebears accessed her service record (knowing that she had been an army nurse) and tracked her down to the hospitals where she had worked. Her last hospital knew about Charlottesville. Hopefully, they could ride under the radar long enough to come up with a better plan.

Sleep was a long time coming, despite the long ride that day. Jack did not talk, but she knew that he was thinking far ahead as they lay there. His strong, hard body was a comfort, but more than that, she knew that together, they had a good chance of out-thinking whoever might come after them. And, barring that, maybe outfight them. This time, she was glad not to be riding alone.

Slowly, she relaxed with her back up against him. They drifted off to sleep at about the same time.

CB CB CB

Jack ended the call and slipped the phone back into its holder on his handlebars.

"Done. We have a room on the west bank of the White River, across from downtown."

Hilda shoved their trash into the recycle bin. "Expensive?"

"More than the only hostel in town, but not much more. The main thing is that we don't have to worry about where to stay, and the motel desk will be open."

The ride from Prophetstown State Park had taken longer than expected, and they still had at least two hours of riding from Lebanon to Indianapolis. With the days getting shorter, they would arrive just after sundown. Hilda turned on her phone to see if there were any calls or emails waiting. She did this as they were about to leave a place so that they would not be there if anyone were looking for her phone.

"Uh-oh," she said. "Three calls from the FBI Field Office in Chicago, all in the last hour."

"Show me the number and use my phone." Hilda showed him her screen and powered down her phone. She took Jack's phone as it was ringing.

"Federal Bureau of Investigation, Chicago Field Office. How may I direct your call?"

"This is Hilda Paisley. I have three calls in my mailbox from you."

"One moment, please."

Hilda sighed, expecting the usual long wait while the receptionist looked for whoever wanted to speak to her. A male voice surprised her in less than ten seconds.

"Miss Paisley?"

"Yes."

"This is Special Agent Norman. My partner and I interviewed you the other day."

"I remember. What can I do for you?"

"It's what we can do for you, Miss Paisley."

"Hilda, please. You're Mike, right?"

"That's right, Miss—Hilda. Anyway, I'm afraid I have some bad news for you."

"Related to the six arrests I saw on the news?"

"We have intelligence that a terrorist organization may be targeting you."

"Let me guess. The Forebears of the Mahdi."

"That's classified! How'd you know that?"

"The *Chicago Tribune.* Page one, the day after I left town."

"Oh." Hilda could hear his embarrassment. "Why aren't you answering your phone?"

"Because of that photo and the report of my involvement leading to the arrests. Let me guess again. The Forebears have a contract out on me."

"Something like that. It's called a *fatwa.*"

"Great. That's worse."

"We've been looking for you since we got the intelligence this morning, to arrange protection."

"Do you know where I am?"

"Not yet."

"Good. Please give me a cell phone number where I can call you to check in. I'm sure that the field office is tapped."

"That's impossible!"

"Please, Mike, you know better." She let the silence linger. Agent Norman gave her his cell number. "Thanks, Mike. I'll call you when I get into town tonight."

"Where—"

Hilda turned off the phone.

"Sorry about that, Jack." She briefed him on the call as he returned his phone to its holder.

"I'll leave the phone off until we need it next."

Thanks to an easy downhill on the Lafayette Road bike trail, they pulled up outside the motel while the sun was still an angry ball behind the building. They could see a supermarket across the street, and a family-style restaurant next to that. Good location for a couple of days in the big city.

After checking in and arranging to lock their bikes in the motel storage room, Hilda considered calling Agent Norman back.

"I'm wondering whether to use your phone again, the motel phone, or a pay phone," she said.

"I have an idea." Jack pulled his wallet from his pannier and dug out a plastic card. "Use my AT&T calling card. I haven't used it since I got a smartphone, but the account is still active. It's only a penny a minute nationwide."

"Thanks." She took the card and walked to the lobby. This place was cheap enough to have guests who still used pay phones. She called Agent Norman's cell number.

"Hello, Mike. We're here, and I don't think that this phone is on anyone's radar."

"M—Hilda, why'd you hang up on me?"

"It should be obvious. I have to stay off the grid until I'm no longer interesting. With a *fatwa* on me, that could take a while. I may be here for a couple of days."

"What's a *fatwa*?"

"Think of it as a kind of religious curse. Any believer who kills me gets max brownie points. Maybe even a go-straight-to-Paradise ticket. Even better than plenary indulgences in the Catholic Church."

"No money involved?"

"Not directly. In addition to the professionals and the jihadi, I'll have the one-off crazies looking for me."

"Where are you now?"

"Come on, Mike. My safety depends on not being found. I'll check in with you regularly, so you'll know that I'm keeping in touch."

"Hilda, this is crazy. I didn't know you were so paranoid."

"Ever dealt with the Forebears, Mike?"

"No."

"I've treated their victims and dodged more than one of their bullets already. But none were as personal as this. Trust me, I'm not paranoid. If you can tell me where I am when I check in, I'll know that they'll probably find me soon. Then we can discuss protection."

She hung up. Twenty-five seconds. With Norman on a

cell phone, and her on a landline, they probably could not run an interstate trace in that time.

"Aren't you being a little rough on him?" Jack asked as she turned away from the phone.

"Maybe, but I feel safer out here with you than in any kind of protection program—until this won't work, of course."

"I mean the way you talk to him. From what you told me about him, he can't be many months out of the Academy."

"Actually, he's relatively senior, but he's never been posted outside the Midwest. He doesn't understand what we're up against."

"Why the first names?"

"Guys like that lean on their titles like some doctors. This keeps the conversation at eye level. I know he's uncomfortable, but there's not a thing he can do about it. And I have to keep the conversation short, so I can't make nice talk before I hang up."

"It just sounds like you're antagonizing him."

"I might be, but I don't think that it'll be a problem. During the interviews, he got used to the first names and seemed to enjoy the less formal atmosphere. After I check in a couple more times, he'll know that I won't disappear on him."

Jack and Hilda walked across the street to buy breakfast to have in the room—muesli, yogurt, and a pint of raspberries. They split a half-gallon of orange juice in the room to replenish their body fluids. Then they showered, changed, and walked to the restaurant for supper. It turned out that a local Greek couple owned it. The other patrons were having pizza, but

Hilda had *moussaka* while Jack ordered a *souvlaki* plate. That pleased the owner so much that he brought out a complimentary glass of red *aresinato* wine for them. The leisurely dinner, chatting with the owner and his wife, did much to ease the tension Hilda was feeling about her situation.

"So, where to in the big city?" Jack asked as they sipped the last of their wine and drank water. "You were talking about the zoo and the Museum of Art."

"Let's do both. There's a bike trail that passes right in front of the zoo and the museum."

"That's convenient."

After dinner, they walked down to the river.

"It's hard to make a river scenic running through a big city," said Hilda.

"I agree. But this city has parkland on both banks for most of the river. At least it's not all concrete and steel."

They found an empty bench. Jack put his arm around Hilda's shoulders, and she snuggled in. It was noticeably colder now that the sun had set for a while.

"Let's enjoy Indianapolis," she said. "I'm afraid that as soon as I need to draw some cash from an ATM, the Feds will locate me. I never mentioned that I was on a bike, but it shouldn't take them long to figure that out and draw a radius of our max travel."

"We could throw them some curves." Jack wiggled his eyebrows, then grinned. Hilda smiled at his boyish enthusiasm.

"How can a guy who's been through what you have act like this is a game?"

"It's that, or let depression and PTSD take over."

"Good point. What kind of curves?"

"We could get on a train or a Greyhound and leapfrog north or south of here. Norman knows we're going east. I'll bet they'll check airports and rental cars before they think of Amtrak or the bus."

"Step it up. We ride to a small stop on the line we want and get on there. I make a withdrawal in a big town, but we get on a train the same day and go in a completely different direction."

"Getting off in a small town again."

They walked back to the hotel and checked Amtrak and Greyhound routes. Jack got tickets to the zoo and the museum before they turned in.

3

MARYLAND

J ACK SHOUTED, "Let's stop at the next place with some cover." Hilda pointed to an abandoned gas station on the road running next to the bike trail. They pulled in and leaned their bikes against the columns holding up the roof.

Jack found a stick and cleaned out the thickest mud between his tires and the fenders. The rain was not particularly heavy, but after four hours, the Great Allegheny Passage (GAP) Trail was becoming difficult.

"You know," said Hilda, "if this rain continues, we'll have to get back on the highway."

"It turns into asphalt in Maryland. We could reach Cumberland by tonight."

"Good. I'm looking forward to a real bed and dry sheets."

They sat on the platform where the fuel pumps had been and ate some nuts and dried fruit.

"Do you need an ATM yet?" asked Jack.

"Maybe, but we've done so well so far. With just the daily phone calls from both cell phones and landlines, I can't imagine that the FBI has been able to interpolate our track yet. He keeps guessing, but the closest he has come is 'somewhere in Indiana' the last time I used my cell phone."

"That was brilliant, remembering your college friend on a farm outside Jackson. That was way off the grid. Indianapolis, Cincinnati, and Dayton were fun."

"Yeah, she was wonderful—especially driving us to Columbus in her truck. I enjoyed the ride to Pittsburgh from there."

"You always did like the steep hills more than I." Jack grinned. "But I like the view when you take off like that."

Hilda gave him a friendly punch on the arm. "The view's not bad when you're pacing me on the flats, man." She checked her watch. "Let's check in with Norman for today. Then we can spend the night in a different state." She powered up the phone. FBI Agent Mike Norman was at his desk. He brought her up to date on the search for them and for the Forebears of the Mahdi. She turned off her phone in less than a minute.

"He's getting pretty good at that, isn't he?" Jack said.

"He's okay with it. He knows I'll check in every day, so he seems happy that we're under the radar. Besides, the office has so much else to do, that I don't imagine they think much of us between calls. They're probably more worried about other Forebears and possible future attacks."

"No need to hit the ATM in Cumberland if you want to keep riding. This trip isn't costing much, and I'm okay paying for both of us."

"I want to pay you back, but let's take it a day at a time. We're far enough east that we have lots of options for jumping on trains or buses and getting far from the ATM before the alarm bells go off."

The rain was a noisome drizzle when they mounted up and rode back onto the trail. If anything, the cold was becoming more of a bother than the rain. An hour after passing through Meyersdale, Pennsylvania, they hit asphalt outside Frostburg, Maryland. The climb to the college town kept them both warm, then it was downhill among the evergreens to Cumberland. The rain stopped on the way down. By sundown, they were checking into a cozy B and B in the city center, which catered to cyclists. They unpacked, showered, changed, and washed out their kits from the muddy day's ride. When the laundry was hung in the bathroom, they went out in search of supper. Their host recommended an Italian restaurant nearby, which did not disappoint.

As they sipped their wine between the pasta and the veal course, they both felt a warm sense of pleasure. Could there be anything better than being on the road with a friend, with good food and a cozy place to sleep? They spent a long time just looking at each other, smiling. Jack broke the trance.

"Thanksgiving is next week. We told Joe we would be there Tuesday, give or take a day."

"It's not supposed to rain for the rest of the week. I think we could ride the C&O Canal all the way to DC. It's only three days, taking it easy. Then what?"

"If you want to hit an ATM in DC, we can do that. Taking the bike route on US-40 to Joe's house in Aberdeen, we'd be there the same day."

"Do you think we should brief him on our problem before we arrive?"

"Yes, but I don't know how much." He asked her opinion with raised eyebrows.

"He's retired army. He doesn't need much. If you tell him that we need for no one to know that I'm there, he won't slip up. Promise to brief him when we get there."

"That should do it. I'll call after supper."

The *scaloppine alla marsala* arrived. Conversation paused while they savored the wine sauce and the soft white meat.

After dinner, they took a walk to a café on the Potomac River, then back to the guesthouse.

ଓ ଓ ଓ

The next day dawned with the promise of brilliant sunshine and unseasonably warm temperatures, which in November meant comfortable. The hosts fixed a big breakfast and sent them on their way by nine o'clock. The Chesapeake and Ohio Canal Towpath was familiar to them both from past rides before they met. The surface was still muddy from the day before, especially in the shade, but they were able to maintain a decent pace all the way.

They camped at Fort Frederick the first night and near Harper's Ferry the second night. They had both visited the attractions before (John Brown's house, the Armory, the 1756 Fort Frederick), so they packed up each morning and hit the road. Hilda called Agent Norman from a pay phone each afternoon. They checked into the HI Washington Hostel by sundown on the third day.

Over breakfast in the hostel dining room, Hilda considered what to do next.

"I don't think I'll hit the ATM unless Norman figures out where we are, or at least guesses that we're biking. Then they'll have something to go on. Or, of course, if we get suspicious about our surroundings. I don't feel comfortable in this city. It's a magnet for the people we're dodging."

"I agree. Let's set out for Aberdeen today. Once we get there, we can make a better plan."

"My old CO is at the Proving Ground. It'll be good to see her. Do you think we could set up a secure phone call? I'm sure Mike Norman would appreciate a long conversation."

"Great idea. I know the provost marshal. Let's go."

They packed after breakfast and soon were riding to Baltimore. Most of the roads had bike lanes, and there were long stretches of separate bike paths. They were past Baltimore by early afternoon. They ate lunch at a picnic table near Herring Run. Hilda decided to call Norman just before leaving Baltimore.

Jack watched as Hilda's expression darkened.

"You're partly right, Mike. I'm with friends, but no, I'm not telling who. I'll call later." She powered down the phone and looked up at Jack.

"They finally thought to check the HI Hostel in Chicago and found out that I had a bicycle there. So, Mike figures that I'm hiding somewhere nearby because I can't go far on a bike."

"But we're a long way from Chicago."

"That was the good news. The bad news is that someone also asked who else had a bicycle, and there were only four cyclists. Bicycling isn't so popular in November, y'know."

"So as soon as they figure out that you did not leave alone—"

"He said that they did not know if I left alone or with a friend, but that they would find out." She paused and took a breath to calm herself. "When they figure out that I'm with you, it'll only be a matter of hours before they establish your credit card trail from Chicago."

"Well, we made it this far. The last data point was the Washington Hostel, and we can make it to Aberdeen before they find us. Let's ride. If it takes too long, I'll call Joe to come get us on US-40. If they know I'm the one, they'll find out that I have a brother. I'd like to be there when they do."

Hilda felt the dread returning. If the FBI figured out where they were, the Forebears of the Mahdi would probably find out not long after. They pedaled with a renewed sense of purpose, covering the last thirty-five miles in two and a half hours.

Joe and his wife, Linda, came out as they rolled up the driveway. Jack and Hilda briefed them on the situation as they walked the bikes to the guesthouse.

Jack's brother lived on three acres on an island in the Chesapeake Bay, just outside the Aberdeen Proving Ground. The guesthouse was by the dock, where a trim inboard-outboard boat was tied.

"Ready for a getaway by land or by sea," Joe quipped.

Joseph Rathburn had been Jack's hero growing up, which was probably why Jack followed him into the army. Joe went to the Military Academy at West Point, but Jack had developed a liking for police work as a teenager, so he majored in criminal justice and joined the ROTC at the University of Illinois. While Jack was in Iraq and Afghanistan, Joe was doing his last two tours at the Proving Ground. Having only retired the year before, the older brother still had most of his friends among the personnel there. Indeed, the only road access to the island passed through the army base, so it felt as if they had not left.

"Check out this view," Jack said, standing in front of the window as he buttoned his shirt. The fall leaves had not all dropped on the opposite shore. The confluence of the Susquehanna River into the Chesapeake Bay provided a panorama of nature and human activity.

The guesthouse had an upstairs bedroom with a bathroom. Hilda was drying her hair.

"Did you say something?" she asked as she came out. Her shining hair fell behind her. She was wearing a white bathrobe.

"I was admiring the view from the window, but you're a far more beautiful sight."

Hilda smiled and stepped to the window.

"Gerrit Dou would have loved to paint that," she said. "Have you seen his work?"

"There was a special exhibit at the National Gallery of Art a while back. I know what you mean. The Dutch Masters loved landscape, and he was one of the best."

Hilda dressed quickly into her all-purpose black dress. They walked downstairs and up to the main house. Dinner was a simple affair, but it was in the dining room, rather than the kitchen, and Joe had dug out a 2015 Montepulciano d'Abruzzo to go with the meal.

"I called the base CO and the commander of the Kirk Clinic—your old CO," he said. "They both want to help, and Lieutenant Colonel Smythe especially wants to spend some time with you, Hilda."

"She was more than a CO." Hilda looked at Joe over her glass of wine. "She became a good friend too." She put down her glass. "She's also the main reason you still have a brother."

Jack put down his knife and fork. "I only remember you pulling me into your Humvee and messing around with my guts before I blacked out."

"Karen Smythe was the surgeon in triage when we got you back to the base. I could not have patched you up for evacuation to Germany in the truck, Jack."

After a somber moment, Joe continued. "Anyway, my friend Colonel Harper would be happy to let you call the SAC in Chicago on a secure line. He'll set it up in the morning."

"I'll email Agent Norman, so he can be prepared for a long conversation. I don't know how this'll go down."

"Well, if it's any help, Nate Harper said that they could put you two up in the Visiting Officers Quarters on base if you need better security. I don't expect that the Forebears will be able to get to you, not without some careful and time-consuming preparations."

"It's a big base," said Jack, "but I don't relish the idea of staying there for a long time."

"We'll know more in the morning, Jack," Hilda said. "Being able to talk for a while will allow us to find out just how big the threat is. By now, the bureau should know more about the Forebears, especially how many more there are and who's unaccounted for."

"Good point. I feel safe with the base between here and the mainland. But we need to find out more about them if we ever hope to stop running."

"It's agreed, then," said Joe. He looked at Linda. "Shall we take this conversation—and the rest of the Montepulciano—to the living room?"

"Sure. I'll clean up."

"No, you won't. You show Hilda your pictures, and Jack and I will clear the table."

The evening was spent catching up, laughing over past misadventures, and generally enjoying family and friendship. About ten, the yawning began, so Jack and Hilda bade the others good night and started back to the guesthouse. They were holding hands walking down the path, something new for them because usually, they were pushing their bikes when walking.

Halfway back, Jack said, "Don't look now, but I think I saw a flashlight moving through the trees to the left."

"I saw it too."

"That's supposed to be undeveloped wetlands. There shouldn't be anyone there at night." They gently increased their pace and quickly reached the guesthouse. Jack checked the door and the soft earth around the house before they let themselves in. The only tracks were their own. Hilda locked the door and the windows while Jack made a careful search for signs that anyone had been in the house.

"Are we being paranoid?" Hilda asked as they went upstairs.

"I don't think so. I wouldn't come to the house the first day either, but I'd set up surveillance as soon as possible. I'd want to know the regular movements of the inhabitants before going into the house."

"Probably safe for tonight, then?"

"Probably. But let's keep alert when we go out tomorrow."

As Hilda drew the drapes on the big window, she considered the beautiful landscape at night. Ships were plying the waters of the bay, their running lights passing in front of the Elk Neck State Park like fairies in the darkness. Havre de Grace and the traffic crossing the Susquehanna River looked like a distant light show. She shivered.

"Now, that view scares me a little."

"Me too. I'm glad we're here and not in a tent tonight."

There was an urgency to their lovemaking that night because neither was ready for sleep. But they slept at last, overcome by the exhaustion of the day, the emotions of their situation, and the warm comfort of the bed.

4

ABERDEEN

HILDA AWOKE WITH A START. Jack was hyperventilating, his body rigid and shaking, sweat starting to soak the sheets. He was sleeping, but not resting, that was for sure.

"Jack," she said softly. "Jack, wake up." She touched his head gingerly from the top. As she expected, Jack doubled upright suddenly, eyes wide in terror. She slid her arms gently around him. "Easy, soldier, you're safe here."

Jack's body relaxed as he took in his surroundings. He turned to bury his head in Hilda's long black hair. "Oh, God, I thought I was past that." He hugged her as his trembling subsided. They fell back on the pillows. The alarm clock on the nightstand glowed "04:25" in red digits.

"I'm sorry about waking you," he said.

"No problem there." She stroked the side of his head. "It's been a while. Did you have any episodes while I was riding from Seattle?"

"No. I guess it's been six months." He took her hand and kissed her fingers. "I still hate putting you through my problem."

"*Our* problem, Jack. We were taking turns when I came back and ran into you last year."

"Yeah, I guess we were." He smiled. "Does that make us compatible?"

"We have the same nightmares." She turned toward him. "Do you want to try to go back to sleep?"

"I don't know. I'm keyed up. What I feel like doing is going online to find out more about the Forebears of the Mahdi. I want to see if there is anything else we can find out before you call Agent Norman, and I talk to Ted Tinsley."

"That's your friend who was at Central Command in Qatar when we were in Iraq?"

"Yes."

"Let's do it, then. I forgot to email Norman when we came back from dinner."

Dressed in matching bathrobes and slippers that the Rathburns had left for them, they made their way downstairs. Jack made coffee in the kitchen while Hilda opened her laptop on the table and composed an email to Mike Norman in Chicago.

Jack came in while the coffee maker gurgled away. He booted up his machine and started with the obvious open sources—Google, Wikipedia, and a few major newspapers. Then he logged into his account at army.mil.

Hilda scooted over next to him. "Any luck?"

"Not much. In fact, only two hits before the scene in Chicago. For all the damage they did in Baghdad, they may be smaller than we think."

"We'll get an update from Norman."

"I'll check the NCIC before we go. There might be something." The National Crime Information Center.

"You still have access?"

"Uh-huh," Jack grunted, his face intent on the screen. Hilda slapped him gently on the back of the head.

"You're still on active duty! Why didn't you tell me?"

"You never asked." Jack grinned. "I've been on medical leave. On paper, I'm assigned to the provost marshal at Walter Reed until my next checkup in March. I'm hoping to be certified as fully fit for duty."

"I thought you had your twenty years in already."

"Not quite. I can retire in May. If I don't pass the checkup, I'll be retired medically in March."

"A man of dark secrets, Jack Rathburn." Hilda rose and went to the kitchen. She came back with two mugs of black coffee. The darkness was weakening outside the living room window. They went back to their research, sitting side by side. Hilda surfed through German, English, and Arabic websites. Jack set up a virtual private network and moved into the law enforcement databases.

"Here's a piece on the *fatwa*," said Hilda as she read the Arabic *Al-Jazeera* news. "It seems that the imam who issued it in Mosul last month has recanted it."

"That's good news."

"Yes, but will the word get out to all the crazies before one of them finds me?"

"Good point. I hope it means that the Forebears can call off their teams."

"They may have a personal grudge, you know. Even without a *fatwa,* they blame me for their six brothers getting arrested."

When the sun began leaking around the living room curtains, they shut down the computers, made breakfast, and went up to get dressed. Columbia® shirts and trekking trousers were the extent of their "street clothes," but that seemed more appropriate than spandex bicycle kits for the offices they would visit that day.

They pushed their bikes up to the main house, their senses keen for movement or sounds on either side. Whoever had the flashlight the night before was either gone or well hidden.

Joe and Linda were finishing breakfast. Over coffee, they reviewed the day ahead.

"You don't need your bikes, Jack," Joe said. "I can shuttle you around."

"Actually, Joe, I don't mind if we take your truck to meet Colonel Harper, but we have separate places to go after that. Let's throw them in the back so you won't have to stick with us all day."

"Makes sense." Joe turned to his wife. "Need anything from the commissary, hon?"

"Thanksgiving's all stocked up, but what about some things for Jack and Hilda?"

"That's okay, Linda," said Hilda. "We can shop for ourselves. Just having a fully equipped house is wonderful. Jack and I can meet at the commissary to get groceries before we come back. By then, we'll have an idea of how long we'll be here."

At nine o'clock, Jack, Hilda, and Joe walked into the commanding officer's office. Nate Harper was a big man, with no fat on his frame.

"I'm honored to meet you, Major," he said, extending a hand to Hilda. His handshake was firm; Hilda guessed that he could probably crush her fingers if he wanted to. "Major Tinsley told me about what you did in Iraq, but the Chicago stories have made a real hero of you."

"It's all a little embarrassing, sir. I just did what I was trained to do."

"But Chicago isn't Baghdad," said Joe.

Nate Harper nodded at Joe, then said to Hilda, "We'll do everything we can to protect you. Has Joe shown you around yet?"

"Yes, sir. We got the windshield tour on the way here. We can find all the places we need to visit today."

"Good. We thought it might be handy to call Chicago from the provost marshal's office so Major Tinsley can make arrangements as soon as you hang up."

Outside the headquarters building, Jack and Hilda donned their insulated jackets and took the bikes from the truck.

"Linda hopes you'll be back for supper," said Joe, standing by the door to the truck. "Just let us know either way. We know you both have friends on base who are anxious to see you."

"That's true," said Hilda. "We'll let you know."

Joe climbed into the truck and drove off.

"Ted's office is on that next block." Jack pointed across the street. "Let's walk over." They pushed their bikes to the unremarkable brick building and locked them outside.

The reception area resembled a police station in any town, with its collection of wanted posters, plain walls, and hard plastic chairs. An MP in desert utilities stood behind the glass at the reception desk. He smiled at them in a professional manner.

"Good morning, sir, ma'am. Can I help you?"

"Good morning, Sergeant. Major Rathburn and Major Paisley here to see the provost marshal."

The desk sergeant straightened noticeably. "Yes, sir! We've been expecting you." He pushed a button on the intercom, which brought out another MP in a green service uniform. She approached them quickly and saluted Jack.

"Major Tinsley said to bring you in right away, sir. You, too, ma'am. I'm Sergeant Jones."

She led them to an office just behind the reception area, motioned them in, and closed the door behind them. The office was as unremarkable as the building, with a minimum of furniture, and a large desk with only a few files on it. A short man with powerful shoulders and arms stood facing the large window that gave out on the parade ground. He turned around, and Hilda noticed that his brown eyes twinkled with humor from an otherwise stern face. The face melted into a grin when he saw Jack.

"Rathburn, you old reprobate! I was afraid I'd seen the last of you when the report came in from Baghdad."

They stood a moment clasping each other's arms, speechless with emotion, then gave each other a hug. Hilda felt a lump in her throat, knowing how much healing an old friendship could carry. Jack turned their attention to her.

"Ted, this is Hilda Paisley." Ted's grip was strong in her hand.

"I've heard about you, even before Jack told me that you two had met again. It's an honor to meet you, Hilda."

"Likewise, Ted. Thank you for helping us out."

"The least we could do. Want some coffee?"

They assented, and Ted called Sergeant Jones in.

"Sergeant, could we have some coffee, and could you check on the secure phone setup?"

"Ready when you are, sir. We tested it with Chicago earlier."

Ted winked at Jack. "As usual, the sergeants stay ahead of us. Thank you, Jones. What time did you give them?"

"Ten-hundred. Twenty minutes, sir."

"Good. Would you join us with the coffee? You and I may have to take care of some of the details personally."

When Sergeant Jones came back, Jack and Hilda briefed them both on the entire story from when each of them arrived in Chicago. Ted asked enough questions to understand everything in each of Hilda's phone calls to Agent Norman.

"So, they don't actually know about Jack?" he asked at the end.

"As of yesterday morning, they had guessed that I had left with one of the other three cyclists who were checked into the hostel. They must have figured out who it was."

"But I have not used a card since then," said Jack, "so they'll know only that we were in DC yesterday. Since I'm officially stationed there, they may be planning to contact Gerry McQueen at Walter Reed today."

"Does Gerry know about this?"

"No." Jack looked at the two MPs. "Until we got here, only Agent Mike Norman knew anything, and never our location. We've told Joe and Linda, and Colonel Harper, of course."

"Good. Depending on what the FBI will accept, we can probably offer you as secure a place to hide as anywhere."

"It's 09:55, sir," said Sergeant Jones. They all stood, and Ted led them to the communications room. They waited around a console while the MP called Chicago and set up the secure connection.

"I have Special Agent Norman on the line, sir," she said to her CO. Ted gave Hilda the phone.

"Hello, Mike. It's Hilda, checking in." She grinned at Jack. She could hear the FBI agent's smile.

"Good morning, Hilda. I hope you won't hang up on me today."

"Not today. I take it you know where we are this time."

"Yes, and I guess Major Rathburn is with you."

"Indeed. Mike, I have the provost marshal, Major Tinsley, his assistant Sergeant Jones, and Jack Rathburn here. May I put this on speaker?"

"Sure. I have Special Agent in Charge Louis Jefferson here."

The communications technician flipped a switch to turn on the speakerphone. Ted gestured for her to wait outside by the door. She picked up a handheld radio that was squawking with police traffic and closed the door. Ted motioned for everyone to pull up a chair near Hilda.

"Who goes first?" asked Hilda.

"I think you should, especially after all I put up with. Do you know that you have almost everyone in the bureau pissed at you?" They could hear SAC Jefferson chuckling.

"I'm sorry about that, Mike, but we made it here safely, didn't we?" She went on to brief the two FBI agents about their ride across the eastern half of the country. Agent Norman and his boss occasionally asked for details, obviously so they could check out the story at each of their stops. Finally, Hilda wrapped it up and asked, "What do you want from me now?"

The SAC answered. "We still want you in Witness Protection until the trial of the six suspects. Things got interesting after you left. We had two attempted jailbreaks, so we have ten Forebears in custody. The US Attorney is sure that he can get convictions on all ten because the breakout attempts help make the case against all of them."

"From what we could learn, it's not a big group," asked Jack. "Have you any idea how many more of them are out there?"

"Can't be more than a half dozen left," said Jefferson. "It was a very exclusive group, maybe three dozen in Raqqa and a dozen in Mosul. The Mosul crowd was from Baghdad originally. The Raqqa group was killed or captured. We accounted for all of them. According to the sources, the Baghdad slash Mosul unit had been planning to come to the US for a long time. That means there can't be more than two of them unaccounted for."

Hilda spoke again. "And the *fatwa?* We learned that it was recanted. Can you confirm that?"

"Yes, we can. I'm surprised that you knew about that."

"*Al-Jazeera.* It was on the internet."

"The latest we had from *Al-Jazeera* was the announcement last month. The cancellation came to us from classified sources." Agent Jefferson did not sound happy.

"Well, it's public information in the Middle East. Not everything *Al-Jazeera* broadcasts gets translated, which makes me worry that someone in North America may still be trying to earn a ticket to heaven."

"That's why we want you in Witness Protection."

Ted spoke up. "Agent Jefferson, Major Paisley is on a high-security army base. It would be very hard for a lone actor or an outside organization to target her." Hilda frowned and shrugged. There was a pause on the line.

"I see your point, Major Tinsley. Tell you what. Now that Ms. Paisley has stopped moving, I can pass this case to the SAC in Baltimore, and you can work it out with him." Hilda started to talk, but Ted motioned her to be calm.

"That sounds like a plan for now. We have a good working relationship with Pete Sayfield and his team."

"Works for me, Major. I'll brief Washington on this, then call Baltimore. Do you think she'll be safe over the holiday?"

"She's staying with the Rathburns on base. Imagine our embarrassment if anyone tried to breach security here. From what you say, there are only two Forebears left. They or any freelancers probably couldn't organize an infiltration that quickly."

"I agree. Special Agent Sayfield will probably contact you on Monday."

"And, Mike, thanks for everything," Hilda said. "I know I was not easy with you."

"Forgiven, Hilda. After the third call, I knew that you'd be okay."

The two FBI agents ended the call. Ted hung up the phone while Sergeant Jones called the communications MP back in to take over the console.

Back in Ted's office, he motioned for the three of them to sit.

"I'm surprised that the bureau didn't just drop you into our custody, Hilda. They usually pass the buck easily."

"My guess is that this is a high-profile case, and they want control," said Jack.

"It does not look good from where I sit," said Hilda. "I'll go stir-crazy trying to ride around the base. I don't care how big it is."

"Relax, Hilda," said Ted. "You were going to be here through the Thanksgiving weekend anyway, right?" Hilda nodded. "Pete Sayfield is one of the good guys. He's a former MP himself, but, better than that, he doesn't have the CYA attitude of some of his colleagues. You'll like him. Trust me."

"So, do you want us to do anything in particular?" asked Jack.

Ted thought for a short while.

"With the holiday, I don't want to increase patrols. Seems like a waste of effort. There's just one thing that bothers me." He looked at Sergeant Jones.

"An attack from the Bay," she said.

"She's been bugging me about that since I got here, and she's right. The islands have more coastline than we can patrol, so our effective perimeter is around the mainland part of the base."

Hilda frowned again. "I have a job to report to in January."

"Let's see what happens over the weekend, then work up a plan with Pete Sayfield next week. I'll call him today. I'll also call the Maryland State Police and local law enforcement to tell them that there may be intruders trying to use the islands. It's way off-season for tourists, so any boats will attract attention."

"We saw a flashlight in the trees last night," Hilda asked. "Isn't that undeveloped wetland?"

Ted looked at the big map of the base on the wall. "Yes, it is. But it's also a favorite haunt for nighttime poachers. I'll send a detail around to check for tracks. They should still be there if anyone was moving around. That should tell us if they were hunting you or the local critters."

They rose. Jones went to make phone calls, and Ted walked them back to the entrance.

"How about lunch at the O-Club?" Ted said. "It has become a very nice, regular restaurant overlooking the Bay. On me."

"Thanks, Ted, but no. You and Jack have catching up to do. I'd like to visit Karen Smythe. We may see you there if she doesn't take me home."

Ted smiled. "She has quarters on base, but don't go to Havre de Grace for lunch."

"Promise. On base." She looked at Jack. "Meet you at the commissary at two?"

"Sure. Let's text if either is delayed."

Ted shook hands with Hilda. He and Jack went inside. Hilda unlocked her bicycle and rode to the Kirk Army Health Clinic.

આ આ આ

Thanksgiving at the Rathburn house did more to ease Hilda's concerns than almost anything could. She felt as much at home as she did with her parents in Kaiserslautern. She and Jack relaxed, took the boat out for picnics in the state park, and generally let the tension flow away for a while.

Ted's MP's did find tracks near the house where they had seen the flashlights, consistent with poachers. One MP even recognized one set of tracks as belonging to a local repeat offender. The tracks showed a sudden turn away from the path by the house, so Hilda and Jack had probably scared them off just being there.

The week after Thanksgiving, Hilda agreed to stay through Christmas. An early snowfall in mid-December had put everyone in a holiday mood.

"I'm so glad you agreed to stay through Christmas," Linda Rathburn said as Hilda handed her the angel topper for the Christmas tree.

"I have to admit that this has been a safer and friendlier place to wait than anywhere else. You and Joe have been wonderful."

Linda climbed down and reached for her hot apple cider on the table. "The truth is, we're a little selfish. It's hard to get Jack to visit or to stay for more than a couple of days. Joe misses him a lot when he's gone."

"I noticed that they are closer than most brothers who aren't twins."

"They're third-generation army. With all the moving and their father gone so much, they only had each other growing up."

"I wish I'd had a brother or a sister."

"Where was your father stationed when you were young?"

"After Stuttgart, where I came along, we went to Fort Benning, Georgia, which I don't remember. I do remember living in Argentina, then Kaiserslautern. We stayed there for two tours while he was in Afghanistan and Qatar, then moved to Hawaii. He took a twilight tour in Landstuhl, so he could retire to Kaiserslautern, my mother's hometown. I grew up there."

Linda handed Hilda a box of tinsel, and they walked around the tree, putting on the final touch.

"I think what you're doing yourself is simply brilliant," Linda said. "I'm happy not to be moving every three years, but your riding around between temp jobs in hospitals sounds like a lot of fun."

"The nomadic lifestyle suits me. It's not for everyone."

"It seems to suit Jack too."

"It does. We both found out that it's great to ride on your own, but it's even better with a friend."

"Well, you two are fantastic together. I hope you can keep it up."

"As long as our health holds out, I can't see why not."

"And the Forebears stay off your case."

"That too."

They heard Joe's truck pulling into the garage. The two brothers came into the house, laughing hysterically about some shared memory. They regained their self-control by the time they entered the living room. As Joe went over to hug his wife, Linda asked what was so funny.

"I told you the story of Jeb Moran in fourth grade, didn't I?"

Linda smiled and chuckled. "Yes, that was funny." She turned to Hilda. "I think you had to be there for it to be *that* funny." Hilda grinned. Jack gave her a hug and a kiss.

Linda pointed to the tree and the decorations. "I hope you two are hungry, and that you did something about it. We've been too busy, as you can see."

"Fresh fish for supper," Joe said. "We even cleaned them at the pier and put them on ice."

"We can make that work."

Supper was a community affair, with everyone fitting into the Rathburns' spacious kitchen. Conversation at dinner revolved around old memories and prospects for the future.

"What are you going to do after Hilda has to go to work in Charlottesville, Jack?" Linda asked.

"Probably ride back up to DC and check in with Gerry McQueen. I'm still attached to the hospital there."

"You can always stay here."

"I know, and thanks." He took another helping of new potatoes. "You two have been so generous with us."

"You're family," Joe said. "Both of you."

"Come to the guesthouse for dinner tomorrow or the next day," said Hilda. That got a quick assent from all concerned.

After dinner, Hilda and Jack walked comfortably back to the guesthouse.

"Any idea where you want to ride next?" she asked.

"Not really. I'd rather be tracking down the Forebears or taking on another case."

"You're not going to handle retirement very well at this rate." She squeezed his arm and smiled. "Do they have temp jobs for cops like they do nurses?"

"I could be a PI or a consultant, but that doesn't appeal to me. Maybe I'll stay in Aberdeen for a while. Make myself useful with Ted Tinsley. Everyone's understaffed everywhere."

The next morning, they rode to the commissary together after agreeing on what they would fix for supper. It all fit in Hilda's panniers, so Jack rode over to the provost marshal's office to do some research and find out the latest on threats to Hilda.

Hilda cranked up to twenty-three miles per hour, crossing the causeway on Spesutie Island Road. She blew past the gate, exhilarating in the smooth pavement and the westerly wind behind her. She gained speed and did not slow down for the gentle curve.

Coming out on the straightaway, she caught a glint of light among the trees to her left. Before she was consciously aware of what was happening, she was braking and steeling herself to jump or drop the bike just as she felt a powerful thump hit the left pannier.

The bike began to swing out from under her. Instinctively, she corrected to the right, which took her flying into the grass toward a clump of trees.

She heard the crack of the rifle as she leaped from the bike and rolled on the ground. She stayed down, rolled again to get behind a tree, then stopped.

She heard a man shouting, "*is'ad bil-balam, hasseh!*" then the sound of an outboard motor gunning. From the sounds, she guessed that the boat backed away from the shore and sped toward the open part of the bay.

She waited in the silence, then moved from tree to tree to examine the line of trees on the shore across the road.

She was alone.

She moved back to the bicycle, pulling out her cell phone. She righted the bike and leaned it against a road sign. Orange juice and red wine were leaking from the bullet hole. She was sure that the eggs in the right pannier were well-scrambled.

"911. How can I help you?"

"Major Paisley here. I'm about seven hundred meters past the gate on Spesutie Island Road. Someone just took a shot at me with a rifle from the beach at Sand Cove. No injuries, and whoever shot at me seems to have escaped in an outboard boat with at least one accomplice."

"A patrol car is on the way, Major. Are you okay?"

"I'm fine, and the pannier seems to have collected the bullet. I'll wait here. Are you in the APG police station?"

"Affirmative, ma'am."

"Would you please let Major Rathburn know? He should be with Major Tinsley in the provost marshal's office."

"We'll pass it on."

Hilda ended the call and dialed Jack's number.

"Hey, beautiful. What's up?"

"Not feeling so beautiful, Jack. I just got shot at from the beach. A patrol car is on the way, but if you want to join me, I'm about seven hundred meters past the Spesutie Island gate, near Sand Cove."

"The messenger just walked in to brief Ted. We're on our way."

As Hilda pocketed her phone, she heard the sirens. Two cars showed up. Fifteen minutes later, a full crime scene investigation was underway, with MP's combing the beach with dogs. Hilda's panniers were taken into evidence after the CSI team checked for trajectory from the bullet hole at the spot where the bike was struck.

Pete Sayfield from the Baltimore Office of the FBI called Ted, who assured him that an emergency run was not needed, but he could see everything later that night when the FBI agent could get there from the scene he was working close to Washington.

After taking photos and measurements, the CSI techs let her take the bike. Joe showed up with his pickup truck. He insisted on taking Hilda to the health clinic.

"I know you're not hurt," he said, "but Ted and the FBI will need to have the scratches documented by the clinic. Besides, we'll need to swing by the commissary again, won't we?"

Karen Smythe was waiting for them and took her friend into the ER. They cleaned up the abrasions, took photos, and promised to send the report to the provost marshal right away. Joe, Jack, and Hilda swung by the commissary to replace the food that had been impounded by the MP's.

"You and Linda are still coming to dinner, I hope," she said.

"Absolutely." Joe smiled and backed the truck out.

"You know what's missing?" Hilda said as they rode to the house.

"What?" The Rathburn brothers spoke as one.

"Reporters. In Chicago, it was a zoo. Here, the MP's could work unmolested by the press or the public."

"They'll be around," said Joe, "but they won't be snapping photos of you for Page One this time."

"Thank God. That's how I got into this mess."

Dinner was delicious, but the atmosphere was more somber than the night before. Ted and his MP's determined that two men of about the same size had come ashore. One had set up the ambush while the other smoked unfiltered cigarettes by the boat, which was a Boston Whaler type of fiberglass craft.

"My guess is the Forebears," Jack said. "There are two unaccounted for, and a one-off fanatic would probably not be that organized."

"Obviously, they've been watching us after all," Hilda said, fiddling with her salad. "It was too good to last, wasn't it?"

The phone rang. Joe got up to answer it. He came back in just a minute.

"That was Nate. You're to transfer to the Visiting Officers Quarters on the main base tonight." He looked at Hilda. "He's not asking. He can only order Jack around, but he really means you."

"It's his base. He and Ted assured the FBI that we'd be safe." Hilda sighed. "Let's finish dessert. Jack and I don't need more than a half hour after the dishwasher starts to pack out."

"Let Linda and me clean up while you pack. Okay?"

Hilda got up and brought out the chocolate cake while Jack poured some port. An hour later, they locked their bikes in the courtyard of the VOQ and carried their bags up to the suite that they had been assigned on the second floor. The Rathburns joined them in the dining area of the suite. Joe called the base commander to let him know that the two were safely in the VOQ.

"Nate said that he would check on you tomorrow."

Joe and Linda stayed for only one drink. In the silence after their departure, Hilda felt the day crashing in on her. She sat at the dining table.

"Suddenly, I'm exhausted."

"This battle is over. Time to come down." Jack massaged her shoulders as he talked. "I'm glad you took Joe up on his offer to drive you to Charlottesville in the truck."

"You and your brother have done so much for me. I could never—"

"Don't say it. You taught me the words 'pay it forward' when I started talking like that last year. You'll get your chance. Besides, I owe you my life already."

Hilda got up, turned around, and hugged Jack. They remained there immobile for a while, savoring the feeling of safety in each other's arms.

After washing up the glasses, they retired to the bedroom and unpacked their panniers. Everything they had fit into one of the dressers.

An hour later, Hilda lay staring at the Venetian blinds leaking light into the room. She began to shiver.

"I felt that." Jack rolled over to face her back and put his arm over her. "Tell me."

"Had I been riding any slower, he'd have hit me."

"People make that mistake a lot with you, Wonder Woman. You ride faster than anyone expects."

"It's less than six inches from that pannier to the heel of my foot."

Jack squeezed her and held her still. "Breathe and focus on something else. You dodged that bullet to fight another day, Nurse."

Hilda relaxed. She breathed deeply and slowly. She turned around and kissed her soldier fiercely, channeling all the fear into her passion....

5

WEST MAIN STREET

TWO WEEKS AFTER THE AMBUSH at Aberdeen Proving Ground, Joe, Jack, and Hilda were driving slowly south on Interstate 81 down the Shenandoah Valley. The winter storm pounding the East Coast was less severe west of the Blue Ridge, so Joe decided to head west above Baltimore to Hagerstown and down the Shenandoah Valley. From the radio reports, they knew that the main I-95 corridor from Aberdeen south was impassable. On I-81, the convoys of long-haul trucks on the "New England Expressway" between Atlanta and Boston helped the snowplows stay ahead of the falling snow.

"Aren't you glad you didn't try to ride this?"

"You won that argument before Christmas, Joe," said Hilda. "I would have holed up somewhere and had to make my way to the train. Still doable, but this is better."

Joe grinned and took the ramp to Waynesboro and Charlottesville. Half an hour later, they could not see past the taillights of the truck ahead of them. They monitored the GPS on the dash to know when to expect bends in the highway, turns, or other events invisible in the whiteness. Interstate 64 led them past Waynesboro and up the side of the Blue Ridge. Fog lights embedded in the pavement kept them on course, albeit at a crawl.

They knew they had topped the Blue Ridge when the GPS showed the Parkway crossing overhead, and the highway dipped downhill.

It took an hour to cover the twenty-three miles to the Residence Inn in downtown Charlottesville. Hilda had chosen a suite there instead of one of the hotels closer to the hospital, in case she had trouble finding an apartment quickly. She booked and paid for a room for Joe, too, insisting that he have a place to park his truck out of the storm. It was late at night by the time they pulled into the garage. The storm stopped as they were moving into the adjoining suites.

The next morning, Hilda walked down West Main Street to check out three of the available apartments that she had found on the internet. She selected an apartment in a brand-new building just three blocks from the emergency room where she would be working. By the time she got back to the Residence Inn, Joe and Jack had returned from Wegman's south of town and stocked the room. They were sitting in the living area of her suite, with a hockey match on the big-screen TV.

"You guys look at home," she said. They raised their coffee mugs in greeting as she moved to the kitchenette to pour a mug for herself. "I have a place on this side of the tracks just west of here. It wasn't that much more to get two bedrooms, so we can all stay there tonight."

"We bought staples and at least three days of food," said Jack. "We'll help you move it."

Hilda checked out of the Residence Inn while the men loaded the truck.

By midafternoon, they had Hilda moved into her new apartment, which was on the third floor. There was bicycle parking in the garage in the basement, but the elevator was big enough for her to roll her bike to the apartment if she wanted.

They walked to the Downtown Mall, a pedestrian area which had been swept clear by the time they arrived. Movie theater, upscale restaurants, boutiques, city hall—everything seemed to be conveniently located.

After dinner at Himalayan Fusion, they walked back to the apartment. Joe retired early to call Linda from the guest bedroom. Jack and Hilda went online to check news stories about the attack in Aberdeen. The mainstream media had fallen quiet after a week, but every other day or so, someone posted an "update" on the story.

"Uh-oh. This doesn't look good." Hilda swung her computer around, so Jack could see the full-screen picture of her, cropped from the *Chicago Tribune* picture that had started it all. The caption in all capitals blared out the intention of the Forebears of the Mahdi to have revenge. A reward of $10,000 was offered for her death. "It's been shared on Facebook and Twitter. So far, I've only found it on Arabic sites, but if it keeps going, it will be viral soon. That's a lot of money."

"It doesn't say how to collect the money, does it?"

"No, but that won't slow down the excitement." Hilda slumped her shoulders. "This gets me down sometimes."

Jack moved his chair next to hers. "Let me see." He took her computer and surfed some of the leads from the post. "Correct me if I'm wrong, but does that say that Abu Namr has called for your execution?"

"Yes, Abu Namr himself. Isn't he dead?"

"No. He moved to Mosul when we were in Baghdad. He must still be the leader."

"Of an army of two."

"It might not be he. They might just be using his name." Jack saw her put her head in her hands, elbows on the table. He put his arm around her shoulders. "And you're not alone in this. Special Agent Sprouse told us in Aberdeen that he would check in on you as soon as you got here. We'll call him before Joe and I leave tomorrow. We'll get an update on Abu Namr. He might be one of the ones in jail, for all we know."

"I never thought to ask about names."

"Neither did I. But I'll be working on this full-time from Aberdeen. I'll keep you informed." Jack's gaze went to the screen. "Does that say what I think it does?"

Hilda read the new post. "I'm supposed to be hiding on the army base at Aberdeen. It calls for helpers to keep me from escaping."

"They have no reason to expect you to read Arabic, so it's probably not misinformation intended for you."

"They'll find me soon enough."

"But not before we can talk to Greg Sprouse and organize something ourselves."

They shut down their computers and went into the bedroom. They turned in silently.

Hilda's mood was torn—sadness that Jack was leaving in the morning; anger at having to worry about the Forebears and wannabe bounty hunters; excitement about the new job; fear that she might be attracting violence to her new coworkers.

Jack sensed her thoughts.

"You've been through worse, Hilda. How did you handle it?"

"That was there. It's not normal here."

"What if this is the new normal? What are we to do?"

Hilda sat up. Staring at the wall still empty of decoration, she remembered her daily routine and the threats behind it—bombs in Baghdad and Kabul; terrorists in Chicago; snipers in Somalia. Then she remembered the children in the streets near the base in Baghdad, the families gathered in the waiting area when she came out of the ER in Baghdad, Seattle, and a dozen places around the world. She remembered Jack's smile as he slipped into unconsciousness in the Humvee bouncing to the base.

"Been there. Done that." She turned to Jack. "Mission accomplished, Major. I can handle this."

"I thought so." He laughed when she leaped on him from her seated position....

ଔ ଔ ଔ

Jack and Joe left in the morning. Hilda walked to the Medical Center. She knew the first day or two would be filled with paperwork, interviews, and meetings, so she chose a light tan pantsuit with a white shell, which she had bought at the Post Exchange at Aberdeen. Personnel, newcomer orientation, and interviews with the director of nursing and the chief of Emergency Medicine. She found out where ER was, but never got there. She came home with three sets of hospital scrubs, fixed supper, and went online. Nothing new, but Jack called her on Skype when they got into Aberdeen. She slept soundly.

The next morning, Suzie Bennett stood at the nurse's station as the tall nurse with a ponytail walked in.

"You must be Hilda."

"Right." Hilda nodded at the nurse's large abdomen. "And you must be Suzie."

"Any day now."

"I'm glad I could get here in time." Hilda reached for her ponytail. "I picked up scrubs yesterday, but I was hoping we had bonnets here."

Suzie came around and showed her where the supplies were. They toured the ER and walked through the procedures for incoming flights by the Pegasus helicopter. It was a mercifully quiet day after the dozen flights they had handled in the aftermath of the blizzard.

Turnover went more quickly than expected. The ER department was well-organized, and Suzie had prepared an extensive binder of information for Hilda. Young Antoine Bennett arrived only two days after Hilda. Suzie went into labor at work.

"How are you holding up?" Jack asked on Skype in her apartment, the day after Suzie was wheeled from ER to delivery. "You look good."

"Okay, I guess. Suzie went into labor, so I'm it. You know it's a part-time position, but I'll be working every day for the first two weeks to get up to speed. Then Monday, Wednesday, and Friday, in case you want to know when my phone will be off. Day shift for the first three weeks, then we'll see." She paused. "Any news?"

"It turns out that Abu Namr is in custody. He was one of the original six. I told Pete Sayfield about the reward, and the FBI tracked it down to a leak in the jail. They put Abu Namr in solitary. The bureau has a couple of Middle East specialists working the case, so they are monitoring the Arabic sites—and writing posts to contradict the reward scam and to remind readers that the *fatwa* was recalled."

"I saw some of that. Nicely done. I couldn't tell that it was the FBI, but it sure has the chat rooms confused."

"I can't say that you're safe from the one-off nut cases, but we have solid evidence that there are only two Forebears at large—the two that took a shot at you. We almost caught them in Havre de Grace, so it seems that they were still convinced that you were on base at least as of yesterday."

"We?" Hilda watched him smile.

"I'm TDY to Ted Tinsley's office in Aberdeen. He put me on the case, working with Pete and the local law enforcement officers. It frees up his people to focus on their normal duties. I thought Pete's name was familiar.

He was stationed at Camp Ederle in Vicenza when I was in Livorno."

"Sounds like you're having fun."

"I wouldn't call it that. Not until we catch the last two. But it beats wandering around Walter Reed Medical Center without a job."

"Meanwhile, ER here looks like a break room for the FBI and the local police. I think they make up excuses to hang around after bringing in the usual crash and shooting victims."

Jack laughed. "They probably want to watch the beautiful new nurse at work."

"Stop it, Jack. I can't punch you through the screen." Hilda grinned. "Besides, half of them are women."

"Any cyclists?"

"Four of them ride bicycle patrol when the streets are clear. I wouldn't try to beat any of them in a sprint."

"So, you're meeting people?"

"Of course. I'm already a regular at the Starbucks on the Corner, which is like another PD and hospital break room."

"After just two days?"

"Great staff. They knew my name and my drink the second time I showed up."

"You are memorable, Hilda. I'm glad you're settling in."

"Beats wandering around UVA Medical Center without a job."

Jack smiled and slapped both hands to his chest. "Got me!"

They signed off, both feeling better.

Hilda got into a routine that she learned working in combat zones, which was not to be routine. She had several different routes to the ER from home, and sometimes she would ride instead of walk. With her UVA ID card, she could also use the city or university bus systems to get around. She never arrived at work at the same time twice in a row. Sometimes she worked out at the gym downtown, but sometimes she went to the University Aquatic and Fitness Center or a gym north of town. She enjoyed variety, so mixing up her movements was no hardship.

She especially enjoyed the Corner, the business district adjacent to the University, only two blocks from the hospital. Besides Starbucks for coffee breaks and post-workout refreshment, she liked the teeming variety of people there: students, faculty, tourists, local schoolchildren and residents. She heard at least a dozen different languages each time. And she discovered a church that used much of the same music that she had enjoyed growing up in Kaiserslautern.

By the time the yellow forsythia bloomed, Hilda was an old hand around the hospital. Only rarely would anyone recognize her from the Chicago picture. It was normal for law enforcement to be in and out of ER, so the frequent visits by the Charlottesville and UVA police, and Greg Sprouse, the FBI Resident Agent, did not attract notice. *It would have been different if I'd taken an assignment in OB-GYN or pediatrics*, she often thought.

PART TWO

EMILY

6

THE WRENCH

"BYE, DEAR. Have a good day." Emily heard her mother's voice as her stepfather closed the front door. Her mother walked into the kitchen as Emily came downstairs. The smile turned to shock.

"What happened to you?"

Emily put her hand to her left cheek. "Oh, that. I skidded on some leaves on my ride yesterday. It's nothing."

Her mother came over, looking anxiously at Emily's face. However, closer inspection revealed no more than a bruise around the scab. "I worry about your riding all over, and now you're hurt."

"Mom! It's nothing. Really. Falling off a bike is no big deal. I know how to fall, so nothing serious happens. Jo—" She bit her tongue to keep from saying more. "We've been over this. It'll heal, and I'll be fine."

Her mother's face relaxed a little, but Emily could see the alarm in her eyes. It had been six years since her father had died—an event that had transformed her mother from a daredevil, extreme athlete into an overprotective "helicopter mom." She missed Daddy, too, but she also wanted some space.

Thank goodness Mark had come along. He seemed to be a tower of wisdom and a rock to her mother. He brought balance into their lives. Her mother's face cleared.

"Let's have some breakfast so you can get to school."

They served up the rest of the bacon and scrambled eggs on the stove and sat across from each other in the dining area of the kitchen.

"Do you have anything after school today?"

"Not really, but when I get back, I want to take the bike to K-Bikes for a checkup." She had two bikes, but the Colnago was *the* bike.

"Mark and I have separate meetings in Wichita this afternoon. Could you heat up the casserole in the refrigerator about six? We should both be back by seven."

"I can handle that. Dinner at seven. Would you prefer red or white with that?" Her mother looked up sharply. Emily grinned. Her mother's shoulders relaxed.

"Stay out of the wine cabinet, wise guy." Her mother smiled. "After the party last night, neither of us will want anything but water, I think."

Emily got up and cleared the table. Her mother loaded the dishwasher and set it to run. They met again in the garage. Emily wheeled her trusty Bianchi Volpe out and slipped her combination pannier/bookbag onto the rear rack. Her mother backed out the Mercedes C-230 Kompressor. They waved and headed off to work and school.

℞ ℞ ℞

That afternoon, Emily swapped out her sneakers for cleated bike shoes and rode downtown to K-Bikes on her Colnago. Jake Smith, the team mechanic, was manning the counter. Bicyclists call their mechanics "wrenches"; Jake looked the part. Skinny, strong, and reeking of bicycle grease, he sported spiky brown hair that came off the top of his head in two peaks, like the grips of an open-end wrench. He often stroked the spikes absentmindedly. Except for his spikes, hands, and apron, he was, in fact, clean.

"What happened to you?"

"I got that a lot today, Jake. I crashed on some wet leaves yesterday. The part that shows isn't what hurts."

"You okay to ride?"

"I got here, didn't I? My hip looks like hell, but it's already healing over. I had to trash my team kit. All bloody and shredded."

"Matt can get you a new jersey. You want to buy shorts today?"

"Not today. What I need is a new front wheel. Here." She rolled the bike behind the counter. "It looked like a pretzel, so I know it needs to be replaced."

Jake picked up the bike and spun the front wheel.

"You three fixed this?" he asked.

"Well, no. I was alone. Joanna and Mary backed out at the last minute."

Jake whistled. "Where'd you learn to true a pretzeled wheel?"

"I didn't. A tourist came along. She had a spoke wrench and showed me what to do."

"Cool. This is a really good job."

"She said that I should get a new wheel before going out again."

"She's right, but you could tool around town forever with this. You just wouldn't want to race it."

"Can you get me a new wheel?"

"Of course. We have spare wheels for all our racing bikes. That's what a team sponsor does, you know."

"Oh, great," Emily sighed with relief. "Can I put it on now? Then I won't have to walk home."

"No problem. Wait here." Jake went into the back room and came out with a new wheel. He picked up a new tire and an inner tube and walked to his bench.

"Jake?"

"Yes?"

"Could you show me how to put the tire on? I learned how to put the wheel on last night."

"Oh." Jake looked around the empty store. "Okay. Business is slow." He had her take the inner tube out of the box and showed her how to put one bead of the tire on the rim. He had her inflate the tube slightly, then push it into the tire around the wheel. Then Emily put the other bead on and checked to be sure that the inner tube was not pinched anywhere.

"Sometimes you need tire irons to get the tire on. Sometimes not," said Jake.

"Just never use a screwdriver, right?"

"Whoever she was taught you well." Jake brought over a floor pump while Emily mounted the wheel. He showed her the two types of valves that the pump would handle, then let her pump up the tire.

"Is that it?"

"I guess you can call the ride home your road test. Bring it back if there's a problem. This weekend, I'll show you how to check the tension. Think you will have ridden a hundred kilometers by then?"

"Of course." Emily spun around, looking at the shelves in the shop. "I also want one of those small tool kits for under the saddle, with tire irons, patch kit, and a spoke wrench."

"Over here on the wall. You'll probably want a lightweight multi-tool, too, for loose nuts, or getting parts off." He picked out the items and added a small compressed air cylinder. "And you should probably carry this on training rides if you're thinking of fixing flats. You'll need to pump it up when you're done."

"Thanks." Emily put the tools into the bag and strapped it under the saddle.

"That's a sight, a Colnago with a tool kit."

"Some of the guys always carry a tool kit on training rides. I may not have a tourist come by next time."

"Was that you that signed up last night for the Thursday maintenance class?"

"Probably. It was the first thing I did when I got home."

"Great. I'm teaching it."

"How much do I owe you for all this?"

"Thirty dollars for the tools and the tool bag. Nothing for the wheel."

"Nothing? That's a completely new wheel set!"

"Nothing. I'll tell Matt that you were on a team training ride, and we'll cover the new wheel. I may give you that hub for the wheel-building part of the maintenance course."

"Thanks, Jake." Emily pulled her wallet out of her jeans and paid cash for the tools.

She had just turned onto the bike lane on Kansas Avenue when she heard a familiar voice behind her.

"Em, what's with the jeans?" Joanna pulled up alongside. Her skin glowed from her workout. She was wearing her team kit. There was no traffic on the street, though that would change soon.

"Not training, Jo. I'm just running an errand."

"On your road bike?"

"I took it to K-Bikes for some work and stuff."

"Like the little bag under the seat? Looks like Randy's seat." Joanna winked. Emily blushed and gritted her teeth.

"I guess you like Randy's seat, I got this for me. Thanks to you and Mary, I was all alone when I crashed yesterday."

"Well, excuuuuse me. Like you've never had to change your plans."

"I found out that you set up that date with Steve a week ago. You could've told me sooner than just as we were supposed to roll."

Joanna stood on her pedals and sped ahead, her long blond ponytail flowing behind her helmet in the wind. Emily wondered sometimes how her best friends could be such jerks. She did not feel like giving chase, though she could easily catch Joanna, even riding in jeans. Instead, she rode to Sand Creek and took the bike paths on both banks, just to see how it felt to push herself. Her left hip ached a little, but she felt good. She also calmed down.

She turned east back toward Kansas Avenue, passing a pair of bicycle tourists following US-50 through town. At the McDonald's near Twelfth Street, she saw a half-dozen heavily laden touring bicycles leaning together on the wall. She stopped by the tables, where the riders were gathered with orange juices and Quarter Pounders, poring over a map of the area. Three men and three women. None seemed over twenty-five. Unlike the other tourists that she had noticed, these were wearing regular bicycle kits, and their stuff was all out of sight in their panniers, like Hilda's last night. The bicycles were sturdy models, like Hilda's also, but brands that Emily had never seen—Koga, Gazelle, Batavus.

"Can I help you guys?"

"Thanks." One of the men had a clipped accent. He was blond, sunburned, and tall. "We are trying to find the campgrounds at Bethel College."

"I don't know about that," Emily said. "May I see your map?" She looked over the AAA map they were consulting. Two of them had Google Maps up on their phones.

"See? There is a campground indicated on the phone here, but we are not sure."

Emily pointed from one of the phones to the map. "I see. That's the Sand Creek Community Gardens. I think it's run by the college, but it's actually for gardening." She considered their eager stares. "You know, growing vegetables and such."

"Oh, yes. Like an allotment. We have those at home too. But the camping?"

"I think that they'll let you camp on plots that're not being worked. It's a large area, and the growing season's basically over. Try the phone number there on Google."

A short phone call established that the group could camp, which caused no small relief among them. While the tall one made the arrangements, the others introduced themselves. They were Dutch university students from Arnhem, taking a semester off to cross the United States. They all spoke excellent English.

"Do you have trouble finding places to camp?" Emily asked.

"Not usually. Everyone has been very generous, and the way you let bikers camp in the parks is fantastic." This from one of the women, Elise. "We just got very behind today. We normally decide where to stop by two o'clock, but we were so close to your town that we went for it as you say. We've ridden a hundred and twenty kilometers today. I don't know the miles."

"About seventy-five," said Emily. "Our coach makes us keep our training logs in kilometers, so the whole team set their bike computers to metric."

The tall student, Lucas, ended the call. "It's arranged, but we have to stop by the gatehouse before they close at four."

"It's three and a half miles from here," Emily said, "about five kilometers."

"That will take us under a half hour," said Elise, "but what if we get lost?"

"I can show you how to get there. It's not on the AAA map, but there's a bike path along Sand Creek almost all the way. Come on."

They gathered themselves and soon were speeding up Sand Creek toward the college. Emily paced them, but not so fast as to make them string out. She was surprised at their ability to maintain twenty to twenty-two kilometers per hour with the loads they were carrying. They arrived with fifteen minutes to spare. A Mennonite woman at the gatehouse was waiting with a big smile. She gave them a map showing them where to pitch their tents and told them where to find water, food, and the toilets.

Emily watched the scene with growing pleasure. After the gatekeeper wished them all a safe journey and walked away, the Dutch students came over to Emily. They each wrote their names, addresses, and emails on a sheet of notebook paper.

"Emily, you will always be welcome in Arnhem, so let's stay in touch. Is there anything we can do for you?"

"I'm fine. I'm sure you'll find some way to pay it forward. And maybe I'll be racing there someday."

"We certainly hope so. Or just come for a visit. You have six homes now." Elise gave her a hug, and the seven of them mounted their steeds to ride off.

Emily was home by five. Plenty of time to finish her homework and still have dinner on the table when her parents came home.

7

COLORADO

EMILY GRITTED HER TEETH AND PUSHED. Her legs were burning from her hips to her ankles, and her toes might be numb or in pain—she couldn't tell anymore. She couldn't get enough air, either. Up ahead, she could make out the top of the St. Francis Medical Center, poking up behind the 7000-foot contour line. She had a line of sweat running down each lens of her sunglasses, but there was nothing she could do about it.

The team had come to Colorado Springs ten days ago, so that they could acclimate themselves to the altitude before the US Air Force Academy Invitational, a new race for aspiring professionals. Only Under-23 and junior amateurs with USA Cycling cards could compete, and scouts from the various pro teams in the USA had been invited to come watch. K-Bikes had partnered with a bike shop in Denver, which also had a small team. Together, the two shops fielded a team of twelve strong riders, enough for a peloton and a couple of leaders. It would be the first time for the young women to compete at a high level, using the tactics and techniques of team riding to the utmost.

Emily had done her best this summer, and she was far and away the strongest rider on the K-Bikes team. But the steepest hill in Kansas was a ramp to the interstate.

The idea of her taking a week off from school had triggered the first argument her mother and stepfather had ever had. Katherine was against it but finally yielded to the combined pressure of Mark and Emily, with some phone calls from Matt, the K-Bikes Shop owner, and a half-dozen parents who had been following Emily's successes during the summer. Mark and Katherine would both be at the race, but they each had to work that week. Katherine was especially upset that Emily was going away without her.

"Katherine, she'll be fine," said Mark. "We know everyone on the team, and the organizers have taken all sorts of precautions for this race."

"I know, it's just-" Emily's mother left the room. They could see her shoulders shaking as she went into the master bedroom and slammed the door.

Mark put his hands on Emily's shoulders as they stared at the door. "Give her a moment before you go in. It's not easy watching your baby go out on her own. She knows this has to be, but she doesn't have to be happy about it."

Her teachers took it better than her mother, allowing her to take the only quiz that week early, and giving her the homework assignments on the Friday before. Working Friday night and in the team van, Emily had the homework done by the time they arrived in Colorado Springs. There were only four riders coming from Newton—Emily and three women who had been a couple of years ahead of her at Newton High. None of the other teenagers had made the cut.

"Go for it, Em!" she heard Matt shout from the back of the motorcycle in the next lane. "You can catch your breath on the way down!" His voice seemed distant. Her vision was narrowing, and she knew that soon she would black out. She stood on the pedals for the last 200 meters, barely in time not to be dropped by the woman who appeared on her left.

Suddenly, she was over the top. Woodmen Road stretched out before her in a long, beautiful downhill. The police motorcycle escort sped up and left them plenty of room. Emily felt the load come off her legs as she shifted into her highest gear and pedaled, still standing, until she reached fifty kilometers per hour. Then she tucked into an aerodynamic pose and gave those pedals all the spin she could. She began catching up with the motorcycle escort, which caused them to scramble.

She had tried standing while racing downhill after reading about the Italian racer Fausto Coppi, who was famous for riding uphill seated and coming out of the saddle for the downhill sprints. During the summer, she was sure that the technique had given her the edge more than once over more experienced riders, and it was paying off here too. Soon she was fifty meters ahead of the next rider in the race.

The whole week before had been grueling and full of surprises. She had expected painful training rides after first arriving, but they were required to rest every other day, to let their bodies recover and acclimate to the altitude. They had stayed in a training camp in

Northwest Colorado Springs, at 7400 feet. That was higher than the ridge that Emily had just passed. She knew that the climb up to the US Air Force Academy would be steeper, but much shorter. Then there would be a downhill sprint to downtown Colorado Springs.

During the recovery days, the racers were treated to tours of the US Air Force Academy and feted at various events. The cadets from the USAFA Cycling Team were assigned to escort them places, run errands, and generally keep them company. One day, they rode the track railway to the top of Pikes Peak, where they could see the city below and the plains all the way to Kansas.

The youngest rider in the event, Emily found herself blushing often as cameramen, reporters, and cadets enthused over her performance. Not having raced at this level, she did not know that anyone had been watching.

Approaching the first curve, Emily came up slightly off her saddle, which lowered her center of gravity to her bottom bracket. She held herself vertical as she leaned the bike into the curve, taking it at something over forty-five kilometers per hour. There weren't many curves, and they were more like lane changes, compared to the switchbacks that she had seen on TV coverage of major bicycle races. She put her full concentration into the curves, which could end a race, a career, or a life in a split second. Woodmen Road was a major thorough-fare, with plenty of lanes for the riders to maneuver. Emily had been amazed to see the route, which was a joint effort of the towns in the area, eager to attract high-level bicycling.

The race blew past an enormous Walmart and the Woodman Plaza Shopping Center, applauded by spectators gathered next to the road. The whole field of riders gained speed heading toward Academy Boulevard. Emily was first to round the intersection, and she geared down for the climb to the Academy. The hill began to take its toll as the solar collectors and the airfield passed on her right. She couldn't afford to sightsee. The redhead from Ogden, Utah (*what was her name?*) and the semi-pro racer from Sacramento, California, (*Augusta something*) were taking turns passing her. The three leaders were showing the strain, but also their shared determination to lead the race. It was a credit to the organizers that the three women in front were only thirty or forty meters from the pack. This could be anyone's race today.

Emily and her teammates did not have the experience or skill to play the waiting game, hiding their sprinter in the peloton until the last few miles, then drafting her into a position to jump off the pack and take the lead at the last minute. But they knew that there could be a potential slingshot rider in the peloton. Emily's teammates had trained hard at last-minute sprinting, so they could snap out of the field and challenge any potential leaders hiding in the pack. Emily's job, meanwhile, was simply to stay in the front of the field for the entire one hundred miles of the race.

It was a short race by international standards, but the concept was new, and none of the organizers were sure how the young women amateurs would do. They were surprised to see Emily and "her" trio riding so fast for so long. The police were hard-pressed to clear the traffic up ahead because the whole field was arriving earlier than scheduled.

The climb ended at Falcon Stadium. They tore around it and took a spin around the parade grounds at the Academy before returning to Stadium Boulevard and Pine Drive for the last twenty kilometers into downtown Colorado Springs. The redhead risked a crash to elbow Emily on a curve coming off Pine Drive and pulled ahead. At that point, there were no observers. Emily swore, and in her anger, found an unexpected reserve. Emily took the lead just as they turned onto Willamette Avenue for the sprint to Boulder Park near the US Olympic Training Center. The last ten blocks were flat—just like Kansas. Emily hardly heard the crowd as she tore past the tape, still bent down. Only after passing the stands did she rise in her saddle and slow.

The cool-down circuit was inside the Training Center. She rode straight there and did the required 500 meters to recover her heart rate and her sanity—and to calm down. Matt and Jake were waiting at the end. She gave them each a big hug, then climbed into the van while Jake snapped the bike to the rack.

"I knew you would win this one, Em," said Matt as they drove back to the finish line.

"How'd the team do?"

"Great. All in the top twenty, which means the combined team is either in first or second place. The whole field was spread over only five hundred meters, one of the tightest races anyone has ever seen. And no one was dropped. Every woman finished the race."

"That's amazing," said Jake. "There's always someone who crashes or bonks or something in every men's race I've ever seen."

"So much for the weaker sex," said Matt.

"The course really could have been longer," said Emily. "Maybe we should have just raced the same course as the men."

"And embarrass them with your faster times?" Matt wiggled his eyebrows as they laughed.

Back at Boulder Park, Emily stepped from the van and began walking toward the stands. Suddenly she stopped, her mouth open and her heart racing.

"This is like one of those big races! So many people." She started to turn back.

"Easy, Em. This is probably just the first one of these scenes for you. They should all be friendly here," said Jake.

"And they speak English too," said Matt. "Wait till you have to listen to speeches in Dutch or French."

Emily squared her shoulders and headed toward the officials. Then she saw her mother and Mark at the edge of the stands. Oblivious to everyone else, she ran toward them and buried her face in their chests.

The crowd was silent, then began to applaud. The youngest rider had won the race. It was a Cinderella moment for some, and a shock for many.

Aware of the attention she was getting, Emily stood back from her parents. She turned to the officials, and let them escort her to the podium, where the redhead from Oregon (Colleen O'Reilly, Emily remembered), and the semi-pro racer (Augusta Bivens) were waiting. The speeches were brief and focused mainly on the hopes of USA Cycling to develop a field of talented racers, both men and women, which could return the Stars and Stripes to the podiums of racing venues worldwide. The crowd cheered. Emily and the others waved and posed for photos.

The team was waiting to hug Emily and congratulate her. More posing for photos. An hour after the end of the race, Emily finally got in the van with her teammates. All she wanted was a shower and a nap.

That evening, Emily and her teammates were escorted to a reception and dance at the Air Force Academy. More photographs, with the handsome cadets vying to get selfies with Emily.

Augusta Bivens found Emily standing on the side of the dance floor during a break. Augusta turned out to be pleasant. She opted for professional racing after high school and worked in Silicon Valley as a programmer when she wasn't racing.

"I expect to see you around a lot, Em," she said. She clinked her glass of champagne to Emily's Coke and moved away.

"Hello, Emily. You're quite the star tonight." Emily turned to her mother, who glowed with pride.

"It's a bit much, Mom. I'm ready to go home already."

"Mark and I are leaving in the morning. Want to come with us?"

"I'd like that, but I should really ride home with the team. The others worked so hard for this win. I owe it to them to make the trip back with them. Besides, I want to hear about what kind of trouble the *domestiques* cause after the party."

"That sounds terrible."

"Oh, Mom." Emily rolled her eyes.

Katherine laughed and patted her arm. "I think I understand. I know I didn't look forward to this before, but I'm very proud of you. I would've been proud if you had finished off the back of the pack. Thank you, Emily."

"For what?"

"For helping me see that parents need to grow up with their children. This is a big moment in my life too. From now on, I plan to enjoy your milestones, not fight them."

8

KANSAS

EMILY WRAPPED HER SCARF TWICE AROUND HER NECK and stuffed it snugly in her jacket before starting down Twelfth Street again. The snow had come suddenly—it had been sunny and pleasant on the way to school. By the time she turned north into her neighborhood, the white stuff was beginning to stick, in that dangerous phase where the road is most slippery. Fortunately, she did not have any turns or hills ahead, and her Schwalbe Marathon tires were reliable going straight.

She blinked the snow off her eyelashes as she unlocked the garage door and stowed her bicycle against the far wall. Shedding her jacket and shoes, she went into the house to drop her bookbag panniers in her room. Then she went into the kitchen to see how long it would take to bake the *mostaccioli* that her mother had prepared. She had two hours to finish her homework and have dinner ready when her parents got home.

The pasta dish was almost done, and Emily was setting the table when she recognized the sound of her mother's car easing into the garage.

"Hi, Mom. Dinner in about twenty minutes."

"Thank goodness." Katherine Dempsey came in from the mudroom off the garage, minus her heels and her overcoat. "What weather! It's not even Thanksgiving yet." She stopped, remembering that Emily had come home on her bicycle.

"How was it getting from school?"

"No problem. The snow didn't start until I was almost home. Cold, though."

"Good. Mark will be home soon. We have big news, but first, let me change."

Katherine gave her daughter a hug, then went to her bedroom. She came out in jeans and a sweatshirt just as the garage door opened again. Mark Dempsey's Tesla did not make any noise at all. He came in, with his shoes in one hand and his briefcase in the other.

"Hello, Emily. That smells good."

"Disclaimer, Mom made it."

Mark kissed his wife. "Then it smells even better, but the fact that it's hot and ready on a miserable day like this is all your credit, Em. Thanks." He tossed his briefcase on the desk in the home office, swung by the bedroom for a pair of slippers, and joined them in the dining room.

"Mom says that you have big news," Emily said, holding out her dish to Katherine, who dumped a quarter of the pan onto it.

"We both do, Em. You want to go first, Katherine?" He held out his dish, then made a mocking show of comparing his meager (normal) portion to Emily's. Katherine shook her head and smiled.

"No, dear," she said. "You start the show."

Mark poured hot cider for everyone as he spoke. "I got a call from Tim this morning."

"Who's Tim?" Emily asked.

"My college roommate, and possibly my best friend after your mother."

"The best man?"

"That's Tim." He took a bite and relished it, chewing slowly while the others watched and waited. Food was not hurried in the Dempsey household. "Anyway, Tim has asked me to take over his company as CEO. He wants to move to California, where he has several start-up ventures."

"Is it like what you do for the Air Force?"

"It's another defense contractor, and the Air Force is one of his big clients. It's a good fit. I would like the work because it's what I did before I came to Wichita."

"We would have to move," guessed Emily.

"Which is why I'm bringing this home to you and your mother before I call Tim back."

"Where?"

"The company is in Richmond, Virginia. Although I would be going to Washington and military bases in Hampton Roads a lot. We could live almost anywhere in the state."

Emily looked at her mother, who had just taken a bite of salad.

"Is your news the same?"

Katherine finished chewing and took a sip of cider. "Similar. I got a call from a friend on the faculty at the

University of Virginia. There's an opening coming up for a tenured position. It will be advertised tomorrow. They're hoping to fill it between semesters."

"They want you?"

"They can't say so officially, but it's a very small field. I know all the others, and none of them could take it on such short notice."

"Couldn't they hire a temp of some sort? What do you call them? Adjunct something."

"They could hire an adjunct instructor for the undergraduate classes, but they have graduate students in their PhD pipeline. They hope to find someone who can advise and direct research as well as teach."

"Do you want to move?" Emily looked back and forth at the two of them.

"Well," said Mark, "the question is do *we* want to move. I can do just fine staying here or moving, and I think that you're in a good position at Wichita State, aren't you, Katherine?"

"Yes," said his wife. "But what do you think, Emily?"

"Richmond, where they held the World Cycling Championships?" Emily spread her hands in amazement. "What do you think I think?"

"But what about your friends here?" Katherine remembered how tough the transition to Chisholm Middle School had been on her daughter. Except for a few Air Force kids, no one had been anywhere else. Emily had been mercilessly bullied in seventh grade by the local students.

Emily thought about that for a while. "All my real friends ride bikes. Jocks don't hang with us, and neither do the nerds. Joanna and Mary would be happy for me.

There are hills in the east. Real ones. I think the team would want me to take them along."

Mark winked at Katherine.

"Maybe we better find a place with a guesthouse and an extra garage for a sag wagon," said Mark. They laughed.

"Speaking of that, where would we live?"

"Your mother and I have been talking about that. We both like Charlottesville because it has great schools. It's very pretty, and we think that you'll be able to fit in quickly. Charlottesville is not only very diverse. It has a sizable transient population, so there are always new kids coming in."

"You could train on the TransAmerica Trail," said Katherine. "The climbs up and over the Blue Ridge aren't just scenic. They're steep and curving. We wouldn't have to drive you to the next state to train for a high-level race."

"It sounds like a done deal. When do we go?"

"Not before the end of the semester here," said her mother. "I need to apply right away and serve notice to Wichita State if they accept me."

"They won't be happy."

"They have others who will be."

Mark took another helping of casserole. "I'll write to Tim tonight. Then we can start working on the details."

The rest of the meal was an exciting mix of dreams and possibilities.

It took less than a week for the University of Virginia to make a formal offer to Katherine. By then, Tim's company had announced the change in CEO's to the press, and Mark flew out to Richmond to meet with the management team. He already knew almost everyone on the board and most of the senior management. It would be an easy transition.

Emily did not tell anyone at school until the weekend when the team gathered at K-Bikes for coffee and socializing. The snow had not cleared enough for a training ride.

"Can't say that I'm happy for the team, Em," Matt said. "We're taking a big hit. But I'm seriously happy for you. We love you here, and I hope we will see you on the road and on TV."

"K-Bikes has the best coach ever. I'm sure we'll see a lot of each other if I can get on the circuit back East."

Joanna started to cry. "Em. I'm sorry I was cruel to you."

"Huh?"

"When I made you crash because I went on that date with Steve."

"Oh, that." Emily hugged her. "I forgot already. Besides, I slipped on the leaves all by myself. It made me take Jake's class, so I can always get a job as a wrench if I need to." She winked at Jake, who beamed.

"In another year, Jo and Mary could be as fast as you were," he said. The two youngest women on the team blushed and smiled.

Emily rode home feeling good, but also wistful. She wished she could take her friends with her, but she also had the feeling of passing a big milestone. Somewhere in the East, another team was waiting, a new school was waiting, and new friends were waiting. It was scary and wonderful all at the same time.

9

VIRGINIA

"ENOUGH SLACK, YOU TWO," Emily shouted and grinned. "Race me home!" Emily opened on them until she was a small dot in the distance. Mark and Katherine were already drenched with sweat, but the effort was keeping them warm on a freezing day. Fortunately, it had not rained or snowed since they arrived in Lancaster, Virginia, but this was the first day of a long cold snap.

"I don't have any calories left from your mother's Christmas dinner," gasped Katherine as she dug down for reserves to keep her daughter in sight.

"Me, neither," Mark grunted. Although a fine athlete all his life, he could never ride as fast as his wife or her teenage daughter. "That girl is keeping us trim anyway."

By the time they rolled up the driveway of the antebellum mansion to which Mark's parents had retired, Emily had already parked her Colnago and wiped it down.

"Did we just ride forty miles in two hours?" Mark asked Emily as he and Katherine pushed their bikes into the garage.

"Yeah, pretty slow, huh?" Emily winked. Katherine gave her a soft wallop up the side of the head. "Hey, Mom. You were the triathlete, remember?"

"Not anymore. Chasing you is workout enough."

"You should go out for seniors racing or something. I remember when you used to compete. You were awesome."

"I was never as fast as you are, Emily." Katherine looked at them and sighed. "Besides, that was a different lifetime." Mark took her hand and squeezed it. Katherine smiled at him and leaned her head on his shoulder as they walked to the main house from the garage.

They paused inside the front door to remove their cleated bicycle shoes.

"Y'all are back earlier than I expected," Mark's mother called out from the kitchen. "Supper won't be ready for another couple of hours."

"That's okay, Mom," said Mark. "We need to cool down, shower, and change."

"Don't tell me you were trying to keep up with Emily?"

"Well, she held back for us, but I think Katherine and I both rode a personal best today." They paused at the kitchen door. Dorothy Dempsey was poring over a half-dozen cookbooks. He gave her a kiss on the cheek.

"Can I help?" asked Katherine.

"She's a pretty awesome cook, Gramma, and I could help, too, you know."

"Sure. But let me figure out what to have. With a team of *sous-chefs*, I could get carried away. Go upstairs, clean up, and come back later."

Emily had liked her Gramma D from the first time she met her, which was at Mark and Katherine's wedding. Mark's parents had come out to Kansas a few other times, which had helped both Emily and Katherine adapt to their new life with Mark. They felt like a family now.

"What do you think she'll do after that feast at Christmas?" Katherine said as she and Mark were dressing after their shower. Emily had a post-ride routine of stretches, so she was in the shower.

"I can't imagine, but Mom loves cooking. This gives her an excuse to pull out the stops."

"I won't need to eat again until final exams next spring."

"You'll burn it off if we go riding with Emily as much as I'd like."

"We can't, Mark. She's on a different level completely. We'd just stunt her training. I know she's enjoyed riding with us since we got to Virginia, but we can't ride as hard as she needs to."

"Point taken, but you're a serious challenge for me. Let's you and I ride together and let her ride ahead. We've covered all the good routes around the Northern Neck, so she knows her way around."

"The visibility on some of these roads is terrible." Katherine looked worried.

"I know, honey, but she's a better rider than we are, even in traffic. Let's just agree in advance which route she'll take." He smiled. "If something were to happen, we'd be on the scene almost right away." He hugged her gently as she buried her face in his chest.

"I'm being a nervous Nellie again. Thanks."

"You're welcome, and your concern is well-placed. The important thing is to have a plan and be ready to be there to help her."

Katherine straightened up and checked herself in the mirror. She took a brush to her hair and pulled it into a ponytail.

"Where did you say your father was today?"

"He's in DC for a meeting of the Military Officers' Association. He should be back for supper."

Retired General James Dempsey did return as expected, about a half hour before dinner. Dorothy kicked Mark out of the kitchen, so he could chat with his father. She kissed her husband and ordered a glass of white wine for herself and her dessert chef. Katherine was whipping cream and watching the shortcake baking in the oven while Emily was chopping vegetables and greens for a salad. The conversation was lighthearted and relaxed.

Despite all the cookbooks earlier, dinner was simple—coq au vin, with braised Brussels sprouts and sweet potatoes, followed by cheese, fruit, and strawberry shortcake. Mark's father uncorked a bottle of Malbec from Cahors, which he had brought back from his last tour on active duty.

"Have you heard back from that real estate agent in Charlottesville?" he asked as they each took selections from the cheese plate.

"She called this morning, Dad. She wants to show us three places to rent, so we can settle quickly. We may have to wait until the spring turnover to have a good selection of places to buy."

"Not a bad plan. Where are the places she proposes?"

"They're all in the city of Charlottesville limits, so Emily can go to Charlottesville High School. Two in the Greenbrier neighborhood and one off Jefferson Park Avenue."

"Good for you. She'll graduate from one of the best public high schools in the state." He looked at Emily and smiled. "Are you anxious to get started?"

"Yes, sir," she said. "School starts next week, so it'll be a little crazy at first."

"Well, your stepfather's an old hand at sudden moves to faraway places, even if he never talks about it. You'll all do fine."

ʘ ʘ ʘ

The next day was their last ride before packing the car up for the final trip to Charlottesville.

As planned, Emily rode out ahead along the back roads south of Lancaster to Kilmarnock, around that town to White Stone and the Rappahannock River, then back up to Irvington Road north past Kilmarnock again, turning back to Lancaster after she passed Mount Olive. She sucked in the smell of the thick pine forests and the cold fresh air, delighting on the curves and the ravines that gave her mini-intervals. On Route 200 north of Kilmarnock, she overtook a peloton of riders on a training ride. She joined them for about a mile, but they were going too slow, so she sped up and lost them before turning west at Mount Olive.

Katherine and Mark set out with her and enjoyed riding as a couple. They kept her in sight until they all warmed up, and Emily disappeared on Harris Road south of Kilmarnock. They maintained a steady twenty miles per hour, but they had no idea how far behind Emily they were for the next hour.

"Omigod," shouted Katherine as they came out of the pines on Mount Olive Road, surrounded by fallow fields. "Is that Emily up there?" She stood on the pedals and began sprinting toward the small figure on the side of the road about a half mile ahead.

Mark tried to keep up, but there was no catching the panicked mother.

Emily had her bike upside down and was sliding the rear wheel into the hangers. She looked up and smiled.

"Hi, Mom! Got a flat." They dismounted with worried expressions. "You must not have been very far behind me."

"Are you okay?"

"Of course, Mom. It's just a flat. I can fix those on the road, you know."

Mark relaxed immediately. Katherine took a couple of deep breaths, but she, too, settled down. Emily centered the wheel, tightened the quick-release levers, and reached for the frame pump. She pumped up the tire, then waved the pump at Mark.

"Want to put some muscle on it since you're here?"

"Sure." Mark pumped until Emily deemed that the tire was tight enough.

"Thanks. See you at the house?"

They both nodded. Emily was on her bike and halfway out of sight by the time they picked up their bikes and mounted.

"Last year, she'd have been on the side of the road crying," Mark said. "She's come a long way, darling."

"I know. It still scares me sometimes."

With the unscheduled rest stop, they lost their rhythm for the ride and arrived a half hour behind Emily.

ଡ଼ ଡ଼ ଡ଼

Emily carried her cleated racing shoes into the kitchen. She had her long-sleeved winter racing kit on, with a bright orange microfiber buff around her neck. Katherine motioned to the table and set out bacon and eggs. Emily put the bread in the toaster.

"Why the bicycle kit, Mom?" Katherine was wearing a winter riding outfit, but with sneakers.

"It's comfortable."

"We've gone out past Earlysville to Dyke before. You don't have to drive a sag wagon every time I ride."

"I know, but I want to, and, besides, I enjoy the back roads."

"Why not ride with me?"

"You're too fast. I'd only hold you back."

"Not that much. Mark's the slowpoke."

Katherine looked out the window. The second weekend in January was brilliant with sunshine and unseasonably warm. Especially compared to Kansas. She sat at the table.

"Okay. After breakfast, I'll get my cleats while you clear the table. How far do you want to ride today?"

"At least sixty kilometers." Emily's bike computer was still set to metric.

A half hour later, the two women were blasting up Berkmar Drive on the new bike lane. They rounded the south end of the Charlottesville Airport and headed west toward the Blue Ridge Mountains. Traffic was light, mostly shoppers headed the other way to the Hollymead Town Center or to US Highway 29. They kept up a fast pace, breaking seventy kilometers per hour on the downhills, and not dropping below eighteen on the climbs, one ravine after another. Katherine was working hard but noticed that Emily had a sweat stain down her back too.

The sun climbed to their left, high enough not to cast annoying shadows from the bare trees. On the flat stretches, large farms extended away from the road, some with horses, others with grapevines, and still others with cows. They climbed Simmons Gap Road to Nortonville and turned right on Dyke Road. They overtook a foursome of women in University of Virginia colors riding toward Dyke. With a friendly shout, Emily and Katherine passed them, which started an impromptu race to the Dyke General Store.

Emily led the pack to the side of the store, where they leaned their bikes and introduced themselves. Two sophomores ("second-years" in UVa-speak), one junior ("third-year"), and their coach, who was racing while working on her PhD.

"Emily Hampstead!" said Mariana, the coach, a Latina with jet-black hair. She might have had more curve if racing had not burned off all her fat. "You were on the cover of *Peloton* magazine last summer."

Emily blushed. "Yeah, that was me." She looked down.

"You beat Augusta Bivens in the Air Force Invitational. That was awesome!"

"No wonder you blew past us," said Megan, a redheaded second-year.

"You all are strong riders," said Katherine, taking some of the spotlight from her embarrassed daughter. "Is there a team at the university?"

"The Cycling Club at UVA is sanctioned and races on the intercollegiate circuit," said Jane, the third-year. "Are you at UVA?"

"I am," said Katherine. "We just arrived this week."

"That's unusual, transferring in the middle of the year. Where were you before?"

"Wichita State. I didn't have any Part Two courses in the spring, so it's a clean break."

Emily interrupted. "Sorry, guys, but I think we need to ride. I'm cooling off too much." That led to a general donning of helmets and clicking of cleats on the concrete as they returned to their bikes.

"If you're looking for a coach and a team," said Mariana, "I can introduce you to the CRC people and the UVA team." They swapped numbers on their phones.

"Thanks," Emily said.

The UVA group turned back toward Charlottesville while Emily and Katherine continued north.

They bent east to Amicus and then down Buffalo Mills Road to return to Earlysville.

"Thanks for distracting them, Mom," Emily said as they slowed to cool down on Earlysville Road by the airport.

"You're welcome. I never did get used to the attention when I was competing."

"I don't think that they realized that you're a professor."

"If so, I'll take that as a compliment."

"Let's ride by Blue Ridge Cyclery to ask about the Charlottesville Racing Club. It's here at the Hollymead Town Center."

"Okay."

The coach and the team were out training. The wrench, who was manning the counter, gave them the USA Cycling forms Emily needed to transfer her license, and a schedule of local rides.

Back at the house, they changed and spent some time online checking out the other teams and stores in the area. Mark came back laden with groceries from Costco.

"Didn't you have a meeting in Richmond?" Katherine asked as they formed a brigade to carry the groceries into the kitchen.

"I did, but I took the shopping list off the refrigerator with me."

"I love you." She gave him a kiss on the cheek, careful not to drop the heavy box of almond milk.

"'Cause I'm domesticated?"

"That too." Katherine grabbed the four-place bike rack and closed the lid. "We met our first UVA students today."

"Oh, I thought you weren't going to go on campus until Monday."

"It's 'the Grounds', not 'the campus,'" Emily said. "It was a foursome from the Cycling Club at UVA on Dyke Road. We raced them to the Dyke General Store."

"If they're any indication, Emily should have no trouble finding A-level rides for training around here. The ravines in this area really burn the legs."

"You rode, too, I take it."

"Could I waste a day like this?" Katherine pointed to the sunbeam coming into the living room window.

"We stopped at the store that sponsors the local racing club on the way back. They have rides on Tuesdays after school in season." Emily snagged a banana from the bag of fruit and began peeling it. "One of the riders we met is a coach at UVA, who recognized me from the *Peloton* article."

Mark chuckled, looking at Katherine. "So, the world-famous professor of feminist literature meets the student body at UVA, but Emily is the celebrity?" Katherine shrugged and grinned.

"I'll have the last laugh. I recognized her name. Mariana Vásquez is a PhD student in the department, and I'm replacing her advisor. Imagine her surprise on Monday."

"I'm pretty sure that they thought Mom was a student. She just said she was 'at UVA' when they asked."

"I would make the same mistake if I didn't know her," said Mark.

Katherine punched him playfully on the arm. "C'mon, you're supposed to say that. But thanks anyway." They hugged while Emily did an exaggerated eye roll.

The next day, they went to church at Saint Paul's, which was next to the university. They found that it offered a five thirty service on Sundays, which was geared to university students but attracted all ages.

"That's an option for those Sundays that you have races or team training rides in the morning," said Katherine.

"I like the music," said Mark. "What do you think, Emily?"

"Works for me. I missed going to church on all those Sundays in Newton. Some of my best friends were in the youth group." They had lunch on the Corner near the church and resolved to come back.

ಢ ಢ ಢ

Monday, Emily walked to Charlottesville High School, which was only on the next block from their house. It was her second week of school, and already she looked forward to class each day. Newton High was a good school, but the variety of backgrounds of her classmates at CHS, and the level of the teaching impressed her. There weren't any dull teachers, although she heard kids complaining about one or two that she had not met yet.

"Hey, Em! Over here!" Emily carried her lunch over to the table where Fran Monroe was sitting with a girl who had to be a freshman. "You have a fan."

"Oh?" Emily looked at the younger girl, who sat immobile, staring wide-eyed at Emily. Her big brown eyes were set in a chocolate face.

"This is Taniqua Jackson. She asked if you were Emily Hampstead, and I ratted you out."

Emily noticed that Taniqua had her hair cut short evenly all around.

"Hi, Taniqua." Emily extended her hand. Taniqua took it cautiously, then shook it with a firm grip.

"I saw you on the cover of a magazine at Community Bikes. I thought you lived in Kansas."

"I did. We moved here over Christmas."

"I ride, too, but nothing like you."

"What do you mean?"

"I ride to school, and to church, and everywhere else. But I can't race."

"Are you fast?"

"I don't know. I never raced anyone, but I try to get everywhere as fast as I can."

"Taniqua lives next door," said Fran. "We all take the bus, but she convinced her mother to let her take her bike when she started CHS, and she has ridden every day, except during that blizzard."

"School was closed for that, anyway," said Taniqua.

Emily looked at Taniqua, then thought of something.

"Hey, Taniqua, I'll bet you know where everything is. Could you show me around on your bike? My folks don't know the town any better than I do, really."

Taniqua grinned. "Sure. Where?"

"I don't know, just around. The downtown mall, bike stores, where the movies and churches are, the different neighborhoods, whatever."

"Do you have your bike here?"

"No, but I only live over on Foxbrook Lane. We're renting a house there. I can get my bike and meet you after school any time you want."

"Okay. I'll ask my mom. She works afternoons at the UVA Medical Center. She won't mind as long as she knows what I'm doing."

"I'll check with mine too." The bell rang. "See you later. Ciao, Fran." She packed up what she hadn't eaten and headed for World Studies in the B concourse.

The rest of January and most of February, the days were pleasant and sunny more often than not. Emily settled into the routine at CHS easily, making friends with Fran's friends, some of the girls who were also in Girl Scouts (not many at that age), and a couple of classmates who had arrived in the fall. Taniqua showed her around Charlottesville so that soon Emily could find her way across town faster than Mark or Katherine could in the car. She could drive, of course, but she preferred her bike. She found that most of the motorists were used to bicycles because there were so many of them on the streets.

Mariana showed a serious interest in Emily and invited her to ride on the A+ rides with the club. That kept Emily in shape, waiting for the racing season to begin. Jane and Megan became good friends.

Emily joined the CRC and quickly made her place on the juniors team. She was easily the fastest rider, so that after only three rides, the coach, Sam Wallenborn, suggested that she train with the older USA Cycling riders. She registered for the Cavalier Criterium near Richmond and the Tidewater Winter Classic in Williamsburg, both in late February. As a high school student with a USAC license, she could race in the junior category intercollegiate races.

ርঙ ርঙ ርঙ

"Mom, could we bring Taniqua with us to Richmond?" Emily asked when she came home after a training ride. "She's never seen a race, and I think that she'd just love it. She loves everything to do with cycling."

"Sure, honey. Tell her to have her mother call us."

Taniqua was beside herself with excitement. Her mother was pleased, having followed the growing friendship between her daughter and Emily. Taniqua rode to the Dempsey house the night before the Cavalier Criterium with her backpack in a milk crate on her bicycle rack.

"I don't have any luggage or much to put in it," she explained.

"It's just for tonight. You won't need much." Emily showed her where to put her bike and carried the backpack up to the bedroom with her. Staying with Emily was like an old-fashioned slumber party for the two of them, except that they both went to sleep early.

A criterium race consisted of multiple laps over a short, closed course. It was challenging because the mass start could be messy. There were many turns, and it required a lot of individual technical skill. It was not Emily's best event. She excelled in the longer races, where endurance counted as much as speed. Nevertheless, she placed second in the Women's Collegiate A race and third in the Women's Open A race a few hours later. The youngest racer in those events, she became something of an instant sensation.

Mariana and her team were at the Criterium because the UVA Cycling Club hosted the race. Jane was in the collegiate race with Emily, coming in fourth. It was her best position to date, and a personal best, so she was happy for herself and for Emily. Mariana almost crushed Emily with her hug after the podium ceremony. Emily cried, more from the love these women had for her, a newcomer, than for any other reason.

The next weekend, the Dempseys were off to Williamsburg for the Tidewater Winter Classic, again with Taniqua. As they cleared the traffic on the east end of Richmond, Taniqua fell silent.

"Something wrong, Tani?" Emily asked.

"My bike is such a clunker. I could never ride like you."

"It's not a clunker. It's a Bianchi Volpe, in the original Bianchi celeste color. I have the same bike, which you know I ride more than the Colnago."

"But yours is all clean and shiny. My mother got mine at Community Bikes. It was donated by some guy they said rode it thousands of miles. It's got dings and chips, and the chain is rusty."

"You can fix all that."

"We can't afford to take it to a shop."

"You can fix it yourself."

"How?"

"I didn't know anything about fixing a bike until last year. I took a course in bike maintenance. I could show you. We could fix it up together."

Taniqua brightened up. "You're the best, Em. I never had a friend like you."

"I like having a friend like you, Tani. Nobody knows the back roads of Charlottesville or the county like you do."

They lapsed into a companionable silence until Mark pulled into the motel in Williamsburg. He had reserved a room for the girls and another for the grown-ups.

The Tidewater Winter Classic was a 9.5-mile race on mostly flat land. Being too young for the Women's Open race, Emily had registered for the Collegiate A event. That meant racing alone because she wasn't a member of any college team, and none of the young riders on the CRC team had qualified for that level. The older CRC riders were racing in the open event.

Emily broke from the pack on the last lap of the race and dodged the *domestiques* from Virginia Tech who tried to move out to stop her. She overtook the pack and caught up with the race leaders in the last 200 meters.

Sprinting past the Tech rider, she managed a third-place finish behind Jane from UVA and a Dutch woman wearing a Cornell University kit.

During the awards ceremony, Mariana, Megan, Taniqua, and the Dempseys jumped up and down with excitement. That made Emily smile from the podium, which delighted the photographers.

The third of March, a massive winter storm came out of Canada and blanketed the East Coast with record-breaking amounts of snow. Power was out for only a day in Charlottesville, but schools were closed for a week while the city dug out. Emily hated riding spinners at the gym, but she had no choice.

By the time the roads were all clear, it was only two weeks until her first local event, a new international race along the Blue Ridge Parkway. The CRC team stepped up the training, riding three times a week to get ready. This was going to be a long, regular road race, requiring teamwork and strategy. Emily was expected to be the leader, but they trained hard, taking turns as leaders and guards, sprinting, changing positions, and simply riding long and hard to build endurance.

Emily and Taniqua met after school on Mondays in the garage of the Dempsey house. Emily and Mark showed Taniqua how to clean and oil the drive train, change parts such as the cassette, the cables, the brakes, and the chain, and how to true a wheel. The young Charlottesvillean especially liked learning to repair a flat.

"I have a bunch of inner tubes at home with holes in them. I'll have spares for life." Mark gave her a pair of tube repair kits from their stash in the garage.

"Do you have a place to work on your bike at home?" he asked.

"No, but Community Bikes is just down the street. They'll let me put the bike on their stands and work on it for free." She wheeled her bike out to the driveway and turned on the lights. Waving to Emily and her stepfather, Taniqua rode back across town to finish her homework before her mother came home.

03 03 03

"It's just above freezing, Emily. I can drive you to school." The kitchen was bright with the sunlight reflecting from the winter wonderland in the backyard.

"I'll ride the long way around, Mom. It's clear all the way, and there is plenty of room on Rio Road and the John Warner Parkway to avoid any frozen puddles." Emily finished her breakfast and started clearing the table.

The Dempseys had not expected to find a home in the winter because most of the moving took place in the spring. They were surprised to find several homes in the city that met their needs—room for the cars, three bedrooms and a home office, and room for the bicycles and the repair stand. They settled on a home on Brandywine Drive in the Greenbrier neighborhood. The large covered driveway could hold both cars and the van. The basement became the bicycle storage room and repair shop. It was only a mile from the rental on Foxbrook Lane, and close enough to CHS for Emily to ride to school. The hills were challenging first thing in the morning, but she did not mind arriving each day with her heart pumping and her brain awake.

They had moved in the middle of March as soon as the snow from the blizzard was cleared. The weather had disrupted Emily's training for the Blue Ridge Parkway International. The spinner indoors would never make up for the real thing on the road. On days when the black ice on Yorktown Drive made riding through the neighborhood dangerous, she went the long way around. Either way, she was enjoying the commute to school more than the training time in the gym.

"Why don't you ride to work, Mom?" Emily asked as she closed the dishwasher and picked up her bookbag/pannier.

"I will. I'm still hauling stuff between the office and the house, getting settled."

"For two months?"

Katherine eyed her with a stern look, then smiled. "Okay, I'm a little lazy, but I'm about out of excuses to myself. The last one is that I don't have a good bike for commuting, like your Bianchi."

"You could use a backpack like Professor Gualtieri next door."

"And leave my Pinarello in a bike rack on Grounds? I wouldn't press my luck, even with the Honor Code."

"Seems that you need a bike."

Katherine thought for a moment. "Mark won't be back until Sunday. Want to go bike shopping with me Friday after school?"

"Sure."

"Good. I'll meet you at school. We'll go from there."

Emily went to the garage, where she clipped her pannier to the rack on her bicycle, donned her helmet and rode carefully to the end of the street. The melted runoff tended to collect at the bottom of Brandywine Drive then freeze overnight. Today the intersection was clear and dry. The last vestiges of the blizzard disappeared by the end of the week.

Friday, they rode to five different bike shops, Katherine on her Pinarello and Emily on her Bianchi. They had fun with the same routine in each shop. Katherine would walk in first. The Pinarello would command immediate respect. After allowing time for her mother to size up the sales staff (did they see a rich sucker or a serious rider?), Emily would come in. At that point, the store owner would show up and start offering discounts to make a sale to the phenom's mother.

She settled on a Specialized Diverge with fenders, racks, lights, and a gel saddle. The owner lived in Greenbrier and volunteered to drop it off on his way home that evening. Emily and her mother rode home from the south side of town while the wrench was putting the accessories on the bike.

"Not as fast as the Pinarello or the Colnago, but it will get me everywhere in any weather and take any kind of road—or even dirt," Katherine said. "And I loved the feel. That bike fits me like this one but feels as solid as a truck."

"I never pictured you on anything with shocks and wide tires."

"You weren't in the picture when I was shredding trails in Marin County, dear. Even your father hadn't shown up for that yet."

"I've seen the pictures. Somehow it doesn't seem real, but I'm glad to see you riding again."

"This bike will just be for around town and anything the Pinarello wouldn't be right for."

"Like a little dirt?"

"Maybe."

They reached the house, parked their bikes, and went in to fix supper. The new Specialized Diverge arrived as they were clearing the table.

The next day, they both rode to UVA. Emily joined up with the Cycling Club for a fast training ride. Katherine ran errands between her office, Alderman Library, and the house. She also swung by Whole Foods to do some shopping. She was putting away the groceries when she heard the basement door open. Emily came in, covered in sweat and grinning.

"That was a good run. We averaged forty kilometers per hour even with a climb up Afton Mountain."

"Where the Blue Ridge Parkway meets the Skyline Drive?"

"Uh-huh. It's a serious workout."

"Won't that be the finish line for the race at the end of the month?"

"Yup, and guess what."

Katherine raised her eyebrows and shrugged.

"The National Park Service will let anyone who is registered for the race use the course even while it's closed to the public. They finished the paving and only have to put up signs and paint stripes before they open it to the public."

"Doesn't that give the locals an edge?"

"No more of an edge than locals at any race venue. Teams will be coming early to scope out the course and train. It's going to be big-time Bike Week here for a while."

They heard Mark pull the handbrake in the driveway (the only thing on his Tesla that made noise). Emily and Katherine turned as he walked in.

"You're home early."

"I called, but you both had your phones off. We finished this morning in time for me to catch a flight back today."

"Well, we just got back ourselves." Katherine held up the groceries. "Nothing's planned. Want to take us to lunch?"

"Sure." Mark brought his suitcase in while Emily ran to her room to stretch then shower.

They took Mark's car to Stonefield for lunch. Conversation was light with the two women restoring their carbohydrate balance as they talked. While they were having coffee, Mark's phone rang.

"The office on a Saturday. Must be serious." He got up and went outside to take the call. When he returned, he looked puzzled.

"DOD put out a notice about possible terrorist activity around military facilities, but it's so vague, no one knows what to do with it."

"What kind?"

"They don't know, but a small fringe group called the Forebears of the Mahdi is supposed to be planning something around a base in the mid-Atlantic area."

"I heard about them last fall," said Emily. "They attacked the Sheraton Hotel in Chicago."

"I remember that," said Katherine, "but weren't they arrested rather quickly?"

"Apparently, not all of them." Mark sipped his coffee. "I'm glad we don't live near a base."

"What are you supposed to do?"

"According to our security people, nothing except to be alert. We don't even know who or what to look for, but we get called because contractors like us are moving on and off base all the time."

"Maybe they'll have something more specific when you go into the office on Monday."

"Probably. If not, I'll make a point of getting a briefing at Langley Air Force Base. We'll be there Monday and Tuesday."

Mark called for the bill. He paid, and they walked silently back to the car. At home, Emily took a nap, then rode across town to see Fran and Taniqua. They were going to see *Black Panther* together, which was still showing on the Downtown Mall. They had already seen it, but it was fun to catch things that they missed the first time.

10

THE BLUE RIDGE PARKWAY

WITH FIVE KILOMETERS TO GO, Emily broke from the peloton and sprinted for the finish line. Sylvia and Tashiqua pulled alongside her, blocking any moves by the riders in the field. Everyone knew what was happening. After the races last fall and the two this spring, Emily was becoming famous in women's cycling, not only as the fresh new face on the circuit but for her ability to sprint after grueling hills. No one understood why a girl from Kansas could do that (except her mother, who did not grant interviews).

As the trio cleared the front of the pack, the two *domestiques* fell back and took their turn leading the peloton. Neither could have kept up with Emily anyway. The hills of the Shenandoah were cloaked in a thin layer of bright green, which signaled a new spring, but no one had time to admire the view.

The organizers were especially proud of this race. It was being held on the last weekend before the Blue Ridge Parkway reopened to tourist traffic. It had taken years of negotiating with the National Park Service to do it, but finally the growing interest in bicycling—and in women's sports in general—wore down the career bureaucrats. That Sheila Barstock, the new Director of the NPS, had been a gold medalist in the Olympics put the lie to any excuses about the seriousness of women's athletics.

Emily pulled up to the pair of leaders, Augusta Bivens from California and Céline Daubry from France. For about one kilometer, they rode essentially abreast, then Emily began inching ahead. With only two kilometers to go, the other two pulled up, but never quite even. Emily dug down for that last bit of reserve that she kept for finish lines.

There were still at least six sharp curves to the tape. The police escort was struggling to stay ahead of the racers. Escorting professional bicycle races was not something that they were trained for, and they had not expected the women to be so damn fast! It was as if they did not even slow on the curves. They did not know that these three women trained on curves to increase their speed until any of them could round a hairpin at speeds that would push a sedan over the edge.

Five curves later, Emily was alone in front. She had no interest in where anyone else was as she took the last curve. The road flashed, and she saw it—a large oil stain. Then she was flying straight over the guardrail.

In slow motion, she saw her Colnago sliding on its side and wedging under the guardrail. She twisted instinctively and tucked. She recognized a white oak from her *Girl Scout Handbook*, then everything went black.

PART THREE

EMILY & HILDA

11

UVA

A VOICE. Familiar. But who?

"Hey, Emily. Over here." She felt a hand on her cheek and opened her eyes. Bright blue eyes, high, sharp cheekbones in a black face, big smile.

"Hilda." She tried to move, but excruciating pain seared up her back.

"Down, girl." Hilda stroked her cheeks gently. "Take it easy. We have to patch you up first, then you can fix the rest yourself. I'll check in on you."

Emily tried to smile but could only croak "thanks" as she fell asleep.

More voices. Her mother, her stepfather, a man, two women. Slowly, she opened her eyes. The overhead light blinded her, and she squeezed them shut again.

"She's awake!" her mother shouted. Emily heard the commotion but kept her eyes shut. She turned her head and opened her eyes again. She knew she was in bad shape from their worried expressions, but she felt no pain. Just a floating sort of well-being.

"Hi, Mom," she croaked.

A nurse on one side and a doctor on the other (she guessed, one with a lab coat, the other not) began fussing about adjusting IV drips and checking the sensors attached to her.

Her mother took her hand. Emily squeezed it.

"She's heavily sedated," said the doctor. "Please keep it short and simple. Details later." He looked at Emily and smiled. "You're going to be okay, Emily."

"Thanks." Emily drifted into a blissful, dreamless sleep.

The surgeons at the University of Virginia Medical Center managed to set all the broken bones (three ribs, a clavicle, and a humerus). The punctured lung and the concussion worried them more, along with the dislocation in her back, which could have left her paralyzed, had the extraction team from the Pegasus helicopter not been as skilled as they were. The inflammation from the dislocated vertebrae healed first, the lung next, the bones last.

Hilda visited every day after Emily began staying awake. She could not stay with Emily any longer than any other visitor, but the younger woman looked forward to those visits like nothing she had ever experienced. Every other day Hilda would show up in the afternoon, wearing scrubs.

"You were the first person I saw after my crash," she said one day. "Where was that?"

"In the ER. They had just flown you in on the Pegasus helicopter."

"Oh. You work in the ER?"

Hilda nodded and smiled. Emily took her hand.

"I never expected to see you again."

"Small world, isn't it?"

"Was that you who fingered the terrorists in Chicago? I thought I recognized you from a news photo."

"I hardly fingered anyone. I just answered some questions for the agents, and they figured out the rest."

"Anyway, I thought it was cool. I wasn't sure it was you."

"My time's up, Em. I'll see you tomorrow." She squeezed Emily's hand and started for the door.

"Hilda?"

Hilda stopped and turned around. "Yes?"

"Thanks. I'm glad you're around when I get in a jam."

"I'm glad, too, Em."

By mid-April, Emily was able to return to their new home on Brandywine Drive.

"With her youth and all her exercise, she should recover quickly," the head surgeon had told Mark and Katherine. "Get things to normal as fast as she can take it."

Emily spent her days exercising and studying. She knew that she could pass with the grades she had before spring break, but she hoped to be able to graduate on time and with her usual grade point average. She was in the rehabilitation wing for only a week, then her parents took turns driving her to day-long rehab on their way to and from work. "*Get things to normal as quickly as she can take it.*" Emily had insisted on her parents returning to work as soon as possible.

Hilda came by rehab on her days off. The exercises in rehab were as tough as anything Emily remembered on the bicycle because they were working muscles that she had taken for granted—arms, shoulders, back, etc. Hilda knew the team in rehab, who let her monitor Emily's workouts. After rehab, Hilda would wait with Emily in the lobby for her mother to collect her. Occasionally, Hilda would ride to Brandywine Drive to have dinner with the Dempseys.

At last, the therapists agreed that she could go home and come back three times a week for just an hour.

"When can I ride?" she asked on the last day.

"Whenever you feel ready," Dr. Morgan, her attending physician, said. "Just have someone nearby when you first set out, in case we were wrong about something."

Emily rode to school the first day, with her mother trailing in the Mercedes. Her classmates made a brief show of welcoming her back as they gathered their things in their lockers.

C3 C3 C3

A couple of weeks before final exams, Emily walked into the nurse's office. It had been all she could do to finish the essay in Advanced English Composition, and she had bolted from the classroom, leaving her backpack at her desk.

"What's the problem, Emily? I'm not surprised to see you after what you have been through." Josepha Gladdins had raced bicycles before college, marriage and two children had taken her away. She had returned to her hometown only last year—minus the husband.

"It all hurts, Ms. Gladdins. I've got a pounding headache and pain all over."

"Didn't they give you painkillers when you left the hospital?"

"I took the last one two days ago."

"Do you remember what it was?"

"Percocet."

"What was the dosage?"

"Up to three times a day as needed."

"And I take it you 'needed.'"

Emily sighed and looked down.

Josepha looked at her for a long time, then took a pencil flashlight to her eyes, mouth, and ears, and squeezed different parts, especially the arm that had been broken and her shoulders. "Does the pain change?"

"No, but the headache is worse. Do I need to go to the doctor?"

"Yes, you do, but let me warn you about Percocet."

"It's an opioid, right? We learned about them in physical education."

"It is and a powerful one. I'm concerned that the pain isn't where you were injured. It may be a sign of withdrawal."

"You mean I'm an addict."

"I did not say that. But you need to be careful. The doctor may give you more painkillers because they often do for people recovering from severe trauma, like you. But you need to pay attention to the pain, not just dull it or go for the high."

"But—" Emily's eyes got wide with alarm.

"Easy, Emily. I have an idea, but you, your parents and your doctor need to buy into it, or I would be out of line. You know about the endorphin high, don't you?"

"Of course, I get mine about thirty kilometers out."

"I guessed as much, watching you on TV." Emily blushed as the nurse continued. "It's not a high as much as the endorphins acting as super painkillers, allowing you not to feel the stress you're putting on your body."

"Still feels good."

"What is feeling good is the dopamine that the body releases into the brain as you exercise. Here's the catch. The opiate painkillers not only dull pain, but they dull the body's ability to create the dopamine high by deadening the brain's receptors. That way, you get all this pain after the opiate wears off."

"What can I do? This pain is killing me."

"What would you do if you had a choice between an endorphin high and taking a pill?"

"Get on my bike!" Emily almost shouted. It made her head pound. "But I only started riding two weeks ago. Mom trails me on my ride to school. Pretty lame."

"I thought so. That's why you must be careful. The painkillers will deaden your receptors if you stay on them, so it will be harder to get the dopamine high to kick in. But endorphins will always do some good. How much pain did you have in rehab?"

"None, but I had the painkillers then."

"Good point. You probably should have supervision, or at least keep your doctor and parents informed, but I say get back on that bike and get in racing form as soon as you can. You may find that the headache goes away while you're exercising, even if it comes back until you get over the withdrawal."

"I can handle that. I think."

"Good. I have some acetaminophen I can give you just to get home but don't take more than six of these a day. Bad for the liver." She put some Tylenol in a small pouch and gave it to Emily.

"Thanks, Ms. Gladdins."

"I hope that I will be on the sidelines watching you again soon."

"I hope so too. Maybe after this summer."

Emily trotted back to her homeroom. It made her head hurt at first, but she pushed that down, determined to get her heart rate up.

"Emily! Over here!" Her mother waved from the parking lot. Emily wheeled her Bianchi Volpe out to the asphalt and mounted.

"Come on, Mom. Race you home!"

"Emily!"

Katherine jumped on her Diverge and followed her young speed demon across the parking lot. Emily's head stopped hurting by the time she crossed Grove Road and hit the hill on Concord Drive. She was going to be okay. She knew it.

12

RECOVERY

THE GREENBRIER NEIGHBORHOOD WAS AWASH with brilliant white and pink dogwoods. The sun filtered through the trees as Emily made her way to school. Hilda trailed her as they navigated the curving, narrow roads.

"You're getting stronger, Em," Hilda said as Emily locked her bike to the rack outside the main entrance to the school. "How do you feel?"

"Great, but I'm not in racing form yet."

"What about when you're not riding?"

"I only have a dull throb in my head and kind of a twitchy feeling in my arms and legs. It goes away if I can do something physical. A lot less than last week."

"Good. Any nightmares or panic attacks?"

"Nothing like that. I relived the crash in my dreams in the hospital, but nothing since going home."

"Also good. Just don't be scared or surprised if you have a flashback at night now and again. It's normal, and it will get less and less."

"Is this like PTSD?"

"You had a terrible crash. Yes, it's like that."

"I guess you've seen a lot of that."

"I've had it too. It doesn't stop my life." She motioned toward the door. "Don't be late."

"Okay. Bye." Emily hefted her book panniers and ran into the crowd of students getting off a bus.

Hilda rolled out the driveway to her shift at the UVA Hospital. It made her feel good to be able to spell Katherine Dempsey from having to follow Emily to school every other day. She liked the girl, so bright and positive. It made her smile just to think of the way Emily approached almost everything she did.

That week, Emily had a follow-up appointment with Dr. Morgan right after school. Katherine was pleased when Hilda volunteered to accompany Emily to the appointment because it conflicted with the final class of the PhD seminar. It was one of Hilda's days off, so she was at the bike rack when Emily emerged from the main doors at CHS. They blew down the bike lane on the John W. Warner Parkway and followed the bike lanes up to West Main Street to the UVA Medical Center.

"You're doing great, Emily," the physician said after the usual prodding and questions. "You can resume normal activity."

"I don't need an escort to school?"

"No. But don't plan on returning to the race circuit this summer. Build back slowly. There is still healing going on in there. A full recovery by September is certainly possible."

Emily's face fell.

"Can't I race at all?"

"Not competitively. You need to keep getting faster and stronger, but I don't want you to push your body to make a finish line and tear down the progress you've made.

"Looks like you'll have to race against yourself, Em," said Hilda.

"Well put, Nurse Paisley. Does that make sense, Emily?"

"I guess. It just seems like so long."

Dr. Morgan looked at Hilda as if asking for an idea.

"Em, you can ride with your mother or even me. There's no shame in beating Katherine Dempsey. I've seen you two on the road."

"It's like a whole summer of recovery rides."

"Maybe we can make it interesting. Let's discuss it with your mom."

Emily shrugged with resignation. Dr. Morgan thanked Hilda for her involvement with Emily and wished them both a great summer.

"What was that about?" Emily asked as they unlocked their bikes. "'Keep working with me'?"

"I may be a friend, Em, but I'm still a nurse. I think he trusts me with you."

"Oh, yeah. That makes sense."

"Hey, it's early. Let's get a Frappuccino at Starbucks."

 C⒭ C⒭ C⒭

Studying for final exams consumed Emily's attention. Hilda was asked to work full-time as the university closed out the academic year and prepared for finals, then Beach Week. For many undergraduates, this consisted of an alcohol-hazed week at Myrtle Beach, South Carolina. Most made it back safely, but there was an uptick in ambulance calls and Pegasus missions to parties and automobile crashes.

During the week between finals and graduation, Emily rode around Albemarle County, often with Taniqua or with Hilda. Taniqua had a growth spurt in the spring and began to lose her skinny, gawky look. The rising sophomore walked with confidence. Her skin shone with health, and she had no extra fat anywhere. The cycling did what it usually does to a woman's legs.

"Are you doing anything special this summer, Tani?" Emily asked as they sipped iced tea outside the Jackson home. Mrs. Jackson had just left for work.

"Mom gets two weeks in July. We usually go to Tennessee for a family reunion."

"Where's that?"

"Davidson County. A place called the Hermitage."

"Are y'all *that* Jackson?"

"Uh-huh." Tani took a sip of her tea. "Weird, isn't it?"

"So, is this a reunion of all the Jackson descendants?"

"A lot of them. My great-great-great-something grandfather was a blacksmith on the plantation. My dad was named Aaron for him."

"Wow. That's special. Like me being a Daughter of the American Revolution—which I'm not, of course."

"That's weird, but it makes sense, kind of."

They fell silent for a moment. Emily was first to speak.

"You never talk about your father. Is he around?"

"He died."

"That must be his picture next to the flag in the living room. I'm sorry."

"No problem. I was too young to remember him. He was killed in Iraq."

Emily cast about for something to say. "It's not easy. I remember my dad dying. Sometimes I wish I had been too young, like you."

"You've got Mr. Dempsey."

"Mark is great. Mom and I were in pretty bad shape, and he changed everything."

"I wish my mom could find someone again. She works so hard. With her hours, I don't know if she'll ever meet anyone. She says there's not many good men around, but I keep hoping."

Emily's phone rang in her jersey. "Hi, Mom… You're home early… I'm at Tani's. We just got back… Okay. Be there in fifteen minutes … Yes, ma'am, twenty-five minutes." She ended the call and stood. "Gotta go. Mom's home and wants to go out with me as soon as I can shower and change. And she doesn't want me to race home." They giggled at that, thinking of the speeds they had already reached on their ride that day. They carried their glasses into the kitchen.

"See you Saturday."

"Yeah. Big one." Charlottesville High School graduation attracted so many people that it no longer fit in the high school auditorium. The arena at the university would be packed.

ભ ભ ભ

Memorial Day weekend. Tourists replaced the throngs of students on the Corner, but there was still a sense of calm having the crowds of intense young people missing. Emily and Hilda locked their bikes to the rack outside Starbucks and paused to cool off and catch their breath.

"Whew! That was a bear of a ride." Hilda wiped her face, stretched to her toes and bent back while Emily held on to the bike rack and stretched her legs. "How do you climb that fast?"

"I'm not sure," said Emily. "I've always been able to climb hard. I think it comes from my mother."

"She's amazing. What did she do to get like that?"

"She was into extreme sports when I was young. I remember Daddy taking me to single track races in the George Washington National Forest and triathlons at Virginia Beach. She has a box full of trophies and medals for cycling, running, snowboarding—you name it, she's done it." Emily held the door for Hilda. They walked up to the register and ordered grande Frappuccinos. They each picked a banana from the basket too.

"And your father?"

"He did triathlons. That's how they met. Mom won the Ironman that year and had a faster time than he did."

"You're kidding!"

"Well, she won the women's race, but still she came in third overall. He was right behind her, to hear them tell it."

"You spring from a great gene pool."

"I guess." Emily blushed a little. They took seats in the comfy chairs by the big window, where they could keep an eye on their bikes outside. "You're no slouch. You were right with me going up Afton Mountain."

"Having no panniers does make the old bike feel like a road racer. I could get used to riding around without a load, you know."

"But you go so fast. Most of the touring cyclists I remember in Kansas never went over about twenty kilometers per hour."

"I like to push myself."

"I love hearing your stories of all the places you've been. I would love to do that, too, someday."

"Do what?"

"Ride around from job to job. Seeing the world, but still riding my bike."

"It is fun, I admit. It's why I do it."

"With Nurse Bennet back, what are you going to do?"

"Not sure, Em. I like it here, so I put in for a couple of temporary positions at UVA and at Martha Jefferson Hospital. There are private practice physicians advertising for nurses too."

"You mean you'll stay?"

"I didn't say that, but I wouldn't mind coming back, or maybe taking another job here for a while. Nothing starts before September, so I have all summer off. I could keep the flat and come back.

"What about you? Are you all going anywhere this summer before Moving Day at the university?"

"There's talk of going to the Northern Neck for a while, but Mom has agreed to teach some summer session classes, and Mark is still settling in with the company. He has a lot of changes to make in his first year."

"The Northern Neck is where Mark's parents live, right?"

"Uh-huh. Are you going to tour this summer?"

"I think so. I'd like to ride to Montréal. It's a beautiful city, and Québec is glorious in the summer."

"All those cities—Washington, Philadelphia, New York. Exciting, but it sounds more dangerous than scenic."

"I know a route that goes to Norfolk, up the Eastern Shore to New Jersey. I take a hydrofoil to Manhattan and a ferry to Long Island, then ride to Port Jefferson. There, the ferry goes to Connecticut. By following the Connecticut River all the way north, I can get from here to Montréal without ever staying in a big city."

"Amazing. I wish I could tour. I love riding long distances, and we still have all my camping gear from Girl Scouts."

"Are you serious? What about your racing?"

"I can't do that this summer anyway, but I do worry about what touring would do to my racing form."

"It's different. Like being a Mack truck hauling cargo instead of a sports car. You can get up to speed, but slowly. After time, the fast-twitch muscles make room for the stronger, slow-twitch muscles."

"That's what I've been thinking about."

"Well, keep thinking about it. And talk to Mark and your mother because if you want to learn how to tour, you can come with me."

"Really?" Emily almost knocked over her Frappuccino. "Oh, Hilda, that would be awesome!"

"I think it would be fun for both of us."

They said goodbye outside at the bike rack. Emily raced up Rugby Road back to the Greenbrier neighborhood while Hilda slowly biked the few short blocks to her apartment near the medical center.

After a shower and slipping into the long nightshirt she preferred for lounging around the house, she started assembling the ingredients for a lasagna casserole. The Bennetts had invited her for supper. She had insisted on contributing the casserole. Suzie only put up token resistance. Hilda looked forward to playing with little Antoine.

She heard the familiar warble of a Skype call on her phone on the counter. Wiping her hands, she tapped the screen.

"Hey, Jack, what's up?"

"Hello, gorgeous. You're a sight for my eyes." Jack looked relaxed. Trim and tanned, with a smile that stirred Hilda in all sorts of places.

"You look like you've been getting some sun. Retirement agrees with you."

"Not much has changed. Ted got me called back as a special investigator. It keeps my clearances and access active. When we're not working the coast of the Bay checking leads, I'm out fishing with Joe. That's a lot of sun."

"So, what's the threat assessment this week?"

"It's lower. Hassan and Abdul were identified in Montréal by facial recognition at the airport. The RCMP is checking whether they were going or coming and where."

"You know that's where I'm planning to ride this summer."

"Yes, but at least we know they can't get at you this week. We'll find them before you get there. Greg Sprouse says it's quiet there." Hilda had been surprised to find out how many security and intelligence assets were devoted to Central Virginia. It made her feel safer for having chosen to work in Charlottesville.

"It's quiet, thank God. I've been riding a lot with Emily—you remember the girl I met in Kansas?"

"Yes."

"It keeps me extra alert having her around. Speaking of which, are you still planning to meet me heading north?"

"Wouldn't miss it for the world. It already feels like years since my retirement ceremony last week. I like having you around."

"Would you mind some extra company this time?"

"Emily?"

Hilda smiled. "She can't race this summer, and she's thinking of touring with me to Canada. It's a big choice because it'll change her conditioning and her cycling form to tour that far. She also has never left home for so long by herself. I told her to discuss it with Mark and Katherine and to make her mind up slowly."

"I think that would be swell. I've never done a group tour before."

"Three people is hardly that, but we wouldn't have the privacy we usually do."

"She gets her own tent, I hope."

"Of course. She's a rising college student, not a little girl."

"I think it would be great to have her along. Besides, after all you've told me about her, I'm dying to meet her. I checked her out online. She's hot!"

"She was jailbait in those pictures, Jack." Hilda put on a mock scolding tone. "She only turns eighteen next month." Jack laughed.

"I was referring to her racing form and what I read in the articles." He made an innocent face. "She had some amazing wins until that crash in March."

"True. I didn't tell her this, but at her age, she could always retrain and return to racing, probably even stronger."

"Why not tell her?"

"She's so excited about the idea that I didn't want to influence her decision."

"Okay. Anyway, I'll be happy either way as long as you're along."

They chatted some more about the Rathburns, and Hilda's job search, then ended the call. Hilda returned to the casserole, singing an aria from *Die Fledermaus*. While the casserole baked, she checked job listings one more time, then changed into a green skirt and a white shell with low-heeled pumps. With the casserole safely wrapped in an insulated carrier, she walked to West Main Street and caught the bus to the Belmont neighborhood where Marcus and Suzie Bennett lived with little Antoine.

13

NEAR MISS

HILDA SWITCHED ON CHANNEL 29 NEWS while the coffee maker gurgled on the countertop. She didn't watch much TV, but she would rather let Dave Rogers tell her what the weather would be than look it up on her computer. She assembled a three-egg omelet as the commercials droned on. She was not really paying attention, but she perked up when the commercial was interrupted for breaking news.

"At the university medical center, shots were fired in the emergency room. UVA and Charlottesville Police were on the scene and report that the shooter has been stopped. We'll update the story as events unfold. Here's Dave Rogers with the weather."

She turned off the stove and sat at the counter. She tried to picture who might have been in the ER at that moment. She got up to pour some coffee and spilled it when her cell phone rang. She put down the carafe and looked at the screen. "Greg Sprouse, FBI." She took a deep breath and tapped the answer icon.

"Good morning, Greg."

"Hello, Hilda. Did you hear the news?"

"Just a breaking news flash about a shooting at the ER. Was anyone hurt?"

"Suzie Bennett took a grazing shot on the arm. She'll be fine. It was the shooter's bad luck that Walter Johnson from CPD was there with his cousin Shariq from UVA Police. They put him down with a bullet each."

"Where are you?"

"At the scene. We're still working it, but I need to see you. There is already a plainclothes CPD officer on his way to your building to keep a lookout for anyone trying to get to you. We don't want to tip off where you live, in case there are more behind this. Please don't open to anyone before I get there."

"Okay. I hope you'll have more details when you do."

"I will." He ended the call.

The weather seemed irrelevant, though Hilda noted from the graphic on the screen that it should be a beautiful day. The omelet had cooked itself in the hot pan. She wiped up the coffee she had spilled and put out another mug. She considered changing out of her bicycle kit but decided to eat breakfast while she waited. She could change clothes or not depending on what the FBI agent had to say.

The news returned. A lone gunman had walked into the ambulance entrance of the emergency department with an assault rifle. As he raised his weapon to aim at the duty nurse, the two policemen by the water cooler to the left of the door both pulled their guns and fired. The attacker's first rifle round grazed the left arm of the nurse. The next three rounds went into the floor in a line as the gunman fell to the right from the force of the two shots by the officers. "The gunman remains unidentified. Identity of the nurse is being withheld pending notification of next of kin, but she is not seriously injured."

Hilda had just put the breakfast dishes in the dishwasher when the doorbell rang. Greg Sprouse was outside, rocking back and forth on his feet. Hilda undid the chain and unbolted the door for him.

"Coffee? You take it black as I recall."

"Thanks."

Greg went to the kitchen with her.

"I'm glad Suzie is okay. I'm stewing here, hoping that this doesn't have to do with me."

"I'm afraid that it might, Hilda." Greg sat at the table where she had put his coffee. He pulled out his notebook. "We identified the shooter right away, but we don't want to tell the media just yet."

"And?"

"Richard Lee of Richmond. He goes by the name Abu Sayed, which he made up himself. We had been keeping an eye on him, so when he left Richmond this morning, we passed him off to the state police as he drove up I-64. They handed him off to CPD."

"Is that why Shariq and Walter were there?"

"Not really." Greg grinned. "I don't think that they knew that you left."

"Oh." Hilda smiled quickly. Shariq was cute, Walter was drop-dead gorgeous, and neither seemed to notice that Hilda could have borne either one of them.

Greg continued. "Lee has a rap sheet as long as your arm, but the short of it is that he was a very disturbed young man, who was radicalized in our own penitentiary system. He started out as an angry white boy in high school and fancied himself a white nationalist when he was arrested for buying and selling firearms while underage."

"He could do that?"

"In spite of recent changes, it's still too easy in Virginia. Anyway, that's what got him sent to jail the first time. He turned eighteen in prison. He embraced Islam while there. I hesitate to call it conversion, considering what a hodgepodge his beliefs were. He attracted the attention of the bureau when he was recruited by a radical cell we know about in Richmond."

"The connection to me?"

"What you might expect. We knew that he followed *Al-Jazeera* in English and a few dark-web sites. He had downloaded the old *fatwa* on you and your picture from the Chicago newspaper last summer."

"Didn't you say, 'white nationalist'?"

"I also said 'very disturbed young man.' He may have conflated his devotion to Islam with his racism."

"Weird."

"Yes. We need to investigate the case further, to determine if this was a hate crime or a terrorist act. We're also making sure whether he was acting alone or not. Lee, as a one-off hater, doesn't pose as much danger as a potential extension of the Forebears into Virginia."

"Have you talked to Jack?"

"He's checking the whereabouts of the various Forebear contacts that we've been watching in this case."

At that moment, Hilda's phone rang.

"Hi, Jack. Greg Sprouse is here, and he's briefing me."

"Hi, lovely. That saves me a phone call. Can we go to speaker?"

Hilda put the phone between Greg and herself and tapped the speaker icon.

"Hi, Jack," said Greg. "Any news?"

"Pete Sayfield has a total of fifteen people that Hassan and Abdul met with in Maryland and DC, and all are accounted for. Very quiet here."

"Okay, then. We're checking Lee's contacts from this end."

Hilda spoke up. "Speaking of Abdul and Hassan, anything from the Canadians?"

"I was going to call you this morning, but this came up first. The RCMP confirmed that they came over the border in Vermont in a rental car, which they dropped at the airport in Montréal. The credit card they used was stolen in Havre de Grace, near here. They may have been trying to get a flight out, but they slipped off the radar after being filmed walking around in the ticketing area for a while. Facial recognition was overloaded and picked them out only as they walked out the sliding doors. That was the day before yesterday."

"Thanks, Jack," said Greg. "Does Pete know this?"

"Pete is the go-between with the Canadians. Almost all our info comes through his office in Baltimore. How are you doing, Hilda?"

"More than a little shocked. The injured nurse was the one I was spelling. I only left the other day, you know." She looked up at Greg with a smile. "Greg has me under house arrest with all the exits blocked."

She heard Jack laugh. "Good. What's the plan, Greg?"

"We just want to make sure that Lee is a loner. If the media continues to speculate about disturbed young men randomly running around with assault rifles, we may be able to avoid the ramifications of either another hate crime in Charlottesville or a perceived terrorist event. Of course, the connection to Hilda may leak out at some point, which would change the game completely."

"How long to figure it out, one way or the other?" Hilda asked.

"Not long. Fortunately, we know Lee and his contacts. I'll let you know as soon as I can."

Jack spoke up. "Hilda, when were you planning to leave town?" Greg raised his eyes in surprise.

"I was thinking as early as the end of next week. Emily is still talking to her parents, and I'm having dinner at their house on Friday." She looked at Greg. "I was planning to tour on my bicycle this summer."

"I heard from Pete about your under-the-radar bicycling." He looked relieved. "Depending on what we learn between now and then, that actually might be perfect."

"We'll be keeping in touch this time unless it looks like our communications have been compromised."

Greg smiled. The months-long search for Hilda after Chicago had become an FBI legend. They ended the call after agreeing to touch base again the next day, or if the connection to Hilda leaked to the media.

ૠ ૠ ૠ

Meanwhile, west of town, Katherine and Emily were riding toward the Blue Ridge at a steady thirty kilometers per hour, working up a sweat and not talking much. As the sun climbed behind them, they geared down for the hills beyond Crozet, turning around about halfway up Afton Mountain. Traffic was almost nonexistent on the country roads with most of the residents at work.

After they had sped down the mountain and reached the rolling landscape on the TransAmerica Trail, Katherine slowed to a conversational twenty kilometers per hour.

"How are you feeling, Emily?"

"Good, Mom, why?"

"You're recovering quickly. Clearly, you can already outrun me any time you want. I appreciate the fact that you don't."

"Dr. Morgan doesn't want me competing. You know that."

"What I mean is that you've been talking about touring with Hilda. I've been thinking a lot about that."

"And?"

"I just worry. That's all."

"Oh, Mom." Emily rolled her eyes. "You're *supposed* to worry. It's your job."

Katherine laughed lightly. "I know. Still, I wonder whether I need to worry about keeping up with you all summer or take up chewing my fingernails while you're gone. We've never been apart as long as this tour would be."

"You don't think I haven't thought about that?" Emily's speed crept up, and her expression became grim.

Katherine was about to call out when her daughter fell back to rejoin her. "Sorry, Mom. That was kind of short."

"No problem. At least I know it's bugging us both. Given that, how are you feeling about touring or racing?"

"I can't settle on it quite yet. I keep putting off the decision."

"Want to talk about it? I've tried to keep out of it, but I can see that you're torn."

"Let me think on the way home."

"Okay."

They sped back up and soon were pushing their bikes into the basement bike shop/storage on Brandywine Drive. After stretching and showers, they met in the kitchen with a bowl of fruit and a pair of protein shakes between them. They stared at each other in silence as Emily pulled an orange from the bowl. Katherine chose a banana. Emily finally blinked.

"I want to go with Hilda."

"Okay. Just to be sure, what's your rationale?"

"I can't race all my life. Even if I can come back to racing next fall, how old will I be when I retire? Thirty?"

"You could tour then."

"But what are my chances of doing my first tour with a teacher as awesome as Hilda? She's not just an expert at bicycle touring, she's a combat-trained nurse. There's just about nothing that can go seriously wrong. I feel so comfortable with her."

"I admit that knowing that you would be with her does ease my Mommy-willies. What about the muscles, slow-fast, and all that?"

"I'll just have to find out. For one thing, I already have the power muscles for climbing hills, and Hilda is a strong rider. I have a hunch that I wouldn't get that far behind with just one tour."

Katherine took a swig of her protein shake. She looked at Emily, then out the window, where the backyard was bright with brilliant flowers and bright green trees. She looked back.

"I'd like to run this by Mark—no faces, Emily. I accept your choice. He's a smart guy, though. He might have some ideas."

"He already said he would support me either way. He even offered to drive to REI in Richmond if there is anything I need that we can't find here."

"I know. Hilda's coming to dinner Friday night. We can all agree on the details and get ready."

Katherine's phone rang. It was Mark.

"Hi, dear, what's up?"

"Have you seen the news today?"

"Uh, no. We just got back from a ride." She motioned to Emily to turn on the TV. "What's happening?"

"A shooter at the UVA Hospital ER. I was hoping you had more details. Isn't Hilda there?"

"No. She left the day before yesterday. Mrs. Bennett came back to work."

"Oh. I was worried. Anyway, Charlottesville is back in the news again. Not many details, but apparently no one was hurt seriously, except the gunman."

"That's a relief. We'll check on it. You'll be home tonight."

"Maybe even a little early. See you then."

"Drive safely, honey. I love you." They ended the call.

Katherine and Emily waited for the news at the top of the hour. The nurse, Suzie Bennett, was only lightly grazed. The shooter was dead, and police were investigating his identity and the motivations for the attack.

"Would this have anything to do with Hilda?" Emily asked.

"I can't see why? She wasn't even there, but we can ask her. By then, maybe the police will know more."

"I'm going to call her, just to see how she is."

"Fair enough. Just don't take too long. She'd be too nice to tell you if you're interrupting something."

After washing out their blender bottles, Katherine went shopping at Whole Foods while Emily went to her room to call Hilda.

"Hi, Em. Nice to hear from you."

"I just saw the news. Are you okay?"

Hilda laughed. "I'm fine. I haven't even been out of the house. Thanks for your concern. Maybe I should've called you."

"We just got back from a ride. If Mark hadn't called us, we wouldn't have known to turn on the news."

"I've got the TV on too. Terrible, isn't it?"

"I know you're not there anymore, but you were the first person we thought of when we saw the bulletin."

"My lucky day, I guess, although Suzie Bennett is a friend, and I'm really bummed about her getting shot at. As soon as the police clear the scene, I hope that I can see her."

"She's still at work?"

"For a little while longer. I called her husband Marcus. He says that they're going to give her the rest of the day off. She should be home soon."

"I'm glad you're not hurt."

"Thanks. Are we still on to ride Thursday?"

"Sure. Then Friday you're coming to dinner."

"Absolutely. How are you coming deciding on the tour?"

"I've made up my mind. I want to come with you. Mom wants to see if Mark has any ideas, but he's already agreed either way."

"Okay, then, I'll come prepared to get into details. This will be fun."

"I'm excited."

Thursday, Emily and Hilda rode a fast one hundred-kilometer circuit north parallel to US-29 into Orange County, east to Gordonsville, then back to Charlottesville along Highway 231 and US-250. Not much conversation as the older tourist worked to keep up with the teenager on her Bianchi. Since deciding to tour, Emily chose to ride the Bianchi, for its extra weight, and its handling on bad road surfaces and in traffic. She was good about not letting the distance grow between them, which kept her from inadvertently overextending herself. The Dempseys were both out when they returned to the house on Brandywine Drive. Hilda waved goodbye and rode home. Emily let herself in and went to her room. After her stretching and a shower, she began laying out the things she planned to take on the tour. Hilda would be back the next day to review them with her.

14

BRANDYWINE DRIVE

FRIDAY EVENING, HILDA RODE TO BRANDYWINE DRIVE. The flowers and bright green leaves were reaching their peak in the heat of the late spring. Soon, just crossing town like this would be a sweaty affair, even with the shady tree cover of the Greenbrier neighborhood.

Mark had fired up the grill. Dinner was set up outside on the deck. As she walked around with a glass of Riesling, Hilda noticed how private the yard was. A ravine ran between the houses to the rear, where the woods thrived in a small stream that led to the Meadow Brook. Emily and Katherine joined her.

"When do you want to leave, Hilda?" asked Katherine.

"That depends on my partner here." She smiled. "By myself, I'd be gone already, but we want to see that Em is outfitted properly, don't we?"

"Let's go tomorrow!" said Emily. The two older women laughed.

"Sure, Em. Is your gear ready for inspection like we talked about yesterday?"

"That sounds very army, Major Paisley," said Katherine.

"I have everything laid out on my bed," said Emily. "Do I have to pack it?"

"Let's have a look after supper. If it will fit, you could pack it up, but even if it won't, the main thing tonight is to draw up a shopping list of what's missing and pull out what won't fit. I can come back each day to help." She looked at Katherine. "Even with any shopping, we should be able to set out by next Friday, don't you think?"

Katherine nodded. Just then, Mark called them to the grill to load their plates.

"What about your gear, Hilda?" asked Mark as he piled a steak and two baked potatoes on her plate.

"It's packed. I keep it that way, except for the toilet kit. I've been airing the tent and sleeping bag since arriving in Charlottesville, but I packed them yesterday."

"How long does it take you to get going in the morning?"

"About twenty minutes if the tent is dry."

Emily sloshed her drink on her arm. "That fast?"

"I don't expect that at first, but I'll lay odds that one of us will usually be packed before the other after a while. When I'm riding with Jack, he's the slow one."

"That's Jack, your army friend?" Katherine asked.

"Yes."

"Will he be joining you?" Mark asked.

"I hope so. He's at the Aberdeen Proving Ground and should be able to catch us in Delaware before we get to Lewes."

"What's he like?" Emily was wide-eyed, but her parents leaned in with a different kind of interest.

"Oh, I guess six-four. Sandy hair, cut regulation style. Hazel eyes—and, of course, fit and hard." She winked at Emily, who blushed. Katherine and Mark laughed.

"MOS?" Mark used the abbreviation for military occupational specialty.

"Military Police. He's a major, just retired. He's back on active duty at Aberdeen to help the provost marshal."

Mark sat back. "So, we're sending our little lamb into the world with a police escort and a rolling emergency medical department."

"Something like that." Hilda smiled.

"How much could go wrong with that?" Mark said to Katherine, who looked relieved.

Hilda took a big bite of steak while the others did the same. She thought during the silence as they chewed.

"Actually, Mark, I don't want to deceive you. A lot could go wrong. But I try to be as ready as possible for it, and so far, it's worked out. Broken chains, thunderstorms, crazy drivers, and clueless pedestrians— they're all part of the mix. I've watched Emily, and she can handle all that already."

"Even pretzeled front wheels," blurted out Emily. She clamped her mouth shut in shock.

"What's that about?" asked her mother. Emily looked distressed. Hilda put her hand on Emily's forearm.

"It's how we met, Katherine. I gather you didn't tell them, Em."

"I wasn't supposed to be out alone, but my two friends stood me up. I was afraid to tell Mom, so I just said I fell on some wet leaves, which was true."

Hilda turned to Mark and Katherine. "She was walking home on the road from the abandoned base, with her bike over her shoulder. She would've made it home late for supper, but otherwise safe and sound—except for the bike."

"Hilda showed me how to snap the wheel back into shape using a spoke wrench. That's when I decided to take Jake's maintenance course."

"I have to admit that you're a decent wrench, Emily," said Mark.

Katherine sighed. "So, you've known Hilda since last summer. Probably not the first revelation we'll have as we grow older." She squeezed her daughter's hand. "That was before Colorado, dear. Everything's been different since I decided to let you follow your dreams."

Over dessert, Mark asked about the attack at UVA earlier in the week. "Did you see anything?"

"No. I left two days earlier. I'd been temping for Suzie Bennett, the nurse who was wounded, while she was on maternity leave."

"Lucky for you."

"Yes, but Suzie's a friend, and I'm still upset about it."

"The police said it was a kid from Richmond. Some kind of disturbed loner who had applied for a job there some time ago."

"I saw that report too." Hilda took a spoon of ice cream. Emily was staring at her. Hilda guessed what she was going to say and froze.

"Was he after you, Hilda?"

Damn, she's too sharp, thought Hilda.

"Why would he be?" asked her mother.

Emily looked from Hilda to Katherine and froze. She felt like she had spoken out of turn in class. Her face blushed deeply.

"Go ahead, Em. I think I know what you're thinking." Hilda urged her on with a gesture.

"Chicago."

"Chicago?" Mark and Katherine said together.

Hilda sighed, more with relief than worry. "Chicago last summer. Emily's referring to my picture on the front page of the *Chicago Tribune*. Right, Em?" Emily nodded. Hilda put down her spoon. "I was wondering all day how to bring this up because you need to know. Do you remember the incident she's referring to?"

Mark shook his head. Katherine thought for a moment, then said, "You were the nurse at the Sheraton who fingered the attackers."

"Well, not that dramatic, but, yes, I was there. The ATF and FBI agents asked me a bunch of questions, and the answers helped them narrow their investigation."

Mark's expression brightened as he recalled the incident, "They made arrests just two days later. Is there a revenge thing going here?"

"We don't know, but Chicago is the reason that the FBI and the police kept a close watch on me after I started working at UVA. They've been keeping me informed. For example, the *fatwa* to kill me was canceled, but not before the social media echo chamber started going.

"What I'm about to tell you is still confidential. Richard Lee, the shooter in the ER, was already on the FBI and local police watch lists. They've determined for sure that he was acting alone because he had no connection to the Forebears of the Mahdi, who orchestrated the attack in Chicago. Lee applied for jobs at UVA, Martha Jefferson and VCU in Richmond. He had that Chicago photo of me in a folder with his job applications, photos of teachers he hated in high school, and the Krispy Kreme doughnut shop where he was fired last month. Was he disgruntled about UVA or gunning for me?" She raised her hands, palm up.

Katherine was stunned. "You're not seriously planning on taking my daughter into this, are you?"

Mark put his hand on her arm. Katherine took a deep breath. Emily was looking wide-eyed at all three of them. "This worries me too," he said. "Hilda?"

"I won't sugarcoat this, but I'll tell you what has happened so far, and let you check some things out yourselves to reassure yourselves—or not."

"It was so long ago," Emily said. Hilda smiled.

"I remember when time ran as slowly as it does for you, Em. It hasn't been a year yet, has it? You know what happened in Chicago. I was there to meet Jack. We rode through Indiana, Ohio, Pennsylvania, and Maryland. Three months later, we arrived at Aberdeen Proving Grounds, where we had planned to visit Jack's brother for Thanksgiving. We stayed below the radar until we got there. We figured that an army base would be about as safe a place as we could find."

"You mean you dodged a nationwide search by a global terrorist organization?" Mark was impressed.

"Something like that. We were mainly trying to avoid the FBI because I didn't trust our location not to leak if they found us."

"The FBI is looking for you?" asked Katherine.

"No, not now. I called the Chicago Field Office every day along the way, so they'd know that I wasn't hiding. But they never figured out who was with me or our whereabouts until the day we left DC to ride to Aberdeen."

"How did you manage to do that for three months?" Mark asked. Hilda looked at Emily, who was bursting.

"Easy," said Emily. "They were on bicycles!"

Hilda let that sink in. Katherine seemed to struggle to recover some normalcy.

"Coffee?" she asked. Hands went up. Emily stood.

"I'll make it, Mom." She left the door to the deck open, so she could hear.

Mark and Katherine sat in stunned silence for a while. Katherine closed her eyes, leaned back, focusing her thoughts and feelings. She sighed deeply, opened her eyes, and sat back up.

"This makes a pretzeled front wheel look lame." She took another breath. "You and Emily knew about this all along?"

"No, Katherine. I never talked about it. But Emily kept that photo from the paper. She mentioned it in the hospital after her crash."

Mark spoke. "You were in the ER when she arrived on the helo, weren't you?"

"Yes, I was. She recognized me before falling asleep again."

Katherine stood and said to Mark, "Are we sending Emily out to be hunted by terrorists?" He rose and put his arms around her.

"No, we're not. But we haven't heard the rest of the story." He looked at Hilda. "You were saying that you 'try to be as ready as possible for it, and so far, it's worked out.' What's your plan for this?"

"The fact is, the Forebears themselves aren't the major threat. Jack has been assigned full-time to a multinational police operation on this case. There are only two Forebears left. They tried to get me at Aberdeen before Christmas. As of last week, they thought that I was still there. Jack and the Maryland police almost caught them. They managed to flee to Canada. The Canadian police will pick them up. Their American contacts are accounted for and being watched. Jack knows them all, practically by name.

"The problem is loners like Lee. But someone like that has to be lucky enough to see me, recognize me, and mount an attack on short notice."

"You do stand out in a crowd, Hilda," Mark said.

"I know. Not always a good thing. Anyway, only the police and the FBI know that he had my photo. The other potential targets are coming out from the people who knew him. That is why the 'disturbed young man' story continues to get play in the media. The gun-control issue is dominating the news, and the police aren't going to volunteer the fact that he had my photo."

Emily came out with a tray with the coffee carafe, sugar, and creamer. Mark moved mugs to the table.

"Go on, Hilda," he said.

"It's like lightning. The chance of being hit is never zero, but there are things one can do to reduce the odds. The safest place for me is on the road, and the bicycle has proven itself to be incredibly low-profile. People in North America simply don't think of it. I won't be so bold as to say that Emily would be safer with me, but I want you to consider the incremental risk among all the risks you were already willing for her to take—crashes, illness, rednecks throwing beer bottles, potholes, drainage grates, drunk drivers, and even lightning. You should talk to Special Agent Greg Sprouse, the FBI resident agent here in Charlottesville. He can give you background, which I'm not allowed to divulge. Jack and I promised not to keep the FBI blind again, so Greg'll also almost always know where Emily is all summer."

"You mean the FBI will be following you?"

"Not quite, but almost. Greg can explain how it works."

"Do they let you know what's going on as you travel?"

"When we check in, yes. Jack has all the necessary clearances to work with any law enforcement agency, so they're completely open with us. In fact, he's something of a legend."

"Is he armed?" Katherine asked.

"If you mean a gun, I don't think he rides with one. It's heavy and bulky, and I would have noticed. But don't let the man anywhere near you if you don't have good intentions. In Iraq, I saw him take down three armed soldiers with his bare hands."

Katherine shook her head. "I don't know. This scares me."

"Mom, it's my trip. I'm not scared. I trust Hilda."

Katherine hugged her daughter. "I know, dear. And I know the thrill of doing something risky and stupid. In fact, on a scale of risk, I've done stupider things than what you and Hilda are proposing. But I wasn't a mother then."

"We don't need to make a firm choice now," said Hilda. "You and Mark need to discuss this with Emily. You need to talk to Greg, and maybe Jack in Aberdeen. If that isn't enough, Pete Sayfield, the Special Agent in Charge of the Baltimore Field Office, can put in his two cents' worth. Jack, Greg, or I can give you the contact information. Even if Emily does not go, let's look at her gear to see what she needs. She could tour locally if she doesn't go with me."

They finished their coffee in safer conversation. Hilda was a frequent guest, so cleaning up was a team effort that took no time with everyone pitching in. Mark had the grill scrubbed and covered before the dishwasher was loaded.

They retired to Emily's room. Posters of Megan Guarnier, Dalia Muccioli, Laura Trott, Annemiek van Vleuten and Lizzie Armitstead covered the walls. A drone shot of a peloton racing down the Passo dello Stelvio in the Alps was taped to the ceiling over the bed.

Hilda was used to Emily's tidiness, so the pile of clothes, camping gear, and bike accessories on the bed made her laugh.

"Where are the panniers, Em?"

"I only have my book panniers, so I haven't bought those yet. I thought you could help me figure out what I need to carry all this."

She messed Emily's hair and laughed. "To carry all this, young lady, you will need a pickup truck, not panniers. Let's see what you have."

An hour later, Emily had put away a week's worth of underwear, cotton blouses, skirts, and shoes. She kept three bike jerseys, two pairs of shorts and a Marmot rain jacket. The bike accessories were reduced to a spare inner tube. The camp stove and cooking kit were put away because Hilda and Jack had those. The tent from Girl Scouts was too big and heavy, but her sleeping bag would be adequate for the summer and early fall. A new tent went on the list. Mark had also written down panniers, collapsible bowl and cup, air mattress, touring shorts with gel liners, titanium eating utensils, and bicycle touring shoes with SPD clips.

Hilda pointed at the bed. "Put all that in a pillow-case." Emily began filling the case.

"I can't get the sleeping bag all the way in."

"That's okay. You'll have two panniers. Between the two, you can pack everything here and on the shopping list. The tent can go on the rack."

Mark tapped his pencil on the clipboard. "That's amazing. You crossed the country with just two pillowcases—I mean panniers?"

"Basically. Along the coasts or in Europe, just two panniers. When I must carry food and cook, I add two front panniers."

With the pillowcase filled, Emily's room was as tidy as usual. Hilda bade them good night and rode back to her apartment. They would meet again the next day. This time next week, Hilda would be riding under the radar again. Would she have Emily's irrepressible enthusiasm with her or not?

ଊ ଊ ଊ

Emily and Hilda stood in the sunshine outside the store in White Hall. They finished their Magnum Dove Bars, put the wrappers in the trash, and took swigs from their bike bottles. Hilda swung smoothly onto her bicycle throwing her right leg over the saddle and coasted to a halt to watch Emily put her leg over her top tube and slide to a position straddling her bike. With some wobbling, she got rolling and picked up speed. Hilda waved her on and rode up alongside as they headed back toward Charlottesville on the TransAmerica Trail.

"Wow, I've never felt so clumsy in my life," said Emily. "Will I get used to it?"

"Sure. You're already doing better than this morning at home. You didn't drop the bike this time."

"My book panniers are heavy, but this is worse. And the bike handles more sluggishly with thirty-two-millimeter tires."

"Your load's also spread out wider. That changes the handling too."

They slowly picked up speed. With her new panniers packed for the trip, Emily no longer blew away from Hilda as they made their way down Garth Road at a respectable twenty-five kilometers per hour. Emily adjusted quickly to the heavier handling of her bicycle in motion, so the occasional debris or pothole did not pose a problem.

"Agent Sprouse is cooler than I expected an FBI agent to be," Emily said after a mile of silence. "Mark and Mom absolutely howled when he described the search for you and Jack."

"I like him. And I'm glad he convinced them that you would be as safe with me as anywhere else. I don't know if I rate that kind of endorsement."

"Anything less would not have convinced them, especially Mom. I think that they're happy."

They flew into the ravine to cross the Mechums River, then pulled up the steep grade on the other side.

"I'm going to be sore tomorrow, Hilda. I can feel the strain of pulling this weight through all these ravines."

"That's why we're doing this today. You should be fine by Friday, and there's nothing this steep east of Charlottesville."

"If you say so."

Six miles from White Hall, they spied the Hunt Country Store.

"Hilda! I have to stop. Omigod!"

Hilda slowed and stopped. She looked back at Emily. Blood was running down her right leg. Emily's face signaled a mix of surprise, anguish, and embarrassment.

"Period?" asked Hilda.

"This is scary. My pad is useless."

"Let's ride over to the store." Hilda gestured to the store. "They have a bathroom. We can get you cleaned up and a fresh pad."

"What's wrong?"

"Probably nothing, Em, but we'll take a look."

They rode the two hundred meters to the store and parked their bikes.

"Since we're packed, we have everything we need, don't we?" Hilda began to open her right pannier. Emily looked helpless. "Let me guess. You don't have pads or tampons." Emily shook her head. "Don't worry. I was going to suggest switching to mine since whatever you're using isn't going to be enough. Grab a clean pair of shorts and your towel."

Emily got her shorts from her pannier. Hilda knew where the bathroom was. Inside, Emily cleaned up and put Hilda's pad in her fresh shorts. She rinsed out her bloody shorts, and Hilda showed her how to ring them out almost dry using her camp towel.

"Feel better?" Hilda asked as they buried the bloody paper towels in the trash can.

"Much. I only started having periods last year, and they have never been like this."

"That's because you've been a top-level athlete since puberty. You know what athletic amenorrhea is?"

"Lack of a period. It's common with athletes."

"True. And not a problem for someone who eats well and sleeps regularly, like you. But you're looking at the other side. You stopped exercising that hard when you had your crash, and your body is catching up.

With normal periods you're going to need the larger pads, or tampons."

Emily frowned. "Just what I need. Something else to pack."

Hilda laughed. "It's not that bad. You can get what you need anywhere, so you only need to carry enough for one period. We can split a pack between us."

"Okay."

They went out into the store and bought a carton of orange juice, which they finished before continuing back to Charlottesville.

"How was your first mini-tour?" Katherine asked as they trooped into the kitchen. Hilda carried Emily's tent.

"Mom." Emily dropped her panniers and hugged her mother. Katherine aimed a questioning look at Hilda.

"Her athletic amenorrhea ceased with a vengeance. She'll be okay. I had a bigger size pad in my pannier."

"Oh, that." She patted Emily's back. "Hilda's right. It happened to me too. Scared the hell out of me the first time." She held her daughter out by the shoulders. "You feel better?"

Emily nodded, then picked up her panniers with a slight grunt. "It was a good idea to do this on Wednesday because I'm going to be sore tomorrow. It's a whole different ride with big tires and loaded bags."

Emily and Hilda took the gear to Emily's room. Emily put her shorts in the laundry hamper.

"I plan to have no laundry left over when we go Friday," she said.

"Good idea."

Emily hugged the nurse. "I'm so glad you're around. You're my best friend. Ever."

"I'm glad, too, Em." Hilda disengaged. "See you tonight."

That night, the Dempseys turned dinner into an early birthday party for Emily. Mark and Katherine had already bought her panniers, tent, and everything on the shopping list, but there were still presents on the table. Hilda gave her a Road ID bracelet. Katherine had mail-ordered a Shebeest sleeveless bicycle jersey in bright orange, red and black.

"No fair," said Mark. "Why are all the best-looking bicycle kits only for women?"

They toasted Emily with a 2015 Chardonnay and made jokes about her being a bargain. "Other kids are getting cars," Mark said.

"Dad, I don't want a car. You've always gotten me the best of everything I've ever wanted."

"What did you call me?"

Emily put her hand to her mouth in shock. Then she laughed. "That came naturally. May I?"

Mark rose and went to her place to hug his step-daughter. "Of course, and I'll always try to earn it." Hilda saw that tears suddenly ran down Katherine's cheeks. She felt a welling in her own eyes.

"Eighteen is too late to adopt you, but I would have at any point." Mark looked at his wife. "I think you both know that."

Hilda slipped into the kitchen while the three of them had a group hug. She found the cake and the gas lighter and lit the bonfire of candles. She waited until the family disengaged before intoning "Happy Birthday" as she came back into the room.

15

HAMPTON ROADS

Thursday, Hilda got emails from several Warmshowers hosts in the Richmond area and called a family that lived in the Fan District to confirm. Then she booked a tent site at the campground at the Joint Expeditionary Base Little Creek-Fort Story. She emptied her refrigerator and carried what she could not eat in the next twenty-four hours to the graduate student couple next door. She had almost sublet her apartment for the summer, then thought better of it. *What if the Forebears or unknown crazies figure out where I live while I'm gone? Better to have the place empty.* She checked the air in her tires and oiled the chain again. Emily and she had both their bikes overhauled and tuned on Monday and Tuesday.

She made a big salad with baked cod and vegetables, clearing out the rest of the refrigerator, and took it to the westward-facing window of the main room. The sky over the Blue Ridge was a blaze of brilliant reds and oranges, and she remembered the adage a navy friend had taught her, "Red sky at morning, sailor take warning. Red sky at night, sailor's delight."

Indeed, Friday dawned clear and sunny. Hilda rose with the sun, dressed and finished the rest of the milk and the last bowl of cereal. Nothing would be left behind for mice or ants or people. An hour after rising, she was riding down the John Warner Parkway to Rio Road and on to Brandywine Drive.

By eight, the hugging and fretting were over. Emily and Hilda were riding down US-250, almost the last segment of the TransAmerica Trail.

The land here rolled gently downhill toward the sea. On either side in Fluvanna and Goochland Counties, they passed farms with horses, livestock, or crops maturing in the sun. The corn was already high enough to block the view in many places.

The highway paralleled Interstate 64, which carried the high-speed, long-haul traffic. For that reason, most of the traffic passing them was local, with very few large rigs, and almost no speeders.

They stopped at Zion Crossroads to drink some water and stretch.

"You've been quiet, Em."

"I'm so excited, I want to burst, but I don't know what these first few days will be like, so I'm trying to conserve my energy. It doesn't sound like much to ride a hundred and twenty-one kilometers, but I worry about doing it with the bags."

"You'll be fine. As long as you remember your sunscreen every day."

Emily gave a little gasp and turned to her left pannier. "Thanks for reminding me. Lucky you don't need this stuff."

"Oh, but I do, Em. I blister as bad as anyone else. It just doesn't show until it's too late. I use the same SPF as you."

Emily finished applying her sunscreen. They mounted up and rode on. Emily went thoughtful again for about ten miles.

"Hilda?"

"Yes?"

"Have you ever been attacked on the road?"

"Kind of late to back out, isn't it?"

"I don't mean it that way. I just wonder about all the stories I hear about women being assaulted. Have you have been harassed?"

"Too often, but the only man to walk away from it was the very first one—my drill sergeant in boot camp."

"What happened? I'm sorry. You probably don't want to talk about it."

"You brought it up, and the problem is real, so we might as well talk about it. He fancied himself some kind of stud. He was also tall, about six-seven, so he could look down at me, unlike most of the others. He ordered me into his quarters one night and ordered me to strip for some R&R."

"R&R?"

"Rest and relaxation. I told him no and started to leave. He grabbed me and started to force me toward his bed. I screamed, which brought the other drill sergeants to his room. He tried to BS his way out of it, but the other drill instructors knew what was going on. They told me to go back to the barracks and make like nothing happened."

"Was he punished?"

"No. The whole thing was ignored. I kept my head down and graduated the following week."

"But that sounds like attempted rape."

"That's what it was. Overall, more than one-third of women in this country have been sexually assaulted and in some places over half. It's not pretty."

"What did you do after that?"

"As soon as I got to my first duty station, I signed up for a martial arts and self-defense class. The rest was a matter of attitude."

"Attitude?"

"I don't act shy, and I don't take any guff."

"Uh—I think I noticed that about you. I like it."

"I also follow that time-honored motto, 'the best defense is a well-directed offense.'"

"You strike first?"

"Not exactly, but I do strike at the slightest touch if a man isn't behaving properly."

"Wow. I don't know what I would do if someone attacked me."

"I can show you some moves that might make the difference. The rest is in your head. You have to be ready to do damage."

"Gosh. That sounds scary."

"We're not looking for trouble, Em. But if it comes looking for us, it's better to be ready for it."

"Okay. Teach me something, would you?"

"We'll start after Richmond. I wouldn't want to put off the nice family hosting us tonight."

Hilda had told the family in Richmond that they would eat an early supper, so that they would not need to be fed, but that they would be there before sundown.

They stopped at the big shopping center at Short Pump and bulked up on *rigatoni all'arrabbiata* and garlic bread. After supper, they each downed a protein drink from the GNC store. Hilda bought a box of fancy chocolates for their hosts. Then they rode into the city against rush hour. There was plenty of bicycle traffic, and the drivers seemed used to it. It was not quite six o'clock when they found the place. The family lived in a spacious home on Hanover Avenue. They locked their bikes in the little yard behind the building.

After introductions and showers, Hilda and Emily joined the family, who had just finished supper. Jane and Robert Macalester were Scottish, both working in Richmond for an engineering company. Their three little ones played with the two strangers for an hour, then were trundled off to bed.

"Now for some grown-up time," Robert said when they returned from the children's room. "We can't tell you how special it is to have you here."

"How so?" asked Hilda.

"Well, look," Jane said, pointing at Emily, "we had no idea you were bringing Emily Hampstead with you. She's a legend!"

Emily blushed while Hilda grinned. "She is that, isn't she?"

"Have you retired since the crash?" Robert asked.

"No. But I can't race until next fall. So, I'm going on tour with Hilda. She's the legend."

"We did some touring before we came to the States, but nothing as ambitious as you're doing."

"Where did you ride?" asked Hilda.

"Our long one was Hadrian's Wall. Only two hundred kilometers, but it was great."

"I've always wanted to ride that. It's so beautiful—and varied from what I could see."

"It is that. Would you like an after-dinner drink? Some port, perhaps?"

"That would be nice. Emily?"

"I've never had port."

"I'll give you a taste. What are you pouring, Robert?"

"Sandeman. It's what we could find here."

"That'd be good."

Robert got up while Jane set out cordial glasses from the sideboard. Hilda let Emily take a sip.

"It tastes like the communion wine at church."

"See? You've had port after all."

They chatted for another hour while the sun finished setting. By ten, they were all ready for bed. The guest room had two twin beds in it.

"There's a nightlight in the hall, in case you need to find the loo."

"This is lovely. Thank you so much," said Hilda.

"Good night, then. We'll see you in the morning."

After setting out their bicycle kits for the next morning, brushing and flossing, they packed their panniers as much as they could and turned in.

"This is really very nice, Hilda. I thought we would be roughing it."

"Don't worry, we will. Warmshowers ranges from this to camping in the backyard, where the dog left his fleas, and everything in between. We may have to share a bed sometimes."

"I think that would be okay. I don't know if I snore or toss about."

"We'll find out, won't we?"

"Yes." Emily yawned.

"Good night, Em."

"G'night, Hilda."

Lying in the dark, Hilda tried to map out a loose lesson plan to teach Emily some self-defense moves. She also tried to picture ambush locations along the route. There were not many of them. Most of their route would be open spaces until Connecticut.

She heard Emily's soft breathing almost immediately and smiled to herself. *Such innocence, but what courage.* She relaxed and drifted off.

ଔ ଔ ଔ

The next day, the family was up at the same time as their guests. They had to drop the children at day care before work. By eight, Emily and Hilda were making their way to Fourteenth Street, where they picked up the Virginia Capital Trail along the left bank of the James River. They had lunch in Colonial Williamsburg, which both had visited before. The sun was especially pleasant eating outdoors on Duke of Gloucester Street.

In the afternoon, they rode past a sign for Langley Air Force Base.

"Too bad Dad had to go to DC today. He could have given us a tour."

"Have you been there?"

"Oh, yes. There was a father-daughter day back in January. His office was a mess because they had just changed contracts and assignments, and everything was being rearranged."

"Maybe we can go there after we get back."

An hour later, they were loading their bikes on the front of a city bus in Newport News, which took them through the Hampton Roads Tunnel under the Elizabeth River and left them in Norfolk at Ocean View. They rode along the coast on US-60 to the Naval Amphibious Base at Little Creek. Beyond the base, they could see US-13, the Military Highway, stretching out over the water, where it became the Chesapeake Bay Bridge-Tunnel. US-60 was flat, and where the traffic seemed heavier, there were bike lanes and bike paths. Soon they were checking in at the campground, which was outside the base perimeter. This meant that Emily did not need a visitor's pass. Their site overlooked some wetlands and woods. It was hard to believe that they were in a city, except when the occasional siren wailed down Amphibious Drive between the campground and the base.

Practicing in the back yard paid off. Emily had her tent up just before Hilda. They left their panniers in the tents and rode to the commissary less than a mile away. It was also outside the perimeter. They approached the ID check station at the entrance, where Hilda presented her ID card.

"Can she get a pass to stay with me," she asked, indicating Emily, "or is there somewhere she could wait?"

The gray-haired man at the counter looked at Emily.

"She less than eighteen years old?"

"Yes."

"No problem. She just has to stay with you, and she can't buy anything herself."

"That's a relief. Thank you."

Emily was amazed at the size and scope of the place.

"This is bigger than Walmart or Costco," she said.

"It might be. It serves thousands of military families in the cities around here. Not the greatest selection for natural or organic foods, but the prices are unbeatable on name-brand items."

"How do they do that?"

"It's part of the Defense Logistics Agency, so the merchandise is shipped with the stuff for the mess halls and canteens of the troops. The markup only has to cover the operating costs of the stores themselves. You can still find something cheaper at Food Lion or Kroger, especially if it's a loss leader."

They picked up some fruit and trail mix for the road, some muesli and two small yogurt cups for breakfast, and a roast chicken with potatoes for supper, with another carton of orange juice. They strapped two bags to their rear racks while Hilda hooked the bag of chicken and potatoes over her handlebars. Back at the campsite, they made a small fire and sat at the picnic table to enjoy dinner.

"Let's shower tonight. You'll find that there is always a crowd for the showers in the morning."

Emily speared a roast potato wedge. "Okay."

By sundown, they were fed, washed, and ready for bed. With their air mattresses inflated, they put all their gear inside and crawled into their respective homes.

"This is fun. Thanks for bringing me along."

"You're quite welcome. Good night, Emily."

"G'night."

They listened to the frogs and insects singing in the wetlands as they drifted off into the happy sleep of those who have pedaled well.

16

THE EASTERN SHORE

E MILY AND HILDA DRAPED THEIR TENTS OVER A RAILING while they ate their muesli and yogurt. The sun had climbed above the Chesapeake Bay Bridge-Tunnel and was creating ground fog as it warmed the wetlands around the campground.

"This could be the easiest or the worst day so far," said Hilda.

"How so?"

"Because we can't plan where we'll be tonight. It won't take long to cross the Bridge-Tunnel, but when the pickup truck will take us depends on who else needs a ride, and when the truck shows up."

"How does that work?"

"The state transports bicyclists and pedestrians in a pair of king-cab pickup trucks. The bikes and any luggage go in the back. If the truck is sitting there and there isn't anyone else expected, great. We pay our thirteen dollars, same as if we were in a car, and the truck gives us a lift to Cape Charles. If the truck just left or is sitting on the other end, we have to wait."

They finished breakfast, washed up their bowls and spoons, and packed up. It was still cool when they rolled onto US-60 and rode the short distance to the ramp for US-13 North and the Bridge-Tunnel. At the Administration Building, Hilda walked into the lobby while Emily watched the bikes.

"Sorry, ma'am, the truck just left. But the other one is on its way here, and the driver has had his break, so it won't be long."

"Can we wait in here?"

"Certainly. You can lock your bikes out back where the truck loads if you like."

"We'll do that. Thanks."

She went out and showed Emily the loading dock at the back of the building. They locked the bikes to each other around a signpost, then went into the lobby. While they waited, they plugged their phones into a charging station.

A half hour later, the agent told them that the truck was ready. A half hour after that, they stood on the pavement by US-13 on Cape Charles.

"That was not bad. We should make it to Chincoteague in plenty of time for a little self-defense training tonight."

"Cool! Let's go!"

They stopped at Wendy's in Onley, Virginia. The highway was monotonous after a while, in the way that the beauty of a landscape fades if it doesn't change after an hour or so. The wind had come around to the south, warm and steady behind them. The push was welcome, but they were going through their water bottles faster than they planned. Vegetable farms stretched out to the pines on the coast, and cigarette stands proliferated as they got closer to the Maryland border.

"Is that for real?" Emily pointed to the biggest cigarette offer yet. The billboard stretched for twenty yards, facing south. "LAST STOP FOR CHEAP SMOKES!!"

"I think so," said Hilda. "There's the state line." She pointed to a small sign in a stand of trees on the right side of the road.

They stopped at the convenience store to refill their water bottles, and to split a half-gallon of orange juice.

"You okay?" Hilda asked.

"Sure. The wind makes a difference, doesn't it?"

"It does. Let's try for Pokomoke City. That's where we leave US-13, and there's a nice campground at the State Park there."

"Let's go."

They rolled into the Pokomoke River State Park an hour later, having stopped at a grocery store at the intersection of US-113. There was plenty of time to set up camp, fix supper, and relax. Hilda made an online reservation for the next night at Cape Henlopen State Park in Delaware.

They had the area to themselves, so after they cleaned their bikes and oiled their chains, Hilda had Emily take off her shoes and socks. They walked to a grassy area.

"This is more effective with shoes, but we don't want to hurt each other, do we?" Emily shook her head. "Let me walk slowly through the sequence. Sandra

Bullock in *Miss Congeniality* made this famous. It's called SING."

"SING?"

"SING. It's a mnemonic for solar plexus, instep, nose, groin. Stand facing me."

"Do I come at you?"

"You could, but it would be distracting. Just watch."

Hilda gently pushed her right fist into Emily's chest, then stepped on her foot and bent her head down to touch Emily's face on the nose, almost immediately raising her free knee into Emily's crotch.

"Can you imagine that at full speed?"

"It's scary enough in slow motion. What if the guy is too tall for me to reach his nose?"

"Skip it and concentrate on kneeing him while holding down that foot. You try it."

Emily went through the sequence. On the second try, she used her head on Hilda's chin.

"I wouldn't try that, Em. The chin is hard bone, and the nose is soft cartilage. Just skip it if the guy is too tall. Let's speed it up."

Emily repeated the sequence until she was getting fast and not having to think about it. Hilda had her react to a man coming on.

"Don't hold back. I'll let you know if it hurts."

Twenty minutes later, Emily was drenched in sweat, and Hilda admitted that she was fast enough to deck the typical idiot or untrained fighter.

"One more thing. Turn around. How do you react to this?" She squeezed Emily's butt, close to the crack in her cheeks. Emily squeaked and jumped.

"I don't know. I'm facing the wrong way."

"Right. There are a couple of moves you can do behind you, but getting into position for a SING is easier to remember. Almost all the time, you can catch the guy off guard."

She turned around and had Emily make a pass at her rear. Hilda reached back, caught Emily's wrist, and spun around, using Emily's weight to add speed. She used her other hand to tap Emily's solar plexus and stomped with her foot on Emily's.

"Get it?"

"Let me try."

Emily ran through the full sequence a dozen more times.

"That's good. You notice what's different?"

"Well, I was expecting the pass on my butt."

"That's the difference. You didn't squeak and jump. You just reacted because you were expecting it."

"What if someone surprises me?"

"Attitude, girl. You've had your last surprise already."

"Huh?"

"Always expect a pass in a room with even one stranger in it. Restaurant, bar, workplace—even a church social."

"Really?"

Hilda gave a single, solemn nod. "When you walk into a room, pause just a second. Not enough to draw attention, but to check out who is where, especially any men you don't know."

"On this trip, that's going to be everyone."

"You're getting the idea."

Emily looked disheartened. "But—"

"You can still have fun, Em. Most men are just fine, but if you know where they all are in the room, you can be aware instead of surprised. You just develop a habit of checking out any room you enter. We're not expecting trouble, just trying to be ready for it."

Emily was silent for a while. "Is that it for today?"

"I think it's enough. Let's shower and turn in."

On the way back from the showers, Emily caught up with the taller woman. "Hilda?"

"Mmm?"

"What you said about entering a room. It made me feel sad somehow."

Hilda put her arm around the teenager's shoulder. "I can understand that. I'm sorry, but not as an apology. You left home a bubbly teenager, surrounded by parents and friends. When you get back, you'll be a young woman, strong, confident, and pleased with herself. Travel like this does that to a person."

"I don't know—"

"Don't worry, Em. I'll be with you almost all the time. Watch me. Learn to be in charge when you enter a room. That keeps most of the would-be Lotharios at bay. You will never be a timid teenager standing uncertainly at the door, will you?" She smiled and arched her eyebrows.

"No. Thanks." Emily passed her arm around Hilda's waist and gave her a hug. "I'll need more practice."

"Every day, and we'll try new moves."

"Okay."

As they settled into their respective tents, Emily noticed the strong smell of salt air and the noise of the various creatures waking up on the riverbank. It felt new and exciting. She fell asleep with the image of Hilda's gaze upon entering a room. She had seen it often enough, and now she understood.

Hilda sent a short message updating Jack on their progress. As she curled into her sleeping bag, her phone dinged with a reply. She fell asleep with a smile and dreamed dreams she would not share with Emily.

೨ ೨ ೨

"You gonna sleep all day?" Emily flicked a finger on the top of Hilda's tent.

"I'm awake. Just getting dressed. Ouch!"

"What was that?"

"Just a little tender in the solar plexus. That was more drill than I realized last night."

"I'm tender in the saddle area."

"Sorry about that."

Emily turned out to be a natural at pannier organization. Their tents were not damp, so in less than forty-five minutes, they were rolling north on US-113. The landscape in Maryland was as flat as Virginia, but with more trees, so there were not as many wide-open vistas. The highway itself was mostly four-lanes with a generous shoulder. It might be boring to some, but they delighted in the warm tailwind again.

"We only have to ride about a hundred kilometers today," said Hilda as they remounted after a water-and-snack break. "We'll be at Cape Henlopen by mid-afternoon."

They turned east on US-50 in Berlin, Maryland, and traveled to Ocean City. Tourist traffic was heavy, but not moving fast past them.

Emily pointed to the sign marking the end of US-50. "This time last year, I was riding this highway in Newton."

"And I started on it in California."

They picked up a pair of packaged salads and a *panino* at the OC Food Market and ate them on the Boardwalk. The surfers were not having a good day, but families and couples were enjoying the sun and the sand. It felt good to catch some rays and relax.

By one o'clock, they were riding north on the series of barrier islands that protected the Eastern Shore of Maryland and Delaware from the Atlantic Ocean. Water lapped the low-lying sand beaches on either side of them, with only some sparse seagrass on either side of the road.

By four o'clock, they had passed Dewey Beach and Rehoboth and were riding into Cape Henlopen State Park. Hilda sent a text message to Jack when they had their campsite assignment. They pitched their tents, showered and did their laundry. They practiced the SING maneuver front and back, and Emily learned to do the Instep and Groin combination behind herself.

About six, they were relaxing at the picnic table when Emily noticed a tall man on a loaded touring bicycle rolling slowly over the crest of the hill. When Hilda jumped up, Emily knew exactly who this had to be. *Now who's the bubbly teenager?* she thought. He dismounted as Hilda ran into his arms. He let the bike lean heavily against them as they embraced and kissed.

Disengaging, Jack grabbed his handlebars and led the bicycle to the campsite. He took off his helmet, revealing close-cropped sandy hair. Emily stood her ground, unsure how to greet him.

"You must be Emily."

"Major Rathburn, I presume," she said with a theatrical lilt. Jack's hearty laugh both surprised her and made her feel at ease.

"Please, call me Jack." He reached out and shook hands, with a firm grip. "You're every bit as impressive in person as in the videos," he said as he leaned his bike against the picnic table. Emily blushed and looked at Hilda. The nurse shrugged and smiled.

"Not as impressive as Hilda. She's my guardian angel."

"Granted. We share the same angel, I think. But in addition to the race footage, I'm impressed with your travel. I didn't expect you to be here before tomorrow."

"Smooth roads and tailwinds," said Hilda.

"You haven't had supper already, have you?"

"No. I knew you'd be here before that."

"Good. Let's ride to Lewes for a proper sit-down seafood dinner to celebrate."

"Sounds good to me. Emily?"

"Great! I could eat a horse, but fish will do."

Jack laughed again, which pleased Emily.

"Hilda, would you make reservations at Striper Bites or Gilligan's while I shower?" Hilda gave him a thumbs-up, taking her phone from her pocket. Jack pulled his toilet kit, towel, and clean clothes from his panniers and headed for the bathhouse.

"Wash your kit while you're there," Hilda shouted. "There's space on our line here." Jack gave her a thumbs-up and waved without turning around. Hilda made a call to the restaurant.

Emily looked at the man dance-skipping down the path to the bathhouse.

"He's a cheery type," she said. "I like him."

"I'm glad you do. I'd hate to have you practicing your SING moves on him." They shared a laugh.

"You're in love, Hilda. I never saw you look the way you did when he showed up."

"Well, you can't camp with a friend for as many months as we have without becoming close. And we have our shared nightmares too."

"Iraq?"

"And Afghanistan. We were helping each other a lot in the first year after we got back. I was just retiring in Washington when he was being discharged from Walter Reed. I ran into him at the discharge office, where we were both being processed. I told him about my plan to ride to the West Coast, and he asked to come along. The rest is history."

"But you were alone in Kansas when I met you."

"Yes. In Chicago, he turned north to go visit his college roommate and some friends in Canada. I went to work at the Puget Sound Naval Hospital for three months, then started riding to Charlottesville. You know the rest of the story."

"It's kind of romantic."

"I guess it is, isn't it?" Hilda smiled and looked toward the bathhouse. "Anyway, I'm also glad he's with us, for your sake as much as mine."

"Why? You're awesome."

"Oh, we can take care of ourselves, Em, but Jack is like having a nuclear warhead going into a fistfight. And he has *so* many connections everywhere. Almost every ex-military policeman in the country knows him either personally or by reputation."

"That's cool."

They sat there for a minute. Hilda suddenly stirred.

"Let's get his gear in my tent, so we can go to dinner right away." She pulled his sleeping bag from the open pannier, closed it, then unsnapped them both. The two women put the bags inside the tent. Emily blew up the air mattress, and Hilda spread out the sleeping bag.

Jack came back wearing a trekking shirt and shorts. He had on his bicycle shoes and was carrying his damp bicycle kit. He hung it on the line while the women zipped up the tents and gathered their bicycles.

Dinner was as good as Jack and Hilda expected. Emily enjoyed being included, despite the frequent silences when the two of them paused to stare at each other.

"You two are googly-eyed, again," she said at one point, which brought out more pleasant laughter. "How far are we going tomorrow?"

Jack answered, "If you two would like it, I was thinking of going as far as Atlantic City. It's only sixty-six kilometers, but have you ever been to a casino?"

Emily shook her head. "Let's get a place in the city and visit a casino, just to check that off your bucket list. I think we can walk through the gambling areas just looking. Except for the gambling, they're like shopping malls on steroids. What do you think?"

"I'd like that!" Emily said.

"Works for me," said Hilda. "I know a motel halfway between the Tropicana and Caesars—they won't give us a hard time about bikes in the room."

"Good thought," said Jack. "Let's do it, then."

Emily finished her dessert as Hilda booked the motel, and Jack got tickets on the ten o'clock ferry, then notified Pete Sayfield where they would be the next day. Jack signaled for the bill.

"Pete Sayfield is the FBI agent in Baltimore, isn't he?" Emily asked as they rode back.

"Right. She *is* checked out, isn't she, Hilda?"

"Fully briefed, Jack. She has Greg Sprouse on speed dial, I think." Another one of Jack's warm laughs.

Emily tried to stay up listening for sounds from Hilda's tent, but the riding, the exercises, and the full dinner forced her eyes shut. She slept the deep, dreamless sleep of the truly tired.

For their part, Hilda and Jack were quiet. After all, they knew how to move without letting the enemy know they were there....

17

ATLANTIC CITY

MV *Cape Henlopen* EASED INTO THE MOORING AT CAPE MAY with only a slight bump. Emily, Hilda, and Jack wheeled their bicycles down the ramp and soon were riding up Route 9. Between the commercial centers, the land was mostly sand and pine trees, with stretches of wetlands among the neighborhoods.

"This is a pretty town," said Emily as they turned north off the causeway to ride through Stone Harbor.

"But I'm not sure I'd want to live here permanently," said Hilda.

"Looks like a lot of people agree with you," said Jack, "if the out-of-state plates parked in the driveways are any indication."

"How are you doing, Em?" asked Hilda.

"Great. You were right. It's been easy riding since Charlottesville."

"The tailwind helped. This area gets north-easterly winds often, then it's like climbing a single hill all day."

They fell into single file as the road narrowed leaving Avalon and they lost the shoulder. Only twenty-two kilometers from Stone Harbor, they picked up bike lanes in Ocean City after riding along the beach. They stopped for lunch at Berenato's Corner Deli downtown before taking the bridge and the bike-laned coast road into Atlantic City. By three o'clock, they were checking into the motel. Emily's single room had more floor space than Jack and Hilda's room, so Hilda put her bike in with Emily's.

"Now you get to wear those street shoes, Em," Hilda said as she left Emily's room. "See you at five?"

"I don't need that long to shower and change."

"I don't know about you, but Jack and I need to make some phone calls, and I might lie down for a while. If you want to go out, just stop by our room to let us know."

"Okay. But I might call Mom and some friends too."

Jack was on the phone to Ted Tinsley. He hung up as Hilda sat on the bed. She raised her eyebrows to signal him to talk.

"Ted says that four of Abdul and Hassan's friends left town today, heading north on I-95. Pete Sayfield notified Homeland Security. They were tracked through the toll plazas all the way to the Holland Tunnel, so they don't appear to be coming at us. They might be headed to rendezvous with Abdul and Hassan farther north."

"JFK or La Guardia?"

"Homeland Security already put a notice out to the airports and train stations. My guess is that they'll drive secondary roads after losing any tail in the city."

"Do we know whether Abdul and Hassan have crossed the border?"

"The Canadians and the border patrol are both on alert, but a little cross-country walk might get them in anyway."

"This doesn't look good, Jack."

"I know. But I have an idea."

"And?"

"If they are still at large by, say, the time we get to Vermont, why don't we take a detour?"

"Which way?"

"Either west to Niagara Falls or east to New Brunswick. We could still double back to Montréal and see some neat stuff along the way."

"We were going to visit Ottawa and Québec City as well as Montréal. We could just change the order." Hilda pondered silently.

"It would also give more time to flush out Abdul and Hassan."

"And they would have even less idea about which way we are going. I like it, Jack. Any preference for east or west?"

"No, and we don't have to choose now. Let's make our way through Connecticut and Massachusetts and see what develops."

"And brief Emily."

"Of course. In fact, I think she should make the choice if we divert. You and I have both seen Niagara and New Brunswick."

"Good idea. Let's get showered and whatever. I told Emily five o'clock."

"That's time for plenty of whatever." Jack grinned. Hilda punched him gently on the arm and started to stretch....

At quarter to five, the phone in the room rang. Jack picked it up like a live bomb.

"Hello?"

"Jack. It's Emily. Can I come over? I'm ready, but I didn't want to barge in early."

"Sure, Em. But why are you calling us on the house phone?"

"I forgot to plug mine in. It's almost dead."

"Come on over. We're almost ready ourselves."

Hilda disappeared into the bathroom for a last-minute check of her lipstick and her hair. When she came out, Emily was sitting at the table with a glass of orange juice. She stood and considered Hilda with admiration.

"Hilda, you look fabulous! How do you do that with just two panniers?"

"It's my do-it-all dress and a pair of flat pumps."

"You told me about that, but I never understood how it could look. I feel dowdy with a blouse and skirt."

"You look fine. Blue is a great color on you, and by matching them, it steps it up a notch, like a dress." Hilda looked over to where Jack was rinsing glasses and back to Emily. "You know, this would be a good place to start looking for a black dress for you."

Jack turned from the sink. "Hey, Em, isn't this your real birthday?"

"Yes. You noticed!"

"I did, and I'm the only one who didn't get you a present yet. Let me get the dress."

"Watch out, Jack," Hilda said with a grin. "We're talking two women in the casino shopping mall."

"So? What else have I had to spend my money on, living with my brother on an army base?"

"Jack, that would be wonderful." Emily ran over and hugged him.

"And if we don't find the perfect dress here, we'll check along the way. If Hilda can't pick it out, it hasn't been made yet." He winked at Hilda.

They gave the room a once-over and walked out. The sun was still high in the sky, and it was warm as they walked to the Tropicana. The wind began picking up and backing to the east.

Inside, Emily was impressed by the opulence of the place, but also something else.

"Everything is so big and glitzy. It strikes me as just a little cheesy. Does that make sense?"

"My feelings exactly, Em," said Hilda. "But I don't think the tourists and gamblers notice. They are drinking and flowing to the slots and games."

They walked up the stairs and paused at the entrance to the casino's main room. Emily noticed how Hilda scanned the room. Then she saw that Jack was doing the same thing. She tried to look carefully around, but there were so many people and so much movement, she could not pick out anything. After just a moment, Jack and Hilda flanked her, and they walked in.

"I can't gamble here, can I?"

"No," said Jack. "We're allowed to walk across the game room on our way to the shops and restaurants, but we can't stop. Under twenty-one, you're not even allowed to watch us play a slot machine."

"That's a bummer for you."

"Not for me," said Hilda. "I come into these places with a single roll of quarters—that's ten bucks—and I make myself leave when it's gone. I'm not very exciting to watch."

"How about you, Jack?"

"I've only come to a casino either to arrest someone or undercover, spending your tax dollars to build a case. The house had to give the money back if I didn't win, but if I won, the government kept the money."

"Egad. That's worse." The two grown-ups laughed. "Why is there a disco ball here? There's nowhere to dance."

"Those are security cameras."

"Oh." Emily gave a wave to the disco ball as they moved on past the slot machines to the entrance to the mall. "That felt weird."

"Why?" asked Hilda.

"You two kept scanning the crowd even after we walked in. It felt like having bodyguards."

"Well, you do. We're not letting anything happen to our precious charge, are we, Jack?"

"No way. Besides, Em, it's habit for us. Noisy, crowded places just put us on alert. Nothing personal."

"I tried looking around like you do, but I don't know what I'm looking for."

"We'll talk about that," said Hilda. "We're not actually looking at anything or anyone. Just trying to notice anything out of place at first, in addition to noticing where the men are."

"And, of course, I notice where all the good-looking women are."

"You would." Hilda gave him a gentle slap on the back of the head. Emily giggled.

The mall was not as big as some of the larger shopping malls, but the major upscale brands were represented. In a boutique of designer fashions, a salesclerk in stiletto heels approached them as they walked in. Emily wondered how she walked in those shoes for a whole shift. She wore a gray and black suit with a pencil skirt and a cream-colored shell.

"May I help you find something?" She had a slight accent, which made her sound precise and professional.

"Yes, something quite specific for my friend here," said Hilda, pointing to her own dress. "Like this. Simple, black, fully crushable and washable so that it comes out of the bag or off the line ready to wear. It needs to be versatile, from afternoon tea or a lunch meeting to a gala event. She can accessorize to make the difference."

"And one other thing," said Emily. The clerk and Hilda both turned to her. "It can't look just like hers. We're together, but not sisters." They laughed.

"Of course, miss. Come this way. Many of our customers have those same requirements."

The clerk led them to the back of the store and brought out a half-dozen dresses in a variety of fabrics. Jack opined that they all complimented Emily's figure. Hilda had her raise her knees, spread her legs forward and sideways to test for full movement.

Hilda looked at the pile of discarded dresses, then at the clerk and Emily. The clerk remained pleasant and professional while Emily suddenly understood what Hilda was trying to find for her.

"I get the feeling that there is something that you need, but you are not seeing," said the clerk.

Emily held up a hand as Hilda was about to speak. "If I had to run for my life, what dress should I be wearing?"

The clerk hid her surprise quickly. "Look at this," she said as she picked up a catalog, and flipped to a Michael Kors dress. Simple, black, washable, crushable for travel. An apron top from the neck, sleeveless, flared from the hips but hemmed above the knee.

"I like it. Hilda?"

"I like it too."

"We don't have this dress, and the nearest place to buy it is at Nordstrom's in Philadelphia or New York." She scanned the store, then lowered her voice. "But I can point you to a place that might have something like this."

"That's very kind of you," said Jack.

"Personally, I shop at the Tanger Outlet." She turned to Emily. "You are rather tall and athletic. Your size often ends up at the outlets. I think you could start at Charlotte Russe."

"Brilliant. Thanks," said Emily. Jack and Hilda added their thanks.

"Will you be here until closing?" Jack asked. Hilda looked up, then winked at him. The clerk hesitated then nodded. "Okay, Anya." He pointed at her name tag. "I'll be back before that."

They walked to the Tanger Outlet Mall, which was less than 800 yards from the Tropicana. Anya was right. They found the dress at Charlotte Russe, steeply discounted. It was in a synthetic fabric like their other technical clothing, so washing and drying would be easy. This dress came with a lightweight jacket in the same material, which made it even more versatile.

Jack beamed as Emily modeled the dress. He bought a fifty-dollar gift certificate when he paid for the dress and put the gift certificate in his pocket. He handed the Charlotte Russe bag to Emily. "Happy birthday, Em."

Emily gave him another hug, and they left the store. After dropping the bag in Emily's room, they went to supper at a Greek restaurant on the same street as the motel. Coming out, Jack turned left to go back to the Casino to deliver Anya's gift card. Emily and Hilda walked slowly together back to the motel.

As they passed a bar halfway back to the motel, they heard a commotion inside. Hilda took Emily's wrist and pulled her aside. Suddenly, four men pitched into the street, the last one pushed off the step by the burly waiter inside. "When the man says 'no more', he means no more. Go home and sober up!"

Hilda and Emily waited while the last drunk got up. Then the four men noticed the two women.

"Hellooo, ladies," said the first of the men to come out of the bar. "We're looking for a good time. Would you care to join us?" He was about Emily's height, with a beer belly and a two-day beard that was not attractive.

"No," said Hilda. Emily saw the anger flash in her blue eyes. "And you're blocking the sidewalk. Would you excuse us please?"

"Certainly, madam" He backed up with a satirical bow. "After you."

Hilda pushed Emily gently in front of her as the two walked past the foursome. Hilda knew instinctively when he would put out his hand. She was already turning when she felt it on her buttock. She grabbed his wrist, pulled him forward into her raised knee, and head-butted his nose. Then she ran her free hand into his solar plexus. He crumpled to the ground. The other three stood still, not sure what to do.

"Look. Don't touch," she said. "Now do what the man said. Take him home and sober up." They hastily grabbed their leader's wrists and hauled him to their shoulders. Then they staggered away in the direction of the Tropicana.

"Let's go, Em. Walk smartly. Don't look back."

"But, what if—"

"If they come this way, we'll see them in that store window across the street."

Emily straightened a little more and walked proudly back to the motel.

They were just opening the door when Jack appeared.

"Saw three drunk guys hauling a fourth and bitching about some black Amazon back there," he said. "Was that your work?"

Emily blurted, "She was awesome! She—"

"Em, please." Emily clamped her mouth shut as Hilda finished opening the door. "We'll discuss it inside." They filed in, and she shut the door.

"Yes, Jack. The waiter threw those four in the street just in front of us and told them to go sober up. The leader invited us to join them for a good time, then broke the rule. I convinced them to take him home and heed the waiter's advice."

Jack grinned. "You never give me a chance to help, do you?"

Emily asked, "What's 'the rule'?"

Hilda arched an eyebrow and waited, then said, "What were my first three words to them?"

Emily thought back. "Oh. 'Look, don't touch.'"

Hilda asked her, "What did you learn tonight?"

"I'm not sure. It was all so fast."

"Then ask me questions, and let's pick it apart."

"Why didn't we just go the other way?"

"I never backtrack. On foot or on my bike."

"You wouldn't have had to hurt that guy."

"Who made the bad decision to make a pass. Him or me?"

"He did."

"Right. So, isn't it better to give him a chance to make the right decision than to make my own wrong decision by running away? He hadn't done anything to me yet."

"But there were four of them."

"You saw them stumble onto the street. Tell me about them."

"Well, the last one fell when the waiter pushed him. He wobbled, trying to get up."

"What about the others?"

"I didn't notice them until the one guy said, 'hellooo, ladies.'"

"But I *did* look at them. The leader was looking critically at the other three, and the two in the middle were almost not there. They were waiting for him to tell them what to do."

"That's why you called him the leader."

"I knew he would be the only one to do anything, and the others wouldn't move unless he told them to. So, when I pushed you in front of me and out of the way, how many people was I really dealing with?"

"One." Emily saw that Jack was leaning against the table, smiling at the lesson. "You figured all that out in the time it took for him to say something?"

"I didn't really 'figure it out.' I recognized the types from all the room-scoping and previous encounters. After a while, you don't have to think about it. You know who will do what and who won't act."

"Gosh. I can't do that."

"Yes, you can. Starting now. What will you do the next time a group of men is in front of you?"

Emily shrugged and gave Hilda a helpless look.

"Let me rephrase that. Which ones will you look at?"

Emily paused. "All of them."

"Right. And where will you look if one of them is doing something, like falling down or crying or puking?"

"Tonight, I looked at the guy falling, but I should have looked at the others."

"Right again. Starting with whom?"

Emily seemed confused. Jack shoved himself off the table.

"A hint, Em. The leader is usually the one farthest from the action. Someone standing where he can see the others."

"Oh, so I scan from the farthest guy out."

"It's a good start," said Hilda. "Just don't take too long, and don't make too much of it. Get your impressions, then follow your instincts."

"But I don't have instincts for this."

"No, but you already have eyes in the back of your head. I saw the videos of you racing. You can sense someone coming up behind you without looking, can't you?"

"Well, yeah. But that's different."

"Not as different as you think," Jack said. "When you're racing, you seem focused on the road, but I know that you're keenly aware of all the other riders—and other vehicles too. You don't even think about it."

"The new instincts will come with time," said Hilda. "We'll quiz you on what you observe along the way, and you'll get better at noticing your surroundings as we travel. Then you'll be able to make faster and safer decisions on your own."

"And I thought the scenery would be the main point of the tour."

"Oh, we'll see that too. And the best scenery is where you don't have one heartbeat to evaluate dangerous people."

They stood silently for a short while. Then Emily brightened and said, "It was still pretty awesome, Hilda!" They laughed.

Jack reached into the refrigerator and pulled out the orange juice. "Nightcap, anyone?" They assented, and he grabbed three glasses from the drainboard.

"Did you give Anya the card?" Hilda asked.

"She was still manning the door, so I was only there long enough to thank her again. She turned away as I left. I think she was going to cry."

"Good move, Jack."

"Hey, she saved me a bundle on Emily's birthday dress."

"I know you better than that. She gave up her commission to give Emily that advice, and you knew it."

Emily put down her glass suddenly. "How did you two know that?"

"If you ever work retail, you'll never forget what a hell it can be," Jack said. "And if you just watch how other people treat waiters, salesclerks, and baristas, you'll know what I mean."

Emily pondered that. "I see. I just never noticed."

"Part of the change, Em," said Hilda. "You're learning to look and see. And with your natural ability to see the good in people, you'll learn to empathize too."

"Wow, that's a lot to learn in one night."

"It is," said Hilda. "Let's call it a day and get some sleep."

Jack added, "And remember to plug in our phones tonight."

18

THE JERSEY SHORE

EMILY AWOKE WITH THE RISING SUN BURNING INTO HER EYES. She had forgotten to pull the shades. She leaped out of bed and looked out the window. The sea rippled with occasional whitecaps as it rolled up against the long line of white sand. The beach was almost deserted, except for one jogger, and a dozen seagulls dive-bombing a torn garbage bag.

Showered and dressed in twenty minutes, she packed her panniers and went next door for breakfast. Jack opened the door. Hilda came out of the bathroom as Emily was putting out plates for the muesli and fruit that they had bought the day before. Hilda stopped at the door, still holding a hairbrush.

"Emily, how do you do that with your hair?"

Emily put her hand to the back of her head. "You mean the French braid?"

"Yes. I've never learned how to do that, and on windy days like this, I wish I didn't have such a long ponytail—not a word, Jack!"

Jack laughed as he took the yogurt out of the refrigerator. The coffee maker gurgled happily on the counter.

"I can't imagine riding with my hair loose, Hilda. You really never braided yours?"

"No. I wore my hair short in the army. I've tried, but the German tresses I learned as a girl don't work. They're still too long. YouTube gave me an idea, but I can't do it myself. Could you teach me to braid like that?"

"Well, I can try. Have a seat."

Emily stood behind Hilda and combed out her hair with the brush. She had Hilda put her hands behind her and feel as she wove the fine black hair into a braid, pulling it from the top. By the time they had worked down to the end, Hilda's hair extended just over the collar of her jersey.

"You may have to let out your helmet a bit, depending on where the top fits, but it should press down easily."

Hilda went to the mirror. "That's great, Em. I love it. Thank you so much." She gave the teenager a bear hug. "It's a stretch getting back there with both arms, though."

"You should get used to it."

"I can understand why I usually see those braids on athletic women," said Jack. "It looks like a yoga workout from here."

They sat down to breakfast. By eight, they had cleaned up the meal. Jack and Hilda finished packing. Soon, they were riding US-30 past the wind farms at the north end of town, heading for Absecon on the mainland. The terrain became rolling or, rather, jerky as they climbed and dropped over small hills, ramps, and abutments. They could not continue on the coast because the bridge over the Mullica River was closed to bicycles. The long detour on Route 342 took them past the Swan River Wildlife Management Area and the Bass River State Park, which was certainly more scenic than the Garden State Parkway.

The turn north and east also put them into the wind, which tested their endurance on the simulated climb. Emily hunkered down on the drops and pulled ahead of them, showing that her famous hill-climbing talent was still there. She would drop back before she went out of sight, just before Hilda and Jack started worrying about losing her.

After one hundred kilometers of steady headwinds, they were grateful to pull into the Cedar Creek Campground south of Toms River and set up camp. They went shopping in the camp store for their supper.

"It's a real pleasure to have a home-cooked meal for a change," said Jack as he put another steak on the grill. "We can have ice cream at the café for dessert if you like."

"I'd like that," said Emily, with her mouth full. "Oops. Sorry."

"That's okay. I'm hungrier than you are, I think," said Hilda. "Thanks again for the braiding lesson."

"You were really stroking there, Em," said Jack.

"Not really. I just put my head down and imagined a long hill with a sprint waiting at the top. I was going well below race speed."

"Just so you don't bust a gut while you're still recovering," said Hilda. "You had us worried there. If I hadn't been watching the speed on my bike computer, I would've been hollering for you to ease up."

"I was watching the computer, too, but I was also enjoying the challenge."

"I'm glad you were," said Jack. "Hills and headwinds are necessary evils in my world. I'd have lost you."

"Speaking of losing you two, could we stop at a bike store and get me a rearview mirror like yours? It might be better for knowing when I'm getting too far ahead than to keep turning to look."

"Good idea," said Hilda. "I'm sure we'll find one in Toms River."

"It's only eighty-three kilometers to Atlantic Highlands, so we'll have time to stop," said Jack.

"Do you want to cross to New York tomorrow?" Hilda asked Jack.

"Wasn't the idea to avoid major cities?" asked Emily. "Where would we spend the night if we go all the way to New York tomorrow?"

"Good point," said Hilda. "The Gateway National Recreation Area is the last spit of the barrier reefs and islands. If we camp there, we'll have ridden the full Eastern Shore. We can catch an early ferry and stay in Port Jefferson—or even in Connecticut depending on traffic."

"I like that idea," said Emily. "It feels good to get away from the built-up areas." She waved at the wooded area where the tent campers were enjoying their suppers and visiting with each other. A den of Cub Scouts was playing two sites away, squealing and shouting with delight. "This is more fun than the casino."

Jack pulled out his phone. Five minutes later, they had a site reserved for the next night. They finished their steaks and salad, then washed the dishes at the common sinks before walking to the café. They sat outside, eating their ice cream while the shadows lengthened. It was still warm, and the evening chorus of birds and insects had not yet started up.

"Let's check in," said Hilda, "There's no power at Camp Gateway, so they should know that we might not call tomorrow night."

"Okay. I'll call Ted. You want to call Greg or Pete?"

"Pete."

Emily pulled out her phone. "I'll call home."

They ended their calls together. Jack grinned. "Who goes first?" He pointed to Emily.

"Mom wants a picture of the black dress. I told her we were camping, but I would send her a photo from the first indoor place we stay." She nodded to Hilda.

"Pete says that Abdul and Hassan turned up at the Montréal airport again. There was a chase in the ticketing area, but they got away. The APB has been elevated, and all local jurisdictions are looking for them."

"At least, that means they have not come stateside," said Jack. "Ted tells me that their four cronies dropped off the radar after leaving the Holland Tunnel. Best guess is somewhere on the roads between New York and Montréal. He'll have photos of all four in the morning and send them to my phone."

"When would they reach the border?" Emily asked.

"If they're still in their car, they could do it in a day, but I would expect them to take two days, so they don't attract attention and can use secondary roads."

"Does that mean that they are already in Canada?"

"Probably not, Em. The border patrol and the Canadian Border Services Agency are both waiting for them. They could get near the border, but not cross it on a road. They would have to hike through the woods and pick up transportation on the other side."

"Which would take a day or two more," said Hilda.

"So how do we find out what they did?"

"A couple of things can happen. Local law enforcement has the data on the vehicle and the four men. They'll be looking around on their patrols. If the police find the car empty, we'll know they were trying to hoof it over the border, and the tracking teams can go after them. Someone local may have seen them, so spotting the car—wherever they left it—would tighten the search considerably."

"They could also be spotted in Canada," said Hilda.

"You said a couple of things."

"Yes," said Jack. "They could be waiting near the border for Abdul and Hassan to come back on foot. The longer they wait, the more likely their being discovered is, so they'll want to keep moving."

"Vermonters are nice folks," said Hilda, "but four Middle Eastern men won't go unnoticed."

"If it's the four guys that I think it is," said Jack, "their English isn't very good, so they speak Arabic to each other. Definite attention-getter."

"They have it tougher than we do," said Emily.

"Good point, Em," said Jack, "but these guys have a support network that helps them get from one place to another unnoticed. And we don't have any idea really what they are doing, or what their plans are. They may have nothing to do with Abdul and Hassan, although they are wanted as material witnesses in the case against those two."

"Do you think they're looking for Hilda—or you?"

"That's a possibility. We'll be extra careful about our surroundings once we get to Connecticut, especially if there's no news. From here on, we're within a day's drive from the last place they were seen."

"We're just lucky that they don't know we're on bikes, eh?"

"We can't even be sure of that," said Hilda. "I was riding a bike when they shot at me in Aberdeen. They could guess that I might be on a bike again."

"How would they know which way you went?"

"Asking around. Not them directly, but friends they might have in Charlottesville could've learned that we were going up the Eastern Shore or riding to Montréal. Didn't you tell your friends about the tour?"

Emily paused to think. "Just Tani and Fran."

"And either of them could have been discussing how cool it was or how they envied your going with me—and had someone else hear them talking about it."

Emily looked crestfallen.

"Cheer up, Em. I didn't make it a secret either. And your parents probably talked about us at work."

"But we could be in real danger."

"We've always been in real danger," said Jack. "These men are just another danger, along with the traffic, the drunks, and the crazies. We'll be okay if we keep our wits about us."

"I may need to learn more moves."

"Maybe," said Hilda. "It'll be dark soon. Let's discuss what you observed on our way back to the campsite."

Emily surprised herself by being able to recall more things than she realized at first, including several signs hidden by trees, vanity license plate numbers, and which passing trucks and cars were driven by men and which by women along the beach roads.

She went to sleep feeling better about the trip, but still a little nervous. The kind of nervous that raises awareness rather than incapacitates.

The next morning dawned as glorious as the day before, but the wind had veered to the southeast, so it was not directly in their faces. In fact, it pushed them to Toms River and did not bother them once they reached the barrier islands at Seaside Heights.

They stopped at A-1 Bikes in Point Pleasant, which was just opening when they got there. Emily bought a handlebar-mounted mirror. The shop offered free air, so they left with tires pumped up, and the nuts and bolts checked for tightness. In the middle of the workweek, traffic was light as they rode along the flat, white, and sandy beach. The towns were densely settled, but there were seagrass and pine woods in the open spaces. They picked up supplies for supper and breakfast in Monmouth Beach.

At Camp Gateway, the park ranger gave Jack a smart salute when Jack showed his Veterans Park Pass.

"Thank you for your service, sir."

Jack returned the salute, and they rode to the parking area.

"I'm not sure how I feel about all that thanking yet."

"Me neither," said Hilda. "They seem so sincere that I have to smile."

"It makes them feel better, I'll bet," said Emily.

"You're probably right, Em."

At the parking area, they dismounted and pushed their bikes to the campsite.

"Not bad for *camping sauvage,*" said Hilda.

"What's that?" asked Emily.

"It means rough camping. In some places out on the Gaspé Peninsula you'd be lucky to get an outhouse, and there'd be no other facilities."

"We have flush toilets and running water here," said Jack, "but that's it."

"I can see New York on one side and the ferry port on the other, and it's clean and quiet."

Emily and Hilda set up camp while Jack walked to the ranger station to buy some firewood. After dinner, they cooked marshmallows over the fire. The nearest other camping group was out of sight, so Hilda drilled Emily on pulling an opponent off-balance. They used Jack as the aggressor.

"Damn! You're a quick study, y'know." He rubbed his sore ribs and massaged his arm.

Emily looked distraught for just a second, then she brightened. "Sorry, Jack. Did I do it right?"

"Yes, you did. I keep a nurse handy for this kind of work."

Hilda gave him a one-armed hug. "Let's hope a few bruises are the worst I have to patch up on this trip."

"What else have you fixed on him?" Emily asked. Hilda almost answered, then looked at Jack.

"You or me?"

"I'll go first. I was wounded in an IED attack in Baghdad, Em."

"IED?"

"Improvised explosive device. A homemade bomb. Usually deployed on a road to disable our Humvees and other vehicles."

"Was it bad?"

He gestured to Hilda to pick up the tale.

"Yes, it was bad. Jack had arrested some soldiers who had started a fight in town. I was in the ambulance behind Jack's Humvee with a soldier who was hurt worse than the others. Jack was thrown from the Humvee and slammed against the wall of a building. We got him into the medical Humvee and made it to the ER barely in time."

"Her face was the last thing I saw until I woke up in the hospital in Germany."

"What happened to the others in your Humvee?"

"Dead. The driver, my sergeant, and the four prisoners. The Humvee caught fire immediately."

"I guess my moves are no big deal." Emily fell silent. Jack and Hilda let her think for a while.

"Did you know each other before that?"

"Not well. I was the provost marshal on base, and I would see Hilda at the clinic. We met again at Walter Reed Army Hospital in DC later. I recognized her immediately."

"Hilda told me about that. I think you two are living an adventure movie. Romantic and scary at the same time."

The fire gave a great *pop* as it dwindled. The sun was down behind the trees. They put out the fire and walked to the bathroom building together. Dishes washed, bodies wiped down, and teeth brushed, they trooped back to the campsite and turned in.

Emily stretched in her sleeping bag. The insects were settling down so that her breathing was the loudest noise she heard. She thought briefly about how cool Jack and Hilda were, then fell deeply asleep.

19

SKIPPING THE BIG APPLE

THE SUN WARMED THE SAND AND THE PICNIC TABLE as Jack, Hilda, and Emily finished their breakfast. Less than an hour later they were queuing up for the hydrofoil ferry to Manhattan.

Jack pulled out his phone. "I'm sending these photos from Ted to you two. We should memorize their faces. If our paths cross, we need to spot them first."

"But don't they know what we look like?" asked Emily.

"No. They may have seen Hilda's Chicago picture, but that's it. Only Abdul and Hassan have actually seen her from a distance, and they haven't met you or me."

The ferry crew opened the gates. The cyclists joined the crowd of commuters and were directed to an open deck area, where they stood with their bikes. Emily looked at the scene with excitement. Hilda's expressionless face reminded her to scan the crowd more deliberately.

She had never been on a hydrofoil before. The speed was exhilarating as the craft cut a straight wake across the Lower Bay. In thirty-eight minutes, they were tying up to the South Street pier. Hilda was the expert, having ridden in New York City more than Jack.

"There are bike lanes all the way to the East River Park. I'll take point. Jack, you cover the rear."

Jack gave her a casual salute and a grin. He mounted his bike smoothly and fell in behind Emily. Hilda led them quickly along the East River on FDR Drive, tending to ride the edge of the bike lane to have room to move right if a driver became aggressive. Emily noticed that the cars would ease into the bike lane from sheer traffic pressure if the bicyclists did not occupy it. They moved faster than the cars and were soon buying tickets for the East River Ferry to Brooklyn. The ferry had bike racks inside. No point in sitting; they wanted to stay close to their steeds and their panniers. They could also look at the people and the sights.

"I've never seen so many people and so much traffic," Emily said as the ferry backed out and sped toward the South Williamsburg ferry pier.

"Funny, though," said Hilda. "Thanks to Mayor Bloomberg, I feel safer riding in New York than almost any other city in North America. They have sidewalks for the pedestrians, lanes, and paths for the bikes, and roads for the cars. People can get where they are going without hitting one another."

"The little stoplights for bikes are cute."

"We're getting them in more American cities. We just haven't been to any of those yet."

In Brooklyn, Hilda led them on Kent Avenue to Fifth Street and out Grand Avenue to Route 25. Past Mineola, the neighborhoods began to look less urban.

By Hicksville, there were more trees and gardens. They picked up some ready-made sandwiches in Hauppauge and ate them with some orange juice while waiting for the ferry in Port Jefferson. The 1:45 p.m. ferry left them in Bridgeport at three o'clock.

"It's only thirty kilometers to New Haven and seventy-one to Hammonasset Beach," said Hilda. "Do we go for the long one or make two easy days?"

"It's hilly on the coast here, compared to the Eastern Shore," said Jack. "And the wind is still easterly until the day after tomorrow."

"I feel fine," said Emily, "but I'll go with whatever you guys want."

"Let's break it up," said Hilda. "It's scenic, and we might want to take it slower." She pulled out her phone and booked two rooms at the EconoLodge in West Haven. An hour and a half later, they were enjoying leisurely showers and a change of clothes. The bicycle kits were drying in the showers. Emily came over to the adults' room.

"Wow! Hot date tonight?" said Jack.

Emily giggled. "Mom wants a photo of the dress, remember? Would you take it, please?" She gave Jack her phone, then struck a few poses for him, with and without the jacket.

"You really do look great in that dress," said Hilda.

"Thanks. It makes me feel—I don't know—more grown-up maybe."

"It does that," said Jack. "Do I need a tie tonight?"

"No." Emily laughed. "I want to change back into my skirt and blouse unless you two have plans for something fancy."

"Nothing that we couldn't wear our bike kits to. But we'll look for something better than fast food, okay?"

"Sure. I'll be right back."

The wind had died down, making the early evening ideal for a walk. Less than a mile along Highland Street from their motel, they found the Saray Turkish Restaurant. It was still a little early, so they walked south to Elm Street, where they found the Ward-Heitmann House Museum (closed for foundation work). Elm Street led to the West River, where they stopped before turning back.

"We'll come back this way tomorrow," said Hilda. "This bridge is how we get past New Haven without dealing with Interstate 95. We'll hug the coast all the way to Hammonassett."

The restaurant was still empty when they got back. They chose a table near the rear exit to the parking lot. Jack and Hilda sat facing the main entrance. The place began to fill as they considered the menu.

"I don't know what to order. It all looks so good," Emily said.

"Would you like us to order?" Hilda asked. Emily nodded. Jack and Hilda conferred briefly, then decided on a *meze* appetizer dish to share, *sulu köfte* soup, and *alinazik*. The waiter seemed pleased with their choices. The dinner was delicious. Jack and Hilda seemed visibly relaxed in the atmosphere of Turkish music and Mediterranean cuisine.

"How do you know so much about Turkish cooking?" Emily asked.

"Turks are the largest ethnic group in Germany, and Turkish restaurants are everywhere."

Jack was paying the bill when Emily leaned over and whispered urgently to Hilda.

"Hilda, slide down and make like you're picking something up. One of those guys in the photos just walked in the back door." Hilda instantly made herself look much shorter. She turned away from the main area of the restaurant, so her face would not show. Jack dropped his napkin and sneaked a look picking it up.

"Good girl, Em. Try not to stare but let us know what he's doing."

"He's talking to one of the waiters, but I can't understand it."

"I can," said Hilda, still looking down and away. "It's Arabic. The guy is asking if he can get something to go."

"The waiter just went into the kitchen."

Jack continued to sip his water. Hilda avoided looking back but slid slowly until she was kneeling between the table and the bench. From the top, she seemed slightly shorter than Emily. She carefully eased her ponytail under the collar of her jacket and turned to the window. The sun had set, but there was still too much outside light to see reflections in the restaurant.

"The waiter is back with a big bag. The guy paid the bill and is leaving."

"Did he look around?" asked Jack.

"No, but he got his cigarettes out when the waiter came out and had one in his mouth, ready to light as he left. He seemed in a hurry."

"Can I get up?" Hilda asked.

Jack got up and looked out the windows to the parking lot. "Ease up, Hilda, while I make a run past the restroom to reconnoiter."

Hilda rose back up to the seat slowly so as not to attract attention. She checked the window on her side of the restaurant.

"Nothing moving out there."

Jack returned. "Their car wasn't there."

"Or they've changed cars," said Hilda.

"Or the guy is walking back to wherever they are," said Emily.

"Let's give him a few minutes before we leave," said Jack. "Em, that was fantastic. Can you tell me which one it was?"

Emily got out her phone and brought up the photos. She pointed to one.

"Thanks. When we get back to the motel, I'll call this in."

"Jack, should we have the car description too?" Emily asked.

"Absolutely. I should have thought of that." He pulled his phone out and forwarded the email from Ted describing the eggplant-colored 2009 Saturn Astra and the Maryland license plates. Hilda and Emily's phones dinged. They both studied the email.

"Let's go," said Hilda. "I can't make myself look shorter walking home. Let's hope we see them first if they're out there."

Jack held the door while he scanned the street before Emily and Hilda came out. They walked quickly back to the motel, Jack on the street side, Emily in the middle and Hilda away from the street. There did not appear to be anyone on the street and no sign of the Saturn. Three pickup trucks drove by, with lone middle-aged white men driving them.

Inside the motel room, Jack called Ted while Hilda called Pete Sayfield. Emily considered calling her mother but sent an email with the pictures of the dress instead. She chose not to mention what happened at the restaurant.

When they ended the call, Hilda said, "The Connecticut State Police have an APB out for the four men and the Saturn Astra." She turned to Emily. "You were awesome tonight. That was a perfect call, and the right reaction—asking me to get down."

"Thanks. I'm glad Jack had us study those photos."

"That was important, but your reaction is what allowed Hilda and me not to draw attention to ourselves by turning around to check on him. Well done."

Emily blushed. She was more pleased than embarrassed and feeling scared. "Do we have to change our plans?"

"I don't think so," said Hilda. "The coast road has great visibility. It would be hard to set up an ambush, and we should be able to spot an old eggplant Saturn. There aren't that many of them around anymore."

Jack added, "If he never looked our way, we might be safe. Did he seem chummy with the waiter?"

"Not particularly," said Emily. "He seemed awkward at first."

"He tried his English first," said Hilda, "then found out that the waiter understood Arabic. He only placed the order for four *döner kebab* dinners with rice and thanked the waiter after counting the cash for the dinners."

Jack said, "That makes it pretty clear that he didn't know the waiter. I think that we should be safe for now."

"What if they try to run us off the road?"

"Bad for us and bad for them. They'd be unlikely to take out all three of us. The survivor would recognize them and dial 911. Right?"

Emily realized that he was referring to her. She gulped and said, "I hope so."

"We don't know why they're here. They might be on their way to wherever, and they aren't looking for us." Jack filled a glass of water from the sink. "Even if they are, I don't think that they found us."

"But we're definitely inside their one-day search radius," said Hilda.

"Do you want to leapfrog?" Jack asked Hilda.

"Leapfrog?" Emily asked.

"Jump on a train and go far away in a different direction."

"Let's see what tomorrow brings," said Hilda. "I have a good feeling about this."

Emily stood to leave.

"Not so fast, Em," said Jack. "What else did you observe tonight?"

Emily sat and thought for a minute. "There were three waiters, one looked Turkish or Middle Eastern, but the other two looked Hispanic to me. The lady at the cash register just dyed her hair at home, probably in a hurry. There were eighteen men and twelve women in the room and the nearest man was our person of interest tonight, when it wasn't our waiter."

"Impressive. You're learning well. What's with the dye job?"

"She had dye on her scalp and a little trickle that seeped out beyond her hairline. Which makes me wonder, Hilda. Don't you color your hair? I mean, you're over forty, aren't you?"

"Just barely forty, Em. I'm lucky I got my father's coloring. His hasn't turned gray yet either. I don't plan to hide it when it comes. It looks good on my mother."

"Another thing I like about her," said Jack.

Emily yawned. "Did we just go through three states today?"

"We did," said Hilda. "And I'm coming down from that little excitement at the restaurant."

Emily got up again and hugged them both. "Good night, y'all."

"G'night, Em. We don't have to leave early tomorrow. Breakfast at eight?"

"Okay. See ya." She was asleep in her bed fifteen minutes later. This time she remembered to draw the drapes.

"Are you sleepy?" Jack asked as he climbed into bed.

"Not sleepy." Hilda slid her arm under his head.

"I wondered if you need to take your mind off things."

"I think I do." She lifted herself over him....

20

CONNECTICUT

"GOOD THING IT'S SATURDAY," said Hilda as they discussed the route over breakfast. "The last time I was here, getting past New Haven was an off-road adventure in a construction zone. We might be able to get through today."

Jack switched to Google Earth and zoomed in. "Are you talking about the new and improved Exit 44?"

"Yes. See how they're paving it in this photo? It might be finished."

"If it's not, we can go under the Connecticut Turnpike on Kimberley and back under it again to Sea Street."

"That'll work, and on a weekend getting past the ramp exiting I-95 will be easier."

Soon they were rolling over the bridge into New Haven. There was asphalt past the construction zone. They reached Bayview Park easily.

"Feel like riding some off-road, Em?"

"As long as it isn't loose."

"Packed gravel."

"No problem."

The Long Wharf Nature Preserve was a little jewel hiding between the busy interstate highway and the coast. The gravel trail turned to asphalt at Long Wharf Drive, and traffic was light on US-1 crossing the lift-bridge over the Quinnipiac River.

"This is so cool," said Emily. "Those people up on the freeway have no idea, do they?"

"Nope. The Boston Post Road parallels I-95 for most of Connecticut. There are lots of cyclists, so the local traffic isn't threatening."

They waved to a foursome of cyclists racing in the opposite direction, tricked out in flashy bicycle kits.

"That guy has a Colnago like mine," said Emily.

"Feeling the pull?" asked Hilda.

Emily did not answer immediately. She gave a small sigh and said, "A little, but I'm having way more fun touring with you guys."

"I'm glad. I'm sure slowpoke back there would agree with me."

"Slowpoke? Did someone call my name?" Jack geared down to catch up with Hilda, who laughed. Hilda led them off the Post Road to follow the coast.

"I think that there are only two blind curves like that one," she said, indicating the bend up ahead. Jack gave her a thumbs-up.

"You thinking ambush?" Emily asked.

"Anything. Driver turning wide, stalled truck, yes, even an ambush."

They made their way along Route 146 and the Post Road through East Haven and Branford. For most of the way, they enjoyed having no motor traffic at all on the disconnected portions of the Branford Trolley

Trail, which was hard gravel and asphalt. Winding through wetlands and marshes, it flanked the main Amtrak and Shore Line railroad in places and crossed rivers that forced the highway traffic farther inland. When the trail ended, they climbed back up to the 146 and rode into Guilford, with its picturesque village green.

Outside Guilford, they returned to the Boston Post Road. Traffic remained light, and the east wind in their faces abated in the afternoon as the temperature rose. They were sweating when they parked outside the Stop & Shop in Madison for lunch, and to buy food for supper and breakfast. They rode back to the Madison Green to eat their sandwiches and salads, and to split a half-gallon of orange juice.

"Ashley's Ice Cream Cafe is on our way to Route 1. Dessert, anyone?"

Jack and Emily gathered the trash and dumped it in the waste bin. Soon they were enjoying sundaes outside Ashley's.

"We're only five kilometers from the park," said Hilda. "And halfway there, we'll pick up the Shoreline Greenway."

"We'll be there by two," said Emily. "This is a good day for a swim. Is it that kind of beach?"

"Yes."

An hour later, they camped in the last space left that would take their tents and bicycles. Jack rode his bike to all the other camping areas and the RV sites.

"Kind of crowded, eh?" he said when he returned.

"It's the weekend," said Hilda. "These folks probably came down yesterday. Anyone we know out there?"

"No Saturns. No eggplant-colored cars. No familiar faces."

"Let's hit the beach," said Emily.

They enjoyed an idyllic afternoon, swimming and lying in the sun. Emily noticed that Jack and Hilda never lay down at the same time. One of them always was sitting up, usually reading a book on their phone. She moved her towel over next to Hilda. Jack was lying on Hilda's other side, a magazine over his face.

"You two can never relax completely, can you?"

Hilda smiled. "No, not until the two Forebears are caught, and we figure out what the Fab Four are doing in New England."

"That's sad."

"It is what it is, Em. It's a lot easier than being in an active combat zone." She took Emily's hand and gave it a pat. "You can relax. We've got this."

"I wish I could do something too."

"You already have. You stayed alert when we could not see behind us. Keep that up." She squeezed Emily's hand.

They lay there until about four. Jack was lying down again, when Emily said, "Okay if I walk down to the pier there?"

"Sure, mind if I come along? A walk would be nice."

"Mmmff," came from under the magazine. Jack waved.

"Got it. We're leaving our stuff."

"Mmmff."

The two women laughed and started walking south to Hammonasset Point. The crowd was only beginning to thin as a few families began heading to wherever they planned to have supper. Sleepy toddlers were draped over their fathers' shoulders, and ten-year-olds walked somberly, clearly exhausted enough to go home.

A dozen young people were playing volleyball on the beach. The ball came flying toward Hilda and Emily. Hilda put her hands up to catch it, but it vanished as Emily pulled it down in front of her. She spiked the ball back to the far team, who caught it with a shout of thanks and set up their serve.

"Didn't the near team win the ball?"

"No. They blew the serve coming at them and deflected it to us instead of back over the net."

"Very sharp, Em. I was watching the men on the other side of the game."

"Oh, those. Yeah." A half-dozen young men the same age as the volleyball players were gathered around a cooler of beer, mostly laughing at each other's jokes, and sometimes cheering one or the other of the teams.

"Not your type?"

"I like the three guys playing ball. They're doing something."

"I hear you."

"Hilda, what's the drinking age in Connecticut? I never checked."

"Twenty-one in a bar or restaurant, but you can drink with us in private."

"Really? Just like that? Without my mother?"

"She gave me a power of attorney as your legal guardian as long as she isn't with you."

"She never told me."

"No big secret. It just didn't come up. If you want to sample a craft beer with us sometime, just ask."

"On a day like today, I think a cold brew would've hit the spot."

"I agree, but tomorrow a beer might feel even better. It's a hundred kilometers to Windsor Locks, and we'll be climbing some small hills before we follow the Connecticut River north."

"Small hills are often steeper."

"That's true. Especially the first thirty kilometers. No climbs more than a hundred meters, though."

"Piece of cake. But I'll look forward to that beer if it's as hot as today."

"I'll make sure Jack tells his friend Bill to stock something worth riding there for."

They walked out on the pier at the point and looked back at the beach on one side and the Natural Area to their right.

"I didn't know that marshes and seagrass could be scenic," said Emily.

"I like a view without any modern buildings. Even the desert can be beautiful that way."

"I guess. Maybe I'll see that, too, someday."

"If you want. It's all just a bike ride away."

They walked back the way they came. The beer drinkers were louder than before. The volleyball game was over, and the players were packing up.

"I thought the guys with the cooler were with them," said Emily.

"Me too. Guess not."

The men shouted and whistled as Emily and Hilda walked by. Two of them began singing "Brown Sugar" off-key. Emily grabbed Hilda's hand.

"Hilda!"

"I know, Em. Just ignore them but keep both hands free." She reached down and smoothly scooped up sand. "And maybe palm some sand." Emily imitated her. They walked steadily until the men returned to laughing at their own jokes.

Hilda let the sand out of her hands.

"Do you get a lot of that?" Emily emptied her hands too.

"Define 'a lot.' It felt constant when I first came to the States, and the harassment was daily in boot camp. In college and after commissioning, I think it dropped off. I don't tense up anymore if I hear crap like that and the voice isn't coming closer."

"You think in their own drunk way, they're complimenting you?"

"Nope. The beer just loosened their inhibitions and judgment enough to let their inner feelings leak out. Tell me, Em. What do you see when you look at me? What strikes you first?"

"Your height, your eyes, and your high cheekbones."

"Not my skin?"

"It shines, like a wet stone."

"Really? Not that it's black?"

"Well, yeah, there's that. But you asked what I saw first."

Hilda was silent for another fifty meters. "You're a remarkable young woman, Emily Hampstead. Are you sure you're American?"

"Of course. Why?"

"Because the only American who has ever honestly noticed those things before my skin color was Jack."

"Your cheekbones?"

"I think he listed the way my uniform fit before the cheekbones."

Emily giggled. "He would."

They walked back to their spot on the beach in amiable silence. Jack appeared not to have moved.

"Is it alive?" said Hilda.

"Tickle it and find out," said Emily.

Jack's hand shot out and caught Hilda's wrist just as she bent down. She fell on top of him. Jack reached up and tickled her until she convulsed with laughter. Emily laughed until tears ran. They lay there until they caught their breath, then Hilda got up and pulled Jack to his feet. They walked to the campsite, collected their toilet kits, and trooped to the showers.

While they were eating their supper at the picnic table, a park ranger walked by and paused to look at their bicycles stacked together.

"Nice bikes. Where have you come from?"

Emily filled in the silence. "Charlottesville, Virginia."

"My brother lives in Charlottesville. Not now. He's doing what you're doing—living on his bike."

"Cool. Where is he?"

"I don't know. Somewhere in Europe. He was in Italy until last month." The ranger pointed to Emily's bike. "When he came through here a couple of years back, he was riding one of those."

Jack spoke up. "Nice park and beach you have here."

"Thanks."

"This has been the best day yet since I left home," said Emily.

"I'm glad to hear that," said the ranger. "You enjoy yourselves and come back soon." He waved and moved on to check on the other campers.

"Friendly," Jack said to Hilda. "Have you ever had a ranger visit your campsite and not tell you that you were breaking some rule?"

"Never. It makes me want to take him up on the invitation to come back."

The air cooled rapidly as they finished eating. Jack put some water on for tea.

"Let's check in. I'll call Pete this time," he said.

"Want me to call Ted?"

"Sure. He'd probably like that."

"Should I call Greg?" said Emily with a wink. "Never mind. I'll call Mom."

When Emily hung up, Hilda was putting water and tea bags into the mugs.

"Well?" asked Hilda.

"Everyone's fine. They both have things finally to a point where they can go to the Northern Neck. They'll be there until next weekend."

"Good for them."

"And Mom loves the dress. Dad wants to see her in it too."

Hilda laughed. Jack hung up and joined them. They looked at him expectantly.

"Abdul and Hassan are definitely in Canada. They were identified by people in the Muslim neighborhood where they were hiding when they tried to recruit a kid into the Forebears. The *Sûreté de Québec* collected them—I can hardly say arrested—when they crashed a stolen car in a chase in Laval. They're in a hospital in

Montréal, under guard until they can be transferred to prison."

"Stolen car? That means that they have Canadian warrants on them."

"That's right. Grand theft auto. Recruiting for a terrorist organization. Fleeing the police. Not to mention going a hundred kilometers per hour in a residential neighborhood."

"Aren't they wanted here?" asked Emily.

"Of course, but they'll face Canadian courts and jail time before they can be extradited to the US. I don't think that they'll be going anywhere unless they break out."

"There's always that," said Hilda. "But we can stop worrying about them until they do."

"Could they escape?" asked Emily.

"Not likely. According to Pete, their arrest is big news in Canada. People are furious that they were hiding there, and that they tried to recruit one of the local Muslim kids. Their pictures are all over the news. If they escape, there would be nowhere to hide because people would turn them in and anyone trying to help them."

"Why? They seemed to be moving around easily."

"They were using stolen identities," said Hilda. "Muslims in Québec include a large contingent of refugees from Syria and Iraq, just the sort of people who were fleeing the Forebears and their ilk."

"I get it. So, now we have only the Fab Four."

"Ted had news on them," said Hilda. "The Saturn was found in the long-term parking lot at Bradley International Airport this morning. TSA and the

Connecticut State Police were on the lookout for them, so they did not fly out. The consensus is that they rented a car at the airport, but the detectives are still checking that out."

"If they did, we'll get a new car description, won't we?"

"Probably. But having Abdul and Hassan arrested changes the game. What *are* the Fab Four doing in New England? No point in meeting the Forebears, is there, Jack?"

"Like we wondered before, they may be looking for us or be here for something completely different."

"But they would still recognize Hilda if they saw her, wouldn't they?"

"I'm sure of that. Even if it were a complete coincidence."

"And as of this morning, they were between where we are and where we're going." Hilda looked away, exasperated.

"True," said Jack. "Are we ready to leapfrog?"

Hilda started to say something, then shut her mouth. They sat there for a minute in silence.

"We could catch the Vermonter in Springfield, and we're unlikely to see them tomorrow unless they're incredibly lucky. Let's see what develops tomorrow."

"Okay. I'll call Bill to let him know that we'll be in tomorrow afternoon."

Emily waved at Hilda. Jack looked at her, then at Hilda with a quizzical arched eyebrow.

"Oh, yes. Would you ask him to have something cold ready, anything better than Sam Adams, if you get my drift? Tomorrow is going to be hot, with the winds from the south."

"Like Fat Tire, maybe?"

"That would be great."

He pointed at Emily and held up three fingers with a questioning look.

"Sure," said Hilda. "I may drink it if she doesn't."

Jack called his friend in Windsor Locks.

They turned in while there was still light on the western horizon.

"A good day, Jack. Almost like a holiday."

"Who knew lying on the beach could leave me so tired?"

"You should be baked and burned."

"I did wake up every hour to reapply the sunblock."

"Good. Tomorrow will be more challenging, a good workup for what lies north of us."

"Good night, beautiful."

"G'night, handsome."

ʘ ʘ ʘ

The next day, they rolled out of the park before eight. In the cool of the morning, they got a good start, putting the steepest hills behind them on the first thirty kilometers. By midmorning, they were coasting more than climbing. They stopped for lunch in Middletown. By staying on neighborhood streets, they made their way across greater Hartford in the heat of the day, shaded by trees. North of Hartford, they rode close to the Connecticut River. The south wind was warm, but it also pushed them along at a good clip. With little traffic and bicycle-friendly streets, they rolled into Windsor Locks at about three o'clock

Bill Lanman met them at the door of his freshly painted home. He was of average height, thick with muscle, with short gray hair and a ruddy complexion. He gave Jack a big bear hug and introduced himself to the two women. They stowed the bikes in the garage behind the house and carried their panniers into the house. Bill had a pair of guest rooms with dormers on the second floor.

"Bill Jr.'s in Texas, and Sarah's in Oregon. They won't be needing the rooms anytime soon," he explained.

"I'm sorry about Maria," said Jack. He turned to Emily and explained. "Bill's wife died two years ago. I was in Iraq at the time."

"Thanks, Jack. She's with me every day, you know. Life goes on. Moving ahead until we meet again isn't so bad."

"You have a lovely place," Hilda said.

"It keeps me busy. I retired just last year, and I enjoy working on it." He led them into the kitchen. "It's a scorcher today. You guys want a brew before your showers or after?"

"How about both?" said Jack.

"Good enough. I happen to have two six-packs of Fat Tire." He reached in and pulled out three bottles. He got glasses from the cabinet. Then he pulled out a pitcher of filtered water.

"Emily can share mine," said Hilda. Bill got another glass out, and they all sat in the dining area.

"Cheers," said Bill as they clinked their glasses.

Emily tasted her beer. It was cool and not as bitter as the beers she had tried before. It did feel good after a hot ride. "What did you retire from last year, sir?"

"Bill, please. Airport security over there." He waved in the direction of Bradley International Airport. "It's like running a small city or an army base."

They chatted for a while, then the cyclists went up to shower and change. They checked in with Ted, Pete, and Katherine. No news was good news at that point.

"I think the Fab Four would be nowhere near here after dumping their car less than a mile away," said Jack.

Downstairs, Jack offered to take them all to dinner, so that Bill would not have to cook. Hilda suggested that they make dinner together the second night. Bill's favorite seafood restaurant was only a twenty-minute walk across the river. With their stomachs full and feeling clean and relaxed, they only lasted until ten o'clock before the yawning started.

The jets landing and taking off did not disturb them in Bill's well-insulated home.

21

VERMONT

IN THE MORNING, BILL LOADED JACK, HILDA, AND EMILY into his car and drove to the New England Air Museum on the north edge of Bradley Airport.

"It started out as a hangar with a few old airplanes, but it has grown over the years."

"Impressive," said Jack.

"And so big," said Hilda. "The Naval Aviation Museum in Pensacola is this same quality, but smaller."

As they walked back to the car, Jack's phone rang. He stopped walking to take the call, then ran to catch up with them.

"That was the local FBI agent."

"Frank Daglio," said Bill. "I know him. He's out of the Hartford office, but lives here because of the airport."

"Pete gave him my number. A weird breakthrough. They got a lead on the Fab Four after they couldn't find any record of their having rented a car at the airport."

"The Fab Four?" asked Bill. "Are you Beatles fans?"

"Hilda called them that the other day," said Emily. "It kind of stuck."

"What about them?" said Hilda as they buckled up.

"Frank asked Pete if they could see if any of their credit cards were used in Connecticut. It took a while to trace, but one of them rented a car in New Haven just after we saw the guy ordering kebab in West Haven. They probably drove both cars up to Bradley to leave the Saturn in long-term parking."

"Normally, no one would check that parking lot more than once a week," said Bill.

"He'll send me pictures soon. They only just talked to the rental agency in New Haven."

They arrived at the house and went inside. It was already hot outside, so they gathered in the family room with some orange juice. As they sat, Jack's phone rang again with pictures of a gray Ford Taurus with Connecticut plates.

"Couldn't be more inconspicuous," he said.

"They probably realized how they stood out in the Saturn," said Hilda.

Her phone rang. She mouthed *Pete* and answered. They watched her silently as she made courteous noises while the FBI agent talked.

"Bad news," she said after she ended the call. "The team watching the Arabic social media spotted the Chicago photo going around again—this time with a story that I was no longer in Aberdeen or Charlottesville, but probably headed north. And, of course, all the faithful are to be alert and kill me if I'm seen."

"Another *fatwa?*" asked Jack.

"No. It's the hate echo chamber effect, which can be worse because it's so hard to turn off."

"Did anyone mention where you were last sighted?"

"Charlottesville. No mention of you two—yet."

Bill spoke up. "Let me call some of my local friends in law enforcement."

"Just a minute, Bill. Does anyone locally have any reason to know that Hilda was coming to your house? Or me, for that matter?"

"Well, no. I don't run into many folks lately, and I haven't had a reason to talk about you or Hilda."

"Good. Let's not spread the word that you're hosting us. I can talk to Frank directly, and I never told him where we are staying."

"I see. The fewer people who know where you are, the better."

"Right. For now, it's only Ted, Pete, and Greg Sprouse in Charlottesville." He saw the question on Bill's face. "Greg's the resident special agent there."

"Is it time to leapfrog?" The three adults turned in surprise at Emily's question. They had forgotten that she was there.

"I think it may be," said Hilda. "But let's think this thing out. We still have today if Bill doesn't mind."

"You can hide here forever if you like. I can use the company."

"No need for that, but let's get some lunch and lay out our options."

"Speaking of lunch," said Emily, "don't we have to shop for supper?"

"You're right, Em," said Hilda. "Let's see what's here already and get what we need this afternoon."

"Let's take my car to Geissler's Supermarket across the river," said Bill. "You three draw attention on your bikes."

That settled, they repaired to the kitchen, where they found enough lettuce and other things for a big salad with tuna on it, some fresh Italian bread, and two kinds of ice cream.

"Perfect for a hot day," said Hilda. They dropped the subject of the phone call while they ate. Bill and Jack told a few sea stories about their tour in Germany together. Bill had been Jack's first CO overseas, and a mentor to the young second lieutenant. The stories were mainly funny ones at Jack's expense, even when he was telling them.

"Gosh, Jack," said Emily at one point. "You're so cool all the time. It's hard to picture you screwing up."

"I was only four years older than you are." He looked at Bill. "What was it you told me, about the fourth or fifth time you had to chew me out?"

"You can make every mistake in the book. Just never repeat them."

"That sounds like the bumper sticker we had, 'OMG, not another learning experience!'"

Bill got up and set out the two half-gallon boxes of ice cream. Jack put out bowls while Emily found the ice cream scoops in the kitchen drawer. When everyone had topped off their bowl, Bill put the ice cream back in the freezer, then sat. He looked at Emily.

"Is this leapfrog thing what I think it is?"

"We jump on a train and go to someplace more than a day's drive from trouble."

"The Vermonter and the Northeast Regional both stop here, but only the Vermonter takes bikes. It's only fifteen miles to Springfield, which has checked baggage service to load the bikes."

"That's what we were thinking," said Hilda. "From St. Albans, it's only twenty or thirty kilometers to the border."

"With the Forebears enjoying the hospitality of the Canadian government, we're actually safer in Canada than here until the Fab Four are found."

Since they had to ride to Springfield anyway, they discussed going east to Boston or west to New York State but decided to stick with the Vermonter. Jack took out his phone and got their tickets for the train.

"Good thing we booked now. There were just three hooks left for bikes."

Next, they figured out what to fix for supper. Bill offered to pick up the shopping list, but Hilda shook her head.

"Let's all go. You have the car. Jack is our bodyguard. Emily is very observant, and I want to see the market. We may change our minds there."

"Okay," said Bill.

They loaded the dishwasher and drove over the Connecticut River to the supermarket, not far from the restaurant the night before. They picked up some fresh Atlantic salmon, eggs, cream, and more greens and lettuce. Bill was pushing the cart, Hilda was doing most of the looking, with Jack helping her search, and Emily was slightly ahead of them.

Suddenly Emily came back and turned Hilda around.

"They're in the ethnic food section—all four of them!"

Hilda and Emily started moving away.

"I'll get the tarragon. You two go back to the car." Bill tossed Hilda the keys. "Jack, cover their rear."

Jack eased behind them as Bill turned into the aisle where the Fab Four were haggling over two different brands of couscous.

Out in the parking lot, Emily and Hilda looked around as they hurried back to Bill's car. Emily pulled out her phone.

"Look! That's their car!"

"Damn! Parked right next to us. That *is* one inconspicuous car." Jack caught up with them and immediately understood the situation.

"Get in. Let's move Bill's car around the corner."

"I can drive."

"I know, but I want you to duck if they come out. Em?"

"They haven't come out yet."

Jack backed out Bill's car and found a spot out of sight. He called Frank Daglio while Hilda called Bill to let him know where his car was.

"Bill was in the checkout line. They're still shopping."

A few minutes later, Bill came around the corner, and they loaded the groceries.

"I got something extra in the checkout line." He held up an opened roll of red 3M reflective tape. "Who looks at the bottom half of the front bumper of a rental?" He grinned as he started the car.

"Brilliant, Bill."

"I wanted to let the air out of their tires," said Emily, "but they might have come out any moment."

As Bill drove out of the parking lot, two police cruisers and an "unmarked" full-sized sedan were easing into it.

"Let's not stay to watch," said Jack. Hilda muttered.

As they were putting away the groceries, Jack's phone rang. "Frank," he said as he answered it.

"Hi, Frank. Got news?" Jack listened. "Can I put you on speaker, so Hilda can hear?" He tapped the icon. Frank Daglio had a distinctive bass voice.

"I'm glad you called, Jack. Unfortunately, they were coming out just as we arrived and took off on foot. We have an APB out on them, but you never know what they might do or where they might hide."

"But you've got their wheels," said Jack.

"And their shopping cart. They're gonna go hungry for a while."

"I guess that's good."

"That's not all. We found three rifles, two pistols and a helluva lot of ammunition in the trunk. So, unless they were packing something on their persons, we got their arsenal too."

"Thanks, Frank. I'm Hilda. We haven't met, but I would like to thank you personally after this is over."

"I'd like to meet you, Hilda. What are your plans?"

"We'll probably take a train to put some distance between us and them, then resume our bike tour."

"That reminds me. Trains go through here six or seven times a day. I want to cover the station and get their photos to the patrol officers and the Amtrak police. Good luck, both of you." He ended the call.

"Both of you?" said Emily.

"He was probably briefed about Hilda and told that I was with him. Pete may never have mentioned you."

"Oh, that makes sense."

"After you all are gone, Frank is going to kill me when he finds out you were hiding here. We play golf most Saturdays." Bill grinned. "Do you need to do some laundry or take a nap?"

"Actually," said Hilda, "we should do some laundry and some maintenance on the bikes while we have a day off our machines and a garage handy."

"And I was going to buy the groceries," said Jack, reaching for his wallet. Bill put his hand on Jack's.

"I don't have much to spend my money on, living alone. Let me treat."

That afternoon, they cleaned their chains, checked cables, bolts, and wheels, and pumped up their tires. All their laundry fit in one load; that was done before they finished with the bikes. Hilda discovered Bill's collection of classical CDs, so they fixed dinner while Herbert Von Karajan took the Berlin Philharmonic through Beethoven's Eighth Symphony and Sir Georg Solti led the Vienna Staatsoper in *Parsifal.*

"You have a beautiful voice, Hilda," said Bill as he chopped red peppers. "Where did you learn to sing Wagner like that."

"My mother sang in local opera, and my father was her biggest fan. She taught music throughout his career and after he retired to Kaiserslautern."

"Jack and I were stationed there."

"I know. I grew up there but left for boot camp before you arrived."

"Small world. But even in Germany, a teenager wouldn't know the arias from *Parsifal*."

Hilda smiled. "My mother kept the house filled with arias."

Dinner was a quiet, relaxing affair. Afterward, Hilda logged her computer onto Bill's Wi-Fi to check for news of the Fab Four and to scan the Arabic *Al-Jazeera*. The Chicago picture was in a story about the arrest of Abdul and Hassan in Canada.

"Why can't they show the other pictures of Chicago? It was gruesome enough."

"You're photogenic, dear. *Al-Jazeera* probably gets more clicks from your photo than from a dozen pictures of atrocities." Jack massaged her shoulders. She had not realized how tense they were. Emily excused herself to call her mother.

"Are we ever going to get out from under this?"

"I don't know. Maybe it's the new normal. Maybe it will go away. Maybe there will be a new threat."

"I'm just a nurse riding a bicycle, for God's sake! Why me?"

"I know that you're more than 'just a nurse,' Hilda. When the bad guys run into you, they find out too."

"What do you mean?"

"You don't run. You stand up and do what you have to. When attacked, you fight back—and usually win. How many men have you decked for making a pass?"

"I wasn't counting."

Jack laughed gently and rubbed harder. "Let's check in, just in case Frank has not talked to Pete yet."

"Okay." She got up and stretched while they both pulled out their phones. Emily walked in as they were ending the call.

"Mom wants to talk to Hilda. I told her that we saw the four guys from Aberdeen, but that they never saw us. She still wants to talk to you."

Hilda sighed and looked at Jack. "You're not 'just a nurse,' Hilda."

She called Katherine, bracing herself for a blast of emotional angst.

"Hilda, thanks for calling." Katherine sounded calm, like a professor considering a dissertation defense. "Emily told me that she saw the four men who were looking for you, but that they didn't see any of you. I wanted to know what your take was."

"Emily is correct, Katherine. Not only did she see them, but she got me and Jack out of the store before they could see us. Our host finished the shopping. We called the FBI, and the police were rolling in while we were driving away. Your daughter has proven herself to be very observant and quick."

"You're sure they haven't seen you? How did they know to be there?"

"They didn't. Katherine, we don't know that they're looking for us. They left Aberdeen before the police could question them. They are wanted as material witnesses, nothing more. They came here to hide their car in the long-term parking lot at the airport because they must know that the police are looking for them."

"But they got away."

"Yes. They fled on foot. But the FBI got their rental car—and a shopping cart full of food, by the way. We're taking the train out tomorrow, and we hope to be long gone before they can move again, assuming the local police don't find them first."

"Where are you going?"

"Same place as always. Montréal. We should be there by the end of the week."

"What about the two in Canada?"

"I thought Greg would brief you on that. They were arrested for stealing a car and evading arrest, so they'll be behind bars for a long time—even before they are extradited to the USA."

"Well, that's good news. So, you think you have it under control?"

"Yes. And let me add that Emily is a solid contributor to this team. It's not like chaperoning a teenager at all. You will be pleased and surprised by the capable young woman you raised."

"Thank you. I just wanted to hear it from you."

"I understand." She asked about Mark and exchanged a little small talk before ending the call.

Emily was looking at her like a puppy about to be scolded.

"Oh, Em. Get that dog look off your face. She was fine. Worried, but okay. Any mother would want to double-check information from a teenager. She hasn't seen you growing these last few weeks, has she?"

Emily smiled. "No. What was that about Greg?"

"I think that you might ask when the last time Greg talked to her when you call so that we can get a sense of what she might and might not know about the bigger picture. She didn't know about Abdul and Hassan being off the street."

"Should I have told her?"

"Not necessarily. Greg is supposed to let her know about that stuff. You can keep your conversations with your mother about things that happen to you."

"I don't want her to worry with all this stuff about the guys looking for you."

"Thanks. Neither do I. But we don't know that they were looking for me. All we know is that they know that the police are looking for them. They're scared."

Emily yawned.

They all turned in early.

ଔ ଔ ଔ

"Don't you just love small towns?" said Bill. He passed the local paper to them over breakfast. The *Hartford Courant* ran an article in the "Courant Community" section about the police response to the supermarket, with a photo of the police cruisers outside, and full descriptions and pictures of the Fab Four. "I also got an alert on the *Patch,* which is a local online newspaper. These guys won't have anywhere to hide."

"I'll still be glad to be on that train this afternoon," said Hilda. "No reflection on the hospitality. Bill. You've been a lifesaver—literally."

Bill smiled. "Least I could do for this young guy who keeps getting into trouble." He slapped Jack gently on the shoulder.

Bill insisted on following them in his car to Springfield. They could hardly refuse, not knowing where the Fab Four might be.

Before they knew it, they were riding into Massachusetts. Longmeadow was a pretty town in the idyllic way of a Rockwell painting. Springfield lay just beyond it.

While waiting on the platform, Jack got confirmation from a Warmshowers host just north of the Amtrak station in Saint Albans. When the Vermonter pulled in, they walked their bikes to the baggage car and passed them up to the baggage car attendant, who hung them on hooks near the door.

They found their seats as the train began to move. Jack excused himself to go to the restroom. Emily sat by the window. Hilda stood to secure the flap on her pannier better.

Emily gasped.

Hilda followed her gaze and found herself looking at the man who had bought takeaway in West Haven. He stopped, and recognition flashed across his face.

He began running from the end of the car toward Hilda, pulling out a large knife. A passenger screamed.

The scene switched into slow motion. Hilda saw him raise the knife and realized that he was going to try a deep stab at her upper body. She ducked to the floor, pushing herself into him and coming up under him with her hands on his scrotum. Using his forward momentum, she lifted him off his feet and let him fly over her, crashing to the deck, his head resting under one of the aisle seats. She heard the knife clatter to the floor but did not see it. She flipped around and knelt on his back to hold him down, but he did not move.

Jack came running from the other end of the car. A conductor hurried up behind him.

"He's unconscious," Hilda said. "He's alive, and his pulse is strong."

"You're bleeding," said Jack.

Hilda looked down at the long cut on her left arm, which had not begun to hurt yet. She asked the conductor, "Do you have Amtrak police on the train?"

The conductor, a young woman with terrified eyes, suddenly came to and called into her radio. "They're in the café car, and they're on their way."

"Thanks. Jack, call Pete and Frank." Jack already had his phone out. She reached down and continued checking the man for injuries. That done, she pulled his hands back behind him, never letting him move. He stirred slightly and opened his eyes. She leaned over him and whispered into his ear in Arabic. Then she straightened up.

"He's not hurt seriously. I can hold him."

The two Amtrak police arrived. One was a burly man of about forty, the other a thirty-something woman. The man spoke first.

"What the—"

Jack closed his phone and showed them his identification.

"Military Police?" said the older police officer.

"Yes. This man is wanted as a material witness in an attempted murder in Maryland. His three companions are probably on the train. Major Paisley here is their target."

"But it looks like she assaulted him."

"Nope. He attacked her. I alerted the FBI. They'll have people at the next stop to take custody of all four. Here are the photos of the other three." He showed them his phone.

"We have an APB on them," said the woman.

"You go forward, and I'll go to the rear," said the man.

"If I may suggest something," said Jack, "you might want to go together."

The conductor spoke up. "I came from the rear, and I didn't see them."

The two police officers headed to the front of the train, the man talking into his radio. Jack turned to Hilda.

"Are you okay?"

"If I weren't wearing a bicycle kit, I'd have ruined another shirt. Can you get my pannier down? There's a first aid kit in it."

Jack reached up and handed the pannier to Emily, who set it on Hilda's seat and opened it. The first aid kit was near the top. Hilda motioned to Jack and traded places. Emily took a paper napkin that was in the pocket in front of her seat and reached under the seat.

"Do you want this?" She was holding the knife.

"Good for you, Em," said Jack. "Ease that into the seat pocket without touching it. We'll turn it in with Hamid here."

Hilda took out the bandages. Emily helped her wrap her arm. Jack noticed a bungee cord in the pannier and used it to handcuff Hamid, who glared at him, but seemed seriously cowed by Hilda's fierce blue eyes.

The train pulled into Holyoke and stopped. Emily saw a half-dozen police cars, and a SWAT van at the little station. The head conductor made an announcement for passengers to please wait while the police completed their activity. Emily saw the other three men being escorted in handcuffs down the platform, just as three officers and a man in a suit came into their car. The man in the suit pulled out his credential pack.

"Major Rathburn?" Jack nodded. "And you must be Hilda—Major Paisley. I'm Frank Daglio. Very pleased to meet you after all."

"And this is Hamid al-Mansour," said Jack. "I don't know about the other three yet."

"They're coming down the platform," said Emily, "in handcuffs."

Jack shook his head and grinned. "She always sees them first, doesn't she?"

Agent Daglio motioned to the two officers, who produced proper handcuffs, and bound Hamid after taking photos of him on the floor and of Hilda's wound. After bagging Hamid's knife, they led him away. The conductor made an announcement that passengers could debark.

"We're going to need statements," said Frank, "and you should have that wound checked."

"It's shallow and already clotted," said Hilda. "Is there any way that I can avoid being in the same town with those four?"

"Let me work on that." He pulled out his phone and called the SAC in Hartford. After some back and forth, he ended the call. He motioned to the conductor by the door to let the train move on.

"I can take your statements on the way. The bureau will send a car to take me back to Holyoke."

"Thank you, Agent Daglio," said Jack. "You didn't have to do this."

"I know." Frank smiled. "But I didn't know that I would be riding the Vermonter with a celebrity." He put out his hand to Emily. "Frank Daglio, amateur racer and serious fan. Emily Hampstead, isn't it?"

Emily blushed and shook his hand. Hilda mock-rolled her eyes, and Jack laughed. "Not again."

"My fiancée will be totally blown away when I tell her about meeting you, Emily."

"Who's that?"

"Marianne Van der Fleet."

"Cornell University. She was ahead of me in the Tidewater Classic."

"That's the one. She came home talking of nothing except the teenager on the podium with her. We watched all the videos we could on you after that. It looks like you have recovered from your crash. That was awful."

"Partly recovered. I can't compete yet. That's why I'm touring this summer."

Frank suggested that they move into business class, which had enough room for some privacy. They set up at the end of the car out of earshot of the other passengers. Some seemed shocked at the appearance of the three cyclists, one bloodstained, but soon everyone was ignoring them. Frank recorded their statements on his phone. He reminded them to stay in touch because they might need to return if the case were to go to trial. Then they went back to their regular seats. Frank got off in Brattleboro after taking photos with Emily to send to his fiancée.

"What did you murmur into Hamid's ear?" Jack asked when the train started moving again. "I recognized some words, but not much."

"I told him that I was the blue-eyed *djinn* that his *imam* warned him about, and that I'd be waiting for him instead of the virgins in paradise if he didn't mend his ways."

"Omigod, that's awesome, Hilda!" said Emily. Jack laughed until the tears ran.

It was dark when they pulled into Saint Albans, Vermont. Their host was a retired railroad engineer who liked riding the rail trails and hosting cyclists coming through. Hilda and Emily were able to wash the blood out of their clothes and dress Hilda's wound again. They checked in and learned that the incident on the train was already national news. The only video was taken as the four men were bundled into police cruisers. Ted and Pete complimented Hilda on her taking down Hamid. When they ended the call, Emily was holding her phone out to Hilda.

"Mom wants to talk to you. I told her that we knew about the four men on the train and that it was our train. She said that your takedown is going viral on the internet." Hilda sighed and took the phone.

"Hello, Katherine."

"The internet is full of pictures of you kneeling on one of those four men arrested in Holyoke. What the hell is going on up there?"

"They boarded in Windsor Locks. We boarded in Springfield because of the bicycles."

"So, they *were* looking for you." Katherine's voice was rising as she struggled to keep calm.

"No. They weren't looking for us. They were trying to escape from Windsor Locks. One of them went for a walk, maybe to go to the café car. He recognized me, but he was completely surprised. He rushed me, and I put him down."

"Just like that?"

"Just like that. Emily warned me, so I had the whole length of the car to get ready for him when he started running at me."

"And what if Emily hadn't warned you?"

"It might have been more of a struggle, but he was an amateur, not a trained fighter. And Jack came down the aisle just at that moment. Hamid, that's his name, could not have subdued us both, even armed."

"But they know where you are."

"It doesn't help them. Those four are in jail. So are the two Forebears in Canada. Right now, we don't have anyone that we know of looking for us." She could hear Katherine breathing into the phone. She waited.

"I guess that's a relief."

"It is. Has Greg been briefing you?"

"He told us that Emily was in Windsor Locks, and he told us about the scene at the supermarket."

"Good. We'll be crossing into Canada tomorrow. We'll call Ted Tinsley in Aberdeen or Pete Sayfield in Baltimore each day. Whoever we call should call the others, including Greg. Emily will call every third day at least, or if she gets bored with us."

"She's having too much fun for that, I think. Will your phones ring if we call?"

"Yes. And we'll call you regardless if something important happens."

"Okay, then. Let's hope we don't see you on the news anymore."

"We hope so too. Give my best to Mark."

"Will do. Thanks." She ended the call. Hilda returned the phone to Emily.

On their host's recommendation, they changed their plan to ride straight to Montréal. Instead, the next day, they rode the Missisquoi Valley Rail Trail some forty-five kilometers to Richford on the Canadian border. They climbed a steep ridge out of Saint Albans overlooking the Missisquoi River and plunged to the rail-trail. It took them on a gentle climb through the hills of northern Vermont, cutting through breath-taking valleys and around imposing hills. They arrived in Richford about ten thirty and stopped for a snack. After making sure that they had their passports in their pockets and that their phones were on the international plans that they expected them to be, they took the Richford Road toward Frelighsburg in Québec. The road climbed sharply to the border north of town.

The US Border Patrol waved them through, but the Canadian Border Services agent did not look happy to see them, especially Hilda. He scanned their passports carefully. Then he asked Hilda, "Where are you from originally, Ms. Paisley?" His French accent was soft but distinct.

Hilda looked at his nameplate. Jean-Louis Bertrand. "*Allemagne, monsieur.*" His face cleared to something less hostile.

"*Mais comment êtes-vous américaine?*"

"*Par mon père, qui était en service OTAN.*"

"*Bien donc. Passez.*" He returned her passport.

They crossed into Canada before noon. From there, a dizzying downhill run put them on the plain that sloped gently toward the Saint Lawrence River. They had lunch in Frelighsburg, by an organic produce store with a delicatessen, where they bought sandwiches made with the local oka cheese, arugula, and tomatoes.

"I'm in heaven," said Hilda. "Real bread."

"These are delicious," said Emily.

"Bad food is against the law in Québec," said Jack.

"Why did the border agent quiz you, Hilda? Didn't he believe your passport?"

"You followed that?"

"*Bien sûr,*" she said, grinning.

"My, she's full of surprises," Hilda said to Jack. Turning to Emily, she said, "He may have suspected that I was African. The recent flood of African refugees from the US, mostly Nigerian, is making the CBSA lose its famous welcoming face."

"It looked racist to me," said Jack.

"There could be some of that, but it's been the public outcry against using asylum requests to skirt immigration procedures that has caused a crackdown at the borders."

"Well, it was smart to use French with him," said Jack. "He dropped his suspicious attitude when you did that."

"That's because your accent is so good," said Emily. "When I try it, they keep speaking English to me."

"Maybe we can work on that too," said Hilda. "Have you lived in a French-speaking country?"

"No. I took it all through high school, and we had a trip to France my junior year at Newton High."

Jack booked a tent site at Camping Les Cedres. They mounted up and rode out of town. With the gentle downhill slope, they sped past the large farms on either side of the road. Cars seemed to give them plenty of room, and they saw more bicycles on the road than they had seen anywhere except New York City. They rolled through Saint-Jean-sur-Richelieu by four o'clock, in plenty of time to set up camp.

"This place is like Disneyland!" exclaimed Emily as they rode through the RV resort. "This isn't really camping, is it?" She pointed to the water park and pool.

"It's hardly roughing it," said Hilda, "but it'll be more natural in the tent area."

"And the woods should dampen the noise from the RV's," Jack added.

After pitching their tents, they found the showers, changed and washed out their sweaty bicycle kits. They bought muesli and yogurt for breakfast at the convenience store but had supper in the restaurant—*moules marinières, frites,* accompanied by a smooth white wine.

Jack held out his glass and proposed a toast. "To a night without Forebears or the Fab Four." They clinked glasses and sipped their wine with smiles and sighs of relief.

No one had room for dessert, so they were glad for the walk back to their site.

For the first night in almost a year, Hilda and Jack slept deeply and worry-free. Emily dreamed of adventures—and her dreams would come true all too soon.

23

MONTRÉAL

"**D**O YOU REMEMBER MARYSE?" asked Hilda as they snapped the loose dirt off the ground cloth and folded it.

"No. Should I?" Jack wiggled his eyebrows. She rolled her eyes.

"My high school classmate who lives in Montréal. At least she was there on her last Facebook post. I meant to write to her before we left Charlottesville, but the shooting at UVA made us want to keep a low profile."

"Do you want to try to contact her?"

"This close, I think it would be safe. We were best friends, but we only started exchanging Christmas letters last year after losing touch when she moved back to Québec."

"I'd like to meet her. Go for it."

Emily walked up, pushing her loaded bicycle. "You two planning to ride today?" She grinned smugly.

"More people, more stuff. Gimme a break," Hilda grumbled but smiled too.

"Still want to take the *Voie Maritime*? It sounds like fun to me."

"Sure. It's only fifty-five kilometers all the way to the HI Hostel in Montréal."

Riding the broad plain east toward the Saint Lawrence Seaway, Emily was impressed by the size of the farms. She had seen extensive agri-businesses in Kansas, but these pushed the definition of "family-owned." Hilda explained that many of them dated back to the days of New France. After the British won the Seven Years' War and took over Québec, they recognized the titles of the French aristocracy. Thus, the estates remained intact.

Candiac was a prosperous, elegant town with large houses and bike lanes everywhere. They crossed to Saint-Catherine, then took the *véloroute* that ran along the long, narrow island off the right bank of the river.

"This is fantastic!" Emily began speeding down the straight bike path. On their right, low shrubbery and grass separated them from the water. On their left, a long stand of trees gave them intermittent views of the skyline of greater Montréal.

"Québec has taken bicycle transportation seriously longer than any other government in North America," said Hilda. "Let's plan on some touring on the *Route Verte* while we're here."

"I'd like that."

Soon, they crossed the bridge to the Île des Sœurs and then into the city of Montréal.

The hostel was near the train station, convenient to the metro and all the major sites downtown. Jack had reserved the only three-bed mixed dorm, so it was like having their own room. They checked in, presented their HI membership cards, and settled into their room, with their bicycles locked in the bicycle storage room. As soon as they had showered and changed, Jack and Emily spread out maps of Québec and Montréal on the table.

Hilda pulled out her phone.

"*Allo*, Maryse?"

They smiled when Maryse's squeal of delight reached them across the room. Hilda held the phone away from her ear, shook her head, and continued the conversation in rapid French. After a few minutes of catching up, she ended the call.

"Guess what? She wants us to move to her place tomorrow. As long as we want."

"I can tell she's excited to hear from you." Jack pulled the city map closer.

"I explained our tour, and she insists that we base from her house. We can even leave our camping gear when we know we won't need it. The accountant she married is now the CFO of the Bank of Montréal. They have six guest bedrooms in their place in Summit Park."

"You may need your black dress for breakfast."

"Hardly. She says she and Jacques are into skiing and cycling. Bicycle kit is the Uniform of the Day in their house."

Jack pointed to the map. "Not far from here. Looks like two kilometers."

"But it's an average grade of ten percent to their house."

"Ooh, my kind of ride!" Emily grinned.

They spent the afternoon walking to the Museum of Fine Arts near their hostel. They stopped for dinner at a local restaurant on the way back. With her new habit of scanning rooms, Emily noticed two couples, a family of five, and two casually dressed men by themselves at the back of the room.

Hilda appeared pensive as they waited for fruit and cheese after the main meal.

"I'm trying to recall the pictures of me on top of Hamid. I know the news reports did not mention our names, but Katherine recognized me. Is my face showing in any of them?" Jack and Emily both thought for a minute.

He sliced an apple. "She knows you and that Shebeest jersey you wear."

"None of the pictures I saw showed your face." Emily paused with a piece of brie on her fork. "Are you worried about the one-off crazies hoping to kill you?"

"Anyone could guess we went to Canada if we were on the Vermonter."

"But first they need to recognize you, dear. Someone can't even tell your height or eye color from those cell phone pictures. I think it's a stretch that you'd be identified that way."

"Unless someone starts chatting about you to their friends, and so on." Emily speared another piece of cheese and an apple slice.

"Yeah, I guess there's that, but I think we're making too much of it until we get some other indication." Jack looked intently at Hilda. "It'll be a while before we can hope that you're no longer a target. Pete will let us know about the social media chatter, and when it starts to fall off."

"Okay. You're right. Thanks, both of you." She smiled.

A half hour later, they paid and left. As they walked, Emily said, "Did you see the two guys in the back of the restaurant?"

"Yes," said Hilda. "What about them?"

"They finished before we had fruit and cheese but waited until we left to get up."

"I saw that," Jack said. "They're either following us or just happen to be headed south on this street."

"Let's just let them follow," Hilda said. "We can't dodge them before we get to the hostel."

At the top of the steps, Jack took a quick glance as he went in, then turned around inside to look out.

"They stopped when we went in, and one of them made a phone call. They were watching the door after we went in. I don't see them."

Back in the room, they checked their email, social media, and news.

"Marianne van der Fleet got an offer to race with the Boels Dolman team," Emily said.

"Is that a big deal?" asked Jack.

"Like first draft pick in the NFL. It's very unusual for a new racer. She only just graduated from Cornell."

"I'll bet Agent Daglio will have to make some choices if she follows her dream," said Hilda.

"Anything on your spy networks?" asked Emily.

"All quiet tonight, thank goodness."

While Jack called Pete, Emily phoned her mom. It was a much better phone call than the one from Saint

Albans. Her mother was pleased that Emily enjoyed the art museum and that they would be in a home while in Montréal.

Jack waited until she ended the call to brief them.

"No news is good news. The Arabic news channels and social media have not been talking about you, Hilda. Someone in headquarters suggested taking the Arabists off the case, but they're collecting so much useful intelligence, that HQ decided to design a special unit to continue their work. They'll stay in place in Baltimore until the new team is up—and they'll watch out for stuff on you."

"Did you tell him about the two outside?"

"I told him that we spotted a tail coming from the restaurant, but we've no idea why. He doesn't know either, but he'll alert the RCMP and the *Sûreté*. He'll call Ted and Greg."

"Maryse told us to come by in the afternoon so that Jacques can be there when we arrive. We can do some touring in the morning."

They gathered their toilet kits and headed to the bathroom down the hall. Brushed, flossed, and changed into nightclothes, they arrived back in the room together.

"Who gets the top rack?" Hilda asked.

"Let me take it," said Emily. "Either one of you is likely to pull the bed over climbing up there." They laughed and proceeded to plug in their phones and crawl into their respective bunks. Physically, it had not been a demanding day, but they slept peacefully.

ॐ ॐ ॐ

The next morning, they enjoyed the free breakfast in the common room, with croissants and fresh baguettes, sweet butter, and jam. After the meal, they checked out, leaving their panniers in the luggage room.

Sunny days this far north were not as warm as in Virginia, so walking to the Old Quarter got the blood moving. They passed the Bank of Montréal on the way, then turned toward the river. They took pictures at the Clock Tower of the Quai de l'Horloge before starting back.

After a wonderful seafood lunch at a restaurant at the Place Jacques-Cartier, they admired the city hall on their way to the Boulevard Levesque. That took them to the shopping district and the Place des Arts. They could have taken a metro back, but it was such a lovely day, that they chose to walk past the upscale stores and back through the Place du Canada to the hostel.

"I know Maryse's house is only three kilometers away, but with the hills and our loads, I want to change."

Jack and Emily agreed. They used the washroom off the lobby. When they pushed their bikes out, they looked at the few cars parked on the street, but no one seemed to be staked out in front. There were so many cyclists going in both directions that they could not have spotted a tail among them if they tried.

The Pointreau home was easy to find, occupying most of its block, a two-story mansion surrounded by well-kept landscaping and trees that must have once been part of the Summit Woods behind the property. When they wheeled up to the gate, it opened.

Obviously, someone was watching the cameras and expected them.

Maryse Pointreau was waiting on the porch. Elegant, athletic, and slim, she stood taller than Emily but shorter than Jack and Hilda. Her blond hair was up in a French braid, and she wore Arc'teryx trekking shorts and a designer polo shirt. They dismounted their bicycles smoothly and pushed them into the covered bicycle station cleverly built near the entrance. Hilda and Maryse rushed at each other in a big hug, with double cheek-kissing.

"Maryse Pointreau, this is Jack Rathburn," she said in English.

"So pleased to meet you, Jack."

"And this—" Maryse cut her off and extended her hand.

"Is Emily Hampstead. What an honor!" She turned to Hilda. "This is a surprise indeed."

Jack mock-groaned, "Not again!" Hilda laughed.

Emily took her hand. *"Enchantée, madame."*

"Maryse, *je t'en prie. Nous sommes en Amérique, après tout."* The teenager beamed. It was the first time that someone had not returned her French with English. "Come in, everyone. I'm so excited! Let me show you your rooms, then we can do a little catching up. Antoine!"

While they unhooked their panniers, a middle-aged, muscular man came out the front door. Though he came from indoors, he wore overalls and had a pair of Felco shears on his belt and gardening gloves sticking out of his pockets. He took their camping gear so that they could make just one trip.

"Jacques said that he would come home early today, so we can expect him momentarily."

They stepped into a foyer with a polished marble floor and a crystal chandelier. The dining room to the left held a table that could seat two dozen. The living room to the right was expensively furnished. Hilda noticed that everything was spaced so that furniture could be moved against the wall to create room for entertaining. She imagined cocktail parties, ensemble concerts, and lectures in a space like this.

A staircase carried up to the bedrooms. Maryse showed them two rooms with a bathroom between them. Emily's overlooked downtown Montréal. The other two had a corner room with views of the Summit Woods and the city.

"Make yourselves comfortable. I'll wait for you downstairs when you're ready. Oh—no need to change right away. Jacques is wearing his bicycle kit too."

"Thanks, Maryse," said Hilda. "See you in a little bit."

"I like this family already." Emily grinned.

No one needed a shower because neither the hill nor the sun had broken any sweat. They moved their things from the panniers into the dressers, washed up a little at the sink, and went downstairs together.

As they reached the ground floor, Maryse was opening the front door for a tall, slender man in a white BMO team jersey that had already dried. He gave her a hug and a kiss, then removed his helmet and sunglasses. The tan face and crow's feet betrayed much time spent outdoors.

"These must be our guests." His English was slightly accented. "Maryse has been beside herself since you called. Hilda Paisley, yes?"

She shook hands and introduced Jack. Emily came up from behind.

"Goodness, I did not know that we would see Emily Hampstead in our home. Welcome, welcome!" He pumped Emily's hand enthusiastically, which made her blush more hotly than ever.

Jacques waved them toward the living room, and Maryse led them to a south-facing veranda that overlooked the garden with the city beyond. Comfortable outdoor furniture was gathered in groups, and a wet bar stood against the house.

"Wine, beer, other?" asked their host. Hilda suggested a white wine to sip, and Jacques showed her a 2015 Moselle from the bar refrigerator.

"Perfect. This brings back memories, *n'est-ce pas,* Maryse?"

Maryse smiled. "We both like Rieslings and Moselles. It was one of the first things we learned about each other when we met on a bike tour of the Moselle Valley."

"That sounds romantic," said Emily.

"It was." Jacques poured her wine because she was closest. "On the third day, we arrived in Schengen, where Luxembourg, Germany, and France meet. I wanted her to show me where she had lived, so we left the group. The rest, as they say, is history."

"How are your parents, Maryse?" Hilda held her glass out for him.

"They are well. Papa made general after the Germany tour. After two tours in Ottawa, which he hated, they retired to a small house in the Laurentians, only a couple of hours from here by car. We see them often enough."

"It's also fine riding among the most beautiful hills in Québec." He corked the bottle. "So, we don't lack for excuses to visit."

They sat around on the veranda, sipping the Moselle while Hilda and Maryse brought each other up to date, slipping easily into German and French and back to English. Jacques was much taken with Emily. It turned out that he had raced in his twenties, including the Tour de Québec and road races in the USA. He followed cycling news in North America and Europe, so he was aware of the coverage that she had received, and of her crash in the spring.

"Will you be able to race again?"

"Probably, but not this summer. I was delighted when Hilda invited me to tour with her. This is a lot more fun than training rides around Albemarle County."

"*Bien sûr*," agreed Jacques. "When will the doctors clear you to compete?"

"When we return, we'll see what this touring does to my form and whether I can get back in shape for next spring."

"You are young. It should be no problem for you."

"As it is," said Jack, "she has to watch her speedometer to keep herself from going too fast on tour—even with the bags."

"I can imagine. Your form on the videos was amazing, Emily."

She blushed. "I'm not used to all the attention since we crossed the border. Strangers recognizing me and even asking for my autograph."

"We follow cycling, especially in Québec. Potential world-class North Americans get a fan following quickly."

"Wow."

"Hilda was the center of attention when we left." Jack tilted his glass at the teenager. "Looks like Emily is now."

"Well, I don't want the attention she was getting."

"How is that?" Jacques and Maryse looked quizzically at Emily and her.

Jack answered. "Hilda was pursued by some Middle Eastern terrorists and their associates until we got to Vermont. That's why she didn't call Maryse when she set out to come to Canada."

"What happened?"

"The two terrorists were arrested here in Montréal, and the other four were captured in Massachusetts."

"Wait a minute. Was that the two who crashed their car in Laval last week?"

The three Americans nodded. "The Forebears of the Mahdi."

"*Sacre bleu!* They attacked the Sheraton in Chicago last year as I recall."

"That's the group," said Hilda. "The last two had some friends in the US, who ran into us in Connecticut. Luckily, they were all off the street by the time we arrived here."

Suddenly, Maryse reached over and tugged at her husband.

"Jacques! Remember the nurse in the Chicago attack? That was Hilda!"

"Oh, so that's the connection. Why didn't you recognize her then?"

"I was taller than she at seventeen, *mon cher*, and her hair was short the last time I saw a picture of her. We change, you know."

"You haven't, *chérie*." Maryse gave him an affectionate slap on the arm.

Emily said, "I'm just glad we don't have to worry about them anymore."

"Me too." Hilda gave a long sigh. "Me too."

Jack pretended to scan the bushes. "Now our biggest problem is Emily being kidnapped by racing fans." They laughed.

They broke up about six and took showers. Maryse insisted on serving dinner at home.

"Simple fare. *Bœuf bourguignon, pommes de terre et flageolets verts*." She apologized. "We'll do something fancier later."

"Maryse, don't spoil us. We're still reveling in the fresh bread and seafood here."

Over dinner, Jacques suggested that they dine at a restaurant near the house the next night.

"Let us treat you at some point while we're here too," said Jack.

Their hosts raised their wineglasses in assent. "Okay. I hope you will stay long enough to sample our best restaurants."

"We'll need to ride to Ottawa and Québec City to burn that off," said Hilda.

"But we planned to do that anyway," said Emily. "This is going to be the best summer I've ever had." The Pointreaus smiled with obvious pleasure.

"We're serious about your basing from here," said Maryse. "We have the room, and no one is coming."

"Do you have children?" asked Emily.

"Yes. Our son is in the army."

"Which outfit?" Jack asked.

"He's with the Twenty-Second Regiment," said Jacques.

"Québec City?" asked Jack. Jacques nodded.

About eleven, Emily yawned. Jacques had to go to work in the morning.

Maryse rose. "You sleep in as long as you like."

"Please don't disturb your routine for us," Jack said as they walked to the kitchen.

"We won't. I go for a ride in the early morning when he leaves. You'll find fresh baguettes and croissants on the counter when you come down. Whip up a big American breakfast if you like. There are eggs, bacon, fruit, juice, jam, butter, and cheeses in the refrigerator. *Soyez chez vous.*"

"Thank you."

"*Bonne nuit*, Maryse." The two friends exchanged a hug. Then everyone trooped to their rooms.

"You go first, Em." Jack paused at their bedroom door.

Inside, he and Hilda paused for a romantic embrace and a kiss.

"Maryse said that we could use the computers in the studio anytime." She eased out of her shoes. "The password is *routeverte,* all one word."

"Almost too easy to remember."

A knock on the bathroom door. Emily opened it cautiously.

"I'm done. By the way, I used my phone to Google Maryse Pointreau and found out she was Maryse Langlais. A champion rider twenty years ago."

"Before Facebook and email. No wonder I didn't know. She's too modest. Maybe you should check out her training ride one of these mornings."

Emily gave her a thumbs-up. "G'night, y'all. Remember to get some sleep." She winked and closed the door before they could say anything.

After their shower and evening ablutions, Hilda and Jack stretched out in the king-size bed on fresh linens.

"Is there anywhere better than this?"

"Only if you're next to me."

"Major Rathburn, you're impossible!" She rolled over on him....

24

SUMMIT WOODS

T HE NEXT MORNING, JACK AND HILDA WOKE UP WELL AFTER DAWN. Donning the white terry bathrobes and slippers on the bathroom door, they crept downstairs to find that no one was stirring in the house. He started the kettle while she scooped coffee into the French press on the counter. As they put out some juice and dishes, Emily came into the kitchen, also in a robe.

"Good morning, Em." He poured the boiling water into the French press, stirred the mix, and covered the coffee maker. He set the timer for four minutes.

"*Comment es-tu ce matin?*" asked Hilda. How are you this morning?

"*Bon. Ou voulons-nous aller aujourd'hui?*" Where do we want to go today? She and Hilda continued discussing where to ride while Jack put croissants on their plates and assembled a bowl of fruit.

When the coffee was ready, he poured it and set it out. "*Assez! On mange.*" Enough! Let's eat.

To their surprised looks, he added, "I agree. Let's visit the Oratory because it's right near here, then climb the Mont Royal. But I think we should save the Botanical Garden for tomorrow. That takes most of a day itself. After the Mont Royal, why don't we ride down to the Île Sainte-Hélène and the Île Notre-Dame? We could find lunch at the Bon Secours Market on the way."

"I like that," Hilda added. "Depending on the time, Habitat 67, the Biosphere—"

"The Barbie Expo on the way back!" Emily said. "I saw a sign for it walking back from the Vieux Port yesterday and looked it up on Google."

"Why not?" Jack took a bite of his croissant.

They heard the door open and a pair of cleats step onto the marble floor. A moment later, Maryse padded into the kitchen in her socks. "Hello. I hope you all slept well." Her red and black Castelli jersey was wet, but the rest of her was only shining. She was still high on endorphins, but her breathing was normal.

"Good workout?" asked Emily.

"*Oui,*" their hostess said enthusiastically.

"*Café? Nous en avons assez.*" Coffee? We have enough. Jack got up and poured a cup. Maryse joined them at the table.

"*Très bon,* Jack. I did not know you speak French." She took a croissant and a banana.

"I'm not as fast as Hilda, so I usually just listen."

"This looks like a planning session. Where to today?" They shared their ideas. "I have not done those in a while. Would you mind if I came along?"

They sat there another twenty minutes, adding some cheese and more fruit to their breakfast. Then they went up to their rooms to change.

Without the weight of the panniers, riding around Montréal proved easy and invigorating. The staff at the Oratory knew Maryse as a parishioner and let them in free as her guests. After that, she led them on the easiest roads, acted as their tour guide, and even got them discounts at the ticket windows; veterans for Jack and Hilda, and student for Emily.

They had lunch at the Bon Secours Market, rode the islands, and still arrived at the Barbie Expo by midafternoon. This last surprised them—a vast collection of unique Barbies, dressed in original outfits by the leading designers of haute couture.

By five thirty, they returned to the house. Maryse whipped up cheese omelets for a protein-rich snack. They were eating in the kitchen when Jacques arrived.

"We had a wonderful day, dear." She kissed her husband. She told them about it while he got a plate and joined them.

"This isn't dinner," he said at last. "We're going out tonight."

"My treat," said Jack. Jacques shook his head.

"Later, my friend. Tomorrow, we can eat here. What do you think, Maryse?"

She turned to Hilda. "*Qu'en penses-tu?*"

"This is like a NASA lab compared to the little galley in Kaiserslautern. Shall we work together?"

"Of course."

"I hope 'together' includes us." Jacques pointed to Jack and himself.

"*Bien sûr, mon cher.*"

"That'll be fun," said Emily.

Jacques went to the studio to book a reservation at Europea, down the hill from the house. They all showered and changed. The three Americans checked their email and social media sites, then joined their hosts on the veranda.

"No news," said Jack.

"That's good," said Hilda.

Jacques was pouring a 2016 Riesling when Emily arrived.

"Mom's happy I'm here. She's been here before but never knew about the Barbie Expo. She went totally ballistic about it! Grandma had one of the first Barbie dolls and gave it to her!"

They took the car to the restaurant, which lived up to its reputation. They got back after midnight, but it was Friday, so Jacques did not have to go in the next day. Maryse planned to ride about eighty thirty instead of dawn.

ભ ભ ભ

On Saturday, Emily and Maryse cycled past Saint-Eustache to the open country west of the city. Farms extended on either side of them to the horizon or the river. The few drivers they saw passed with care, sometimes giving a friendly toot before pulling back into the lane. They encountered more than a dozen groups—mostly men—riding hard in pelotons, obviously training. In the villages, kids rode trick bikes, and housewives pedaled city bicycles. The bright colors of the riders contrasted with the browns and greens of the fields.

Emily was transported to a happy place, surrounded by like-minded people enjoying her favorite sport.

Maryse rode hard. Her steady thirty kilometers per hour was well below Emily's threshold, but the young rider could read the intensity on Maryse's face and knew that the pace would not allow her to chat. They covered about fifty kilometers by the time they rolled into the driveway. They had omelets and a half-gallon of orange juice before going up to shower. Jack and Hilda were in their room, getting dressed to go out.

"How was it?" she asked.

"Great. She rode hard, so we didn't chat. Lots of cyclists out there of all types."

"Hard for you or her?"

"Her. Only about thirty the whole time. Dr. Morgan would approve."

"Okay. I heard you in the kitchen. You want to go out or eat something else first?"

"I ate something. I'll be ready as soon as I change. You're in street clothes."

"It's only fifteen kilometers away."

Emily went to her room through the bathroom.

Downstairs a half hour later, Jacques and Maryse were trading sections of the newspaper, sitting at the kitchen table.

"Enjoy the *Jardin*." He waved his section. "We'll go shopping this afternoon."

"*Merci. À bientôt.*" Hilda strapped on her helmet.

Jack was right; the Botanical Gardens near the Olympic Stadium were worth their own trip. Amid the topiary in many colors, the Japanese garden and bonsai house, and the Chinese garden with its pagoda, they found natural habitats of different parts of the world, vegetable plots, greenhouses, and many places to relax and enjoy the view. It took the entire morning to cover the displays, including a stop for ice cream.

Since they were so close, they pedaled over to the Biodome for the environmental exhibits. The former Olympic velodrome was an attractive nature center, perfect for school groups and families, in particular, those who might not travel far from urban Montréal.

"So where is the velodrome now?" Emily asked Hilda. "This place is bike-crazy. They must have track racing."

"They do, but the only track is in Bromont, just on the other side of Saint-Jean-sur-Richelieu where we camped. Being outdoors, it isn't as useful as it could be."

"I haven't been to a track race myself. What I've seen on TV seems very different."

"I've only been once—in Bromont, and it is different. Considering the weather here, I hope they fund one of the three proposals for an indoor velodrome."

They rode slowly back to the house, stopping for a light lunch at a brasserie that they remembered was near the hostel. Jack and Hilda chose a table where they could watch the room. Emily excused herself after asking them to order the *salade niçoise* for her.

"Those same two guys who followed us to the hostel just walked in," she said as she returned from the ladies' room.

"I saw them too," said Jack. "Can't do anything except keep an eye out for them without being too obvious."

"Maybe they live in this neighborhood," said Hilda.

"Perhaps. Let's see if they follow us again."

They felt tense as they ate. The pair went to the bar and ordered beers. They seemed to chat.

"They paid for their drinks right away, so they can leave on short notice," Jack said.

After lunch, they walked out to their bikes. The two men came out just as they rode away. Emily checked her rearview mirror.

"Dark blue Peugeot that was parked outside the brasserie," she reported. The car made the right turn with them and followed for a block before speeding up to avoid blocking traffic.

"Did you get the plate?" asked Hilda.

"Yup," said Jack.

"Me too," said Emily.

"Let's look out for them or their car, especially if either shows up outside this neighborhood." Hilda wondered about this new development. She did not think they were foreign (how could she tell in a city as diverse as Montréal?). She hoped that these two encounters were coincidental, but she didn't believe that.

Back at the house, Jack stopped at the entrance.

"You two go in. I want to check the house from the back. I'll ride around the block and be right back."

Hilda waved, and Emily followed her in. On the other side of the house, Jack spotted what he was hoping not to find. He cycled back, parked his bike, and joined the others in the kitchen. Maryse smiled but immediately lost her expression.

"You don't look happy," said Hilda. "What did you find?"

"A blue Peugeot 844-JXD."

Emily gasped. "Here?"

"Around the corner over the wall by the veranda."

"What's wrong?" Jacques asked.

"Maybe nothing, but two men followed us to the hostel from dinner the other night. The same two appeared at the *brasserie* where we had lunch. They tailed us for a block until they had to speed up because of traffic."

"Their car is parked outside your house. Either they're neighbors, or we're being watched." Hilda's eyes did that flaring thing that Emily both feared and admired.

"Easy to check," said Jacques. "I can have a friend in the *Sûreté* run the plates. We can at least make sure it's not a neighbor before we worry."

"That would be an unofficial favor, wouldn't it?"

"Of course. What are friends for?"

"Let me try official channels first." He pulled out his phone. "I have the name and number of a point of contact I'm supposed to call here in Québec. Our liaison with the FBI."

"Impressive. May I know who?"

"Pierre Laurent."

"Chief Inspector Pierre Laurent." Jacques smiled. "You have a well-placed network."

"Is that your friend?"

"Yes. Among other things, he leads the anti-terrorism unit that arrested the two Forebears of the Mahdi. Go ahead and call him but tell him that you're staying with us—and save your dime. Use the phone in the studio."

"Okay. Thanks."

Jack came back as the others got out knives, cutting boards, and ingredients to prepare dinner. There were vegetables to cut, marinades to mix, and dough to rise and fill with meat and fish.

"If I didn't know better," he said, "I would say that's too much for five people, but we'll burn it."

Emily showed him how to use a mandoline on the onions. Hilda and Jacques washed the ingredients for the salad while Maryse prepared the *crème fraiche* and put it in the refrigerator. When everything was chilling, rising or chambering, the phone rang. Jacques took it.

"That was Pierre," he said when he came back. "The car is registered to a company, not a person. He was curious about that, so he ran a check on it. It turned out to be a shell company for an outfit in Miami, Florida. The FBI is interested because of the possible connection to you, Hilda. Pierre said to tell you that Pete Sayfield is looking into it. We'll know something probably by Monday evening if not sooner."

"We know Pete," said Jack. "He's the special agent in charge of the Baltimore office. He's been coordinating the people watching out for Hilda ever since the Forebears shot at her in Maryland."

"They shot you?" Maryse gasped.

"Let's go sit down, and we'll give you the background." They repaired to the living room, aware that the veranda might be subject to eavesdropping. While Jacques poured the now-traditional glasses of white wine, Hilda briefed them on the events since Chicago, and why the FBI was watching out for her. Jack explained his part in it all.

"And I'm just along for the ride." Emily made a funny face, lightening the atmosphere and allowing them to laugh.

"Well, you should be safe here," Jacques said, "but depending on what your FBI comes back with, I can have our private security contractor find out what they are up to."

"We should bring this up with Ted and Pete when we call tonight."

"You check in often?" asked Maryse.

"Every day, we call either the provost marshal at Aberdeen Proving Grounds, who has been on the case from the beginning, or Pete Sayfield. We made a promise when we started out from Charlottesville."

"Because of the three months that the FBI could not find them after Chicago." Emily grinned.

Dinner that night was as special as they hoped. It took two hours to cook it, and another four to consume it. Jacques had a first-rate entertainment system providing music. With conversation between each course, they had no trouble finishing the *baeckeofe*, a four-pound Atlantic salmon, *coq au Riesling*, *piperade*, and *pâté chinois*, in addition to the salad, the cheese, and the berries with *crème fraiche*.

The talk stayed light and happy as they caught up more deeply the lives that had transpired since Hilda and Maryse had parted ways at the Frankfurt airport.

Emily, Jack, and Jacques had become essential parts of those stories.

They loaded the dishwasher (Emily and Jack had scrubbed all the pots earlier) and went to bed after midnight—again.

Sunday morning, they walked with the Pointreaus to the Oratory for Mass, then came home for brunch. Jack slipped around the corner to check on the blue Peugeot.

"Gone."

"If they are following us, maybe they realized that we made them," Hilda suggested.

"We'll know more tomorrow." Jacques opened the gate with a key fob, and they went in.

In the afternoon, everyone took a short nap. They went for a long walk through the Summit Woods behind the house.

That evening, they decided to go to La Lavanderia for Argentine food. The two men who had followed them did not show up.

"They might have turned it over to another pair," said Hilda as they considered their menus.

"If they did, the second team is better than the first," said Jack. "I've been watching."

"This is a protein-rich menu," said Emily. "Good for our ride tomorrow."

"Do you know where you will stay?" asked Jacques.

"There are two campgrounds off the Russell-Prescott Trail, about halfway to Ottawa," said Hilda. "We'll call ahead when we have an idea of which one we'll reach."

"We've booked the Jailhouse Hostel for Tuesday and Wednesday."

"It's a fun place," said Maryse. "The rooms are actually cells in the old city jail."

Jack signaled for the bill, with a stern stare at their hosts. Jacques held up his hands in surrender.

Emily excused herself to go to the restroom.

Two women were chatting as they adjusted their makeup. Emily took the second stall. When she came back out, the two women turned to the door to leave. It flew open, and two men ran into the restroom.

Emily heard two popping sounds. The women crumpled to the floor.

The men pointed their pistols at her, and the one closest pulled the trigger. Another *pop* and a sting in her stomach.

Her vision narrowed and went black.

25

MASTIGOUCHE

S ITTING OUT IN THE RESTAURANT, Jack paid the bill. They waited.

"Jack," said Hilda. "Did you notice the two men at the bar?"

"Not the same ones."

"Yeah, but guys don't go to the restroom together."

He leaped from his seat and sprinted across the room. She was right behind him.

He pushed the door open to the men's room. Empty.

"Jack!"

He ran to the women's room. Hilda was kneeling over two unconscious women with her phone to her ear. "I called 911. Tranquilizer darts. Emily's not here."

Jack ran to the side entrance. In the quiet parking lot, he smelled the exhaust of a cold engine that had left not long ago. He walked back into the hallway with the restrooms. The manager was there, summoned by the wait staff when the two Americans raced across the restaurant.

Jacques and Maryse appeared next. The manager ordered one waiter to ask the other guests to return to their seats. A second waiter went to the street outside to direct the ambulance to the side entrance.

"Where's Emily?" asked Jacques. Maryse held his arm in a death-grip, her eyes wide with concern.

"Kidnapped, I think," said Jack. "Would you call Pierre? I'll call Pete in Baltimore."

The EMT's came in with the police. Hilda identified herself as a nurse and told them that the two women were not in immediate danger but would remain unconscious for hours.

The officers photographed the scene, then let the EMT's carry the unconscious women to the ambulance on gurneys. The manager located the two gentlemen who were with them. A policeman took business cards from each man and instructed them to wait at the hospital. An officer would come for their statements there.

Pierre Laurent showed up just in front of a pair of detectives from the Montréal Police. The officers and detectives recognized the gray-haired giant at once. His gaze paused on each person before shifting to the next one.

"Majors Paisley and Rathburn, I take it."

"Yes, sir," said Hilda.

"And we're missing Miss Hampstead, *non*?"

"We only reported a possible kidnapping, Pierre," said Jacques. "I did not identify her."

"But almost everyone in the restaurant recognized her. Photos of your table went viral while you ate. The dispatcher knew who was kidnapped immediately."

He switched to French and ordered the crime scene set off. While they taped off the area and re-signed the men's room for unisex service, the chief of detectives from the Montréal Police arrived. Laurent suggested that they all move to the restaurant and let the technicians do their work.

"The FBI will be interested in this," he said, looking at Jack.

"I called them. Pete Sayfield said they'll expedite the tracer on the shell company that owns the blue Peugeot."

Time paused in Hilda's world. The unconscious women had been removed, the forensic specialists processed the crime scene, and the policemen brainstormed in French and English while everyone waited for more information to emerge. An amber alert and an APB with Emily's description (as if anyone needed it) had already gone out.

She tapped Jack on the shoulder. "I have to call Katherine."

He put an arm around her. "Want me to call?"

"No. Just be here while I do."

They moved to the quietest corner they could find while she dialed Katherine's cell phone.

"Hello, Hilda. We were just finishing dinner. What's up?"

"Are you sitting down with Mark?"

"Uh—yes, why?"

"Please put this on speaker. I need to talk to both of you." The phone bleeped as Katherine tapped the icon.

"What's wrong, Hilda? You're scaring me."

"Emily's been kidnapped."

There was a long silence on the line, then she heard Katherine scream. Mark was holding her.

"What happened?" he said. "Where? When?"

"Just now. We were paying the bill when Emily went to the restroom. We got suspicious about two men going to the restroom and raced after them, but by the time we got there, they had shot two women with tranquilizer darts and disappeared with her."

"I could smell the exhaust fumes of their vehicle when I ran outside, but they were gone," said Jack.

Hilda relayed his comment to Mark and Katherine. "The police and the *Sûreté* chief inspector are both here, and the authorities will move heaven and earth on this case."

"But why Emily?" Mark asked. Hilda heard Katherine sobbing against him.

"We just don't know. All along we expected some fanatic to take a shot at me. Emily is a celebrity here, which we did not expect. I don't even know if a ransom request is going to come, or what. I don't think they harmed her because they didn't use firearms, and there was no blood or signs of a struggle."

"Wait. Someone at the door." Mark went to the door while Katherine slowly regained control.

"Where are you, Hilda?"

"At the Lavanderia restaurant. Obviously, a sophisticated gang has been following us. We spotted the pair who tailed us yesterday. Not knowing what to make of it, we reported it to Pete Sayfield. We're waiting for information about the car they were using."

Mark came back on. "It's Greg Sprouse."

"Hi, Greg."

"Hello, Hilda. Is Jack with you?"

"He's right here, but I'm not on speaker because the restaurant is full of police and others."

"Okay. Pete called me and asked me to call on the Dempseys. I figured you'd phone before I got here."

Hilda relayed to Jack.

He took the phone from her. "Hi, Greg. Are you starting your kidnapping protocol?"

"Yes. We'll have people here soon, and I'll go over it with Mark and Katherine."

"If I may suggest something, be ready to think outside the box on this one. It may or may not involve ransom. I can't see why it would be revenge, even against Hilda. Emily is famous here. People have been asking for autographs and taking pictures of her everywhere. The only thing we have not had are paparazzi, but they'll be on us, I'm sure."

"So, you're saying the motives are unknown and could be confused."

"Right. We'll know more when Pete finishes tracking down the car ownership lead. Maybe."

"What can we do?" asked Mark. Jack passed the phone back to Hilda. She heard the question and Greg's answer.

"Sit tight. They have the ball. We must be ready for it."

Katherine muttered almost inaudibly. "I never should have let her..." Hilda could hear the guilt and pain in her voice. She could imagine Emily's mother bending over in grief, but Hilda also knew that she could never know what it felt like, being an only child and childless herself.

"Greg, can you handle your end?" she asked. "The police are still working the scene here."

"We've got it. The team from Richmond should be here any minute. We'll organize this with Pete and the SdQ from here."

"Thanks. Let us know if you need anything." She ended the call.

Hilda looked out the window of the restaurant as she put her phone away. The street was ablaze with the hot lights of TV news crews. The shadow of a satellite truck climbed the wall of the building behind it. There were more police outside than people inside, trying to keep the crowd back. She turned to Jack, standing with the Pointreaus.

"How do we get out of here?"

"We don't yet," he said. "As long as Pierre Laurent is here, I think no one will leave. Any new information is going to come to him."

Jack's phone rang. "Pete," he said as he answered. "Hello, Pete. Any news? Sure." He put the phone on speaker and called out, "Chief Inspector? I have Special Agent Sayfield here. He wants to talk to all of us."

The big policeman came over, motioning them back to the quieter corner away from the restrooms. With a wave of his arm and a stern gaze around the room, he made the noise level drop to hushed whispers from the people working the scene.

"Hello, Agent Sayfield."

"Hello, Chief Inspector. I have some news on the shell company in Miami."

"That's good."

"Our people in Miami have been investigating them for a few months under the RICO statute."

"Money laundering? For whom?"

"That's what's interesting. We have leads to the Colombian drug cartel, the New Orleans and Las Vegas mafias, and MS-42 of all people."

"The gang?"

"Yes. MS-42 is more complex than the street gang it used to be. The drugs run one way, of course, but they also run money both ways for people buying services or muscle."

"And they developed kidnapping as a revenue stream in the past."

"Noted. But why they targeted Emily is something we may not find out until a demand comes in."

"Is Mr. Dempsey wealthy?"

"He's well-off, but he's no millionaire. The company has kidnap insurance on him because of his travel and his government connection, but no one thought his profile required insuring his family."

"Interesting."

"What about Emily as a target herself, independent of ransom?" asked Hilda. "Is there something related to her celebrity status?"

"I have to defer to the chief inspector on that," said Pete. "We know so little about the bicycle racing world, that we can't even imagine what her popularity in Québec is like."

"We're working on it, Agent Sayfield," said Pierre. "We've worked up two or three scenarios. The most unlikely one is the obsessed fan. This was a preplanned, sophisticated operation."

"I agree," said Jack. "Pete, want me to call Ted with a short brief?"

"Done. It seems tangential to Hilda, but we'll keep him in the loop because of her."

"Thanks, Pete," she said.

"I think that we need to keep up the search for Emily, but we can do that better from our Headquarters," said Laurent.

"Let's stay in touch, Chief Inspector. Call me anytime."

"Same here. Anytime." He gave the phone back to Jack. "Let's organize a way to get you four past the news cameras and the paparazzi."

Jacques had parked on the back of the block. Pierre arranged for them to slip into a pair of police cruisers by the side entrance away from the media crews out front. Twenty minutes later, they walked from the garage to the house.

"The paparazzi won't take long to appear," said Jacques as they trooped into the foyer. "I want to call some people before I go to bed. They may have some additional information that the police can't access."

"Private detectives?" asked Hilda.

"*Oui*, but mainly our security contractor. They perform a wide range of services for us. As you can imagine, executive kidnapping is in our budget and our contingency planning."

Maryse hugged him. "I forget sometimes that you are not a humble accountant."

"Giles will have some good ideas."

"Let's face it," said Jack. "I may have been the only one at the table tonight who was not a likely target."

No one appeared sleepy, but they all felt the exhaustion of the post-adrenaline comedown. Jacques switched on the eleven o'clock news. Emily's kidnapping was the lead story, and the subject of three follow-on reports. A terse statement by the chief inspector provided little information, so most of the half hour was taken up with TV footage of her racing, and her high school graduation. Katherine was described as a schoolteacher and Mark as a manager for a government contractor.

"At least that doesn't give the idea of deep pockets," mused Jack.

The program concluded with the Météo report, promising beautiful weather for the next four days. They bid each other good night and turned in.

Hilda lay awake, staring at the ceiling. She realized that Jack was not breathing as deeply as he normally did. She put her arm out, and he wrapped her in his arms.

"Not your fault. And we know that this Christmas tree has a couple of dim bulbs. Let's hope for a break."

He wondered what they could do to create that break.

☙ ☙ ☙

Emily opened her eyes, then shut them quickly to shield them from the sun coming in the window.

Her head pounded, and her stomach was hot—like the feeling as a sudden burn cools off. She felt a little nauseated too. As she lay there, she listened. Whoever brought her here was either asleep or incredibly quiet. Her phone and her purse had been on the table in the restaurant.

When she was sure that she would not throw up, she gently opened her eyes and looked around. She saw an austerely furnished bedroom—pale cream walls, wooden floors, a queen-size bed beneath her, one chair, a nightstand, and a four-drawer dresser. No pictures. Two windows.

Easing off the bed, she walked to the windows. She was on the upper floor of a two-story house. An old house, judging from the high ceilings, which meant that it was a long way to the ground.

One window faced south. From the other window, she saw the sun still low over the mountains beyond the thick forest that started at the edge of the fields around the house. The rows of corn ran east-west. The fields to the south went to more woods, but with no mountains behind them.

The windows opened easily and quietly. However, it was too high to jump, and she saw no protrusions that would allow her to climb down. She closed the windows and checked the rest of the room.

The door was locked. She found a chamber pot in the nightstand. She used it and put it back.

The closet held a man's wardrobe. Mostly flannel shirts, overalls, and a single dark gray suit. Two pairs of work boots, one tall and one ankle-height. One pair of sneakers. No dress shoes.

She expected the dresser to be empty, but it contained more personal items. Whoever lived in the house was organized—socks, underwear, jeans, sweaters, T-shirts, belts, etc. neatly folded in their assigned drawers. The top drawer held the small things that go in a man's pockets: gas lighter, Swiss army knife, handkerchiefs, a tin with spare change, pocket comb, and a tiny flashlight.

Why leave a knife where I can get it? she wondered.

She sat on the chair and considered her situation. The house was deathly silent. She opened the window and listened. Only an occasional bird. No traffic noise. She could not see a road at all. She leaned out the windows to check as far to the sides as she could see, but the view was the same. Fields leading to the forest. *If there's a driveway, it must head northwest from here.*

She reckoned it was still early morning, from the height of the sun, and the fact that no one had checked on her. *That won't last. Someone will be back for me.*

She decided to act and hope that no one was here or coming back soon. She took a denim jacket from the closet. With her tall frame, it was not ridiculously big, and it had lots of pockets. Into them, she loaded the lighter, the knife, the change, one belt, and a couple of the handkerchiefs. She put on a pair of socks. She would need to hike a long way if she got out.

After putting the chair under the doorknob, she pulled the dresser over and leaned it against the chair and the door. The noise of moving furniture did not bring anyone upstairs.

Next, she pushed the bed against the east window because the forest was closest in that direction. *This works in the fairy tales; it better work now.* She stripped the bed and tied the bedsheets together. Lashed to the headboard, the sheets reached within six feet of the ground. She hoped she could drop that far without spraining anything. She tossed the blanket out the window.

Halfway down, she heard a car engine on the other side of the house, coming closer. She scrambled to the end of the sheets. She dropped to the ground, bending her legs to take the impact. She picked up the blanket and began running through the corn.

Just as she reached the woods, shouting came from the house. She turned right and ran along the edge of the field, just behind the first stand of trees. The shouting stopped, so she figured they were in pursuit. She needed to hide and to find out what was going on. She found a tree with branches she could reach and began to climb.

About twenty-five feet up, she nestled into a crotch created by a major branch. Looking back, she saw the corn moving where men searched through the field. She counted at least four looking for her, but there may have been more in the house. She saw the access road heading in a straight line due west.

They could not see her through the corn and the leaves of her tree. She watched them rustling through the corn and considered her situation, again.

From looking at maps of the Laurentians and southern Québec, she had learned enough to understand a few things. Most of the roads and almost all the waterways ran north-south; so, to find a road or a river, she needed to go east or west. She also knew that the large farms ended where the forests began, so she probably was still within one hundred kilometers of the

Saint Lawrence River. Of course, how far east or west of Montréal, she had no idea.

About midmorning, a Chevy Suburban with another half-dozen men arrived and joined the search. They canvassed the field for more than three hours until the sun almost reached its zenith. Two men passed below her tree twice, going in different directions.

She could tell when they gave up because they moved through the corn from the edges of the field at the same time and returned to the house. *Coordinated by cell phone.* She made another note to herself. *This gang has resources—vehicles, people, real estate. They'll have surveillance drones out next.* She resolved not to traverse any more fields in the open.

After the search party gathered in the house, she occasionally heard more shouting and arguing. After a while, the Suburban left, followed by the familiar blue Peugeot. She waited until the sun had moved noticeably in the sky before deciding to move on. She climbed down and worked her way around to the south edge of the field, then west. She hoped to find a river to camp for the night, or a road where she could hitchhike.

When she reached the southwest corner of the farm, she wrapped as many ears of corn in the blanket as she could carry. With the load over her shoulder, she dove into the woods.

26

SAINT-DIDACE

MONDAY MORNING, JACQUES RODE TO WORK, promising to come home for lunch with any developments or ideas at his end. Hilda and Jack promised to call if the authorities came up with anything.

Hilda sat with her coffee, staring out the kitchen window. Her heart ached for the bubbly teenager who was such a surprising young woman. But mostly she felt deeply depressed.

Sitting next to her, Jack guessed her thoughts. "No, my darling, there was nothing you could have done. You saw those two men, and we were on them right away."

"But couldn't we have noticed them sooner?"

"No," said the MP investigator. "I've been watching, but those were two new people. This gang knows what they're doing."

"Oh, God, just what *are* they doing?"

"Probably nothing yet. I would expect them to keep her safe, someplace isolated and far away until enough time passes for them to know they haven't been found."

Maryse took her hand. "Would you like to go somewhere? Take your mind off this?"

"It would be nice, but I worry about being out."

"It might be good to stay in for two reasons." Jack put his arm around her. "You're still a target for the crazies, and the pictures of us with Emily last night went viral. It won't be long before the world figures out where the famous nurse from Chicago is staying."

She groaned and put her head in her hands. Maryse went to the studio to call her husband. She came back in two minutes.

"Jacques came to the same conclusion you did, Jack. He ordered security for the house. Hopefully, they'll be here before the paparazzi. Hilda should not go anywhere except in a car with a bodyguard until we sort this out. I called Antoine and Yvette, the housekeeper, to give them the day off. They offered to run errands for us."

"Let's do our laundry." Hilda got up, and Jack followed her upstairs. They spent the morning washing clothes, calling Ted, and waiting. The TV was on, tuned to a news channel.

About ten, the story broke identifying the mystery woman with Emily Hampstead. Reruns of the stories with the *Chicago Tribune* photo preceded a pair of pundits wondering whether the young bicycling phenom were in some way involved in international anti-terrorism circles during her convalescence.

Hilda groaned again. "I can't tell if I want to hide under a rock or pick up the rock and kill someone."

"You probably don't want to see them," said Maryse, "but I'll send out for the afternoon papers."

"We might as well know what to expect," said Jack. Hilda hugged him and let him hold her for a long while. She took a deep breath and stood back.

"Maryse, there may be no point in trying to do the job of the *Sûreté*, but could we go online for a while to see what we can figure out? To keep busy if nothing else."

"Of course. You know the password. I'll get some coffee and a snack, okay?"

"Thanks." They went into the studio, where Jacques and Maryse each kept a computer with a large-screen monitor, mouse, and keyboard. First, they did their routine check of the Arabic chat rooms and social media. Nothing about Hilda.

"I'm sure that this has nothing to do with you," he said. "I mean, you won't get a ransom demand."

"I agree. You're the professional investigator. Where do we look?"

He rebooted and set up a virtual private network. He logged into the law enforcement databases that he usually checked.

"About two hundred responses to the Amber Alert have come in. All dead ends. She's been sighted as far away as Vancouver and Prince Edward Island."

Hilda shook her head. Jack brought up a satellite mapping program.

"Let's figure how far they could take her to hole up for the night. When would she be waking up?"

"Depends on the dosage. Can we find out when the other two women woke up?"

Maryse walked in with mugs of coffee. "I heard that. The ambulance would probably take them to McGill University Hospital. It's only a few blocks from the restaurant."

Jack searched on the keyword McGill and got a breaking news alert. "They were released at ten this morning."

"So, I'd guess they woke up at between six and seven," said Hilda.

"The kidnappers would want to settle her somewhere while she was unconscious, so let's see how far they could go in, say, six hours."

"A long drive at night."

"Okay, let's see what looks good four hours away."

Jack drew a circle 200 kilometers around the restaurant and zoomed in. For the next hour, he tagged buildings that sat isolated from the nearest road, inside the circle.

Jacques came home when they had about three dozen likely farmhouses and other structures marked. They showed him what they had.

"Pierre had the same idea," Jacques said. "They narrowed the list to only a dozen unoccupied places. The police are checking those first. They also have surveillance drones doing a pattern search out to the forest line."

"Do you have to go back in?" asked Maryse.

"Yes, but I'll shower and change first. I can't get out now."

"Why not?"

"The paparazzi are blocking the gate. They'll be furious when they find out that I was not a bicycle messenger with a delivery. Raymond will bring a company car around to the back at one."

Jack's phone rang. "Pete, again." He listened, then put it on speaker. "I have Hilda and our hosts, Jacques and Maryse, here. Go ahead."

"Chief Inspector Laurent told me about your collaboration, Mr. Pointreau. Thanks."

"The least we could do."

"I told Pierre that I would pass this on to you, so he can concentrate on the search. They detected a spike in activity this morning between the MS-42 people in Miami and a couple of phone numbers in Montréal. The Montréal Police and SdQ identified them as local muscle for one of the drug gangs, so they have the connection to MS-42. This seems to eliminate Hilda as the target. There's been no ransom demand, so we're still not sure what they intend to do."

"With the car belonging to the shell company," said Jack, "this was not a last-minute thing. They'd rent cars for that."

"Agreed. Meanwhile, Pierre may have news for you. There aren't many likely places. It's just takes time to get out to all of them."

"Has Greg briefed her parents?"

"He's doing that as we speak."

They ended the call. Jacques went to shower and change while the others went to the kitchen to put together some lunch. Conversation was sparse as they ate, each concerned and worried about Emily and knowing that they could not do anything just yet. Raymond called from the back gate at one o'clock. Jacques kissed Maryse goodbye and took his leave.

About an hour later, Pierre Laurent called Maryse's phone and asked her to put it on speaker.

"We had a break in narrowing down the search. A *Sûreté* patrol went out to check a farmhouse near Saint-Didace. It was empty but unlocked. It looked like someone had left in a hurry, with tracks of a full-size SUV or light truck and a smaller sedan at high speed. On their way back in, they stopped at the only gas station nearby. The owner remembered the blue Peugeot, and a black Chevy Suburban, which topped off. What caught his attention was that one of the two men in the Peugeot got into the Suburban before they all drove off. The Peugeot did not gas up."

They carried the phone into the studio. The satellite mapping program was where they had left it before lunch.

"What is that, an hour and a half from here?" asked Jack.

"About a hundred and twenty kilometers," said the chief inspector. "What's more, the blue Peugeot was spotted in a factory parking lot in Laval. Empty and wiped clean, but the police impounded it anyway. Forensics may be able to find traces if it was used to transport Emily."

"CCTV on the Suburban?" asked Jack.

"Yes." Pierre dictated the license number. "We have an APB out on it, and, of course, the CBSA and the border patrol will be looking for it."

"She could be in the Suburban."

"Our thought also, but we're also going to have a closer look at that farmhouse."

"Thank you, Chief Inspector," said Hilda.

"Is there anything I can do to help?" asked Jack.

"Yes. Take care of my friends. The paparazzi are very clever. They may even get into the house."

"*Compris, monsieur.*"

"*À tout à l'heure, alors.*" He ended the call.

ೞ ೞ ೞ

Emily paused almost as soon as she entered the woods. As her eyes adjusted to the deep shade, she felt the air temperature drop considerably.

She continued west, thinking that she would need to make camp well before dark. She chuckled to herself considering what a fashion statement she would make, with her thick socks, low-heeled pumps, little black dress, and a man's denim jacket. She picked her way among the trees, which fortunately had such a dense canopy that the undergrowth was almost nonexistent.

About ten meters in, the ground pitched steeply downhill. She was careful to watch for the sun as best she could, and to notice any moss or lichens growing on the tree trunks.

After about two hours, she reached the bottom. A small brook ran swiftly down the ravine. Continuing west meant climbing back up, but she reasoned that flowing water would lead to a river and then to the Saint Lawrence. She turned south and followed the little stream.

Growling noises ahead caused her to stop. She moved close to a tree and looked around the bushes. A trio of black bear cubs played by the brook. No sign of the mother. She had never met a mama bear and did not want to.

She hooked her bundle of corn on a stub above her. She grabbed a branch, climbed above the tied-up blanket, then reached down to move it up above her again. She repeated the operation as she slowly made her way into the thinner branches. Her heart was pounding as much from the physical effort as the prospect of being chased by something with claws and big teeth.

When she was about fifteen feet up, she found another crotch and settled in to look for the mother bear. Her knees and shins were bloody, and she had a splinter under one fingernail.

Mama bear showed up about a half hour later. She had a fish in her mouth, which she proceeded to share with the cubs. Dinner took another thirty minutes or so after which she led them upstream. She paused where Emily had been walking, alert to the smell of the girl on the trail. She growled and looked around. Emily was downwind, so the bear did not pick up a stronger, fresher scent. She nudged her cubs up the ravine, hurrying them along.

While she waited, Emily took out the pocketknife and used the tweezers to remove the splinter. When the bears were long out of sight, she climbed down and moved as quickly as she dared in the opposite direction.

The sun was halfway down in the southwest when Emily reached a river flowing east. This was out of alignment with what she expected, but she turned left, knowing that the Saint Lawrence had to lie downstream and that the river would take her across roads and into more densely settled areas.

It was slow going because the trees went right to the water edge, leaving no bank to walk on. With the sun hitting the woods by the river, there was more undergrowth. She had to pick her way along the steep hill rising to her left. Scratches from the bushes joined the scrapes on her legs from the tree climbing.

She spotted a small island in the stream. The narrow beaches on the riverbank seemed inviting, but she worried about the bears behind her.

Further on, she saw a small clearing on the island at the end of a series of rocks leading from the bank. On the last rock, she slipped and slid into the river. The cold water made her gasp as she struggled for a handhold on the rock. Her feet settled on the bottom, leaving her waist-deep in the stream. Leaning on the rock, she carefully waded to the island.

The air was warmer in the open. She collected firewood and built a fireplace with stones. She used the knife to trim kindling for tinder and started a fire.

She shed the jacket, dress, shoes, and socks. The dress, the jacket and the blanket she hung on a branch close to the fire, hoping they would dry soon. She set her shoes and socks on the fire stones.

After soaking a half-dozen ears of corn in the river, she cooked them in their husks over the coals, steaming them in just a few minutes. She had been so focused all day, that her hunger surprised her. She burned her hands and mouth trying to handle the corn. With a couple of swear words, she donned the jacket while she let her food cool. The sun went down while she ate.

After supper, she put her dress, socks and shoes on, then wrapped up in the blanket on the beach. The only sound was the river running around the rocks. It masked any birds or insects that may have come out.

The sky was brilliant with stars. She had enjoyed starry skies in Kansas, but there was even less light pollution in this spot in the forest. She knew that she was out of sight of anyone who might be looking for her. She worried about Hilda, Jack, and her mom, who were probably frantic. She hoped that she was not too far from a road or a town, but she would find out in the morning.

27

SAINT-JUSTIN

J ACQUES CAME HOME AT SIX. Supper was a silent affair, with the TV continuing to carry wild speculation about Emily's fate and no calls from their friends in law enforcement. After dinner, Hilda called Katherine, who was as up to date as she was.

"It's unnerving having the FBI technicians here, waiting for a call."

"Are you and Mark able to go out at all?"

"Oh, yes. And we've set the agents up in the guest bedroom with all their gear, so they're not in our faces all the time."

"What is the publicity like?"

"The *Daily Progress* picked up the AP wire story yesterday, and the local TV had a mercifully short mention on the six o'clock news. A few friends called, but that's all."

"Not here. CBC and Québec TV have pundits with wild theories, building on each other. It's crazy. And I'm back in the news because the other diners at the restaurant put our table on social media during dinner. It went viral, at least among the cycling fans."

"I'm sorry, Hilda."

"Thanks, Katherine, but I can't imagine what you're going through. I'm in total agony over this, and with the paparazzi on the gate, we can't go out. Jack is climbing the walls because he can't work on it. He admits that the *Sûreté* and the FBI are doing all the things that he would have done."

"Isn't there something about a forty-eight-hour window?"

"Yes, but don't focus on that. For one thing, there has been no ransom demand, so this is looking less like a traditional kidnapping. Then there's something else that gives me hope."

"What's that?"

"Emily herself."

"What do you mean?"

"She's an amazingly resourceful and quick woman. She's strong, alert, and creative. She has awesome instincts and acts on them fast. You raised a phenomenal daughter in more ways than you can imagine, Katherine. Cling to that."

"Thanks, Hilda. Mark and I want to come up there, but the FBI says we need to be here to receive a ransom demand."

"Go with their advice. Everybody up here, including the bad guys, know where to find us. We need communications open in both places."

They ended the call after promising to keep in touch.

Jacques called out from the studio. "Jack, Hilda, you may want to see this."

He was sitting at his computer, with several windows open on the wide-screen monitor.

"I have subscriptions to *Velo News, Bicycling*, and a few others. The online issues are full of Emily's story."

"That will keep the publicity up even in the US," said Jack.

"I should tell Katherine and Mark, but I just talked to them."

"Tomorrow should be okay. Maybe we'll have more news by then."

They retired to their rooms after the eleven o'clock news, which did nothing to make them sleepy. Both Hilda and Emily were featured. It was as if the Canadian stations were delighted to have something to report besides the latest tweets from their neighbor to the south.

Hilda and Jack lay awake, deeply aware that the bedroom next door was empty. They did not talk or move but rested gently in each other's arms. At last, their combat training kicked in as they forced their bodies to yield to the need for rest. They slept.

At six thirty, they rose and made their way to the kitchen. Maryse was up, with the large French press coffee maker brewing.

"The paparazzi are still outside."

"How long could this go on?" asked Hilda as she poured coffee into three mugs.

"Who knows? Until Emily is found or something more exciting happens."

"Has this happened before?"

"A couple of times, when we had a celebrity house guest. The guards should keep them under control, but they're likely to chase a bicycle, so no morning ride."

Jacques came in, shaved and dressed except for his jacket and tie. He poured himself a cup of coffee. Maryse got up and went to the refrigerator.

"Omelets, anyone?" Three hands went up.

Hilda got out glasses and orange juice while Jack set the table. Jacques sliced a baguette and put out butter and jam.

"I haven't heard anything. You?" said Jacques. The others shook their heads.

The phone rang in the studio. Jacques left to take it. He came back two minutes later.

"That was Pierre. The crew in the black Suburban clearly did not realize that there was an APB out on them. They showed up at the border crossing at Blackpool. When the CBSA asked them to step out of the vehicle, the driver ran through the checkpoint and killed a border patrol officer crashing through the American barrier. The American side is on high alert, and a chase is in progress."

"Oh God, Emily!" said Hilda.

"I asked about her, but Pierre was still getting clarification from the people at the two border checkpoints. I asked him to call Maryse here first. The *Sûreté* and the FBI are on a real-time radio circuit." He excused himself to go upstairs to finish dressing for work.

Hilda let Jack hug her while Maryse quietly cleared breakfast.

"This is turning out to be the worst idea I ever had." Hilda buried her face in Jack's shoulder. "I never should have invited her to come along."

"Don't look back." He hugged her strongly. "It was a great idea. You've always done the right thing, and this is no exception. No one—not even the kidnappers—could've expected her to appear in Québec until she did."

Hilda took a deep breath and sighed. She stood back. "I told Katherine that I was clinging to my faith in Emily herself. It's all I have left."

"Then cling on." Jack gave a Vulcan salute.

"Jack, that's almost not funny."

"Better than dwelling on it, love."

Jacques came in and kissed his wife. "I have a meeting that I can't miss this morning, but I'm going to take half days until this resolves itself. I'll be back as soon as I can." He left by the back gate, where Raymond was waiting with a company car. A pair of desultory paparazzi didn't bother to raise their cameras at the CFO of the fifth-largest bank in Canada.

Jack said, "Let's go read some bicycling magazines online." He looked at Maryse, who had finished loading the dishwasher. "Want to join us?"

As they entered the studio, the phone rang. Maryse answered. "*Dis-le toi-même,*" she said and handed the phone to Jack. "Pierre."

"Hello, Chief Inspector."

"More on the chase. The border patrol scrambled a helicopter while their ground units and the New York State Police chased the Suburban south on I-87. It crashed through a roadblock at the exit for US-11, killing another police officer."

"Is this turning into suicide by cop?"

"Almost. The helicopter joined the chase at US-11, and the crew saw the incident at the roadblock. They opened fire on the Suburban. It exploded and burned instantly."

Jack felt a punch in his stomach. "Emily?"

"Units on the scene report seven bodies inside, but I'm still waiting for more details. Wait—"

Jack briefed the others while he waited. Maryse gasped and sat with her hand on her mouth. Hilda stood frozen, her face pulsating between rage and fear. On the phone, Jack heard radio traffic.

"Jack, I'm back."

"Yes?"

"The bodies are badly burned, but all seven are males. No Emily, apparently."

"Thank God, but what does that mean, and where is she?"

"That is why we are detectives, *non*? Between the drones over Mastigouche and our plodding footwork, we'll find her. The lack of a ransom demand and having our prime suspects out of action is giving me hope. I don't want to think that they killed her."

"Not rational. The MS-42 people are cruel and greedy, but not crazy."

"I agree. Unfortunately, the news cameras are covering the scene, too, so expect more paparazzi at the gate after the media makes the connection. Sorry."

"I'll tell the others. Thanks."

"Later, then." The chief inspector ended the call.

Maryse lit off her computer because she had bookmarks for the various cycling publications. Jack heard a sound in the hall. While the machine booted up, he walked over to the door. Hilda rose to follow him.

A flash blinded him. He leaped toward the source of the flash, swinging at the offending camera. By the time his vision cleared, he was facing a thin man with black hair and unkempt beard, a wool knit cap and a camouflage jacket. He raised the camera again.

Jack grabbed his wrist, twisted and pulled the arm over his knee, dislocating the shoulder with an audible *pop*. The paparazzo screamed in pain and fell to his knees. The camera clattered to the floor, and the lens snapped off. Hilda reached down, picked up the camera, and extracted the SD card.

Jack dragged the trespasser by his good arm to the front door. Hilda ran ahead of them, opening it just as they arrived. With a great heave, Jack flung him out on the porch. He could hear the clicking of the cameras with long lenses at the gate. Hilda tossed the camera and its lens into the grass beyond the steps.

"That should give the evening news something more truthful to report."

"Are you okay?"

"Just some spots in my eyes. They're clearing."

Maryse was standing in the hall with a terrified expression. "Was that a paparazzo in the house?"

"I'm afraid so."

"But you assaulted him, *non*?"

"Just doing my job in this case. Was it not the chief inspector himself who told me to take care of you?"

Hilda smiled. Maryse looked a little less terrified. In the studio, they left the TV on while they read the cycling magazines. At eleven o'clock, the lead story was the dramatic and fiery car chase with armed helicopters on the border. The media had not made a connection with the Emily Hampstead kidnapping yet. A second report showed long-distance photos of the hapless paparazzo outside the Pointreau home. He was generally reported as an overenthusiastic trespasser, with little sympathy spared for his having broken into a home.

"They didn't even get a good shot of you," said Hilda.

"Excellent. I can still go undercover in Québec." They chuckled.

Jacques came home by the back door at one o'clock. He had two days of the *Globe & Mail, Journal de Montréal, Montréal Times, Montréal Gazette*, and even a copy of the free *Métro*. After the headlines of the day before, the story had moved to the sports pages.

They fixed lunch and settled into the living room afterward, trading sections of the different papers. The unspoken worry hung over them.

Every half hour or so, Jack would get up and walk to all the windows, checking for more trespassers. There did not seem to be any more photographers willing (or stupid enough) to risk a dislocated shoulder for a shot of the family at home. By midafternoon, there were only four or five bored-looking men outside.

ભ ભ ભ

Emily woke with a start.

The ground was unfamiliar, and dew had settled on her blanket, leaving her damp and stiff. The sky was light, but it would be a while before the sun cleared the steep cliffs above the river. She rose and hung the blanket on a branch to dry.

Doing some stretches limbered her up enough to scrounge around for more firewood. She cooked three more ears of corn, wishing that she could pluck fish from the stream like the bears did. The blanket was dry when she doused her fire and carefully made her way back to the mainland.

She continued downstream, ducking back into the woods when the riverbank disappeared again right after she passed the island. It was slow going, but about the time the sun cleared the ridge and began shining on the river, she thought she heard a car up ahead. About a half hour later, she heard another one, closer. Then she saw a bridge stretching from the top of the cliffs on her side to the cliffs on the other side of the river. A one-ton stake truck sped noisily across the span and faded off to the south.

Encouraged, she began climbing the steep hill toward the road. It took another hour to make her way through the brush. By late morning, she broke out of the woods and stood by the smooth, two-lane highway. She turned south and walked toward the bridge.

A full-sized pickup truck came up behind her, its knobby tires and leaky muffler making enough noise to scare birds out of the trees near the road.

She put out her hand with her thumb extended. The truck slowed and stopped. The driver leaned over and opened the passenger door. Emily first noticed his bloodshot eyes, brown and deep-set. He had dirty brown hair almost shoulder length and wore a denim jacket much like the one she had on. She climbed in and pulled the door shut.

"Where to, beautiful lady?" American accent.

"Anywhere. I need to find a phone." The cab stank of stale tobacco, spilled beer, and cannabis. Emily sat as close to the door as she could.

"Anywhere? That sounds like a come-on to me. Let's go!" He put the truck in gear and headed unevenly back into the lane. Emily wondered if he were impaired and regretted getting in the cab with him. His long, stringy hair was matted, and his ragged T-shirt and jacket were filthy.

The driver looked over at her more often than she liked. After a half mile she said, "You're making me nervous. Would you look at the road more than at me?"

"Why? The road's boring. You look like more fun." He laughed at his own joke.

"What's the next town up ahead?"

"Ain't no town that I know of. Nothing but fields and woods."

"So, where are you going?"

"My place. I got some good stuff there."

"I need to call the police. Either take me to a town or stop so I can get out."

He accelerated. "Nope. I can't expect an angel like you to fall into my lap like this and fly away, can I?"

"Why? Do you know who I am?"

"Nope. Doesn't matter. Ain't letting nobody call the police."

"Just let me off. I saw a sign for a town back there. I'll walk."

"Nope. Can't have you calling no cops."

Oh, hell, thought Emily. She held her hands to keep them from shivering. *Think!*

"Why are you afraid of the police, anyway? Are you on the lam?"

"I got a nice little place in the woods where nobody bothers me, and I like it that way. You'll like it too."

She watched the pavement roll under them as he drove west past farms like the one from which she had escaped. He drove past the sign for Saint-Justin and headed northwest. A couple of miles later, he turned into a narrow dirt track that led into the woods.

Tree branches slapped the window as he drove deep into the forest. He stopped at a clearing with a small cabin.

"Home, sweet, home, darling."

"I'm not your darling."

"Feisty. I like that. Like the last girl who lived here." She tried to open the door, but he had activated the child lock. He got out on his side, came around, and opened her door with the key fob.

"Okay, sweetheart, come to papa." He spread his arms with a stupid grin.

Emily braced herself and used her powerful legs to fling the door open as fast as she could. It caught him on the face and bowled him onto his back.

She was out of the cab and running down the path by the time he got up. He was taller than she, so she was not going to outrun him. Forcing herself to imagine Hilda's fierce face, she planted her feet, stopped hard, and turned.

He was still running when she hit his solar plexus with her fist as she stepped on his foot and kneed him in the groin. She head-butted him so hard that she felt light-headed as blood from his nose spurt out on her neck and chest. He wobbled. She backhanded him with a fist above the ear as hard as she could swing. He went down in a heap by the side of the path.

Though she worried that he might awake soon, she searched his jacket pockets and found the truck keys and a wallet. A quick glance showed a Vermont driver's license issued to a Gary Whiteside. She took ten dollars just in case and ran back to the truck. Her assailant remained on the side of the driveway, but she was terrified that he might suddenly leap up and chase after her. She started the truck, threw it into reverse, and backed up the narrow dirt track in a cloud of dust.

Back on the highway, she returned to the sign for Saint-Justin. It had a small VIA logo on it. A few miles later, the same logo was on a train station in the middle of nowhere. A sign on the wall identified it as Saint-Justin, but there was no town.

She parked the truck and went inside. The station was unmanned, and a sign informed passengers that this was a request stop. The schedule had been torn down and the holder vandalized. She found two payphones, but both had their handsets ripped off.

She got back in the truck and started it up. Coming out of the parking lot, she spotted a sign for the town of Saint-Justin, five kilometers away.

She slowed as she rolled into the village. While it had a pretty church, there seemed to be no businesses, and the houses appeared to be empty. On a hunch, she drove on, thinking that any road going south had to cross one of the main east-west highways.

The shadows were lengthening. The clock on the dash read "4:55P." She did not know where Montréal was from here, but she hoped that she could find a phone or a police station by dark.

Indeed, the road from Saint-Justin ended in a larger road, the Chemin du Pied de la Côte. A general store with a restaurant dominated the corner. She parked the truck and took off her socks before alighting. She walked to the store, keenly aware of how hungry she was.

Feeling light-headed, she paused at the door. One woman at the cash register. A male waiter (fiftyish) to the right near what must be the kitchen door. One twenty-something man looking at the pastries case.

She crossed to the cash register. "*Excusez-moi madame, j'ai besoin d'appeler la police. Avez-vous un téléphone?*" The woman reached in her apron pocket, pulled out a cell phone and dialed 911. She passed the phone to Emily.

"Hello, this is Emily Hampstead. I'm not hurt, but I need to report a kidnapping—two kidnappings, actually."

"Of course, Miss Hampstead, where are you?"

"Le Magasin général Le Brun near Saint-Justin."

"Stay put. We'll have a unit there shortly."

"Thank you. I'll wait."

Emily returned the cell phone to the woman, who suddenly realized who was in front of her. Before she could say anything, Emily asked for the washroom.

In the ladies' room, Emily tried to straighten out her hair, wash her face and arms as best she could, and rinse the dried blood off her legs and the front of her dress. Fortunately, most of the blood was on the jacket, which she did not intend to keep.

Back in the store, she asked for a rubber band and began to pull her hair back. The lady at the cash register reached into her purse behind the counter and gave her a black-covered hair band.

"Matches your dress, Miss Hampstead." She smiled broadly. "You look hungry. Let me offer you something to eat."

"The police will be here soon, but I wouldn't mind something quick. How about a croissant or a *tarte?*"

"Of course." She went to the pastry case while Emily chose a liter bottle of water from the refrigerator case.

"*Combien-ça?*" she asked. The woman shook her head. "You do me honor to come into my store. Please eat and enjoy."

Just as she swallowed the last bite of the lemon custard pie, Emily heard the siren. She thanked the woman and finished the bottle of water as the *Sûreté* officers walked in.

28

QUÉBEC CITY

KATHERINE AND MARK FLEW TO MONTRÉAL the weekend after Emily's escape. Jacques and Maryse insisted on hosting them in the third guest bedroom. Emily had only some scabs from the scratches on her legs to testify to her ordeal.

When they assembled in the living room after settling in, they found that Pierre Laurent had arrived. During the introductions, Katherine looked worse than Emily until the teenager came into the room. Katherine recovered her composure after some tears and hugs, and glowing accounts of her daughter's prowess.

"In addition to shutting down a criminal network with MS-42," Pierre explained, "Emily took a serial rapist off the street."

"What?" Katherine paled again.

"Gary Whiteside was wanted in three New England states on a dozen charges of rape and assault. Emily gave us the keys to his truck. We had him in custody in less than thirty minutes."

"Omigod, what if—"

"No what-if, Mom. He was so excited to have me locked in his truck that he let his guard down when he had to unlock it. I knocked him down with the door of the truck and ran."

Mark hugged his wife and regarded Hilda with a smile. "Who is she, and what have you done with our daughter?" All but Katherine laughed. She smiled, but her eyes worried.

"Oh, that's Emily, I assure you. She's been like this the whole time. We saw it come out when she applied her natural skills outside of a bicycle race."

"Did you teach her this?" asked Katherine.

"Only a few self-defense moves, which she insisted on learning. I knew it would be a good idea, seeing that she's so fearless."

"And how to size up a room," said Emily.

"That too. The rest you taught her." Katherine raised her eyebrows in a question. "Being observant, sensing threats, even behind her, quick reactions, speed, and thinking on her feet. Putting her in a Girl Scout troop that did rugged camping wasn't a bad idea, either."

Emily's mother shook her head and sighed. "I'm so glad this is over. I can't wait to get you home again."

The girl frowned. Her gaze went to her mother, her stepfather, then the others and back to Katherine.

"Mom, I don't want to go home yet. I want to finish the tour with Hilda and Jack."

Katherine seemed stunned. Mark gave her a gentle hug. She gathered herself.

"After all this?" she asked.

"Especially after all this." Emily waved her arms at the others. "The Forebears are out, their cronies are in jail, the kidnappers have been busted or killed, Gary Whiteside is off the street. Who's left, Mom?"

"Well, uh—"

"No need to answer that yet," said Jacques, standing. "Let's celebrate all these victories first, and you take time to think about it." He went to the bar cooler and pulled out a bottle.

"Dom Perignon, '09?" he asked Hilda. Pierre, Mark, Maryse, and Jack exchanged knowing glances and smiles.

"Adequate, I think, Jacques," said the nurse, with a smile.

As he poured, Maryse came over to Katherine. "Emily has been bragging about your skills in the kitchen. Would you like to collaborate on something special tonight?"

"Emily serves dinner most nights in our house."

"C'mon, Mom, I just heat up what you cook. Maryse runs a democratic kitchen. We've all chipped in each evening."

"Okay. Thanks, Maryse. It would be fun."

"More fun than going out," added Jack, "until the paparazzi wander away."

After finishing his glass, Pierre excused himself to push his way to the *Sûreté* sedan waiting for him outside the gate. Jack watched him from a window.

"That guy is such a giant that he simply scowls at the photographers and they back off. I love it!"

Maryse, Hilda, and Katherine spent some time consulting cookbooks and online food channels while the others went to the studio to check the chat rooms, news, and social media. Jacques sat at Maryse's computer, so Jack could use the VPN that he had set up on Jacques's machine. Mark and Emily used their phones.

"This is not good news," said Jacques. "Internal Communications at the bank reports that stormfront.org is posting diatribes about me, smuggling African immigrants and financing subversion in Québec."

"You have Stormfront here too?" asked Emily.

"Of course. Your Southern Poverty Law Center identified more than a hundred white supremacist groups in Canada."

"Wow. That's a lot."

"The SPLC reports almost a thousand in the US. Our population is one-tenth of yours, so the ratio is about the same."

"The issue is Hilda, again, isn't it?" asked Jack.

"I'm afraid so. The human smuggling and financing are fake news—a natural extension of their racial hatred."

"That won't matter to the faithful readers, will it?"

"No."

Jack was quiet as he tapped a few keys and stared for a minute. "Just as the Islamist fanatic threat is abating, we get this." He got up and walked into the kitchen. When he came back, his face was serious but calm.

"I'm sending an email to Ted, Pete, and Greg." He typed for a while. "Done."

Emily went over and read some of the hatemongering on Maryse's computer screen. "That is awful!"

Jack shut down the sites and the VPN. His phone rang. "Hi, Ted." He listened for a while. "Thank Pete for me. I'll tell the others." He ended the call.

"Ted talked to Pete. He said that the FBI tracks the hate groups. They'll listen for talk of Hilda or the Pointreaus. Greg will brief Mark and Katherine after they return, especially because of the anniversary of the rallies in Charlottesville coming up."

"Mom will love that!" Emily frowned.

"You may win your argument to stay with us."

"Maybe she'd like to come along!"

"I think she would anyway, but she has her classes at the university."

A shout from the kitchen: "Scullery crew on deck!" They joined the three cooks and were assigned various duties prepping ingredients on the counters and tables.

While the ovens cranked away, they gathered in the living room again because the veranda was subject to eavesdropping by the paparazzi. The developments with the hate groups put a new perspective on the threats to Emily and Hilda.

"I still want you to come home," said Katherine after Emily repeated her point about the threat being neutralized. "It's not safe."

"It's not safe anywhere, Mom. Hilda and I are linked in the fake news on the alt-right sites. Charlottesville might be more dangerous than Canada soon."

Her mother thought about that as they sipped their Riesling.

"But how are you going to tour with the paparazzi out there?" asked Mark.

"We've had them out there before," said Jacques." They wander off between two and four days after the newspapers stop carrying the story.

"You all are welcome to stay with us until then. We can drive you to Ottawa and Québec City for day tours, using the back entrance, so you will still see the sights you came for. By then, the frenzy should pass, and you can resume your trip."

"If it runs longer," said Maryse, "We could go visit my parents in the Laurentians."

"Where were you planning to go next?" Mark asked Hilda.

"Well, Ottawa and Québec City, so Jacques's offer takes care of that."

"I'd like to get out of town," said Emily. "The country has been more fun, so far."

"School starts in another month," said Jack. "Why not a bit of the Gaspé?"

"That would be ideal," said Hilda. She looked at the Dempseys. "The whole peninsula is stunningly beautiful. Very quiet, even in the summer, with challenging climbs, free-ranging wildlife and isolated towns that don't much care what's going on in the city."

"How soon before school would you be back?" Mark asked.

"We can agree on that. It should take less than two weeks to round the Gaspé to Campbellton, New Brunswick. At any point after that, we can catch a train and roll into the Amtrak station in Charlottesville a day later."

"This means a lot to you, doesn't it, Emily?" asked Katherine.

"Yes, Mom. I've learned so much, and I want to see it through. I don't want to cut it off because of other people's bad choices."

"Pretty grown-up talk." She smiled and sighed. "Best reason I can think of."

Dinner took four hours, and conversation was light and pleasant. They agreed to use the Pointreaus' van to take a tour of Montréal with the Dempseys after church on Sunday.

Monday morning, Jacques took two days off from work. They drove Mark and Katherine to the airport, then went to Ottawa. They visited the Parliament and the Canadian Museum of History in Gatineau.

On Thursday, they loaded the three bikes on the van. Maryse took them to Québec City, losing the paparazzi on country roads in the Mastigouche before turning south to Trois Rivières and on to Québec City.

At Emily's suggestion, they went by the Le Brun General Store near Saint-Justin, so they could thank the owner. Emily returned the black-covered band, and they sat down for a proper lunch, leaving a big tip, and buying a couple of bags of local products.

In Québec City, they took advantage of a guesthouse maintained by the bank, which was unoccupied at the moment. The old city was no place for a van with three bicycles on it, and the house had a garage.

They walked the quaint streets of the old city, had coffee in the Chateau Frontenac Hotel, and visited the Museum of Fine Arts. Emily had never seen Western landscape painting or First Nations art, and she had never heard of the "Group of Seven." In the museums of Ottawa, Montréal and Québec City, she developed a strong appreciation for their work.

The first night, they had dinner in the house and planned to try one of Maryse's favorite restaurants the next night. During dinner, Jack asked about their son.

"You said Jean-Pierre was with the Twenty-Second, didn't you?"

"Yes, but he volunteered for CANSOF. You know it?"

"The tan berets. Canadian Special Forces."

"He's at the CSOTC school."

"How old is he?"

"He just turned twenty-two."

"They must think very highly of him to take him so young."

"That is what his major said, but I find little comfort." She looked at Emily. "All the time your mother was in our home, I felt her concern for you and thought of Jean-Pierre."

"I'm sorry, Maryse," said Emily. "Is this CSOTC place dangerous?"

"Not really. But I'm sure he'll be sent to Afghanistan or someplace like that. He's as fearless as you are."

"Sounds interesting. Do you have a picture?"

She pulled out her phone and showed Emily her lock screen.

"Nice! I would like to meet him." Maryse smiled while Hilda and Jack exchanged surprised glances.

"You might someday. He's as crazy about cycling as we are. I think that he could have gone pro, but he chose the army instead."

"Does he know about Emily?" asked Hilda.

"Oh, yes. He's the one who told us about you last fall after the Air Force Invitational in Colorado. He called you 'hot' and said he was in love!"

That got a laugh from the table, which allowed them to draw Maryse away from her worry and on to other subjects.

The next day, they visited the Plains of Abraham and the Citadel. The view of the Saint Lawrence from the parapets of the old French fort stretched almost to Vermont. Standing under the seven-inch guns in the clear sunshine, Emily could take in the teeming shipping plying the broad river, and the green, yellow and brown fields of the farms on the other side. Tourists were everywhere, and the atmosphere was festive.

They left the Citadel about one o'clock and walked over to the National Parliament. Maryse and Hilda were chatting ahead, Jack and Emily walking comfortably in silence behind them.

"That is so cool," Emily said as they climbed to the imposing building. "They have containers of kitchen herbs around the stairs." Each large pot had a label describing the contents, its origin, and how it was used in food preparation.

They were about halfway up the stairs when there was a flash above them. Hilda pushed Maryse to the ground, and Jack pulled Emily down before the sound of the explosion reached their ears. Suddenly glass and bits of metal were raining on them as the front doors flew in pieces over their heads.

"Jack! Get them out of here!" Hilda was running up the stairs. Jack jumped up and pulled Maryse and Emily down the stairs as fast as they could move, a firm hand on each arm. When they reached the square at the bottom, they paused in the shade of some trees.

"But Hilda could be hurt," said Emily.

"It's what she does, Em. There's no stopping her. Let's see if we can help from here."

They watched as the EMT's and police converged on the scene. Emily saw the first responders gathering, and the people pressing up on the yellow tape being deployed. She looked to the left toward the street.

"Emily! Where are you going?" Jack shouted. But the young athlete was already running twenty meters away. She ran up behind a man standing under a tree with a clear view of the scene.

From behind, she pulled his arm back, using her momentum to throw him down into a flower bed where she landed on him. The cell phone in his hand flew to the ground.

Jack came up behind her. Before the man could twist around, Jack pinned him down and drew his hands back, kneeling on his back.

"What the hell! Emily?"

"Second bomb! He's the leader."

Jack stared briefly at her and the phone and signaled his understanding. Maryse came up and reached for the fallen phone.

"*Ne touches pas le téléphone, Maryse!*" They both shouted at once. Jack pointed to a *Sûreté* cruiser. "Go get a police officer from that group over there."

When Jack identified himself, the SdQ officer took their suspicions seriously. In less than one minute, the police took charge of the man with the cell phone and called over a technician from the bomb disposal squad. It took no time for the expert to order an immediate clearing of the scene. The wounded had been removed, so the first responders left the dead and cleared out.

Hilda came over. She had blood up to her elbows and across her chest. She was wiping down with a handful of antiseptic wipes as she walked. Jack and Emily checked behind her, but the reporters were still fixated on the bomb disposal activity up at the scene.

"Maryse, we can't let this turn into another Chicago. We need to be out of town before the media connects Emily or me to this." She sat on a bench to reduce her visibility, pulling Emily down with her. "Keep your head down, Em."

"Let's go to my parents. I'm calling Pierre." She pulled out her cell phone and hit speed dial. After a fast conversation in French, she ended the call. "Someone in charge will come find us." She wrote her parents' address and phone number on a note pad from her purse and tore off the page.

"Madame Pointreau?" A short man with thin gray hair and a round face appeared from the direction of the scene. "Chief Inspector Bertrand. My colleague in Montréal contacted me."

"*Enchantée*. We have a problem."

"I can see." He looked at the other two women. "The well-known Hilda Paisley saved several lives up there, and the famous Emily Hampstead saved the lives of the rest of us."

"You confirmed the second bomb?" asked Jack.

"Yes. Are you Major Rathburn?"

"Jack Rathburn."

"Marcel." He shook hands with everyone. "Laurent told me about the problems you had with publicity. We can protect you."

"What we would like to do, Marcel," said Maryse, "is quietly return to our car, collect our things as quickly as possible and escape the city before the press finds out who took down the trigger man here."

"But we will need your statements."

"Of course. We'll be available at my parents' house in the Laurentians. Here is the address and the phone number." She gave him the piece of paper from her note pad. "We can hide there from the media."

"That seems reasonable if you move fast. We will send an officer to take your statements up there."

"Thank you."

"Thank *you*!" he said, eyeing Emily. "I might have been dead a few minutes ago." He turned back to Maryse. "Are you at the BMO house?"

"Yes."

"Let us take you there. The unit will wait and follow you until you are clear of the town. Just to make sure you don't have company on the way out."

"Thank you."

"Go. Now. It won't do for the reporters to see you here."

They got into the cruiser that had been parked nearby. It eased away quietly. As far as they could tell, there were no camera flashes, and no one was taking an interest in them as they left the scene. The reporters converged on Marcel Bertrand as he approached the tape.

At the guesthouse, Hilda changed her shirt. They packed and checked the house for their things.

"Em, I still don't understand how you recognized the trigger man," asked Jack as he cinched the top of his panniers.

"It was what you and Hilda taught me in Atlantic City." She hefted her panniers and started for the door. "I looked away from the commotion and saw one person who was watching everything with no emotion like he was in control."

"The leader?"

"Exactly. I had a terribly urgent gut feeling. I just knew that it would be better to be wrong than to risk being right." She headed downstairs to the garage and checked that the bikes were secure while the others brought their panniers down.

Jack and Hilda were silent as Maryse drove north out of town. The *Sûreté* cruiser eased along behind them, raising the anxiety level of the drivers behind them, who were afraid to pass a police car driving slightly above the speed limit.

The traffic peeled off as they passed through the suburbs. When there was only the cruiser behind them, the officer flashed his high beams and signaled a turn. Maryse waved from the side window, and he tooted his horn as he did a U-turn.

29

THE LAURENTIANS

MARYSE DROVE THEM INTO THE LAURENTIANS. The "small place" had three guest rooms because Maryse's parents remained ready to host both their children at once. They arrived in the early evening. Jack and Emily stood by the van while Hilda ran up the steps into the arms of Madame Langlais. While she was hugging Maryse's father, Jacques slipped out from behind their host to embrace his wife.

"What happened?" he said. "You weren't supposed to arrive until tomorrow."

"Long story," said Maryse. "What's it like at home?"

"Still two or three paparazzi at the gate," said Jacques as they walked into the house. "As long as the newspapers and magazines are buying pictures, there'll be someone outside."

Hilda turned to Jack and Emily. "I'm sorry. General Langlais, these are my friends, Jack Rathburn and—"

"We heard. Emily Hampstead. What an honor." He came down to shake their hands.

"*Enchantée, m'sieur le Général.*"

"*Tutoyons-nous*," he said. "Maryse and Hilda have grown up and so have their friends." He shook Jack's hand. "Jean-Paul."

"Jack."

"And call me Louise," said Madame Langlais from the porch. "Come settle in." She led them into the house. Maryse briefed Jacques on their adventure in Québec City as they went to their room.

There were woods and sky everywhere out the windows upstairs, and a cozy feel to the small, well-appointed rooms. After stowing their things and washing up, they gathered on the shaded back patio.

The bombing at the Québécois Parliament knocked coverage of Emily's escape off the Canadian media. To the amazement of everyone in the house, the police in Québec City diverted attention away from the triggerman by including him in the quartet of suspects they arrested over the next four days. Because the bomb squad cleared the scene early, Hilda was out of view before the press gathered.

The blast was worldwide news for a week. In the United States, however, a school shooting in Minnesota and a hurricane in Florida put the bombing on page two of the newspapers after only a day. It only made TV news that first night.

Marcel Bertrand himself came the third morning, accompanied by a court reporter and a notary, so he could take a fully admissible statement. He was satisfied that they would be safe with the Langlaises.

"I don't know how you did it," said Jack as they were leaving. "But thank you for keeping Hilda and Emily out of the media."

"That is selfish on my part. Paparazzi make our work harder. No one realized that there was a triggerman, so I wasn't going to volunteer the information. It can come out at the trial after the noise dies down."

"We've heard so much speculation about motive. Which one is it?"

"The triggerman is the leader of a small white supremacist group from Trois-Rivières. He had been on our radar, so we recognized him immediately. No one has taken credit for the attack, so we are not sure what he was targeting—blacks, immigrants, Jews, Métis, or the government in general. It will come out when he finally starts talking."

೩ ೩ ೩

Jacques, Jack, and Hilda rode together every day, letting Maryse and Emily disappear ahead of them. Sitting on the 700 m (2300 ft) contour line, the Langlais cottage provided a challenging ride in any direction. The curves in the roads revealed a panoply of views of mountains, lakes, the Saint Lawrence seaway, and the Gaspé Peninsula to the southeast.

Wednesday evening, they were relaxing after dinner, all seven of them savoring the fresh air, the good food, and company.

"Too bad we have to move on," said Emily. "I enjoyed Québec, and especially this place, more than any place I have ever visited."

"I'm glad, Emily," said Louise. "And you're always welcome back, alone or with company."

"How are you planning to reach the Gaspé?" asked Jean-Paul, unfolding a map of the Gaspésie and lower Québec.

"I don't see any way to cross without going back to Québec City," said Jack. "I guess we go there and take the ferry to Lévis."

"I know you don't like to backtrack." Jean-Paul put his finger on Beaupré. "You could go to the Montmorency Falls and down the north shore. You must see the Falls. I have a friend who owns a secluded place on the river just outside of Beaupré, who would be happy to ferry you across to the south side. Less exposure to crowds and puts you farther east on the *Route Verte*."

"That would be awesome!" exclaimed Emily.

"It does seem like a wonderful option," said Hilda, "and I would welcome less exposure as long as the brouhaha hasn't died down."

"Do you want to call him tomorrow?" asked Jack. "We could leave later in the morning."

"I called him back on Sunday to ask him about it. He's excited to be in on the escape plan."

"Not to insult anyone, but what about leaks?"

"Don't worry, Jack. Not his first extraction. He was SAS before he retired. Ran a couple of forays into East Germany for us when we were in Kaiserslautern."

"I take it this isn't a ferry ride," said Emily. "What's SAS?"

"Special Air Service, the British Special Forces. He has a boat with room for the bikes on the fantail. It can run around the Gaspé to Prince Edward Island and back if he needs to."

"Fantastic. Where does he suggest putting us on the south shore?" asked Hilda, looking at the map.

"It's ninety kilometers to his house from here. He suggests that you spend tomorrow night as their guests, then let him put you ashore in Rivière-Ouelle. It's about eighty kilometers downriver from his pier, but a two-day ride from Lévis. There is a pier within a couple of hundred meters of the *Route Verte*, close to the campgrounds."

"It sounds like a plan," said Hilda. "Thank you."

"Did you get all your things from our house?" asked Jacques.

"Yes. Maryse suggested being prepared to continue without returning, depending on the publicity."

"Except I didn't get Jean-Pierre's info," said Emily. "Did you tell him that we stayed with you?"

"*Oui*. I'll send you both an introduction by email," said Maryse. "That way, you'll have my contact data and his."

Emily did a Schwarzenegger imitation. "I'll be back!" That got a round of laughter.

"You are planning to take the train from Campbellton, *non?*" asked Maryse.

"There isn't time to ride all the way to Charlottesville."

Maryse cocked an inquiring eyebrow at Jacques, who nodded. "Campbellton to Montréal is a twelve-hour overnight train with a very tight connection to the Amtrak train," she said. "Spend your last day in Canada with us and catch the Adirondack the next morning."

Jack, Hilda, and Emily smiled together. Hilda said, "That's very kind. We accept!"

"Good. Let us know when you get to Campbellton. You can book a sleeper car and leave that same night if you like."

They turned in after that. Emily's phone dinged as she closed her door. It was Maryse's email to Jean-Pierre and her. She only got her shoes and blouse off when the phone dinged again. He sent a picture and wrote how pleased he was to "meet" Emily. His mother had told him about their adventures, so he hoped that he could meet her in person soon. The photo showed a slim, sandy-haired bicyclist standing by his road bike (a Stevens, she noted), in a BMO team kit, with his helmet hanging on the right handlebar.

She sent a picture back (in bicycle kit without helmet) and reciprocated the feelings. If he was anything like Jacques and Maryse, he had to be a great guy. She really did want to meet him. She went to bed with a big smile.

Jack and Hilda checked their phones for news. The hate groups were still echoing the Stormfront's postings about Hilda, but the tone had shifted into general complaining about blacks and immigrants, without mentioning her specifically. Emily's escape was still on the sports pages, focusing on background and whether she would return to racing or pursue a career in international intrigue.

"It seems the pundits can't leave it alone, can they?" she said.

"Nope, but at least she's off the front page and not making the evening TV news."

"That's something, anyway."

Relaxed and feeling relatively safe, they plugged in their phones and turned out the light. They had other things to do before sleeping....

30

THE SAINT LAWRENCE RIVER

THE RIDE FROM THE LANGLAIS COTTAGE (elevation 700 m) to the Saint Lawrence River (elevation almost zero) was a blistering series of terrifying descents and challenging climbs. Jack, Hilda, and Emily were paying for the three weeks spent without their loaded panniers. Still, they stopped at particularly breathtaking overlooks to admire the view (and to slow down their heart rates).

"Mom had some news last night." Emily looked at the river from a cliff.

"Is everything okay?" asked Hilda.

"Fine. Greg Sprouse is being transferred and guess who's coming in to replace him." Hilda and Jack shrugged. "Frank Daglio!"

"That *is* a coincidence."

"According to Mom, Frank asked for Charlottesville after meeting us. Something about being close to an airport with nonstop service to Europe without having to serve in Headquarters itself."

"A man after my heart," said Jack. "I hated Washington duty."

"It sounds like he's thinking of racking up frequent flyer miles to and from Amsterdam," said Emily. "We'll see how that shapes up."

They mounted their bicycles and flew down the next ten-kilometer stretch. They stopped just beyond Sainte-Brigitte-de-Laval to eat the picnic lunch that Louise Langlais had packed. Then they rode down to the right bank of the Montmorency River. From there, it was a steady downhill along the Boulevards Raymond and Lloyd Welch to Courville, which was where the built-up suburbs downstream from Québec City ended.

They rode to Montmorency Falls by riding through Villeneuve and along the *Route Verte* by the Saint Lawrence River. Beyond the bridge to the Île d'Orléans, the island was a vast expanse of farmland. Mudflats made the shore unapproachable by boat.

"Beautiful." Emily admired the Falls from the bike path. "But I think I like the Laurentians better."

"Me too," said Hilda. "That was so quiet and clean, wasn't it?"

"It was, but I, for one, am not complaining about a well-paved, level bike path along a wide river," said Jack.

As expected, they rolled into Beaupré about three o'clock, pausing to take pictures at the Church of the Blessed Virgin, a major pilgrimage site in Canada.

Following Jean-Paul Langlais's directions, they rode north out of Beaupré exactly 900 meters, then stopped in a bend in the highway. Woods shaded both sides of the road. They could see a development beyond the trees to the left. The woods on the right were taller and denser.

"That must be it." Emily pointed.

"What?" Jack squinted at the forest.

"See the dirt track between those two trees?"

"So there is. Let's check it out. Nothing else here."

"Jean-Paul said it was a long, dirt driveway," said Hilda.

They turned down the path, which could hardly accommodate one vehicle. Occasionally they dodged branches that showed signs of having been broken by passing cars or trucks. About one hundred meters into the dark woods, the road became steep with occasional ruts from rain. Suddenly, it leveled into a clearing right by the bank of the river. Jack caught himself just in time to keep from spilling over, but the two women stopped smoothly and dismounted normally.

"Welcome! I'm glad you made it." A deep voice with a British public-school accent reached them from the back porch, and a trim man with short gray hair came smiling down the steps. "You must be Jean-Paul's friends." He approached them with his hand out. "Jerome Gordon-Smythe. Call me Jerry."

They shook hands and introduced themselves.

"Jean-Paul's directions were excellent," said Jack, "but he didn't explain the driveway well."

"Frightfully sorry about that. We hardly ever use it, so it has fallen into disrepair."

"How do you get in and out?" asked Emily.

"On the river. We almost never need to drive anywhere. When we do, we rent a car in Villeneuve and leave the boat there."

"Makes sense to me," said Hilda. "None of us has a car."

"Come, let's get you settled. I want to hear all about your adventures. What little Jean-Paul told me has me as excited as a six-year-old at Christmas!" He led them to the upstairs, where he had three bedrooms, one of which was obviously his home office.

"I hope this will suit you, young lady." He pointed to the twin bed across from the desk. "We have only the one guest room on this floor."

"That will be fine, sir."

"Jerry."

Emily blushed. Jerry showed Hilda and Jack to the guest bedroom. Like the office, it had a view of the woods beyond the river.

"I'll be out on the veranda keeping an eye out for her ladyship. You can take your showers now or later. No need to change for us."

They opted to clean up, so they took turns using the shower and changed into street clothes.

Jerry was sitting on the veranda looking downriver when Jack came into the living room. Jerry put his book cover-down on the side table and turned around.

"Did I make that much noise?"

"Not at all. Just that sixth sense. What'll you have?"

"A beer?"

"I forgot to chill it."

"If it's a good beer, no problem."

"A civilized man." Jerry crossed to the bar and opened two bottles of Ind Coope Long Life. "Have to leave Québec to get this one, but it's worth it." They clinked glasses and sat. "I hope the ladies aren't powdering too much."

"They're not the powder type, but their hair does take longer to dry."

"I had enough powder on me before the shower." Both men jumped up to find Hilda pausing at the entrance to the living room. She had her trekking clothes on, shirt and shorts.

"That is silent," Jerry said with admiration.

"Are those bottles of Long Life I see on the bar?"

Jerry was already crossing the room. As he poured a mug for Hilda, Emily walked in, also wearing a short trekking outfit.

"Beer for you too?"

"If you don't mind, I'd like something cold. Maybe an orange juice."

"That we have." He reached into the refrigerator under the bar. Soon everyone was seated on the balcony. The stream ran swiftly past the house.

"What's that roar?" asked Emily.

"The rapids in the Saint Anne Canyon. The white-water rafting ends just around the bend upstream." He pointed with his mug. "Ah—there's milady herself."

A Boston Whaler was coming quickly from the south, its bow waves crashing into the riverbank on either side. At the wheel, an athletic-looking woman with a blond ponytail waved to Jerry. She did not slow down as she turned toward the house but went into full reverse to bring the boat to a gentle halt somewhere beneath them. They heard the engine stop.

Moments later, she came into the living room from a door next to the stairs from the bedrooms. She was taller than Emily, fair, well-tanned, and the lines on her face spoke of much time on the water, in the wind and sun. And of much laughter and smiling. Jerry gave her a kiss and turned to the guests.

"Margaret, may I present Major Hilda Paisley, Major Jack Rathburn, and you-know-who?"

Emily laughed. Jack rolled his eyes. Margaret Gordon-Smythe reached out to Emily first.

"So pleased to meet you." She shook hands with them. "Please call me Maggie." Jerry appeared with a glass of white wine. "Thank you, dear. Would you mind bringing up the shopping?"

Jack hastened to accompany him to the boat. The others went to the veranda and sat. The shadows were long, and the temperature was dropping, a combination of the tall woods, the steep hills to the west of them and the water rushing by the house.

"This is quite the hideaway," said Hilda. "I take it you two don't care for cities and crowds."

"This suits us perfectly," said Maggie. "We have friends everywhere, but we like to be able to reach out on our own terms."

"We also like not being easy to find," added Jerry, coming in with Jack from the kitchen. "It allows us to live in something resembling a real retirement."

Jack and Hilda exchanged glances. "I could use a place like this."

"Me too," said Emily.

"You're welcome to stay as long as you like. Jean-Paul only described the barest outlines of your adventures, and I don't trust what I see on the telly. Tell us about it."

They spent the next hour recounting their stories, much to the delight of their hosts.

"But what about you?" asked Hilda.

"Some time in the army and here we are."

Emily was staring at them. "Jean-Paul said that you were SAS. That sounds like more than 'some time in the army.'"

"The best tales haven't been declassified yet, so I must hold on a while longer."

"Jean-Pierre is going into the Canadian Special Forces."

"That's partly my fault, you know. I love that boy, and we got along so well. Maryse may never forgive me."

"Speaking of her, and others I know"—Emily eyed Jack and Hilda—"how did you two meet?"

Maggie laughed. "That story is mostly declassified."

"The embarrassing parts anyway." Jerry winked at his wife. "I served in the Falklands—miserable cold operation, that. I was leading my first team on a raid on the other side of the hill from Port Howard. We put ashore and did what we came to do, then ran into an irate farmer on the way back to the boat. Our orders were not to engage civilians. We got away from him, but he fired a load of buckshot in my derrière as we reached the beach." He gestured to Maggie.

"I had the honor of plucking the little beads out." She winked. "Nice arse, so I decided to keep him." Emily blushed and giggled.

After the laughter died down, Emily asked, "What were you doing there?"

"It was my boat! The SAS didn't have anything that could cross water that rough at the time."

"Maggie already had a reputation throughout the Falklands. She was a one-woman SAR team. Our commander asked her to lend a hand." Jerry smiled warmly at Maggie.

"SAR?" asked Emily.

"Search and Rescue. At the sea rescue station, they put up a list of all the people she brought ashore on a memorial plaque. And she's not even dead yet!"

Jack said, "That explains the dramatic approach this afternoon."

"I had to be careful today. Two dozen eggs in the load."

The banter continued for another half hour. Then they all moved to the kitchen to continue chatting while the Gordon-Smythes put supper together.

"A pleasant thing about living here is English food with the freshest ingredients. The fish and the produce are unbeatable." Jerry heated up the deep fryer. "You've probably been drowning in wonderful French cuisine, haven't you?" They nodded. "Tonight, fish and chips and more warm beer."

The Americans learned that Maggie was born and raised in the Falklands. Jerry came back on leave six months after the war and proposed. They lived all over the world together, but when he had a long deployment, she would fly back to the Falklands until his unit came home.

"The army was a good life, but you can understand why we like the water and a certain isolation," she explained.

The yawning started at ten o'clock It had been a long day on the road. In their rooms, the three

Americans fell deeply asleep with the background noise of the river.

The next morning over breakfast, Jerry showed them where they would be going.

"No hurry," he said. "We can get to Rivière-Ouelle in less than four hours–"

"An hour and a half—tops!" Maggie gave them a wicked grin.

"We should let them enjoy the view. Take pictures. That sort of thing."

"You're trying to save on fuel again."

"Not a bad idea, love."

After breakfast, Jack helped load the dishwasher while Emily scrubbed the pans. Jerry checked out the boat. Emily, Hilda, and Jack double-checked their rooms, then carried their panniers and bikes below to the boat. The mooring area occupied the vast space among the stilts beneath the house, with two slips and a generous dock area around each boat. Jerry lashed their bikes together and to the life rails on the fantail with bungee cords.

Maggie went into the cabin, fired up the engine, and let it purr for a moment. Then she threw the eleven-meter Delta Phantom into full reverse and put the jet drive to starboard, churning up the bottom. Emily and her friends grabbed the rail in surprise as the boat pulled out with its stern pointing neatly upstream. Maggie put the engine ahead slow and let the water carry them to the Saint Lawrence.

"Why not the dramatic show we saw yesterday?" Jack asked Jerry.

"The water is very shallow all the way past the mudflats on the north shore of the Saint Lawrence. The Phantom draws more water than the Boston Whaler, so going fast could suck mud into the engines or damage the jet drive."

Jack joined the others. They came to the channel of the Saint Lawrence River. Maggie increased speed and turned downstream. Emily used her phone to take pictures of the farms on the Île d'Orléans and of Beaupré on the other side. The boat moved nimbly, passing the outbound freighters and keeping to the other side of the river from the inbound ships.

"Is there always this much traffic on the river?" Emily asked Jerry.

"There is unless the river or Lake Ontario freezes over. It can happen."

They enjoyed a picnic lunch about noon, with Jerry taking a turn at the wheel while Maggie ate. By midafternoon, Maggie was bringing the boat alongside the one pier in Rivière-Ouelle. It belonged to a friend of theirs, who was visiting relatives in Manitoba.

"Stay in touch," said Jerry. "You're welcome together or separately."

"Anytime," said Maggie. "It was wonderful to meet you and hear your stories."

After farewells, the Americans mounted their bicycles and rode up to Highway 132, where the *Route Verte* led to the end of the Gaspé Peninsula. On the other side of the Ouelle River, they turned left back toward the Saint Lawrence and soon were checking into the Municipal Campground. They bought food for supper and set up their camp halfway back from the shore.

At Hilda's suggestion, they ate early. With the sun still well above the horizon, Hilda suggested a walk on the beach.

"The sunsets here are unique, and to die for," she said.

"Swimming?" asked Emily.

"It's allowed, but I don't feel like sharing the water with all those ships."

As the sun came closer to the horizon, campers and neighbors gathered on the beach. A group was singing around a guitar, and a half-dozen campfires were going as the sun slowly fell below the Saint Lawrence. The combination of colors ranged from gold to deep purple, shifting constantly and streaking across the wispy clouds.

"This sunset is truly spectacular," said Jack. "Almost as beautiful as you are."

Hilda smiled and gave him a hug. "I don't light up the place."

"Oh, yes, you do."

Emily sat immobile on the sand, soaking in the beauty of the moment, enjoying the music nearby, and feeling intensely happy to be on the road with her friends.

31

The Gaspé Peninsula

"WILL I EVER WEAR MY BLACK DRESS AGAIN?" Emily crammed her panniers the next morning.

Hilda was grunting over her bags too. "It may be time to ship some things home if we're planning to return from Campbellton."

"We never got the blood and stains from the woods out. Maybe a professional in Charlottesville can do something about it."

"Or maybe you need a new dress," said Jack. Both women gave him an icy stare. "After we get back, not now."

They rolled out of the campground by eight o'clock and rode into the sun along the *Route Verte* on Highway 132.

To their left, the Saint Lawrence gradually spread out until it was twenty-two kilometers across by midafternoon. To their right, the farms continued to dominate, but slowly the tall forests behind the fields crept closer and closer to the road.

They stopped in Rivière-du-Loup because Hilda remembered that there was a post office downtown.

They crossed the bridge over the river and turned to the Camping du Quai on the water.

"Kind of ugly," Emily said, "another RV park with water slides."

"The tent sites are in the back. Not very scenic, but quiet." Hilda pointed down the dirt road. "We can shop here for supplies, but we can also take out what we want to ship and go to the post office before it closes. There's a lovely park with a trail on the other side of the river from the town. We can come back that way."

They pitched camp, went through their bags, and each assembled about five pounds of things that could go home. With that in a pannier, they rode into town, bought a box at the Canada Post office and sent it off. Emily emailed her mother the tracking data. Then they pedaled to the park by the rapids. The trail let them out just south of the campground. They picked up some fresh fish and other things at a grocery store and went back to their tent site to fix supper.

"Tomorrow could be our last check-in for a few days," Hilda said as they prepared to call home. "There are no cell towers in some parts, so on any given day, we may not have a signal."

"My kind of place." Emily smiled.

"You're not much of a city girl, are you?" Jack asked.

"I thought I was until I came out here with you two." She tested a roast potato on the grill with a fork. "I love the woods and the mountains and the quiet."

"Even when running from bad guys and bears?"

Emily thought for a moment. "I was scared, especially at first, when I was in the tree watching them look for me. But once I got into the woods, I felt at home. I mean, I had what I needed to survive, and I knew that I couldn't be more than a couple of days from civilization if I followed the water downhill. The bears were more predictable than the people."

"You're a remarkable young woman, Em."

"I don't think so. What about you two? Country or city?"

Hilda and Jack exchanged glances.

"Personally, I prefer the country too," said Jack. "It's why I ride solo most of the time and far away from the beaten path."

"I always think of you two riding everywhere together."

"Only since Hilda retired from the army. We didn't know each other until her last tour."

"What about you, Hilda?"

"I like both. I ride from city to city through the country."

"I think I could easily live like the Gordon-Smythes or the Langlaises."

"Tomorrow, we'll cross into the Gaspésie. You'll love it."

The next day, Hilda's words came into focus as they rode along the south shore of the Saint Lawrence and the towns thinned out. By midday, Hilda was signaling a left turn into the Parc National du Bic. They had to wait for a half-dozen logging trucks and several RVs to pass before crossing the highway.

"Where did all this traffic come from?" Emily asked.

"The Autoroute ended twenty kilometers back, so all the eastbound traffic gets on the 132 with us."

"I'm glad we have this bike lane," said Jack.

They checked in at the gatehouse. Beyond the reception center, RV's sat in neat rows. Hilda noticed the sag in Emily's shoulders.

"Isn't it kind of early to stop for the day?"

"Don't let the RVs fool you, Em. Wait till you see the tent camping. This park is worth stopping for and spending some time hiking around. Tonight, we shouldn't hear the traffic."

They found a campsite off the road, deep in the woods on a hill. Pines trees hid them from the campers on the lower level. The washroom was down there, but it was worth the walk to have the privacy and the sound of the water lapping the rocks. They hiked out to the flats and took pictures and selfies on the shore.

As they finished supper, a pair of motorcycles roared into the site. Emily's hackles went up, but the riders immediately shut off their engines and waved a friendly salute. From their beards and gang-looking leathers, Emily had been ready for the worst. The two bikers quickly set up their camp, just as the sun set, and turned in. She slapped herself mentally for judging them.

"I saw your face when they pulled in," said Hilda. "Surprised?"

Emily blushed and stared at her hands. "Yes. It makes me think of the way Mom would avoid bicycle tourists when we lived in Newton."

"What did you observe?"

Emily did not expect another test on observing.

"First, their beards and leather jackets, and the fact that they rode Harley Davidsons."

"And?"

Emily paused. "They had panniers for their gear. They also set up their tent like they were very used to camping. I guess they had supper somewhere before getting here."

"Colors?"

"One redhead, one brown. Beards going gray. The gang patch on the back—if that's what it was—seemed to be a red octopus or something."

"Not bad. Anything to add, Jack?"

"I'd say they've been married a long time and are comfortable with themselves."

Emily's jaw dropped. "You mean they're gay? How can you tell?"

"Same as any married couple. Smooth familiarity with the routine. Don't need to talk to one another. Two guys that big sleeping in a tent that small? What do you think?"

Hilda winked at Jack and grinned.

"So much for first impressions," said Emily. "I need to watch what people do and don't do too."

That night Emily thought about how she and her mother had changed over the last year before drifting off with the gentle night sounds of the forest and the shore.

After breakfast, they rode back out to the 132 and headed east. They soon became accustomed to the traffic because the cars and trucks gave them a wide berth, even if they didn't slow down.

The forest had completely overtaken the farms by the time they approached Matane. Pine trees grew right by the highway. The north shore of the river had long ago dropped below the horizon.

They stopped at a picnic area for a water break. Emily took a deep breath through her nose.

"The air smells different here."

"Jerry was talking about how your nose can tell you when you get to the Atlantic Ocean," said Jack. "The dead things on the shore are salt-water creatures and seaweed."

In town, they stopped at a supermarket to buy supper and breakfast, then followed the Matane River into the forest. They settled into a secluded campground. The RV's were well separated and hidden by the trees. Their tent site took some climbing and dropping to find, but it was close to the river and private.

"Tomorrow, we'll use the bicycle bridge at the south exit of the campground to cross the Matane River and go back on the other side," said Hilda. "That way, we won't have to climb out of here in the morning."

They grilled fish and roasted corn, then sat around the campfire ring enjoying the evening as the sun went down. When the fire was done, they buried the embers and turned in. They slept the sleep of the peaceful.

The following day, the coast road began to go up over promontories as often as it went around them, a long series of steep climbs and dizzying descents into the next coastal village. At Les Mechins, they saw the water turning a different color, becoming the greenish blue of the Atlantic. The mountains beyond the north shore of the Saint Lawrence had disappeared, so the effect was that of a coastline on the ocean.

Their destination was in the town of Sainte-Anne-des-Monts, about one hundred kilometers from Matane. They parked outside a supermarket and went inside for groceries, and to ask for directions. In the checkout line, Hilda noticed that they were the only shoppers, so she asked the cashier about the camping, in French.

"You must mean the Sea Shack," she answered. "It's where all the young people are tonight. In Tourelle." She smiled at Emily. *Clearly not a cycling fan,* thought Jack.

"Isn't it in Saint-Anne-des-Monts?" asked Hilda.

"It is, *madame*. There are four villages in Sainte-Anne. Tourelle is the last one, about eighteen kilometers up the road." Jack rolled his eyes.

"Are you sure?"

"Of course, I'm sure. My daughter will be there too. A big concert tonight."

They bought some food that they would not need to cook, some extra bottles of water, and mounted up.

"I just saw the sign for Tourelle." Emily pointed. "And see, that one says Sainte-Anne-des-Monts with Mont-Albert in parentheses."

"That's the first village," said Hilda. "Okay, we know how to read the place names." Sixteen kilometers farther, the sign for Sainte-Anne-des-Monts (Tourelle) appeared. By the time they found the Sea Shack, the sun had dipped below the woods.

They had to walk their bikes down a rutted dirt road to the beach with parked cars and motor scooters tightly packed on both sides. Rock music rolled up the hill at them. When they reached the *auberge*, they saw posters for the various local bands, with the Fish-monks scheduled that night.

"They must be popular." Emily stared at the crowd. "Everyone around must be here."

"Exactly what the lady at the supermarket told us."

"Let's check in," said Jack. "I hope we can find a spot." He tilted his head toward the beach. Hundreds of tents covered the shore all the way to the rocky cliffs in the distance.

At reception, the staff told them to find whatever space they could but absolutely not to camp beyond the ropes that marked the dunes. About one hundred meters from the house, they found a patch of sand right up against the rope and squeezed both tents in, sharing tent pegs to create a single footprint. Emily's tent opened toward the music coming from the concert; the other tent opened to the east toward the cliffs.

They settled in as soon as they could, but it was still dark when they made their way past their neighbors to the music. Emily was excited about the idea of a rock concert on the beach.

"They're good too," she exclaimed as the group carried off complicated covers of the most popular American bands. The venue turned out to be a large wooden deck with hundreds of teenagers and twenty-somethings swaying and shouting in front of the stage. The bar ran along the east and south sides.

"I'm all for a beer and a place to sit." Jack bought three beers and found a spot on the steps to the hostel. Hilda and Emily had joined him for less than two minutes when a pair of excited teenagers came out of the dancing crowd and asked Emily for an autograph. She obliged, and then followed them out to the dance floor.

"She's going to be fine." Hilda smiled.

"In her element. Makes me feel like an old man."

"You want to dance too?"

"Not yet. No room and this is the best seat in the house."

"You are really tired, aren't you?"

"Now that I'm resting, I'm okay, but those hills got to me today. This was the hottest day all week." Jack stood. "Let's go see the rest of the place."

He took Hilda's hand as they climbed up to the lodge. It was a hostel and a restaurant, with a common area above reception (leave your shoes on the stairs). No vacancy, of course, but the owners let concert-goers pitch tents on the beach. Better that than having them driving home in the dark, drunk or stoned.

They watched the scene for a while. Emily was still dancing, having a great time with her new friends and admirers.

"I'm not sure whether she's a celebrity here or not," said Jack.

"It looks to me like she has vanished in the crowd. Everyone is so wrapped up in the music and whatever, that they don't notice who's around them."

They walked to the water's edge, then skirted the lapping waves as they made their way back to the tent. They missed it and had to follow the dune ropes back fifty meters to find their site. Two tents over, a foursome sang around a guitar, but otherwise, the camping area was empty.

"I'm all for turning in," said Jack, "but we should stay up for Emily."

"I'm the guardian. You lie down. I'll go back and check on her in a while."

"Right." Jack crawled into the tent carefully, leaving his shoes outside. Hilda removed hers, curled in behind him, shaking the sand off her feet before pulling her legs in. She nestled up against him and kissed his ear.

"Checking on Emily?"

"In a while, I said."

ʘ ʘ ʘ

"*Puis-je t'acheter une bière?*" Can I buy you a beer? Emily's current dance "partner" asked. He was tall, but not gigantic, slender like a cyclist, with the most intense eyes and dark eyebrows she had ever seen. His hair was jet-black, with a curl that fell over his forehead. Pale, clear skin and a strong chin.

"*Oui, merci.*" Emily felt happy and a little breathless. After dancing continuously, she was glad that the band was taking a break. She caught her breath while he ordered a pair of pilsners.

"Marcel Sabatier." He held out her beer and switched to English. "I know who you are."

She reached up and put her finger on his lips. "*Si tu le sais, ne dis rien, je t'en prie.*"

"I understand, but we can speak English, *non?*"

"Fine, but I'm hoping to stay lost in the crowd here."

"Then let's get away from the bar and find a place where they won't be looking around." He led her out to the beach below the stage. There were couples making out, groups walking together to cool off, and some impromptu campfire singalongs scattered along the shore. The distinctive odor of marijuana wafted on the breeze.

They exchanged the usual introductory talk. He was an engineering student, home for the weekend.

"This is more exciting than I expected on the Gaspé," she admitted.

"It's a quiet place, believe me. If it weren't for these concerts, the young people would go crazy, and even more of them would leave and not come back."

"So, this is a retention initiative."

"Probably not on purpose, but we don't have the drain that some other areas of the Gaspé have. You will see some poor and almost abandoned villages on the other side."

The band returned to the stage. Marcel took their empty bottles to the recycle bin. Moments later, they were lost in the music and dancing. Feeling a buzz, she gladly let herself go with the music. At the next intermission, she let a group of three that she was dancing with buy her another beer.

When the band wrapped it up, she thought it was another break. She felt unsteady when she stopped dancing and started toward restrooms, but there was such a crowd that she turned to the beach, thinking to go around to the main building.

As she rounded the corner, walking in the sand, the world spun around and went dark.

She dreamed she was in a small boat just off the beach. The winds were buffeting the craft and howling.

Every time the boat crested a swell, everything shuddered, and her stomach rebelled. The scene fuzzed out and took a new shape.

"Emily! Wake up!" She opened her eyes and peered groggily into the deep blue of Hilda's. The shuddering was Hilda's hands on her shoulders. Her head was spinning. She twisted to the side and threw up. Before Hilda could catch her, she fell face down in the sand again and lay there.

"Don' feel good."

"I guess not. Let's get away from that mess. C'mon." Hilda pushed her until she rolled on her back. "Don't try to get up. You'll bump your head."

"Wha'?" Emily sat up and cracked her head on a diagonal crossbeam. "Ow! Where'm I?"

"Under the dance floor, almost. You must have passed out here and crawled under the building."

"I was going to the bathroom. I think."

"Well, you took care of that already. Don't move while I pull you out."

Hilda backed out then reached in to grab Emily's ankles. She pulled the girl through the sand until she was out in the open.

Emily rolled on her side. She was awake and feeling embarrassed. Her head was still spinning, but her stomach was calm. She tasted beer and vomit but made herself hold it all down. She got up unsteadily and leaned on Hilda. She was covered with sand, and she could smell the urine on the front of her shorts.

"Oh, Hilda, I'm shorry."

"Never mind that. I'm sorry too. I should have come back sooner."

"Wha' happened?"

"Jack fell asleep. I was coming back for you, but I must have dozed off too."

"I mean, here." She looked around. "Where's everybody?"

"The concert's over, and everyone not staying here went home."

"Oh." Emily turned full around slowly. Her vision was still fuzzy, but they were alone under a thick canopy of brilliant stars. She forced herself to focus and saw that the sky and the sea were the same black. Less than a half-dozen campfires still flickered on the beach. She could hear some off-tune singing with guitars or ukuleles.

"What time'zit?"

"After three."

"I think I c'n walk now."

"Good, let's hit the washroom first." They got Emily cleaned up as well as they could. "I'm sorry," she said as they made their way gingerly along the dune ropes.

"You said that already. You'll have plenty of time to think about it tomorrow."

Hilda gave her some bread and made her drink most of a liter bottle of water.

"I'll make you rehydrate more in the morning." She helped Emily ease into the tent backward, getting the sand off her feet. "You okay to turn in, Em?"

"Yes. I think so. I'm not dizzy anymore."

"I'm glad. Get a few hours of sleep. We'll wake you." Hilda leaned into the tent and kissed the girl on the forehead. "Good night."

"G'night, Hilda. Thanks."

Emily was asleep on top of her sleeping bag even before Hilda finished backing out. She zipped up the tent and walked around to her own entrance.

Jack did not stir as she eased out of her shirt and shorts. She lay down next to him and stared at the top of the tent. She forced herself not to dwell on what might have happened, but she could not quell her anger with herself. Sleep was a long time coming.

32

LIGHTHOUSES, PARKS AND BEACHES

E MILY WOKE UP. First, she noticed the smell, then the fact that it did not seem completely dark. She felt grubby from the sweat that had dried on her clothes, leaving white salt marks on her shorts and jersey. She got up carefully. Her head felt tight, but her stomach was not queasy. She unzipped her tent, gathered clean clothes and her toilet kit, and eased out of the tent.

From the east, a pink glow was crossing the sky, swallowing stars. To the west, the stars still twinkled in a perfectly black field. No one was stirring among the hundreds of tents on the beach. She took a deep breath of the salty air and felt better.

She made her way quietly to the showers at the main house, where she cleaned up thoroughly. She washed yesterday's filthy clothes and wrung them out with her towel. After taking a long drink at the water fountain, she walked back.

The groceries were in her tent because she had more room. She carried them to the nearest picnic table, set out three places, the muesli, and yogurt. She drank another liter of water, watching the sun come up over the cliffs.

Jack came out first, waved, and walked briskly to the washrooms. He was back before Hilda emerged.

"You look better than I expected, Em," said Hilda.

"Not feeling one hundred percent, but at least I'm clean and the laundry is done."

"Good for you. I'll be right back."

Jack sat and assembled his breakfast.

"Good time last night?"

"Didn't Hilda tell you?"

"Tell me what? I slept through everything. She was asleep when I got up."

"I got drunk and passed out."

"You're kidding!" He looked over her shoulder as Hilda returned and sat.

"Thanks for rescuing me again, Hilda."

"It's my job, I think." Hilda grabbed the box of muesli and started making her breakfast. "How much did you drink anyway?"

"I don't know." Emily pushed her spoon around in her muesli. "I remember the first three beers. Yours, one with Marcel, and one at the next intermission. They tasted good, with all that dancing."

"The band must have taken more than two breaks."

"It's all I remember. The different people I was dancing with bought the beers. Suddenly, the concert was over, and I couldn't get through the crowd to the washrooms. I tried to walk around the building and next thing I knew, you were shaking me awake."

They ate in silence for a while.

"Who's Marcel?" Jack asked.

"The guy I was dancing with when the band took their first break. I didn't see him after he bought me a beer and we chatted during the break."

Hilda frowned and sighed. "I'm sorry, Em. I'm supposed to be looking after you."

"I should be looking after myself. I feel terrible about this. What could I have done?"

"Looking back, I think that we all missed some cues," said Jack. "We forgot to eat the supper we bought. I'll bet you finished your beers during the breaks, didn't you?" Emily nodded. "Too fast. Next time either sit out the next set and drink slowly or leave the unfinished beer."

"You made me drink a lot of water last night, Hilda. Why?"

"The alcohol dehydrates you. That's what most of a hangover is. How do you feel?"

"Not as bad as I did last night when you found me."

"Headache?"

"Not really."

Jack said, "Here's a tip I got that works for me. I order water first whenever I'm drinking. I try to drink at least as much water as beer or whatever. It slows down my drinking and keeps me hydrated."

"I'll remember that. Thanks."

"Are you up for riding today?" asked Hilda.

"Of course! I may not set any speed records, though. How far?"

"It's about seventy-six kilometers to Madeleine. There's a pretty place to camp by the lighthouse."

"That sounds easy enough."

"Oh, to be eighteen again." Jack sighed and smiled.

They cleaned up breakfast, broke camp, and packed the bicycles. Emily tied her damp clothes to the outside of her panniers and rear rack.

Soon they were climbing and coasting the *Route Verte* on the 132 into the sun. They went through their three water bottles each rather quickly, so they found themselves stopping often to refill. They still got to Cap-de-la-Madeleine by three o'clock, in plenty of time to pick an ideal spot.

After stretching, showering and changing, Emily and Hilda took naps. Jack hiked out to the point with an eBook on his phone to enjoy the sunshine and the breeze.

There was a restaurant below the lighthouse, so they relished the fish chowder, *moules, frites*, and salads. Emily drank water. They had *crème brulée* for dessert and turned in early.

The next day, they rounded the end of the peninsula. The sun stayed in their faces until late in the morning as the road turned to the southeast. The traffic was much lighter, though still about half logging trucks and half tourists. They made sure that they had several extra liters of water on each bicycle.

Emily had recovered, which was fortunate because the promontory climbing was steeper and longer, and they had no shade until late afternoon. They drank all their water, stopping to refill their water bottles from the extra bottles each carried.

About six o'clock, they passed part of the Forillon National Park on their right and found themselves on a flat road with trees on all sides. Hilda stopped and pointed to a sign.

"There's nothing here," said Jack.

"Trust me, it's the driveway. C'mon."

They picked their way down the dirt road to a parking lot. Leaning their bikes on some trees, they walked to the building on the beach.

"The sign says *camping sauvage*," said Emily as they reached the office. "Do they mean it?"

"Yes." In fact, the only running water was in the dishwashing sink. No showers, and the outhouse sat at the end of a long boardwalk over a marsh.

"See why I recommended stopping in Rivière-au-Renard for groceries?" She pointed to another sign on the building. The restaurant had lost its alcohol license, and the kitchen was being renovated. "They had a different problem when I was here last, but it was still no food, no drink."

"It certainly is quiet."

"That it is." They found a pleasant spot among some pine trees, far enough from the outhouse not to smell it. They cooked their salmon and roast potatoes and enjoyed a walk along the beach.

The next day, they rode into L'Anse-au-Griffon. The tiny fishing village devoted more real estate to the piers and fish processing than residential property. Taking a right at the Griffon Cove, they climbed a long, 12 percent road to the ridge deep in the National Park. At the top, they rested, drank more water, and considered the newly paved highway.

"That has to be the longest, steepest climb yet, but no view for a reward," said Jack.

"Kind of a bummer, eh?" said Hilda. "The trees block the view."

"My reward is still ahead." Emily pointed to the highway sign indicating a 17 percent grade. "See you guys at the bottom."

"Wait for us at the T."

Emily waved, swung onto her bike, and vanished.

"I hope we don't have to pick up the pieces on the way down."

"She has a racer's touch, but, still, let's catch up."

Soon they were flying down the hill on seven kilometers of smooth highway, with gentle curves and no traffic. At the intersection, Emily was chugging her water bottle, her face bright with excitement.

"The computer says I maxed at ninety-two point five kilometers per hour. That was fun!"

"I imagine you'd peg a hundred without the bags," said Hilda.

"*Bien sûr!*"

Hilda pointed up the road to the right. "Gaspé is that way, across the bay. Mind you, there should be lots of tourist traffic."

They had lunch at a brasserie near the bridge in the picturesque town, across from the train station.

"After that climb and last night's mosquitoes, I would like to find a bed indoors tonight," said Jack.

"Me too." Emily motioned with her fork.

Hilda got out her phone and, in a few minutes, had a reservation at the Douglastown Hostel on the other side of Gaspé. They walked over to the station and learned about the tourist train that runs on the tracks that once carried people from Montréal every day.

Emily came back after reading a sign in the station lobby. "The VIA train only goes to Campbellton."

They rode along the bay and easily found the hostel. Douglastown was an Anglophone community, which had fallen on relatively hard times after the rise of anti-English sentiment in the 1970s.

"We feel the effect of being so far from Québec City," explained the manager as they sat with the dinner that they had made in the community kitchen. "Our children take the bus two towns over to attend an English-speaking school since our schools were closed."

"Is there a lot of ill-will?" asked Emily.

"At first yes, but over the last twenty years, things evened out a bit. It isn't so big a deal to be Anglophone or Francophone today. It helps to be bilingual, and that's how we bring up our kids."

"Makes sense to me."

They had a room together, with bunk beds and a restroom with a shower.

The next day, they rode past a series of beautiful coastal views and camped on the beach in Chandler. The Rocher Percé sitting in the eponymous bay offered some great photography. They passed farms thick with crops, prosperous towns teeming with tourists, shops and vacationers, and nearly abandoned hamlets with only a tiny IGA grocery store.

"You know, we haven't had a cell signal since Gaspé," said Jack as they set up camp in New Richmond. A stand of pine trees separated them from the water and provided shade. Bicyclists rode by on the path along the beach.

"Campbellton's a proper city. We'll be able to check in there."

They walked the shopping district that evening and ate out again. Emily had some wine with dinner, feeling a little nervous at first, but it went perfectly with the fish terrine and green beans.

"I'm not ready for this to end tomorrow." Emily stared wistfully out the window.

"We still have a train ride," Jack said. "You know how the last one went."

"Omigod. I'll hide in the baggage car!"

"Well, I don't want this tour to end either, but I am looking forward to my new job."

"It should be a lot quieter than the ER." Jack grinned at Hilda.

"Should be. Dr. Osborne is a family physician in an old home on Fifth Street. Prepping patients for routine visits—I'll feel guilty taking his money, at least at first."

"After Chicago, Montréal and Québec City, aren't you ready for some boredom?"

"You betcha!" She raised her glass. "To a boring year!" They all clinked their glasses.

"Not too boring." Emily sipped her wine. "I want to win some races next year."

"I'm sure you will, Em."

After dinner, they walked slowly back to the campground.

"Wait, guys!" Emily tugged on their arms as they passed a *brasserie.* "I saw something about Charlottesville on the big-screen TV in there." They walked in and took places at the bar while the commercials ran. Emily ordered a hot chocolate while Hilda and Jack had a beer between them. The news came on, with a short background story about the Unite the Right rallies in Charlottesville in 2017.

"I forgot all about that," said Emily.

"I did too," said Hilda, "although I did mention to your mother that you might be safer here than there."

"I remember. I wonder what's happening."

"Nothing yet, apparently. I guess if there is anything, we'll find out in Montréal." They sipped their drinks during the commercials before the sports news. Emily finished first and went to the washroom. Jack watched her all the way to the door. When she came back, he asked for the bill.

"On the house, sir, if the young lady will sign this coaster for me." The barman pointed to the screen, where split-screen close-ups of Emily showed her finishing in the USAFA Invitational and getting out of the *Sûreté* police cruiser in Montréal.

"Thanks, Em." Jack grinned as she autographed coasters for the barman and three of the waiters. The barman shook hands with them, and they rose. Emily blushed furiously when the customers and staff applauded as she walked to the door. She turned and waved self-consciously. Then with a little bow of thanks, she went through the door that Jack was holding. Hilda took her arm on the sidewalk.

"Will I ever get used to that?" Emily said unhappily as she walked between them.

"I hope not, Em," said Hilda. "Because that's when fame will have gone to your head. Just grow to be grateful and gracious."

"Good point." She hugged Hilda's arm. "Thanks."

In her tent, Emily checked her phone. Still no signal. She wondered if her mother and Mark were okay. Then she realized that she would still be on a train on the twelfth of August.

On the last day of their Gaspé tour, the weather proved to be fickle and difficult. After they started out, the clouds rolled in, though the heat continued to build. The wind backed around to the west, making it sometimes necessary to pedal instead of coast on the long downhill into Escuminac.

As they approached Pointe-à-la-Garde, the skies opened up. They took shelter under the canopy of a gas station island, already soaked to the skin. When the worst of the squall passed, they continued to ride into the wind and rain for the last twenty kilometers to Campbellton.

The rain finally stopped as they rode across the suspension bridge that led from Québec to New Brunswick. Their cells phones dinged as they parked their bikes by the visitor center. It was only three thirty in the afternoon.

"You call Pete while I try to get tickets for Montréal," said Hilda. "We'll probably sit up in coach all night."

Jack checked in with the FBI while Emily called her mother. Hilda and Jack ended the call at about the same time.

"Must have been a cancellation just before I dialed in. We got a sleeper on the train tonight."

Hilda called Maryse while Emily was still talking to her mother. They ended their calls together.

"Maryse is excited. She'll meet us, and we can all ride up to the house together. How are Mark and your mother?"

"Fine, and happy that we're heading home. She's pleased that we can rest at the Pointreaus before the long train ride south. And nothing is happening in Charlottesville. The various police and city authorities are all pumped and coordinated, but it's quiet."

"Pete said the same. He added that Frank will transfer in September. The bureau doesn't want a turnover anywhere near August twelfth."

"Makes sense."

"We've got nine hours," said Emily. "D'you think we could use the washroom to change and clean up?" Hilda thought a minute.

"Let me call the MacKenzie House. I stayed there last time, and the owner told me about the night train. She asked me to call if I ever come back."

Hilda rang up the Maison MacKenzie and got another earful of enthusiasm. After a short call, she ended the call.

"It sounds like she remembered you," said Jack, grinning. "She's German?"

Hilda smiled. "Yes. She told me to come right over. We can take showers and clean up—even do the laundry if we need to."

"Wow. Some hospitality."

"Her husband makes crêpes to die for. Be prepared to have pancakes for supper if he's in."

The historic house was only a few blocks from the visitor center. The woman who met them at the porch personified Emily's idea of a country hostess—big-boned with a ruddy complexion, straw-blond hair braided on both sides, with a print shift and an apron. She gave Hilda a generous hug and pumped Jack's and Emily's hands enthusiastically.

"I know that this is a regular hotel," Jack said. "Thank you so much for letting us use the facilities. Is there a day rate?"

Mrs. Weatherby looked at Hilda. "*Sie wissen es nicht?*" You didn't tell them?

"I haven't had occasion to talk about it yet."

"Hilda saved my life last time she stayed here. I can't ever repay that."

"Oh, please, Margareta. It's not like you were bleeding out in the ER."

Emily was staring wide-eyed, and Jack wore the half-bemused expression he put on when he was discovering yet another interesting facet of his lover.

"Well, come in all of you. Take the room next to the kitchen. It's empty tonight 'for repairs.' Towels are on the bed."

They locked their bicycles inside the fence and carried their panniers to the room.

After showers and fresh clothes, they gathered in the kitchen while the washing machine ran their laundry. Glasses of orange juice all around. Margareta joined them after checking in a couple upstairs.

Emily frowned at Hilda and Margareta. "Is some-one going to tell us the story?" Jack grinned and rolled his eyes.

"Some enormous brutes attacked me as I was coming back from the grocery store. It was the most frightening experience of my life."

She leaned toward Emily with arched eyebrows and wide eyes. "Then suddenly, they were down on the ground, and Hilda here was kicking them down the street in a fury. When they finally got up, they ran as fast as they could."

"Sounds like Hilda," said Jack.

"Uh-huh," said Emily, looking at the nurse. "What's your side of this?"

"I was just coming back from a walk, and I saw Margareta working the latch of the gate with her arms full of groceries. The two goons were coming from the other direction, heading straight for her. I don't think they saw me in the shadows of the trees. It didn't take much to get behind them and knock their heads together."

"You didn't teach me that one yet." Emily heard Margareta suck in her surprise.

"Not yet, Em. You need a certain height advantage, and you have to do it very fast and with all your strength to make sure it knocks them out." She smacked her hands together with a loud clap. "Otherwise, you just make them angry. Once they're down, though, you can keep them under control when they come to."

"She wouldn't let me refund her stay, so I remain indebted to her. Margareta put her hand on Hilda's arm. "Friends of Hilda's will always be welcome while I'm here."

Jack sat silently, smiling at Hilda with admiration in his eyes.

"What are you googly-eyed about?" Emily snapped his attention.

"I could have used her in the MP's. She can put down a whole bar fight by herself, I bet."

"Cut it out, you two." Hilda smiled. She turned to Margareta. "Is your husband here today?"

"No, unfortunately. He has a job over in Moncton. He won't be back for two days."

"Doesn't he work here?" Emily asked.

"Oh, he helps when he's here, but he is also a lineman for Hydro-Québec. They call him whenever there are power outages."

"I'll miss his crêpes," said Hilda. "Any recommendations for supper?"

"Try the Café Europa just up the hill. The food is good, and you won't wait long for your supper. Before you ask, I have three more couples coming in tonight, so I will stay here."

"We'll get our things out of the room—just in case you need it."

The dryer buzzed. They folded their clothes, packed their panniers, and left the room as neat as they could.

The storm front had passed before they walked up to the restaurant. A couple of hours later, they wheeled their bikes into the station on Roseberry Street in plenty of time to check the bicycles and board the sleeper car.

33

MONTRÉAL, ENCORE

EMILY PAUSED TO SCAN THE CROWD on the platform of the Central Station in Montréal. She saw Hilda making her way through the relatives and hurried commuters to the tall blonde standing behind the swirling mob, keeping her bike from hitting anyone.

"How does she manage to look like a Givenchy model in a bicycle kit?" Emily asked.

Jack smiled. "Something about being more French than English? You'll look like that soon, Em."

"You're kidding!" She punched his arm.

"No, I'm not. Her glow, her looks, and her confidence come from her fitness. You have that too. I've seen you grow this summer."

"Well, thanks, but I still feel like a klutz around her—and around Hilda, too, come to think of it."

"They're quite a pair, aren't they?"

The four of them made their way to the baggage car, where the three Americans claimed their bicycles and snapped on their panniers. Outside, the air was noticeably cooler than it had felt by Chaleur Bay just the day before. Riding through the familiar downtown of Montréal and up the side of the Mont Royal to Summit Woods, they eyed any car that slowed down behind them.

"Am I being paranoid?" Hilda asked as they swung off their bikes in front of the house.

"No more so than I," said Jack. "Probably not a bad thing considering what happened before."

"I didn't see anyone following us," said Emily.

"Even if some MS-42 types are still around, they shouldn't have any idea that we're here."

"Come on in, you three." Maryse grinned as she climbed the stairs to the front door. "We'll deal with the paparazzi and kidnappers later."

Inside, Maryse directed them to their same rooms as before. "Jacques will be home for lunch. Settle in and join us." She headed down the hall to the kitchen while they carried their panniers upstairs.

The CFO came in the back door, in his business suit. "I must attend a financial presentation at Bombardier Aerospace at two, so I'll go from here."

When Emily, Jack, and Hilda came down, they joined the Pointreaus in the kitchen. Over *salade niçoise*, beets and baked cod, they reported on their stay with the Gordon-Smythes and the ride around the Gaspé Peninsula.

"We're still worried about security after the kidnapping," Jacques said. "Pierre and his people formed a joint team with the gang investigations unit to keep an eye on the movements of any MS-42 associates. Abdul and Hassan are out of solitary confinement, but no one has asked to see them. They are on a special watch, so they can't pass messages in or out through other inmates.

"While you were away, there was no activity either from MS-42 or the known terrorist groups, possibly because they simply didn't know where you were. I can't imagine that they'll pick up your trail before you leave tomorrow."

"Let's hope so," said Jack.

"*Allo, y a-t-il personne?*" Anybody here? The front door slammed, and a duffel bag hit the floor. Maryse jumped from her chair with a squeal of delight and flew out the kitchen door while everyone else stood. She returned with a slender, sandy-haired Canadian Army lieutenant with blue eyes under his tan beret. The family resemblance to Jacques and Maryse was obvious. His father gave him a bear hug.

Emily was closest to the door. "Lieutenant Pointreau, I presume." She extended her hand, then grinned. He took hers in two hands with enthusiasm.

"I was trying to surprise my parents, but I am the one surprised." Emily smiled and introduced Jack and Hilda.

"Very pleased to meet you, sir, ma'am. From what my mother says, you've been like Emily's bodyguards."

"*Tutoyons-nous,*" said Jack. "Emily's been the one looking out for us, I think. She has eyes on all four sides."

Lunch was a noisy affair as Jean-Pierre briefed his parents on his training at CSOTC. He was only home for the weekend and expected to join his operational unit by Thanksgiving for live exercises.

Jacques excused himself to go to his meeting. After he left, Maryse looked at her son and her guests.

"No paparazzi yet. I missed my usual workout this morning, and these three will have been sitting on trains for thirty-six hours by the time they get home. Let's ride."

"Great idea," said Emily. "A training peloton."

While Maryse cleared the table, the others went upstairs to change into their bicycle kits. Soon Jean-Pierre and Maryse were leading them on the *Route Verte* on the north shore to L'Assomption. The separate bike path took them through the city into open countryside, past vast farms, and orchards.

Maryse, Emily, and Jean-Pierre held a drafting class for Jack and Hilda, who quickly mastered the basics of following in the slipstream of the rider ahead of them. They took turns leading. At a fruit stand outside L'Assomption, they devoured two fresh blueberry pies.

"That drafting makes a difference." Jack's eyes shone with excitement. "I've never ridden so fast without hurting."

"And that's not racing," said Emily.

"But it would let a tourist cover more ground in a day with as much effort."

They remounted and sped back to the house.

"I can't believe that I just rode a hundred kilometers in four hours." Jack dismounted easily enough, but he was still breathing harder than the others. They went into the house. Jack and Hilda joined the racers for their stretching routine.

"This feels good. Thanks for suggesting the ride, Maryse."

"You'll have plenty of time to recover over the next twenty-four hours."

"True."

"Maybe you two should take your shower first." Maryse cocked her head toward the two younger riders talking excitedly in French as they headed to the veranda. Hilda and Jack both smiled. The three older ones went upstairs.

"The RS is supposed to be an entry-level frame." Emily and Jean-Pierre walked through the garden back to the bicycle parking shed. "But you were very nimble on it today."

"It's much lighter than it should be for the price. The truth is that it doesn't make sense to have a top-end bike like the C60 or the C64 when my racing days are over."

"Why over?"

"I'm an all-around athlete." He gestured with his arms apart. "That's what Special Forces have to be."

"What about after?"

"Afterwards, I'll be too old for professional racing, and this trusty steed will be waiting for me."

"You plan to make a career?"

"Unless something happens to me, I'll stay in as long as I still enjoy it."

"Makes sense to me." Emily smiled at him. He grinned back. She could see the warmth creep up from his shirt collar, and she knew that she was blushing too.

"What about you?"

Emily shrugged. "When I get back, Dr. Morgan will evaluate my condition and clear me for competitive racing again—or not. I can't see why he wouldn't, and then I can start training for next spring. I hope my form has not been ruined by all this touring."

"I don't think so. I was watching your form." She blushed again. "I mean, you were the only one out there not really working today."

"Sure, but that's because I didn't have Marianne Van der Fleet or Cristina Rinaldi breathing down my neck. It's different, as well you know."

They reached the bikes. Emily picked up his Colnago and hefted it. "Lighter than it looks." She put it down. "Where is the Stevens in your picture?"

"That wasn't mine. Stevens provided the bicycles for the BMO team last year." He considered her Bianchi. "Why do you ride a city bike?"

"The Colnago is back home."

"The V2R you rode last year?" Emily nodded. "What happened to it in the crash?"

"The handlebars wedged under the guardrail. Everything else was fine."

"Except the rider." His brows furrowed. "I saw the news videos. That was awful."

"I wouldn't know. I recognized a white oak before I blacked out. Next thing I remember was Hilda's face in the ER. I was unconscious for a week after that."

"So, you know Hilda from Charlottesville."

"Actually, we met in Kansas. She was crossing the country and caught up with me when I was walking home after crashing on a solo training ride. She showed me how to fix a pretzeled wheel."

He lifted the Bianchi Volpe. "This just seems unsuited for long-distance touring."

"Maybe, but I've never toured before, and I use this bike for everything but racing. If I were heavier or riding a more challenging tour, I might have had to buy a touring bicycle, but the Bianchi has been fine."

They talked shop as only those who have "been in the shop" can talk until Maryse came out the front door and waved at Jean-Pierre from the porch.

"If you don't want to fight your father for the shower when he comes home, you might want to come in now."

Emily gasped with surprise. The sun was licking the treetops. He laughed.

"I don't think *Papa* wants to try the new moves I learned at CSOTC, *Maman*." He motioned Emily to go first into the house, and they went upstairs.

The familiar routine of white wine on the veranda followed by supper left Emily with a warm feeling of well-being. Sharing life with Jean-Pierre's family felt so normal, so right. Hilda and Jack obviously felt at home too. They would miss the Pointreaus.

They had checked in with Pete Sayfield already, but Emily called her mother from her room that night.

"Do you have your reservations all the way through?" Katherine asked after Emily reported on their day in Montréal and the sleeper train from Campbellton.

"Yes. We'll spend the night in New York because the Adirondack pulls into Grand Central Station tomorrow night, but the Crescent to Charlottesville leaves from Penn Station the next morning."

"We caught that. Mark has an idea, partly because I'd like to leave town this weekend. We'd like to meet you in New York, then drive to the Northern Neck the next morning. Is Hilda there?"

"She's next door. Let me see if they're still up."

Emily went through the bathroom and knocked on the door. A muffled noise was followed by Hilda's voice. "If you come around the other way, Em, I can get my bathrobe off the door."

Emily giggled. "Really, you two." She took both robes off their hooks, cracked the door, and threw them in. While she waited behind the closed door, she heard Jack mutter something followed by laughter.

Hilda opened the door. Emily walked in to find Jack robed and sitting at the desk.

"Mom and Dad have an idea. They'd like to meet us in New York and drive to the Dempsey home in the Northern Neck the next day." She held out the phone to Hilda.

"Hello, Katherine…We can change our tickets… We're booked into the Courtyard across the street… Sounds wonderful… Tomorrow night, then. Thanks. Here's Emily."

Hilda gave Emily the phone. After the usual love and kisses phrases, Emily ended the call.

"You'll meet Mark's dad, Jack. I know that you two will get along great."

"We should, although he might not want to be reminded about me."

"You already know him?"

"He was my CO for a tour in Korea. I arrested his son for shoplifting at the PX."

"Oh, no!" Emily put her hand to her mouth. "I'll call Mom back."

Jack reached out and put his hand over the phone. "No need. He was fully supportive, and we turned it into another learning experience for the boy. It will be good to see General Dempsey again."

"Wait a minute! Mark—"

"Had already left home, which is why I didn't recognize him in Charlottesville. It was his younger brother Bill. I didn't even make the connection before."

"Let's go down to the studio to change our tickets," said Hilda. "The desktops are faster." That took another fifteen minutes. A half hour later, silence reigned over the big house by the Summit Wood.

The next morning, Jacques called from the upstairs window in the hall.

"There are two paparazzi out front."

Maryse came out of their bedroom to look. Everyone else was also up and joined them.

"*Tabarnac!*" said Jean-Pierre. "I was so looking forward to riding to the station with you like we decided last night." Maryse raised her eyebrows but said nothing.

"What do you think, Jacques?" asked Hilda. "Can we still ride if we slip out the back?"

"Let me ask Giles while we fix breakfast."

They made their way to the kitchen while Jacques went into the study. He joined them almost right away.

"Giles thinks we can lose those two if they're just standing there. However, there are often a few staking out the station and the airport, hoping to catch a celebrity leaving town. He'll have a detail waiting for us." He looked at Maryse. "Take them to the side. Giles will be there."

"We're going to be sort of obvious." Emily tore a piece of croissant. "Three tourists and two racers."

"Not that strange on our streets," said Maryse. "All the different bike tribes ride there."

They finished up and cleared breakfast. Antoine arrived for work, and Maryse asked him to move the bicycles unobtrusively to the back door, out of sight of the pair at the front gate.

A half hour later, the six of them mounted at the back gate and rode toward Gordon Crescent away from the house with its waiting paparazzi. They took the bike trail that circled the Summit Wood Park and coasted down the Chemin de la Côte-des-Neiges into downtown. At the Boulevard, Jacques peeled off to the left on his way to work.

As the others crossed the Boulevard, a motorcycle made a right turn behind them and began to close them in traffic. In her rearview mirror, Emily saw the passenger holding a camera.

"Paparazzi!" she shouted ahead. Jack fell in behind Emily, and Jean-Pierre moved to her left. Maryse flanked Hilda. The group sped up until they were passing cars on the right.

The motorcycle got in the bike lane and closed up behind Jack. The passenger trained his SLR camera over the driver's shoulder and began shooting.

At a wide space in the road, the motorcycle sped up alongside them. Jack reached down and pulled up his frame pump. He stabbed it at the cameraman, then stuffed the pump in his jersey pocket. The cameraman dropped the camera, which jerked on his neck as he doubled over. The movement distracted the driver, and they fell behind while the driver regained control.

Just as he gunned the motorcycle to catch up, a siren and lights came on behind them. A Montréal motorcycle police officer waved the paparazzi to the curb. The cyclists slowed to a more relaxed pace.

"What was that about?" Emily asked Jean-Pierre.

"Driving a motor vehicle in a bike lane is illegal."

"Gee, I wish we had that kind of enforcement in the States!"

"As we expected." Maryse motioned with her head. "They're waiting." Ahead on the right, a half-dozen photographers and journalists were blocking the doors under the marquee of the Central Station. "Follow me!"

Maryse turned right onto Rue E, a narrow, featureless street. She dismounted in front of a nondescript door in the gray concrete wall, where three men in dark suits were waiting. The others followed her lead, and in ten seconds, everyone was inside a service corridor and off the street.

Maryse introduced Giles to the Americans.

"You seem to have done this before," said Jack as he smiled and shook Giles's hand.

"Not our first rodeo, Major. Madame Pointreau seems to attract a fair number of celebrity guests." He led them down the passageway, talking into his earbud radio. At the end of the hall, he held the door of the service entrance to a VIP lounge. "We'll wait here. I notified Amtrak that you are ready. One of their people will come get you, and we'll escort you to the train."

They were a half hour early. They helped themselves to espresso and a brioche. Giles and Jack talked shop and exchanged business cards while Maryse chatted with Hilda, and Emily leaned on a column talking with Jean-Pierre.

A burly Amtrak police officer appeared about five minutes before the scheduled departure. Maryse and Jean-Pierre gave their friends a hug and bade them farewell. With the security detail clearing a path, the three Americans found themselves at the baggage car surrendering their bikes in two minutes and safely in their seats just before the train pulled out.

"I like Giles." Jack watched the Saint Lawrence River pass beneath them. "His work seems much more interesting than the typical security firm at a bank."

"Probably because the Bank of Montréal is such a big one," said Hilda. "The physical plant alone would make his job like a PM on an army base, and then there are all the branches."

"And the paparazzi keep things interesting when the bank robbers and terrorists get bored," Emily quipped.

"If we come back for the trials, I hope I meet him again." Jack grinned as Hilda raised one eyebrow.

The ten hours to New York passed smoothly, though when Emily went for a walk to the café car, Hilda insisted on coming along. A Francophone Canadian family with two teenagers and a little girl recognized Emily. She autographed their train tickets for them. The girl stared apprehensively at Hilda at first, but Hilda's smile and friendly demeanor calmed her. *"Elle est si grande!"* She's so tall, they heard the girl tell her parents as they continued to the café car.

Mark and Katherine were waiting on the platform when the train pulled into Grand Central Station.

Emily ran straight into her mother's arms. Katherine seemed ready to cry. Then Emily disengaged and hugged her stepfather.

"Well, Em? How was it?"

"Awesome, Dad." Hilda noticed how Mark stood a little taller and beamed. Emily chattered as they moved to the baggage car to claim their bicycles. They rolled the bikes to the Courtyard Hotel and stored them in the luggage room. After settling into their rooms, they gathered in the Bistro downstairs for a light snack before turning in.

The next morning, the Dempsey van with the bikes on the rack rolled down I-295 to Wilmington. They dropped into Delaware to avoid I-95 around Baltimore and Washington, taking US-50 over the Chesapeake Bay Bridge and US-301 down to the Northern Neck of Virginia. The time went by quickly with all the catching up they had to do.

James and Dorothy Dempsey came out as Mark parked the van in the driveway of their home in Lancaster County. Emily jumped out and ran to hug Mark's parents. Jack and Hilda paused to watch the Dempseys gather around Emily.

"Does this feel like the end of an adventure?" Hilda asked Jack as they removed the bicycles and panniers.

"I'm not sure." He winked. "There's always something happening when you and Emily are around!"

34

RIDING HOME

EMILY DRAGGED MARK'S FATHER TO THE VAN. "I believe you two already know each other."

"Jumping Jack Rathburn!" Jim Dempsey gave Jack a warm handshake and a pat on the arm. "You're none the worse for wear."

"Neither are you, sir."

"Jim. You don't work for me anymore."

"Okay, Jim."

"Jumping Jack?" Emily asked.

"Never mind, Em," Jack said. "It was an old Rolling Stones song that was popular when we were in Korea together."

"More to it than that." Mark's father gave Emily a theatrical wink. "But that's a story for another time."

Hilda and Dorothy had introduced themselves. Together the group got the panniers and bicycles stored in one trip. The second floor had enough bedrooms to start a small hotel; the general and his wife liked having friends and family stop by. Emily got her own room, and there was a room left over.

"That's Bill's," said Dorothy as they walked down the hall.

"How is he?"

"You wouldn't know him, Jack. He's twenty-eight. I expect he'll check in this evening or tomorrow." Seeing Jack's expression, she added, "Don't worry. Believe it or not, you became one of his heroes as he grew up."

"I never saw him after Colonel—I mean, Jim picked him up that day."

"I'll let the two of them tell you about it." She smiled as she led them downstairs.

They gathered on the rear deck, where the house provided shade. Beyond the lawn, the dark, dense trees of Chilton Woods State Forest hid any highways and muffled any traffic that might be out there. Hilda and Katherine had white wine, Dorothy a sherry. Emily opted for orange juice while Mark, Jack, and Jim opened bottles of Beck's Beer.

"Here's to a safe return home." Jim raised his beer. "We want to hear all about your tour."

"Okay, but I want to hear about Jumping Jack when we're done."

Jack blushed as Jim and Dorothy laughed. When the stories reached the Gaspé Peninsula, Jim fired up the grill and sent Jack to the refrigerator for steaks and cod filets. Dorothy started to rise, but Mark was already up, with his hand on her shoulder.

"Stay here, Mom. We've heard the story. We'll get the sides." He left the French doors to the dining room open while he and Katherine set the table. They brought out the potato salad and green beans waiting in the kitchen.

A heavy engine noise approached the front of the house. Emily stopped her description of the 17 percent descent down the Forillon.

"Bill!" Dorothy ran through the house.

She returned with a marine corps captain in his green Service B uniform. He stood a head over his mother, the same height as Mark, but wider in the shoulders and an easy twenty pounds more muscle in his arms and legs. The rows of ribbons on his chest advertised multiple tours in Iraq, Afghanistan, and Somalia. But the Purple Heart and the Bronze Star with a V for valor in combat caught Jack's eye immediately.

"Omigod. I never would have guessed." Jack stood, amazed.

Bill came over to the grill, smiling broadly. He held out his hand to Jack and gave him a firm shake. "I've wanted to see you again, sir. I never forgot a word of that dressing down you gave me in Korea."

Jack was speechless. Mark came over and hugged his brother, who then hugged their father and mother.

"How long can you stay?" she asked.

"Sunday afternoon." Bill started to say something to Jack but changed his mind. "Let me shift into civvies. Get started without me." He disappeared into the house.

"About the descent of the Forillon?" Jim asked Emily. As they finished laying out dinner and seating themselves. Emily continued the story. She, Jack, and Hilda took turns with their respective takes on the south side of Québec until Bill returned in an olive-drab T-shirt and jeans.

"Almost still a uniform," said Jack.

"My gear is packed back at Quantico." Bill took a Beck's from his father. "We fly out Monday."

"Where to?" asked Hilda.

"Can't say, but not far from the last place." That got knowing looks from Mark and Jim.

"Will you be back soon?" Dorothy asked.

"Probably in two weeks—if the situation stays stable."

"Are you stationed at Quantico?" Emily asked.

"Yes, but I'm hardly ever there." Bill eyed Jack. "I'm jumping around more than Jack here."

"That did it!" Emily put down her knife and fork and stared at Jack and Jim. "Someone tell me about 'Jumping Jack'!" The others laughed, and Jack turned to his old CO.

"You started it, Jim."

The general put down his fork and took a sip of water. "Emily, it doesn't seem so funny all these years later. Sitting on the DMZ trying to stay ready for the North Koreans to move when nothing had happened for decades can make you a little goofy. Jack showed up as my new provost marshal. He had been teaching the SRT course at Fort Leonard Wood, Missouri."

"SRT?"

"Sorry. Special Response Team. Like a SWAT team in civilian police forces. It was a new idea in the army at the time. We weren't sure what it was for, except that qualifying was very hard—like the Green Berets or SEAL's."

Dorothy made a rolling motion with her hands, to which the general nodded.

"Anyway, the first week Jack was there, his MP's were called to the enlisted club, where a brawl had started. By the time they arrived, about a hundred men were fighting, and the MP's called for backup. Jack went to the scene, watched the MP's fighting their way from the entrance, then did the most amazing thing. He ran from the door to the edge of the crowd, leaped over the men fighting, doing a full flip, and landed on the bar. His boots made such a noise that the brawlers stopped to look. He barked them to attention, and everyone went quiet.

"The only sound was the refrain of "Jumping Jack Flash" on the jukebox. He ordered everyone to take a seat and sent his MP's into the crowd. As the medics tended the wounded, his men got the names of everyone there, with brief initial statements. It took two weeks to interview everyone, but they got it all sorted out."

"Did you really do a full flip in combat boots?" Emily's eyes were wide in amazement. Jack blushed slightly and shrugged.

"SRT training is very physical."

"Not what I remember," said Bill.

"You were thirteen," said his father. "What did you remember?"

"He was something of a legend at school. I remember that the MP's kids used to say when he told you to do something, you jumped."

"Good advice, son."

"I just can't believe all these cool stories about you, Jack," said Emily, suppressing the urge to giggle. "You've done so many crazy things in Germany and Korea."

"Enough about me." Jack turned to Bill. "How on earth did you end up in the service—and a jarhead no less?"

The marine laughed. "That's not the half of it. Those guys in your SRT were some of the baddest guys any of us had ever seen. I remembered what you told me about being ready to run into danger instead of away from it." He cocked his head toward his father, then said, "You know that Dad sent me away to Fork Union Military Academy, right?"

"I didn't know it was FUMA, but I recall your leaving."

"They straightened me out. All I needed was a little more structure—more than Mom and Dad could provide. I found that I really liked it, so I joined the marines."

"Why the Corps?"

"Partly to stick it to Dad." He smiled at his father. "But mostly it seemed better not to be in the army as famous as he was becoming."

"Makes sense. I know 'every marine is a rifleman,' but what's your specialty?"

"Security Battalion."

Jack's jaw dropped. "You're an MP?" Bill grinned.

Jim added, "There's more. Those two-week trips he takes? He leads field training and certification for SRT's. I told you that you made an impression."

Dinner continued with lively conversation as they reviewed their respective careers and discussed Hilda's new job and Emily's plans. The yawning did not start until midnight.

The next morning, Jim had a tee-time with Mark and some friends. Bill took Jack for a hike into the Chilton Woods State Forest. Emily and Katherine went for a ride while Hilda helped Dorothy put up the fruit that she had picked for canning. They made preserves and jam, and canned peaches, apricots, blueberries, and blackberries. Working in the spacious kitchen put Hilda in a nostalgic mood. She shared her memories of canning with her mother in Kaiserslautern every autumn.

The two riders returned about eleven.

"Jim called," said Dorothy. "They're going to join Jack and Bill at the deli in Alonso for lunch."

"They walked to Alonso?" asked Katherine.

"I'll bet they never noticed the distance or the time. Between the shop talk and the catching up, can you imagine how much they have to say to each other?"

"As soon as we stretch and shower, we'll be down to help."

"Lunch first, but then you can join us," said Dorothy.

Emily and Katherine ran up the stairs.

"You're riding very fast, Emily," said Katherine as they stretched in the hall. "Is that safe?"

"I'm still using the computer to keep my speed down, but I think I'm ready for training. When I don't have a load on the bike, it's too easy."

"Well, I hope Dr. Morgan agrees with you. Do you want me to schedule an appointment?"

"Done. Next Friday at two."

"Oh. Okay, I guess." Katherine suppressed a sigh. "May I go first?"

"Sure. I have another two routines to do."

Emily's mother went to her room and into the shower, where she let the water hide her tears.

That evening, thunderstorms rolled in from the west, so they gathered in the living room for the six o'clock news. As they expected, Charlottesville dominated the coverage from the local station.

"Charlottesville's been in the news for weeks." Dorothy gestured to Mark and Katherine. "Doesn't that worry you all?"

"Things have been quiet so far," said Katherine. "You probably noticed that all the coverage has been about last year. The city rejected all permits for rallies, but the town looks like an armed camp with all the police preparations. I can't complain about being here this weekend."

"We're happy to have you. All of you." She gestured at the six visitors.

Jim asked, "Are you still planning to go back on Monday? You could stay longer."

"Thanks, Dad," said Mark, "but I need to check in Monday afternoon."

"And I have a faculty meeting on Tuesday morning." Katherine rolled her eyes.

"Emily and her bodyguards don't have to go, do they?" He let the question hang.

Emily perked up. "I have an idea! We could ride home from here. Then we would have biked out and back."

"You haven't had enough?" asked Mark.

"No way. It's only two hundred and ten kilometers. We could leave Monday morning and be home Tuesday afternoon."

Katherine's reaction went from surprise to understanding in a quick stream of subtle expressions.

"I can see Emily's point," said Hilda. "I know the roads out there. Scenic and low traffic. Instead of camping, we could use a motel near I-95. We could put what we don't need in the van."

"After Dorothy's great meals, I'll be ready for another ride," said Jack, rubbing his flat stomach.

"What do you think, Mark?" asked Katherine.

"Sounds like a plan to me."

Supper was another feast, capped with some of the fresh berries that had not been canned, and vanilla ice cream.

The next day was Sunday. They all went to Saint Mary's Church in Lancaster for the 11:15 service. Bill hugged his parents and brother in the parking lot and rode off to Quantico.

Dorothy's gaze followed Bill's motorcycle. "I worry every time he leaves." She looked at Mark. "Why didn't it feel like this with you?"

"For one, I was in the Air Force, and he's a grunt. For another, I was an engineer, and he's SRT. Finally, he's your baby. I was old news when he came along."

"You're sweet." She squeezed his arm. "And you always were so grown-up and wise."

"Is this Mark we're talking about?" Katherine asked. They laughed as they piled into the car.

They drove to the Sandpiper Restaurant for lunch. In the afternoon, Emily, Jack, and Hilda checked their gear and cleaned and oiled their chains. Each packed one pannier to leave in the van and another to take with them. More thunderstorms kept them indoors for the rest of the day. They played Trivial Pursuit, which Emily had not seen, but excelled at in the Entertainment category.

"We should have used an older edition," grumbled Jim cheerfully. "Something with the Beatles, Rolling Stones, and Buddy Holly in it."

"Oh, come on, honey," said Dorothy. "Everybody has their top category. We're all acing Geography and History. Mark has the Science cornered. Hilda and Katherine know everything else."

Emily crawled into her bed that night as the rain pounded on the roof. She felt excited and sad at the same time. Soon she would be back home, and her great adventure would be over. But Tani, Mariana, Fran, Amber, and Megan would be there. She could start training again. And her first year at the University of Virginia loomed ahead like an epic quest on the ocean of life.

The next morning, the air filled their lungs with that cool freshness that follows a cleansing rain. The front took the energy out of the summer air, leaving pleasant temperatures all day. Route 3 out of Lancaster County had more traffic than they expected, but there were generous shoulders or bike lanes through the more congested areas.

They had lunch at a seafood restaurant in Tappahannock. From there, they continued generally west on lightly traveled country roads. At five o'clock, they checked into the Centerstone Inn in Doswell, next to the massive King's Dominion amusement park. Hilda was surprised that they had been able to reserve a room.

"Monday is their only relatively quiet night of the week in season," she said after returning with their room keys.

The Inn had a diner with twenty-four-hour service, and none of them felt like going out. They were asleep by nine.

Tuesday, they crossed under Interstate 95 and continued to Bumpass, Mineral, Louisa, and Trevillians. The land rose ever so gently, rolling rather than flat. Pine woods and forests extended on either side, not as dense as in Québec or the Eastern Shore, but fondly familiar.

They picked up lunch at the K&B Mart grocery store in Trevillians and ate it under the trees at the intersection of US-33 and Highway 22. Motorcycles and pickup trucks roared by on US-33 in both directions.

"Hilda?" Emily said as they bagged up their trash. "Is it my imagination, or have we seen more Confederate flags today than usual?"

"I'm not sure, Em. It seems like a lot to me, but then, the hair goes up on the back of my neck whenever I see one."

"I think there may be more," said Jack. "Most don't have Virginia plates, so I figure they were visiting DC or someplace else over the weekend."

"Well, I hope there's nothing going on when we get home." Hilda's face was grim, and her gaze focused down the road. They mounted up and rode. Emily knew this territory because some of her training rides had been out Highway 22 and back. They were only a couple of hours from home.

They fed onto US-250 (the original Three Chopt Road of colonial times) at Shadwell and flew in single file down the ravine and back up again. The highway bent to the right to go under Interstate 64. They saw blue flashing lights ahead.

On the ramp to and from the interstate, groups of men were waving Confederate flags and shouting at the passing motorists. The police had stationed themselves off to the sides, where they could intervene if anything happened.

"Should we wait or keep riding?" asked Emily.

"Press on and don't stop," said Hilda.

"Okay," said Jack. "Hilda, take point." He fell in behind Emily. They sped up, but the double set of traffic lights turned red before they could make the intersection. As they waited, the men closest to them, on the eastbound ramp, spotted Hilda and started moving toward them. She saw the swastika tattoos and patches and tensed up, even as she stared at the light, trying to keep her calm.

"Looks like she don't know her place," said a burly man with an untrimmed beard shot through with gray. The others laughed.

Jack twisted to see the officers in the patrol car and waved until he had their attention. He gestured to the approaching men. The officer hit the siren in a pair of short bursts. The men stopped.

The lights turned green. Hilda and Emily were going twenty-five kilometers per hour by the time they reached the second light and raced past the second crowd of hecklers. Jack caught up with the women as they slowed on the climb up Pantops Mountain.

"Welcome home?" he said. Hilda glared at him.

"Not local," said Emily. "I checked the plates on their trucks as we went by."

Hilda rode in a dark fury as she led them over the Free Bridge, and along the bike lanes of the John W. Warner Parkway.

The van was in the driveway when they pulled up to Emily's home. Katherine's Specialized Diverge was in the bicycle storage space. She came out as Emily was just about to shout. Her daughter gave her a tight hug.

"I'm glad to be home, Mom."

Katherine held on tightly, then she turned to the others. "Do you want to come in for a while?"

"Thanks, Katherine," said Hilda, "but I'd like to use the bathroom, then pick up my stuff and head home. I'll be back soon."

"Is everything okay?"

"Yes, fine, but I need some time alone."

"We had to ride past a crowd of Confederate flag-wavers with swastikas and attitudes at the I-64 ramp," said Emily. "It wasn't pretty. Jack got the police to scare them off."

Katherine took Hilda's arm. "Call me if you need anything. Your panniers and tent are right here by the door."

Jack had said nothing. He quietly collected the tent and his pannier. He followed Hilda back to her apartment. They took the bikes up in the elevator, which was easier than lugging the panniers and tent.

"You want to be alone?" he asked as she got out her keys.

"From everyone else, yes, but I need you around now more than ever."

Except to slip out for a burger and groceries that night, they did not leave the apartment for two days....

PART FOUR

EMILY, HILDA & JACK

35

FIFTH STREET

F RIDAY MORNING, HILDA HEARD THE COFFEE MAKER gurgling and spitting in the kitchen. She opened her eyes and smiled. Jack's hard body fit her back like a glove.

She could not think of a better way to start her day.

Jack blew on the back of her neck.

"I know you're awake."

"How?"

"Your breathing changed."

"The happy sigh?"

"No. That came later."

"How long have you been awake?"

"Just before you."

"You set the coffee maker?"

"Uh-huh. I found the instructions last night." He put his arm over her and squeezed. "Ready to get up?"

"Actually, yes. Thank you for putting up with me."

"You're welcome. Still resigned to staying in Charlottesville for Dr. Osborne?"

"Not resigned any more. I'm looking forward to it. I really liked him at the interview. Besides, Charlottesville is safer than most other places."

"I would agree with you. Shall we sally forth in domesticity and love, then?"

Hilda turned around and put her face nose-to-nose with his. "What does that mean?"

"I was thinking of taking all the panniers empty to Wegman's and stock up the apartment at least. Do some laundry, then maybe take in a movie tonight or see who's playing at the Pavilion."

"That sounds like a plan." She threw the covers back and sprang from the bed. Jack rolled out, and they both donned bathrobes before trooping to the kitchen for some fresh coffee.

"Emily has her follow-up appointment with Dr. Morgan today. I agreed to go with her."

"Where will you meet her?"

"She's coming here at one thirty."

"Okay. I want to walk to the Corner to check out what's new, but I should be here when you get back."

After the rain Wednesday and Thursday, it was refreshing to ride out the bike lanes on Fifth Street. The sun was brilliant, but the air carried the omen of fall coming soon. There would be more hot, muggy days, but not stretches of them.

They spent an hour in Wegmans supermarket, restocking all the perishables that the apartment lacked. On the way back, Hilda pointed to a two-story brick house set back from Ridge Street. With its broad porch and ancient magnolia trees in the yard, it seemed to welcome visitors who came by foot or got off at the bus stop in front.

"Dr. Osborne's place," she said. "It's not that much farther from my place than the ER was in the other direction."

"Good." Jack pointed to the small wooden sign near the door. "Not much for advertising, is he?"

"He doesn't need to. I talked to some of the families I know from UVA. He's been the neighborhood doctor for twenty years. Grew up here and went to Charlottesville High School. He did his residency in Richmond, and he's been here ever since."

"A real family doctor, then?"

"Yup, like something from a 1950s TV show. Very homey. But he's sharp, and he keeps up with the research better than most of the doctors I've worked for."

"I'd like to meet him."

"You probably will at some point if you stick around."

A short siren burst behind them startled them both. A Charlottesville motorcycle officer pulled up alongside and waved them over. They straddled their bikes and waited for the officer to park his steed in the bike lane and come toward them. He was about Jack's size, and his snug uniform emphasized his excellent physical condition.

Jack was sure that they were not doing anything illegal riding down the bike lane. Then he saw Hilda grin.

"Walter, you son of a gun! You shouldn't scare us like that!" Hilda swung around to Jack. "Jack Rathburn, Sergeant Walter Johnson. I told you about him."

The two men shook hands. "Fast work stopping Lee in the ER. Congratulations."

"Thanks." Walter frowned and looked down. "He was my first one. It still bothers me."

"Sorry. I've been there," said Jack. "If the feeling never goes away, you'll know you're still normal and healthy."

"Thanks again." Walter smiled at them. "Hey, Hilda, I can't believe you're back. The place has been dead since you took off with Emily."

"Not judging from the news."

"At least this time, we were prepared. Oops, that's the third cyclist that has had to go around my bike. I better go. Shariq's having a birthday party soon. How can I get hold of you?"

"Dr. Osborne. I start after Labor Day."

Walter gave her a thumbs-up as he mounted his motorcycle and sped toward downtown.

As they rode the elevator up to the apartment, Jack said, "You haven't been here a year, and you already are tight with the local police, the local Marcus Welby, the local church, and people all over town."

Hilda thought about that as they pushed their bikes to the door and she got out her key. "Makes it home—like all the other places I've lived before."

At one thirty exactly, the doorbell rang. Emily stood in the doorway, grinning. She was in her bicycle kit and holding her Colnago racing bicycle.

"Hi, Hilda. Are you ready?"

"Of course. Want to walk or ride?"

"Can I leave my bike here? The UVA team is having its first training ride for anyone who is here early, and I want to be there."

"Assuming that Dr. Morgan clears you."

"He has to. He even called Mom last week to make sure I got X-rays yesterday."

"Bring in your bike and change your shoes." Emily leaned her bike against the wall and traded out her cleated road shoes for a pair of Keene sandals. "If you don't need the sandals afterwards, I can bring them over tomorrow, so you won't have to carry them in your jersey pockets."

Jack came out from the kitchen area and gave Emily a hug. "Good luck." He looked at Hilda. "Let me know." Hilda gave him a thumbs-up. The two women left him and walked to the UVA Medical Center.

Ω Ω Ω

Emily turned pale while sitting in the waiting room. "Oh, Hilda, what if there's something still not right?"

"After all this time, it's unlikely. But what if there is? We're in the best place possible to do something about it."

"I guess so."

"You have your heart set on racing again, don't you?"

"If nothing else, I want to come back as well or better than before. The touring this summer showed me a life after racing, but I want to race while I can, if I can."

Hilda patted her knee. "You have no bad options, Em."

The nurse called for Emily. Hilda pulled out her phone to read a book, but the nurse came back out right away.

"Emily doesn't need a guardian, but she asked if you could join them. Dr. Morgan agreed."

"Thank you." Hilda followed her down a short hallway to an exam room.

Dr. Morgan waved and pointed to a chair in the corner, then continued checking Emily's lungs with his stethoscope. The X-rays hung on light boxes on the wall. He went through the standard physical routine—tapping knees, testing for sensation in the feet, checking skin and range of motion of her arms and legs. Finally, he stared for a long time at the X-rays.

"Enough in here. Let's go to my office."

The office held a large desk and two visitor's chairs. Medical books lined the walls, with no room for certificates or pictures. Hilda knew what they would have been from his online biography. They took their seats in front of the desk while Dr. Morgan went around to his big chair.

"Emily, frankly, I'm surprised—calm down, young lady. This is good news. Usually, some permanent sign of the fractures should be visible, but I consulted with two radiologists, and they can't see anything either. We've never seen such a complete healing."

"Can I train now?" Emily sat on the edge of her chair, and her eyes widened in expectation.

"Yes," he said with a smile. "You're fully released. Just look out for oil spots on the road."

"I learned to look out for more than that this summer."

"I saw the news. Impressive." He looked at Hilda.

"Nurse Paisley, thank you. I'm convinced that she wouldn't have healed this well without the steady exercise of the tour with you. And I'm especially grateful that you brought her back to me in one piece." He rose, and they shook hands.

Emily was glowing with excitement on the way back to Hilda's apartment. Hilda was glad that her stride was longer than Emily's, or she would have had to run.

Jack had a pair of protein bars in his hands when they walked in.

"I know you won't stay for coffee, but here's a pickup to put in your pockets." He slipped them into her jersey as she bent over to put on her cleated shoes.

"Thanks, Jack. Mariana said that they would be at the Aquatics and Fitness building in about fifteen minutes. I can just make it."

She gave them both a hug and clattered out the door.

"I take it there were no surprises." He poured two mugs of coffee.

"Actually, there were. She healed so completely that her bones showed no marks from the fractures. That's extremely rare."

"Morgan and his friends did some extremely rare work on her, I'll bet."

"They did. I'm glad that we're going to the Dempseys for dinner tomorrow. I can't wait to see how she feels after her first training ride with no holds barred."

They sipped their coffee in silence for a minute. Hilda liked the fact that Jack always waited before changing the subject.

"I called Ted while you were gone."

"Any news?"

"Nothing new on anyone chasing us. He'd talked to Pete. They have two cases that they are collaborating on, in addition to the Forebears. But guess who's in town?"

"Here or there?"

"Charlottesville." He smiled when she shrugged.

"Tony Monroe."

"Your deputy in Baghdad?"

"The same. He's the new PM at Rivanna Station out on US-29 North."

"The National Ground Intelligence Center. Big job."

"Rivanna Station is a small base now, but NGIC is not the only activity. More are coming in."

"I'm happy for him. He impressed me."

"Me too. Anyway, I agreed to ride out to pay him a visit on Monday."

Hilda's phone rang. *Dr. Osborne*, she mouthed with a surprised look.

"Hello, Dr. Osborne. I was going to call you this afternoon...the twenty-seventh? I guess I could. Yes... Until then, sir. Bye." She ended the call. "Seems that one of his nurses was injured in a car crash last week, and he would like me on board before the school year starts."

"That's okay, isn't it?"

"Unless you have something planned."

"Nope. I haven't planned anything farther than Fridays After Five today at the Downtown Mall."

They put their mugs in the dishwasher, then showered and changed to walk to the mall.

ఆ ఆ ఆ

Emily's legs burned, but her main problem was air. There was something different about her breathing. She could not find the balance she needed between frequency and volume of each inhalation.

Mariana, Megan, and Amber did not seem to be working as hard as she was, but no one was much for conversation as they blew down and up one ravine after another until they reached Route 151 and turned south into Nelson County.

Riding parallel to the watershed provided some relief, and she concentrated on her breathing even as she kept up speed with the others. They took turns pacing the drafting line, which became more efficient on the 151 and Highway 6. Before she knew it, they were turning north on US-29 near the museum dedicated to *The Waltons* TV show and heading back to Charlottesville. Long-haul truckers favored this section of US-29, but the women were used to the traffic, and the shoulder was wide and smooth.

By five o'clock they were rolling into Charlottesville on Fontaine Avenue, spinning out easily as they cooled down. They locked their bikes outside Starbucks on the Corner, where they could keep an eye on them from inside.

"I'm buying," said Mariana. "You're on your own the rest of the year."

They lined up at the cash register. Emily recognized the tall blond barista from before her tour.

"Strawberry Frappuccino, no whip and a scoop of protein?" he asked.

"You remembered!" said Emily. She admired him as he ran off each rider's favorite drink and rang up the tab.

"Haven't seen you all summer. How's your handsome lieutenant?"

Emily blushed. "How do you know about him?"

"My Facebook friends in Montréal went gaga over you." He leaned over the register. "With all those paparazzi, someone had to put out a couple of memes of you two. More fun than Megan and Harry."

Emily groaned, but she also smiled. The barista made her feel welcome, and she enjoyed being back where people knew her for herself. She joined the others at the pickup point, and they carried their cold drinks back to the front window.

"How is everyone?" asked Mariana.

Megan and Amber said "fine," but they had been racing all summer and were in top shape.

"I'm not so fine." The coach patted her stomach. "I spent the last month with my family without the bike. How about you, Em?"

"I'm out of shape, but mainly because my breathing was off. I didn't expect that. And I did not miss the ravines touring this summer."

"They're a workout, all right," said Amber. "None of the racecourses have the interval training effect of those ravines."

"You kept up pretty good, Em," said Mariana. "I think you're going to rock again next year."

"Well, don't ask me tomorrow. I'll bet I pay for this little metric century."

Mariana gave her a hug. "I'm so glad that you're back. Look, guys, I gotta run home. See you Tuesday?" They waved and watched Mariana clatter back to her bike.

Emily and her friends finished their drinks, catching up on the races that Megan and Amber had done that summer. They both had followed Emily's kidnapping thanks to *Velo News* but were not aware of her other adventures. Emily did not volunteer much; what they had read was exciting enough. They gave each other a parting hug by the bike rack. Emily rode over to Cabell Hall in time to catch her mother coming out, so they could ride home together.

☙ ☙ ☙

Saturday evening, Jack and Hilda rode to Brandywine Drive for dinner. It felt familiar and safe.

"I'm glad to see you unwound, Hilda. May I ask what upset you about those men on the I-64 ramp? Emily tried to explain it, but I'd like your perspective." Mark and Emily stopped chatting with Jack. They looked at her expectantly. Jack gave her a small smile of encouragement.

"It was more than the clowns at I-64, Katherine," she said. "It was the whole day. Just about from the moment we left Doswell, one truck or motorcycle after another went by flying the Stars and Bars or sporting swastikas or both. I was a wreck by the time we reached that ramp."

Katherine paused. "I know a thing or two about oppression, being a student of feminist literature, but you seemed to handle all that Confederate flag stuff before. What was different on Tuesday?"

"It was the combination, and all that it brought up for me. After I joined the army, I had to learn about being black in America, including learning to understand the Confederate flag as a threat.

"But I'm also half German. As a child, being black didn't mean anything to me, but I grew up keenly aware of the scars my mother's people carry from the Nazi era. Swastikas are illegal in Germany, and everyone's very sensitive about that dark part of our history. Seeing those two symbols flaunted again and again just got to me. I've never felt so depressed and discouraged in my life."

She looked at Jack and put her hand out to him. "Thanks."

"Thank you too," said Katherine. "I've tried to understand how these symbols work. Sometimes just doing my research gets me down. I admire your guts."

They ate silently for a while. Then Hilda asked, "On a different note, you're not limping, Em. How was training yesterday?"

"I'm sore, but not as much as I expected to be. The riding this summer kept things in better shape than I expected."

"It's fun with no load, isn't it?"

"Yes, but they were going much faster than we let me go on the tour. My breathing was screwed up. We rode a hundred kilometers, and I didn't get the balance right until we were almost back in Charlottesville."

"Sounds like you're already working it out."

"Oh, yes. But I'll need to work on those ravines and ride longer distances."

"I think our days as Emily's riding partners are over, Katherine."

"I think so. Would you like to pedal around with an old lady once in a while?"

"Sure. Maybe we could get Jack and Mark to come along—just to make them feel bad."

The two men laughed as heartily as the women.

"Deal, then. If the Pinarello's too fast, I can ride the Diverge to even us up."

They agreed to meet on Tuesdays and Thursdays after work.

That night back in the apartment, Hilda lay in Jack's arms and stared at the ceiling.

"Everyone's home and settling in for a routine year, except you. What are you going to do when I go to work?"

"One day at a time, dear. I've more choices than I want to consider, and I think a couple more may come up soon."

"You mean Giles in Montréal?"

"Or Ted in Aberdeen, or a half-dozen other army buddies who could use my skill set."

"I'll hate to see you go."

"You may not have to. Let's see what happens."

She did not want to think about it. Instead, she rolled over and kissed him....

36

RIVANNA STATION

MONDAY MORNING, SUMMER CAME BACK. Jack rode the bike lanes up Rio Hill and the bike path on US-29 north of Charlottesville under a cloudless sky. He appreciated not having headwinds, but he would have welcomed a breeze. His bicycle kit was soaked by the time he reached the Starbucks at Hollymead Town Center. He stopped there to change into street clothes, glad that he had brought a pack of hospital bathing cloths from Hilda's stash.

There was a decent shoulder for the last three kilometers to Rivanna Station. The concrete and glass complex rose on his right as he coasted to the light. Across the highway, new housing developments sprouted out of the newly turned earth. It would be a while before enough vegetation grew in to make the neighborhood look mature. He took a right turn and climbed to the main gate.

The guard checked his ID and directed him to the Pass & ID office. The MP on duty gave him a crisp salute—and a smile. Jack read the name strip on his desert utilities, "Aspen."

"Major Monroe is expecting you, sir. Your badge and vehicle tag are right here."

"Thank you." He clipped the badge to the flap on his shirt pocket. It was a regular badge with his name and rank printed on it, but no picture. "Your name is familiar."

"Yes, sir. Baghdad. I checked in just before the… uh…the IED incident."

"That was only the day before I left, wasn't it?" Jack recognized the soldier's pleasure at seeing him. Ted, Hilda, Joe, and his army friends had looked at him the same way after his release from Walter Reed Hospital.

"Yes, sir. I thought we'd lost you for sure."

Jack signed the clipboard for the badge. Someone had filled in all his information, correctly. Jack held up the vehicle tag.

"Do I need this for my bicycle?"

"Bicycle?" Aspen recovered quickly. "Er, no, sir. You can lock it over there while I call someone to get you." He pointed to a covered bike rack across the driveway.

"Thanks. I'll be right back."

When he returned, a sergeant in desert utilities was holding the door by the counter for him. With her black hair tightly coiled in a bun and her diminutive stature, one might mistake her for someone's kid sister, but Jack knew she could bring down two men twice her size in close combat. He also knew that her family lived in Mineral, not far away.

"Sergeant Martinez! You too? Has Major Monroe assembled a whole mafia here?"

She laughed. "No, sir. I went back to Brigade HQ in Germany after our deployment. I was there when I saw Captain—I mean, Major Monroe's orders. I was able to time my transfer with this opening." She led him down a hall past the ceremonial lobby and up the stairs to the administration wing.

"I'll bet he's glad."

"It's working out all around, sir." They reached the provost marshal's office. "You still take your coffee black, sir?" Jack grinned and nodded. She smiled as she opened the door and closed it behind him.

The man who came around the desk stood as tall as Jack but outweighed him by twenty pounds—all muscle. He had been a champion boxer at West Point, and the SRT training had only toughened him more. His short-cropped hair was turning grizzled. The hair and the scars from the ring and from combat made him seem somewhat older than a man in his thirties.

"Damn, it's good to see you, sir."

"You don't work for me, Tony. Make it Jack, not sir." He held out his arms. They gave each other the kind of bear hug only men give who have been through hell together.

"I've seen Aspen and Martinez. Are you building a private army?"

"Not on purpose. Martinez got her own transfer, but I would've asked for her if I'd known she was due to rotate. You look great! Is that for real?"

"Pretty much. The first year out of the hospital was a little rocky, but I recovered. I heard about the work you did with the unit. I knew you'd handle it. You're a natural."

"I was scared shitless every day after you left, but the troops fell in and made it work. They loved you, Jack, even when you were giving them hell."

"Well, congratulations, Major—early, but you deserve it! Did I read that you trained up five thousand Iraqi police before you came back?"

"Something like that." Tony dropped his gaze. If his complexion would have allowed it, he would have blushed.

A knock on the door preceded another MP coming in with a tray of coffee and Turkish delights in a small dish. He set it down on the sideboard. Tony pointed to him.

"Major Rathburn, Specialist Hughes."

The MP seemed almost embarrassed, but he took Jack's hand and gave it a sturdy squeeze. "It's an honor to meet you, sir."

"Likewise."

"Anything else, sir?" he asked Tony.

"Tell Sergeant Martinez I'll give the major a walk around, and I won't forget the staff meeting at eleven hundred."

"Yes, sir." Hughes took another look at Jack and pulled the door behind him on the way out.

"Did I scare him?" Jack asked.

"Not at all. You're something of a legend among the MP's here. The ones who didn't serve with you personally followed you in the Eighteenth Brigade or SRT school."

"It feels weird." Jack took one of the sweets. "What's with the delicacies?"

"A civilized custom I brought home with me."

"These are delicious! Not like gummy bears."

"I have them sent over from a Turkish sweets shop in Grafenwöhr."

They finished their coffee, catching up on personal details. The day that Jack was evacuated, Tony's wife Beulah was wounded by shrapnel from a terrorist bomb while shopping at the supermarket in Grafenwöhr. The Brigade tried to fly a relief out for Tony, but the relief never left before Beulah came to in the hospital and convinced the CO to let her husband do his job. They both dealt with PTSD when the MP unit returned from Iraq. He got the assignment at NGIC partly to put them closer to Beulah's family in Richmond.

"She's a remarkable woman," said Jack. "You're both okay?"

"We're fine. I don't think we could have come to know each other as well as we do without sharing that dark year in Germany. It was mostly waking up from nightmares and having someone there who understood."

"I know what you mean." They let the silence linger for a while, each looking beyond the other's shoulders. Tony came to first.

"Where next? No. Tell me on the way. I want to give you the tour in time to get back here for the weekly purgatory." He motioned to the door as they got up.

"Staff meetings that bad?"

"Not really, but we like to joke about them. Colonel Richardson runs an efficient meeting. Never more than an hour, no matter how many tweets come out of the White House."

"Kathleen Richardson?"

"The very same." Tony stopped at the next door. "In here."

"Tony! I wasn't expecting to meet your CO." He indicated his trekking shirt and trousers and his cloth biking shoes.

"Too late. She told me to bring you in." He opened the door. The sergeant at the desk rose. "Major Rathburn to meet the CO."

She turned to the door, opened it, and announced the two majors, then held the door open for them. Jack read her name badge, "Walker."

"You dog," he muttered to Tony. "You set this up ahead of time."

"But of course." Tony grinned. "I'm Rathburn-trained."

The woman at the desk stood five feet, eleven inches, but her presence made her look even taller. She was big-boned, but trim, so that her fitness came across as strength instead of slimness. Her expression at rest appeared severe to Jack until she smiled. Then he noticed that her face had more smile lines than scowl lines. The severity of her face came from the position of her eyes and eyebrows, the former deep-set and the latter turning down toward her nose. She could intimidate without frowning. *A convenient trait*, he thought.

"Colonel Richardson, Major Rathburn," said Tony.

"I'm delighted you could visit us, Major." Her handshake was firm. "I knew that Major Monroe had worked for you, so when I learned you were in Charlottesville, I asked him to have you come by."

Jack was speechless. Tony shrugged. "I told you that you're a legend."

"Indeed," said the colonel, "and I was stationed at DIA with Colonel Harper before he went to Aberdeen. He had some fine things to say about you and Major Paisley when I saw him last month in DC, since she was in the news."

"Sometimes I think we have the smallest army in the world," said Jack, smiling.

Tony covered his surprise with a grin. "I was going to give him a short tour—in time for the staff meeting."

"Bring him along," she said. "I'd like him to see us *chez nous* as it were." She turned to Jack. "You were cleared at Aberdeen, so you can go just about anywhere except the code room." She pointed to Jack's chest. "That's why we gave you a regular ID badge instead of a visitor pass." She indicated the door and shook hands again. "See you at eleven." Tony held the door for Jack.

As they walked down the hall, Jack whispered, "Why do I feel like I'm being set up?"

"Maybe you are. This is an intel command, not a normal base, and Richardson's one of the best. She probably had a full background investigation done on you before I found out you were in town! Here's the Requirements Department." He held another door.

The next hour was more like an orientation tour than a guest visit. Tony introduced him to the people in the various departments and asked them to explain what they did.

Jack knew that NGIC sent battlefield intelligence at the tactical level to the troops in the field. But he was impressed by the detail on their displays and the in-depth knowledge of the analysts and coordinators. Most had been to the places that they were monitoring.

Just before eleven, they walked to the briefing room.

Kathleen Richardson did run a tight meeting. As the different department heads gave their reports, she never let any item turn into a discussion unless it had been scheduled for discussion. Instead, she immediately appointed two or three people to take the subject off-line and report back to her the next day. Items scheduled for "discussion" had been staffed by the stakeholders, so the report was usually descriptive, with confirmation of consensus by those concerned.

When they adjourned, Jack was surprised that only forty-five minutes had passed.

"She could teach management at a business school," he told Tony as they walked back to the PM's office.

"She did—Army War College at Leavenworth."

"I'd better Google everyone I meet today. There are some impressive people here."

They walked down to the cafeteria. After lunch, Jack followed Tony on his rounds. His MP's had the usual guard and inspection duties, but Tony also had people in strategic locations around the building, looking like ordinary employees. Most were able to keep an eye on the perimeter and the undeveloped land around Rivanna Station as well as the sightlines down the hallways outside their offices.

Tony explained. "The army gives everyone more than enough paperwork. They can do that dispersed like this as easily as in a common office. Their weapons are under the desks in special holders. Protective gear in the desk drawers, of course."

Jack was impressed. "Like having an SRT deployed before anything happens."

"Something like that." Tony smiled.

About three o'clock, they were having coffee back in Tony's office.

"The personnel officer, Lieutenant—"

"Robbins. Kirsten Robbins."

"Right. What was she talking about, having trouble filling the vacancy for an IED and network analyst? That sounds weird."

"It's actually two jobs. One is an expert on IED's, either someone from Bomb Disposal or an analyst who has studied them. The other is an analyst who tracks insurgent networks. They're civilian positions, but we can't find the right people. Colonel Richardson has Robbins scouring the Personnel Command for some active-duty types to order in, at least until some veterans from the war decide to leave their high-paying defense contractor jobs to work for Uncle Sam again."

Tony paused to sip from his mug. "The CO'd be happy to get one person for both jobs. There's a good flow of intel built up, so it should not be hard to keep up with the new info coming in on both subjects."

"Why is it so difficult to fill the position? I mean, apart from the pay. This looks like a good place to work."

"I'm glad you think so. If I were about to retire— or maybe when I do—I'd like to come back here. But the IED slash Network Analyst job requires the highest security clearances and reasonably good health.

What kind of shape are most people in, who have become intimately familiar with IED's and insurgents?"

"Good point. That's tough."

"Yeah, it is, but they'll keep digging until they find someone – then Richardson will work the WWW."

"The internet?"

"Her Washington Wonder Woman act."

Jack laughed. "Really?"

"She's awesome, man. You noticed she doesn't wear utilities? That's because she almost always has meetings outside with important people. She can manage a room better than anyone I know."

"Does she ever wear utilities?"

"When she does, that means it's quiet on both sides of the Beltway and in Charlottesville. And that she will visit every one of us that day."

Jack finished his coffee. It was three thirty. "I'd better go. You have paperwork left, and you've been taking care of me almost all day."

"Not so fast. The CO wants me to bring you by before you go. Let me call her."

"I can feel where this is going, but why not? I like interesting women, and she is definitely interesting."

Tony hit a speed dial button on his desk phone. "Hello, Sergeant. Could you tell the colonel that Major Rathburn is about done here? Does she still want him to come by? Got it. Thanks." He hung up.

"She just got in, and she'd like you to come down."

They walked around to the commander's office again. Sergeant Walker rose, smiled, knocked on the door, and opened it for them.

Colonel Richardson was hanging her uniform jacket in the closet. She turned and motioned to the chair in front of her desk. "I just got back from a meeting at the JAG School." She pointed to the other chair. "You can stay, too, Major Monroe, if you like."

"If you don't mind, I'd like to wrap up a couple of things in my office. I think he can find his way back." He saluted and left.

Jack realized that this was not a simple exit call. The colonel walked behind her desk.

"Coffee?"

"Just had some, but I could always have another."

She glanced at her sergeant, who disappeared. Kathleen Richardson sat and looked intently at Jack for a moment.

"May I ask what struck you about NGIC today?" She smiled. Jack understood why she had to smile a lot, even when her eyes remained intense.

"I was very impressed with Major Monroe's operation, especially the idea of deploying his sentries inconspicuously."

"Anything else?"

"A couple of things. The detail of the intel coming in and going out. I was the beneficiary in the field, but I never appreciated what it must look like from this end. The people you have working here are amazing."

Sergeant Walker brought in the coffee, which Jack recognized as an Ethiopian single roast from Starbucks. He had grown fond of African coffees on deployment. The colonel sipped her coffee and invited him to continue with a hand motion. Walker stepped out.

"I'm getting the distinct impression that you set up my visit here—much as I'm delighted to see Tony Monroe again. May I ask why?"

"Let me ask you some things, Major." She put down her coffee and opened a folder on her desk. "Do you recognize these?"

Jack took up the eight-by-ten color photos. Improvised explosive devices in various stages of deployment.

"This is a classic buried bomb, detonated by wire. Most are wireless today, using a cell phone. This is the bomb in a dead animal—in this case, the dog and/or the sheep, not the cat. And this is the undercarriage of a Honda sedan with two sticks of dynamite taped to the rear axle."

He looked up at the CO. "That's getting personal, ma'am. I took that shot."

She put the photos back in the folder and took out a sheet of paper. "Quiz time. I have a hunch about you. I give you a name, you tell me where you know them from or if you don't know them."

Jack met her eyes. They were blue gray, like steel. "It's obvious that you're looking for the IED slash network analyst that Lieutenant Robbins briefed this morning. If you want me, just ask, ma'am."

Her smile turned into a tight line, then relaxed.

"Let's put it this way. I've heard more about you than I want to believe. Let me check you out for myself. May I?"

Jack thought for a moment, then smiled. "Why not? Go ahead."

She read from the paper.

"Forebears of the Mahdi."

"Baghdad, Mosul, Chicago—lately Montréal."

"Montréal?"

"What's left of the group is in jail there and in Chicago."

Richardson's face went into its severe no-expression.

"Islamic Front."

"Raqqa, Baghdad."

"Pashtun Liberation Army."

"Kabul, Kandahar, Peshawar, and most towns in between."

"Daesh."

"Anywhere it isn't called ISIS."

"Sons of the Prophet."

"Kirkuz and Kuwait."

"Kuwait?"

"Not anymore, but they'll be back."

"ZKK."

"Kurdistan and bordering areas of Turkey, Iran, Iraq, and Syria. Are you sure they belong on the list?"

"It's just a correlation quiz. Don't read anything into it."

"Faithful of the Ayatollah."

"Herat and Sulaymaniyah."

"Hezbollah."

"Beirut, Tyre, Bekaa and the valley south to Israel."

She looked up and paused.

"The Black Amazon."

"Charlottesville." He scowled. She smiled.

"I've wanted to meet her ever since the Chicago story broke last year. I wasn't surprised when she turned up with you at Aberdeen."

"You could meet her. She's taken another job here, so she isn't leaving right away."

The colonel closed the folder. "How do you know where all those groups are? You have no recorded background in intelligence or Arabic studies, or anything remotely connected with them as far as I can tell. On paper, you don't fit the job description."

Jack answered, "انا ضابط شرطة" I'm a policeman.

She arched her eyebrows. "So would Major Monroe be as well-versed?"

"Possibly. Give him the quiz someday. A police department has to track where all the gangs are, who's in them, and what they're doing—preferably before even they know. Tony probably knows all the fringe groups in Central Virginia. My people soaked up everything NGIC generated on those groups. Our survival depended on it, and the survival of the Afghan and Iraqi officers we were training."

"And you sent us great local intel too." She finished her coffee. "I apologize for setting you up like this and for using your friendship with Major Monroe."

"Tony and I are happy to connect again, Colonel. Don't worry about that."

"Assuming we can make an offer, would you be willing to come aboard here—at least until we can find a civilian who fits the job description?"

Jack paused before answering. "I told Major Monroe that this is a great place to work. I meant that. But I haven't settled anywhere since retiring last March."

"You're not retired, Major."

"The deal was to work with Major Tinsley at Aberdeen on the Forebears of the Mahdi. All the suspects are in custody. That we haven't returned me to retired status is just a matter of my not being in one place for more than a day or two. Colonel Harper and he may have even forgotten."

She smiled. "They haven't forgotten, and Colonel Harper likes it this way." Jack shrugged.

"Who would I be working for, ma'am? I saw three different departments where this could fit."

"Two of them to be precise, and that is a problem that I have to solve."

"While you work on being able to make an offer or order me here, either way, let me think about it. There are some people whose opinion I value."

She stood. "Fair enough. Even if I could order you here, I wouldn't want an unwilling officer or employee. Would you let us know?"

"Yes, ma'am. As soon as I decide."

She extended her hand, and they shook. The smile reached her eyes this time.

Jack walked back to Tony's office. The PM was packing up his briefcase. He looked up, and his eyebrows said, *How'd it go?*

"It wasn't quite an ambush because I could tell where this visit was going. We agreed that I would think about it while she lines up the ducks to get me here."

"Great!"

"I'm not sure, Tony. You're the first person I want to ask since you and Martinez are already here. Is there anything that could go wrong? I'd hate to lose a friend over this decision."

"No problem, Jack. You wouldn't be working for me, and we're both majors." He clasped Jack's shoulder. "I'd be delighted for you to stick around long enough to meet Beulah and the kids."

"Thanks, Tony. I needed that."

They walked down to the gate. Jack turned in his badge, even though it was not a visitor's pass. Tony told the MP to lock it up but keep it handy.

They shook hands outside. Tony walked to the staff parking lot. Jack unlocked his bike.

He rode past the NGIC rush hour back to Hollymead, where he changed at the Starbucks and pedaled back to Charlottesville. The sun was low, and the heat of the day had broken. It was a pleasant ride, but Jack hardly looked at the scenery as he made his way back to Hilda's apartment.

ਃ ਃ ਃ

That same Monday after lunch, Emily rode out Avon Street to Community Bikes on the south side of Charlottesville. She took her Bianchi Volpe and wore her touring bicycle kit.

"Hey, Tani, what's up?" she said to the wrench helping a ten-year-old boy change a tire.

"Emily!" Taniqua crushed her in a bear hug. They stood back and sized each other up. Taniqua was as tall as Emily, with strong legs and a slim figure. She still wore her hair short, and her face had matured.

"You look different, and so tan. Girl, you could hang with us if you stay out in the sun anymore!"

Emily laughed. "You've grown some more. How's the work here?"

"Okay," said Taniqua. The boy finished sliding the tire back on the rim and looked up.

"More than okay," he said. "She's awesome. She knows everything about bikes!"

Taniqua pointed to the floor pump, and he went to fill his tire.

"When are you off?" Emily asked.

"I finished already, but I missed lunch. Let me grab it, and we can chat somewhere while I eat." She said a few words to the manager and pulled a brown paper bag out of the refrigerator. She zipped it into the rack trunk on her Bianchi Volpe, and the two friends rode to the Downtown Mall.

Sitting on a bench, they caught up on their summer adventures while the tourists walked past them. The two green Bianchis attracted no little attention. The teenage boys ogled the two girls and tried to look cool. Emily enjoyed being able to sit with her friend and not be recognized.

"I see you got shoes with cleats, and clips on your pedals," she said. "You really move out."

"I still wish I could race," said Taniqua as she crumpled the wax paper from her sandwich into her bag and took out a banana. She offered it to Emily, who shook her head.

"Why don't you? There are at least two teams in Charlottesville with junior development programs. I got started in Kansas that way."

"Yeah, but it costs too much—license dues, clothes, those fancy plastic shoes. I don't even have the right bike." She waved at the two bikes. "I love my bike, but I could never ride like you on it."

"If you could ride like me on it, you'd be incredible on a Colnago, Tani. But you could race. You're a natural."

"But I can't go to someone like CRC and ask to ride, then have to drop it when I can't afford things. And what about travel money? Even if I got good, my mom couldn't take me to Richmond and Williamsburg to compete like your folks did. That was so great last year."

Emily and Taniqua sat in silence for a while, the rising high school sophomore slowly eating her banana, the rising university student thinking deeply.

"Tani, you can race if you want to. You just need to train, then approach one of the teams. If you're fast—and I know you will be—money won't be the problem. There are scholarships. They want winning riders, and they'll find a way to make it happen."

"Training means a coach, doesn't it?"

"Sure. How about me?"

"You? But you're my friend and a champion. I'll hold you back."

"No, you won't. Let's ride my training routes on my recovery days. I train on Tuesday and Thursday, so you and I can ride on Wednesdays and Fridays. I wouldn't want to go faster than you on those days, but I could give you pointers. You build up your endurance and speed. When you're so fast that it's no longer a recovery ride for me, you can switch up to the fast group rides on Tuesdays and find a racing team. What do you say?"

"School starts in three weeks."

"UVA starts in two weeks. No problem. We can ride after class like we did last year when you were showing me around."

"Want to go ride? I don't need to be home until five."

"Let's do it!"

They rode out US-250 West, past Crozet and took the Transamerica Bike Trail back, looping North to Rio Road and the bike lanes that cut the city in half from north to south. They rode as fast as Emily normally did during the summer touring, which was a challenge for Taniqua.

Louisa Jackson was walking from the bus stop when they pulled up in front of Taniqua's house.

"Goodness, girl, you're soakin' wet," she said as her daughter dismounted and gave her a hug. "Emily! You two been swimmin'?"

"No, Mrs. Jackson. I was showing her one of my training routes."

"I want to race, Mom, and Emily's gonna be my coach!"

Louisa Jackson's expression darkened, and she considered Emily sternly.

"I only offered to give her some pointers to help develop her form. She's a natural athlete, Mrs. Jackson. I think she could become a fine racer."

Taniqua's mother looked at her daughter. "We talked about this before. I can't afford it."

"Mrs. Jackson," said Emily. "It shouldn't cost anything beyond what you put out to get her to this point. She needs to train first, and that doesn't require special gear. I can ride with her after school on Wednesdays and Fridays. When she's fast enough, she can apply to one of the teams in town. There are scholarships for promising riders, and I'm sure Tani would qualify. She'd be earning her own way."

The woman motioned them into the house. They locked their bikes together outside and went in. Tani's mother put her purse and her shopping on the kitchen counter and took a half-gallon of orange juice from the refrigerator. Taniqua gathered glasses from a cupboard.

"But she needs a fancy bike, doesn't she?"

"Not at first. Her Bianchi is just fine. If the team takes her on, they'll provide the bike, and maintain it too. Riders aren't expected to be wrenches, even though Tani already is one."

"Please, Mom. It's only Emily and me riding at first, just like before."

Louisa Jackson stared at the two of them, then smiled at her daughter. "I guess it'll be okay. Just don't be going off having adventures like this one did this summer!" She cocked her head at Emily. Taniqua nodded vigorously.

"Promise, Mrs. Jackson," said Emily. "I don't want any more adventures either!"

Emily took her leave and rode home in time to beat her mother back from the PhD seminar she was meeting with. Mark returned shortly before supper.

The next two weeks were filled with activity. Training three times a week, alone and with the UVA team, riding with Taniqua, shopping for school, and orientation meetings on Grounds. She had asked for and been assigned a traditional dorm room on McCormick Road. She approached Move-In Day like another tour, planning to pack her panniers, plus a messenger bag for her computer and school supplies.

The weekend after Jack visited NGIC, Hilda and he rode out to the Dempseys for a backyard barbecue. Jack had decided to accept Colonel Richardson's offer, so with Hilda starting work the Monday after Move-In Day, this was the last gathering of the summer for the five friends. They enjoyed each other's company until after midnight when Jack and Hilda rode back to her apartment. The night air felt cool and fresh after the heat of the day, and clean with almost no traffic at that hour.

ભ ભ ભ

Monday morning, Jack took the Northeast Regional to Aberdeen to gather his uniforms and other possessions. Not that there was much. In the afternoon, he called on Nate Harper and Ted Turner because orders transferring him to NGIC had been issued on Friday. The checkout procedure went quickly. He spent the night with Joe and Linda.

"Are you going to find your own place, Jack?" Joe Rathburn asked his brother as he drove him to the train station on Tuesday. "That new PO Box in Charlottesville will be a little tight, don't you think?"

"Hilda asked me to stay with her. The job at NGIC is temporary, so neither of us knows where we'll be next year."

"If Kathleen Richardson likes you, the job won't stay temporary, bro." Joe winked.

"If they want me permanently, they have to let me retire again so they can hire me as a civilian. That, or promote me to lieutenant colonel to keep me on active duty."

"She's perfectly capable of that."

"But on paper, I don't fit the job description."

"They can rewrite that any time they want." Joe punched him and smiled. "I hope you enjoy the work. NGIC is the cutting edge."

Joe drove his truck into the parking lot of the train station. Jack pulled his duffel bag out of the truck bed and walked to the platform with his brother. Both men were aging well, so that the difference in their appearance grew less each year. The train arrived on time. With a hug and a promise to stay in touch, Jack was on his way to the next chapter in his life.

37

McCormick Road

UVA Move-In Day the following weekend was an adventure in its own right. SUV's and cars with trailers were lining up for their time slots as Katherine and Emily rode down McCormick Road and locked their bikes outside Lefevre House on Hancock Drive. A hot summer sun had been beating on the asphalt and the humans for hours, and it was almost at its zenith.

All around them, students were running with their arms full. Parents were crying and shouting, and tempers flared as parents moved their children's belongings to the sidewalk and up to the rooms. Emily unsnapped her panniers and hugged her mother.

"Bye, Mom. I'll call you this afternoon."

"Home for supper?"

"Let me call you after the President's Address. I want to meet my roommate first."

"Okay. Let me know."

"Sure."

Emily headed into the open door but stopped and slipped back out to watch her mother ride up Hancock

Drive toward McCormick Road. Katherine's hand was wiping her eyes as she pedaled to her office.

Up on the second floor, Emily found her room halfway down the hall. She noted with pleasure that she was the first to arrive and blocked the door open. She went to the window and opened it. She looked west over the cemetery, a park-like foreground to Lewis Mountain.

After the fresh air from the trees displaced the hot stuffiness in the room, she let the door swing shut. She picked the bed and desk on the south wall, which stayed in shade all day. Putting her messenger bag on the desk, she unloaded her panniers into the closet and made her bed.

She was standing at the mirror, wondering if she wanted to rent a micro-fridge when the door flew open with a crash.

"Which bed is Cindy's?" shouted a walking mountain of suitcases topped by a purple backpack.

Emily whirled around and leaped backward on to her bed while the pile teetered toward the window. She pointed across the room.

"Thanks." The large man in a red shirt and jeans turned right barely in time to drop his load on the bed. His voice matched his burly appearance, bass and loud.

Emily eased off the bed as he stood back and turned around.

"Hi," she said.

"Hi. Be right back!" He ran to the door, yanked it open and almost knocked over a slender woman about his shoulder height, carrying three totes and another backpack. He mumbled an apology and ran down the hall.

The woman stepped inside. Behind her came a shy-looking girl with blue eyes and blond hair in a ponytail. She looked around the room with a mix of fear and dismay. When her gaze settled on Emily, she smiled weakly and put down the two totes she was carrying.

"Hello," said the older woman. Emily tried to breathe shallowly to avoid taking in the sharp smell of sandalwood perfume mixed with tobacco. "I'm Sandra Matthews, and this is Cindy."

"Hi. Emily Hampstead." Emily held her hand out. Cindy shook it while her mother dumped her load on the bed. Cindy's grip was firm, which surprised Emily. She was about Emily's height, but thinner. Her expression shifted from awe to pleasure, and her smile widened and went up to her eyes.

Sandra turned around and shook hands too. She had dyed blond hair cut shoulder length, and tanned, leathery skin. Emily recognized the wrinkles around her mouth as something smokers get, so Sandra could be any age old enough to have Cindy.

"Need some help?"

"I think this is it. My husband is getting the micro-fridge and the last suitcase." She waved at Cindy, who hurried to open suitcases and empty them on the bed. She had a massive pile of clothing and other belongings on the bed by the time her father pushed his back through the door with a micro-fridge and another suitcase on a dolly.

"I was wondering whether to rent one of those," Emily offered as he swung it into place. Cindy took the suitcase and emptied it on the bed.

"No need. It served her brother fine." He extended his hand. "I'm Alden." His hands were rough with callouses, and his grip stopped just short of crushing her hand. He turned to the others. "Gotta move the truck. Let's get those suitcases out of here."

The family vanished as suddenly as they had appeared, leaving behind a single medium suitcase teetering atop the pile. Emily went to the window and leaned out in time to see them come out the front door. Alden had four empty suitcases on the dolly, and the women had one in each hand. They walked across the street to a four-door, king-cab pickup truck and heaved their loads into the truck bed. Cindy hugged her parents, then waved from the sidewalk as they got in and drove away.

Emily scanned the room. The micro-fridge was covered with decals from Virginia Tech and organizations that she did not recognize. The pile on the bed included wear for every occasion, including two long evening gowns, suits, a fan, a large, professional hair dryer, jeans and T-shirts in every color possible. Emily wondered if Cindy would have to do laundry before Thanksgiving if she changed every day.

She took her plastic water glass from the shelf in her closet and filled it from the sink. She had just finished drinking and putting the glass away when Cindy pushed through the door. She had her cell phone to her ear.

"Yes, Mom… Don't worry. Yes, Mom. Bye, I love you too." She tapped the phone and rolled her eyes as she threw the phone on the desk. "They're still in traffic getting to I-64." She sat on the desk chair with a sigh.

"Where are they going? Home?"

"Virginia Beach. Stopping at Short Pump for lunch."

"I rode through Hampton Roads last spring. Nice place."

"I guess. I never lived anywhere else." She tilted her head toward Emily's closet. "Is that all you brought?"

"Uh-uh. It had to fit in the two panniers down there." She pointed to the floor of the closet. "If I need anything else, I'll get it later."

"I wish I thought of that. We went crazy this week, and Mom went ballistic worrying about what I would need. I got out of the way."

"Is she always like this?"

"She overloaded my brother Matt when he went to Tech. I'll be bringing stuff home on every trip until I graduate!" That made Emily laugh.

"Can I hand you stuff—at least the hanging things?"

Cindy got up. "Thanks."

Together, they had Cindy's closet crammed full in just a few minutes. It took a while to sort out the things she would use to put in the drawers. What was left, she packed in the suitcase.

"First run home." Cindy patted the luggage and leaned it against the wall. The desk was full of items, but the bed was clear. The medicine cabinet and Cindy's side of the sink were full.

Cindy's mother called twice while they were organizing their respective desks. Emily avoided commenting. She guessed that Cindy was the last child to leave the nest. By twelve thirty, they were moved in.

"The President's Address is in a half hour. Want to grab something to eat on the way?" Emily asked.

"Where?"

"Newcomb Hall is on the way to Old Cabell Hall."

"Lemme look those up."

"Don't bother. I'm local. I'll give you the tour on the way."

"Awesome!" Cindy's eyes widened. "I was worried about getting lost. Orientation was such a blur."

Emily did a noir detective imitation. "Stick with me, kid!"

They laughed, grabbed their phones and wallets, and locked the door behind them. In the hall, they joined the flow of students with the same idea, dodging the families still coming upstairs to move in. The noise level reminded Emily of the hallways in high school between classes, except for the deeper voices of the fathers.

The sandwiches they bought at Newcomb Hall they finished on the way to Old Cabell Hall. The two roommates briefed each other on their backgrounds. Cindy's parents settled in Virginia Beach when her father retired from the navy. Matt was about three. The big defense contractors courted Alden for his skills, but he liked working with his hands. He became a custom builder and handyman, and his business was booming when Cindy came along.

Cindy's wide-eyed excitement about Emily's having lived in different places made Emily a little uncomfortable, if only because she had never felt that way. She was surprised that the Matthews family had never vacationed abroad. But considering that a builder's busiest and most profitable season is the summer, it made sense that Sandra and Cindy would take small trips rather than extended holidays.

As they settled into seats in the auditorium, she noticed a student in the row in front of them with an "I registered" sticker on her shirt. Emily had registered to vote before leaving in the spring.

"How old are you, Cindy?"

"Eighteen last month, why?"

"Did you register to vote before you came?"

"No. I don't know how."

"They have a booth at the Student Activities Building. We can stop by there on the way back and take care of it."

"I could vote in Charlottesville?"

"Sure."

"Cool—" Applause cut off whatever she was saying. The provost, the president and a half-dozen other officials walked onto the stage. The students settled down to listen to the speeches.

Emily had met the new president at a reception for the faculty and their families shortly after she returned to Charlottesville. There had been speeches there too. Both officials made much of their newness held in common with the first-year students (not "freshmen" as in other schools).

Emily scanned the audience. Some of her classmates appeared bored, some mildly interested. Many, like Cindy, stared at the stage as if in rapture. Whether the speech or the reproduction of Raphael's *School of Athens* behind the stage attracted their interest, she could not tell.

After the speeches, the two walked to the Student Activities Building.

"No need to make a commitment today," said the student volunteer manning the voting registration station. "But you'll be able to vote if you decide you want to later—and the registration is good as long as you're a student and not registered somewhere else."

On their way back to Hancock Drive, Emily showed Cindy the Aquatic and Fitness Center and pointed out the dining halls and bus stops. The crowd of families and newcomers had thinned considerably by the time they walked up to the second floor. The resident assistants were taking a break in the little lounge at the end of the hall. Emily and Cindy introduced themselves.

"Sorry I didn't get to your room when you arrived," said Brianna, their RA, getting up and shaking their hands. "The mother in 218 was having a nervous breakdown, I think. It took all of us to calm her down and get her back to her car."

"No problem," said Cindy. "Emily here is local. She showed me everything." Brianna crossed her arms and frowned at Emily.

"Well, not everything, but I got us to Cabell Hall and back."

Brianna relaxed. "Where do you live?"

"Greenbrier."

"Have you two made a contract yet?"

"No, but we've got the micro-fridge, and we've picked sides," said Emily. Cindy looked puzzled. "It's a start."

Brianna chuckled. "Okay." She reached down to the end table and gave them a clipboard. "Here. It's only a guideline, but maybe it'll help you remember something that'll prevent an argument later."

"Thanks." Emily took the clipboard, glanced at it, and passed it to Cindy. They shook hands with the other RA's then walked back to their room. They could hear country music coming in the window from the room below them.

"I hope that the whole year won't be like this," said Cindy. "I can feel that boom box through the floor."

"Let's see what the first night is like. Maybe the RA's will settle them down."

"I hope so. I also hope it isn't always country."

"What do you like?"

"A little of everything. Classical, early music, rock-and-roll, hip-hop, opera, R&B, reggae. Even country. Just don't keep it on one button for too long."

Emily smiled. "We'll get along fine, then." She picked a pencil from the desk drawer. "That's one of the items on the list." She checked it off. "Background music while you study or silence?"

"Background."

"Me too." They worked their way down the list until they came to the subject of overnight guests.

"I didn't know that we could do that," said Cindy. "Mom said never to have a boy in my room."

"She can't be serious! Half our neighbors in the building are boys."

"I'm not sure that she realizes how coed the dorms are."

"Residence halls."

"Yeah, residence halls. Picky about the terminology, aren't they?"

"I've been listening to it since January, and you're right. We'll be just as bad in a few weeks." They laughed.

"I imagine you know lots of boys to invite here."

Emily looked out the window and thought. "No, not really. All the guys I met at CHS went somewhere else, and I was away all summer. My other friends still are in high school, but they're all girls."

"Okay with me if you have overnight guests—I think."

"Do you have a boyfriend?"

"I did back in Virginia Beach, but we weren't serious. And he went to Yale, so I won't see him again."

"Not even at Christmas?"

"His mother just got transferred to California. They'll be living in San Diego by Thanksgiving."

"You can start in on the country music fans downstairs." They chuckled.

"I don't think so. I want to see who shows up for the University Singers auditions first. If they don't like music, I'm not interested."

"Do you play an instrument?"

"Piano, but only well enough to accompany myself and rehearse."

"I heard the U-Singers in concert a couple of times last year. They're excellent."

"Don't make me more nervous than I am. You really don't have a boyfriend?"

"I like this guy in Canada, but if it grows, it'll be an internet romance for a while."

Checking off "yes" for overnight guests, they continued down the list, surprising themselves with the things that came out.

Cindy smoked ("occasionally"); Emily hated smoke. Cindy admitted that she only smoked at parties when others were smoking. She did not keep any cigarettes or even a lighter. They checked off "no smoking."

Both said that they rose with the sun. They would have to see how much midnight oil they would burn, but each had eyeshades if needed.

Both preferred seafood to meat. Emily liked to cook, but Cindy only knew how to use a microwave. They agreed that if one cooked, the other would clean up. And so it went for an hour and a half.

"What about supper?" asked Cindy. "That sandwich was hours ago."

"Omigod! I promised to call my mom after the President's Address!"

"She doesn't call you?"

"No. We got out of that habit last summer. It's up to me to call."

"Could your mother give mine some lessons?" Cindy said in mock hopefulness. Emily smiled back.

"She's a teacher, but not that subject." Emily got her phone off the desk. "Want to come to my house for supper?"

"Sure! She won't mind on short notice?"

"It was her idea. I told her that I wanted to meet you first." Emily punched speed dial. "Mom, I'm sorry. Cindy's so cool that I forgot the time…She said yes… Okay… I didn't think about that. We can rent a U-bike for tonight…Okay. Bye." She smacked a kiss into the phone and ended the call. "All set for seven o'clock."

"What was that about U-bike?"

"I forgot to mention it. We live in Greenbrier about four kilometers—two and a half miles—north of here. There's no bus service out there. My bicycle is downstairs, and we can rent a U-bike for you."

Cindy's eye went wide. "Bicycle? Two and a half miles?"

"Don't you ride?"

"I learned to ride my brother's bike, but I've never gone anywhere."

Emily thought about that for a short while.

"I could call my folks to pick us up, but I have an idea. Let's rent a bike and go pick up stuff to stock the micro-fridge. Then if you feel like it, we can ride to my house. If not, I'll call for them to come rescue us."

"Okay, I guess. Where's the supermarket?"

"There's a Harris Teeter at Barracks Road next to the North Grounds. About a mile, and a straight shot from here."

Cindy downloaded the U-bike app on her phone, reserved a bicycle, and got a PIN for it. Her face was a mixture of terror and excitement as Emily gathered her empty panniers. They walked the Bianchi to the U-bike station. Cindy unlocked a bike.

"I don't have a helmet."

"Then let's go to Endeavor Cycles and buy one. They're just past Scott Stadium."

Cindy got on and rode around on the broad concrete promenade near the station for a few laps. When she felt confident, Emily pointed her to the bike lane.

They rode slowly to Alderman Road, then south past the Aquatics & Fitness Center and the stadium. Cindy squeaked a few times as she made her way around drainage grates but settled into a comfortable cadence by the time that they reached the stop sign at Stadium Road. She wobbled a bit getting going, but then the store was right there on the next block. They pushed their bikes across Fontaine Avenue at the light.

With a helmet on her head, Cindy felt more confident. By the time they reached Harris Teeter, her only challenge had been the climbs on Alderman Road and the bridge over the railroad line. Emily took her on the less-traveled side streets, the bike path near the Taco Bell, and then through the parking lots of the shopping center.

"That was fun!" Cindy said as they locked their bikes to the rack at Harris Teeter. "I'll need to catch my breath a lot if we have too many hills like that, though."

"Charlottesville is all hills. You'll get stronger fast."

They picked up some microwaveable meals, fruit, snacking carrots and tomatoes, beverages, and chips to offer guests who might come by. They put the lightweight chips in Cindy's basket. Emily's panniers took everything else, and she lashed a twelve-pack of caffeine-free Coke Zero to her rack. Then they made their way back to the room, taking Emmet Street this time. Cindy had to walk up the ramp to McCormick Road but otherwise had no problems even in traffic.

"You just rode five miles. How do you feel?" Emily asked as she stowed half the Cokes in the fridge.

"No way! It can't be that far."

Emily smiled. "We'll take the easy way to my house. It's about as far as we just rode, and it has bike lanes almost the whole way. Only one steep climb. Our street at the very end. You can walk that if you want."

"I'm already sweaty. I'll be a mess when we get there."

"Cindy, we're a family of cyclists. Everyone's sweaty. You'll fit right in!"

Cindy's phone rang. "Hi, Mom… No, we're fine. The micro-fridge is all stocked, but we're going to Emily's for supper tonight… She lives in town, Mom. Isn't that cool? … Her mom's a teacher… I don't know… Don't worry, Mom, we'll be fine… I love you too. Bye." She ended the call with another eye roll. "This is why they made us turn in our phones at Scout Camp."

"You were a Scout too?"

"I dropped out after sophomore year, but it was fun until then."

"I know what your mother needs, but it's your father's job."

Cindy looked at her with a questioning look, then put her hand to her mouth and laughed until the tears ran. When they both stopped, she said, "I swear, if Mom calls me one more time today, I'll call Dad!"

"Just propose a dinner date. Maybe he'll take the hint." They laughed again as they put the dry goods in Emily's closet because she had room.

They gave themselves an hour to get to Brandywine Drive. The sun was falling toward the Blue Ridge Mountains, and the heat of the day had lost its edge. Cindy did not need to walk until they reached the driveway.

They were a half hour early. Katherine was checking on a baking dish of potatoes and onions in the oven. There were salmon filets on the counter ready to go in later.

Emily introduced her new roommate.

"Pleased to meet you, Mrs. Hampstead."

"Mrs. Dempsey, Cindy, but you can call me Katherine when we're off Grounds." Cindy looked at Emily and back to Katherine. "My husband Mark is Emily's stepfather."

"Where's Dad?" Emily kissed her mother.

"Out riding. He should be back soon."

The screen door slamming in the basement announced the return of the man of the house. He came up dripping with sweat and clearly still high on endorphins. He took a couple of deep breaths, pulled off his bike gloves, and stuck out his hand.

"You must be Cindy. I'm Mark Dempsey."

Cindy shook hands. Mark crossed over and gave Emily a big hug.

"Now I'm sweaty too," she said, looking at Cindy, "like I told you."

Mark went up to change while Emily showed Cindy around the main floor.

"It's so cool and shady out back," said Cindy as they came into the kitchen.

"Perfect for eating on the deck," said Katherine. She pulled out the baking dish, set the fish on top of the vegetables, and returned the dish to the oven. "Ten minutes!" she shouted, which got her a mumbled noise from upstairs.

Emily and Cindy set the table, then helped themselves to some orange juice. Katherine poured herself a glass of Riesling and joined them in the dining room off the deck.

Cindy seemed bursting with curiosity but also intimidated.

"Emily has only given me your name," said Katherine. "Where are you from?"

"Virginia Beach."

"Born and raised," added Emily with a smile.

Mark walked in and drank three glasses of water from the tap at the kitchen sink. Then he pulled the wine from the refrigerator and poured himself a glass. Cindy watched him with interest.

"Do you ride a lot, Mr. Dempsey?"

"Mark. Not as much as these two." Katherine and Emily grinned. "I can't keep up with either one of them."

"Do you teach too?"

"No. I run a small company down on the Peninsula—closer to your home than to Charlottesville."

"Where do you teach?" Cindy asked Katherine.

"I thought Emily would have told you. I'm at the university."

"Omigod, you could be one of my professors!"

"Not yet." Katherine laughed gently. "I teach graduate courses in feminist literature. I'll see you later, perhaps." She smiled. "What are your interests?"

"I don't know. I liked all my courses in high school, so I can't even imagine what I'd like to major in."

"Good place to be. Just enjoy the basic curriculum. Something will strike your fancy, I'm sure."

An alarm went *ding* in the kitchen. Katherine rose. "Put out some water, dear, would you? I think dinner is ready."

Supper was a pleasant affair. Cindy sometimes lapsed into silence, obviously fascinated by Katherine.

For most of the meal, Mark observed without comment, but then asked, "Did you say your father is Alden Matthews? How did he come to be a builder?" Katherine glanced at him and gave him a curious look.

"He got out of the navy before I was born. He said he liked to work with his hands, so he became a handyman and started his own company."

"I admire that. I had a CO once who probably could have been a general, but he retired and became a plumber. Last time I saw him, he was making more money than his friends who worked for the big companies."

"That's my dad. He seems very happy building and fixing things."

"He does fine work too."

"Do you know him?"

"Not well. Matthews Building Company from Virginia Beach renovated our offices at Langley."

Cindy sat quietly, not knowing what to say.

"Small world, isn't it?" said Katherine.

"I'll say! I've never met anyone who knew my dad, except for the people in his company."

"Does your mother work outside too?"

Cindy face darkened a little. "I wish she would sometimes. They told me that she taught music while he was in the navy. He's out all day, so I hope she picks that up or something else."

"Ten o'clock," said Mark. "Are you two supposed to be in at a certain time?"

"No, Dad." Emily waved her ID card. "Twenty-four-hour access with these."

"They dim the lights in the halls after ten, and we're not supposed to make a lot of noise," said Cindy. "I wonder how that will work with the boys downstairs."

Emily rolled her eyes. "We'll see. I wouldn't want to call Brianna the first night."

"I take it that Brianna's your RA?" asked Katherine.

"Yes. She's nice, but I think she'll be firm too."

Mark said, "Let me drive you back in the van. I'm not ready for Cindy's first day solo on a bike to include Saturday night traffic with the students newly back on the Corner."

"I hadn't thought of that. Thanks. If we take the van, we can take my Team USA poster without folding it."

"Good idea. Go up and see if you need anything else." He began stacking the dessert dishes. "I'll be ready in a few minutes."

Emily and Cindy went upstairs.

"Wow! You really ride. I had no idea." Cindy stared in awe at the medals and the autographed posters of Emily's cycling heroes. Emily stood on her bed and carefully took down the poster of Megan Guarnier and the women on the USA Cycling Development Team. Emily had met them at her first Talent ID Camp. She was taken into the program the following year.

"To tell the truth, Cindy, I'm glad you sing instead."

"Why?"

"I'm not sure I would enjoy rooming with a jock or another cyclist."

"But you'll have to tell me about it!"

"Maybe." Emily double-checked her dresser and closet but didn't take anything out. "Tell you what. You Google me and then ask me questions, but wait until tomorrow, okay?" She rolled the poster into a cardboard tube. Cindy agreed, and they went downstairs.

"Want some fruit or anything for the room?" Katherine asked in the hallway.

"No, thanks, Mom. We went to Harris Teeter before coming here."

"I don't know if I'll ever get used to the new you, dear." She hugged her daughter.

"It was our routine every afternoon this summer. It's a habit."

Mark came out of the kitchen. "The Lefevre Limo is ready to leave."

They loaded the bikes on the rack and hopped in the van. Mark stopped at the bike station on McCormick Road, so Cindy could lock her U-bike and sign out.

"You want to come up and see?" Emily asked when the Bianchi was locked outside Lefevre House.

"No, dear," said her mother. "Not the first night after Move-In. Your neighbors don't want grown-ups around, I'm sure."

"We'll come by after classes start," said Mark. He shook hands with Cindy. "You come by anytime. Our home is your home away from home. Is that all right with you?" Cindy nodded.

Emily hugged her mother and stepfather, and the two roommates walked into the residence hall. They climbed the stairs and opened the doors to their hallway.

Emily paused to scan the space. A least a dozen boys and a similar number of girls up and down the hall. Most were shouting at each other in a euphoria of excitement. Emily smelled beer, but there were no drinks visible, so she figured it was coming from bodies, not bottles.

Cindy kept walking—right into an enormous boy falling out of the first room on the right. She screamed, but her cry was drowned out. Emily stepped forward and pulled him off her roommate.

He stood unsteadily, his eyes glassy, then staggered back into the room, leaving the door to swing shut behind him. Emily reached down and pulled Cindy up.

"You okay?"

"I think so. He scared the hell out of me!"

"I don't think he ever knew you were there. He's totally wasted."

They walked toward their room. Two boys that Emily recognized from the first floor stepped up to block their way. Emily eased in front of Cindy. They both stank of beer.

"Step aside, please."

"Wanna have a good time?" said the one on the right. Medium height, curly brown hair, thin frame.

The other did not seem smart, but maybe he was only drunker.

"I was already having a good time. Now move." The boy raised his hand. She looked down at his hand and back in his face. "Rule number one: look, but don't touch."

"Tough one, eh?" He reached out toward her arm.

Emily grabbed his wrist, pulled him off-balance toward her and sank her fist into his solar plexus as she stepped on his left foot. She completed pulling him through and stepped aside so he could fall next to Cindy.

Cindy squeaked and jumped to the side. The boy curled up on the floor.

Emily pointed at his roommate.

"You. Pick up your friend and put him to bed. We can introduce ourselves tomorrow when you're both sober." She took Cindy's hand, unlocked the door to their room, and led her inside.

"Omigod, Emily!" Cindy was pale and on the verge of hyperventilating. Emily took her by the shoulders and had her sit on the bed. She got a glass of water from the sink and made Cindy drink it.

After she calmed down, Cindy said, "Did you do what I saw you do?"

"No. He tripped, didn't he? Those two will wake up so hung over, they may not remember it."

The noise in the hall suddenly diminished. A knock on the door was followed by Brianna's head coming through.

"Are you two okay?"

"Sure," said Emily. "We just got back."

"So I hear." She came in and stood by the closed door. "What happened?"

Cindy was still in shock. Emily looked at Brianna and said, "We had a little trouble getting to our room. First, some giant fell out of the room by the stairs, on top of Cindy here. Then two guys from the first floor were staggering toward us, and the skinny one tripped over me."

Brianna stared at her with a serious expression. "I heard they were harassing you first."

"The skinny one tried. The other one was probably too drunk to know what was happening."

"Tripped, huh?"

Emily nodded and crossed her arms. Brianna looked at Cindy.

"Is that your story too?"

"I was so scared after the big guy fell on me that I don't know what happened. I saw the skinny one go down, but that's all."

"Did he hit his head?"

Emily shook her head. "I grabbed his arm as he went down. He kind of curled up on the floor when I let him go."

Brianna opened the door and paused. "The party was getting out of hand anyway, Good night, y'all." The hall was dimly lit and quiet. She smiled and let the door swing shut behind her.

38

GOING TO WORK

MONDAY MORNING AFTER MOVE-IN DAY, JACK RODE OUT TO NGIC. He had taken a taxi there after he returned with his things, stowing uniforms and toilet kit in the men's locker room. He might not always need a shower each morning, but he did not plan to commute in uniform. *Rolling target*, he thought. Today, he showered and changed before reporting to work. The morning consisted of briefings and the other steps of checking into a highly classified workplace. Tony joined him in the cafeteria for lunch.

"Settling in okay, Jack?"

"So far. Yet to meet my two new bosses, but I finished with Personnel, Security, and Medical."

"You'll like them both. What you don't know about IED's or networks, they've forgotten and moved on."

"Why do they need me?"

"Because they have other things to do, and other specialists to supervise, but they know everyone's job."

"I like that in a boss."

They ate some fish chowder in silence.

"You said you're staying with a friend here in Charlottesville," Tony said.

Jack waved an affirmative with his spoon. "Remember Major Paisley at the clinic?"

"The Black Amazon? What's she doing here?"

"She retired on twenty. Got on her bicycle to see the country. Took a temp job near Seattle, then another one at UVA Medical Center. She's signed on with a local GP on Fifth Street, so she'll be here at least until next year."

"Wait a minute—she was in the IED incident with you."

"In the medical Humvee behind us. If she hadn't been there, I wouldn't be here."

"I remember her. Damn fine-looking woman. Fierce too. Word was, no one touched her without permission. Major Smythe said she was the most competent person in the clinic."

"Smythe's the one who patched me up enough to be flown out. She would know."

"Her name's Hilda, isn't it?"

Jack nodded.

"I doubt she'd remember me. I never got shot before she left."

"Wrong. She remembered you right away when I mentioned you."

"I wouldn't mind seeing her again."

"You will. I'm sure we do more than process paperwork here, don't we?"

They took their trays to the scullery and returned to work. Jack was to meet with his new department heads to determine how his days would be organized.

Arty Monroe ran the Ordnance Division. He was a retired bomb disposal officer who had disarmed almost every kind of Russian, Israeli and American weaponry in the inventory, in addition to the earliest IED's.

Shelby Barnhardt was an active-duty major, selected for lieutenant colonel and expecting orders any day. She led the HUMINT (human intelligence) Division. She had spent half of her career working undercover and a good portion of that overseas. When her cover was blown by WikiLeaks, she almost didn't make it out of Stockholm alive. She was moved to DIA, where she reorganized the way the intelligence agencies analyze and track insurgent networks.

Jack went into the meeting knowing all this about his two bosses and feeling very out of his element.

His jaw dropped when he saw Cynthia Rowling sitting at the end of the table. She was as stunning as ever, but her hair was red instead of blonde.

Her hand shot up. "Hold it right there, Jack! Don't say that name." She indicated the chair across from them. "Coffee?" She pushed the tray with the carafe and mugs toward him.

Jack moved to the table and shook hands with his other boss. Arty Monroe looked like anyone's next-door neighbor—medium height, balding white hair, waist gone thick around the middle, wearing slacks, a white dress shirt with no tie, and steel-rimmed glasses. A ready smile. He watched the two of them curiously but mercifully kept silent. Jack was not prone to blushing, but he could feel the heat at his collar.

"I might as well go first," she said when Jack sat. She turned to Arty. "Jack and I served together in

Germany a long time ago." She looked at Jack. "I hope you're not disappointed."

"Now that the shock has passed, no. To paraphrase *Casablanca*, we'll always have Stuttgart."

"I agree. And memories they'll remain." She motioned toward the man sitting next to her. "Arty and I have agreed to divide your days in half, one of us in the morning, the other in the afternoon. We'll consult with each other if a big project or overtime is needed."

"You're new to this, Jack," he said. "So, we won't set this in concrete. Based on what you know already, do you see a preference for mornings or afternoons in a particular division?"

"Will I physically be working in two different spaces?"

"Unfortunately, yes. You'll be one of only a half-dozen people here with the compartmentalized clearances to work in both divisions, but what you'll be working on must stay in our spaces."

Jack thought for a moment.

"Let me ask a personal question, Arty. Are you a morning person or a night person?"

The ordnance expert opened his mouth, closed it, then said, "Morning, I guess. Early to bed, early to rise and all that."

"Perfect." Jack winked at Shelby, who smiled despite herself. "Let's start with mornings in Ordnance and afternoons in HUMINT."

"What about TDY?" asked Shelby. Temporary Duty Travel.

"Already?" asked Jack.

"Not right away, we hope," said Arty, "but every-one here expects to fly to the scene occasionally to analyze details on-site, especially when we discover new ordnance."

"Or we need to interview new players in-country," added Shelby.

"I guess we'll cross that bridge when we come to it," said Jack.

"Good for a start. Let's do HUMINT the rest of today, so you can get oriented in Ordnance first thing tomorrow."

They rose. Arty shook hands and walked out. Shelby and Jack went upstairs to the HUMINT Division. It could be an office anywhere. Just desks and monitors, with shelves of books and file cabinets. Shelby introduced him to the other half-dozen people who worked there. Each seemed to specialize in a cultural area, so the effect resembled nothing so much as a mini-United Nations.

"You and I are the only ones who see the networks and how the HUMINT coming in connects. Your skill at noticing patterns is what we need here."

"My skills can't match yours."

"That's why I'm the boss. But for what it's worth, I recommended grabbing you to Colonel Richardson when your name came up at the staff meeting in June."

"That long ago?"

"Yes. You were still making your way up the Eastern Shore."

"I'll be damned."

"It didn't hurt that Arty had read your intel reports on IED's from Baghdad, either."

"I smelled a set up when I first came here, but I wasn't aware that it ran so deep."

Shelby laughed. "To her credit, the CO did devote the whole summer to finding someone matching the job description."

She showed him his desk, then arranged for each of the others to brief him on what they did. She told him to stop at 15:00 and spend the rest of the afternoon with the briefing books she had placed on his desk. She gave him the combination to his safe and disappeared into her office behind him.

ನ ನ ನ

That morning, Hilda rode out West Main and Ridge Street to Dr. Osborne's office. What looked like a two-story house from the street had ample parking and storage on a floor below street level. She wheeled her bicycle into the garage and climbed the stairs to the main floor. The door let into the reception area.

Dr. Osborne was sitting at the receptionist's station, in his white lab coat and bow tie. He stood when he saw her come in, then shook her hand.

"Hilda! I'm so glad you're here." He noticed her looking at the desk. "I came in early to check the schedule. Doris gets in at eight thirty, and the first appointment isn't until ten. I can give you a tour and help you settle in."

"I heard you were shorthanded, but I've never seen a doctor at the receptionist's desk."

"We've been doing so much so fast with so little for so long—"

"That we can do everything with nothing immediately."

"That's about it. Coffee?"

Reginald Osborne led her down the hall to the kitchen, which served as the break room. He stood six inches shorter than Hilda, but he walked with poise. His close-cropped hair was turning gray, but his face was smooth, except for a few laugh lines by his eyes. She liked his eyes. They twinkled the way she imagined eyes should twinkle in the stories she loved as a child, and he had the most expressive face she had ever seen.

He poured two mugs of coffee from the coffee maker and handed her one.

Hilda sniffed hers. "French Roast from Starbucks? I like this place already."

"I ask a lot of the staff, so I try to make the place livable in any little way I can."

The house had several exam rooms, a modest X-ray room with a digital X-ray suite. The exam room nearest the front entrance had most of an ER suite installed. Hilda admired the setup.

"This is a small hospital."

"We need one. Many of our patients won't go to the regular hospitals, but their families bring them here." He waved at a computer workstation. "You can access monitors and keyboards in every room and office, and the place is wired centrally. Automatic backups every fifteen minutes."

A locked door secured the hall closet for the controlled drugs. "Only you and I will ever hold the keys to this place. My office is there, and your place is there." He pointed to the two rooms across from the locked door. "In addition to the closed-circuit TV in the hall, we can each verify that the other is going into the room."

"TV inside?"

"Of course."

Hilda noted the cameras in the hall. "Better security than most army hospitals."

"I wish I could say it's overkill because most of our drugs are free samples. But we've had several attempted break-ins, so the systems do their job."

"What about the other nurse, Mrs. Shifflett?"

"She took ill last month. Mary Lou went full-time while we advertised for someone to replace Susan until Mary Lou's accident."

"I'm sorry. If I'd known, I could have come in two weeks ago."

He shrugged. "We got by, and now you're here. And Mary Lou should be back at some point."

He spent the next hour showing her the medical records and briefing her on the status of his current patients. While they were talking, Doris Abernathy came in and took over the receptionist's desk. A sturdy woman in her fifties, she looked like the kind of person who could keep an entire classroom of randy teenagers under control, which she had done for many years.

"Lordy me, the famous Hilda Paisley in person," she said as she shook Hilda's hand. "I was telling Dr. Osborne here, I didn't think you'd show up, being a celebrity."

Hilda faced Dr. Osborne with a question mark on her face. He smiled. "Chicago. Every sister in the health care system in Charlottesville knows who you are, Hilda."

"They never let on at UVA last year."

"My dear," said Doris, waving at her, "it's one of the things we like about you. You're so modest." She put her purse in her desk drawer and offered to get more coffee. As she went down the hall, Hilda was still shaking her head.

By the time the first patients showed up for their appointments, Hilda knew which rooms were used for what, and where the emergency supplies and equipment were. She figured that she could ask about anything less urgent.

Dr. Osborne came into the room where she was finishing up working on a boy's cut arm. "Don't forget to take your lunch break." She glanced at the clock, stunned that so much time had flown by.

They had three more patients in the afternoon. About four o'clock, a car came to a screeching halt outside. Doris called down the hall. "The Michaels boys again!"

Dr. Osborne came out of his room, walking quickly down the hall.

"Clean up in the ER and be ready," he said as he passed Hilda's room. She excused herself and went to the ER. Doris stuck her head in.

"You finished with Mrs. Edwards?"

"Basically. I was just putting an Ace bandage on her knee."

"I can do that. I'll sign her out."

Dr. Osborne came in, followed by two young men holding a teenage boy between them. Hilda took the injured boy's legs and helped them swing him onto the table.

He was bleeding from a gunshot wound in his thigh. Hilda ascertained from the blood flow that no arteries or veins had ruptured. No exit wound, so this would be a bullet extraction. She started an IV while Dr. Osborne waved the two men out of the room and began cutting the pant leg away.

"Standard saline. It looks pretty clean."

"Hold the antibiotic, then?"

"Yes, we'll start it if we need it."

Hilda assembled the tray of instruments and brought them over. Dr. Osborne preferred to get the instruments from the tray himself, rather than call for them, so she had time to admire his skill. He had the bullet out in less than two minutes, then asked her to clean and close the wound.

Without a word, Hilda finished the job.

"What do you think, Nurse? Clean or dirty?"

Hilda paused. No doctor had ever asked her opinion on something like that before. "Clean, sir."

"I agree. Let's skip the antibiotic unless he develops an infection. And thanks. I never expected to find everything I needed on the tray."

"Not my first bullet wound, Doctor."

"Of course. Let's brief him and get him out of here. The police should be waiting."

"I don't want no cops," shouted the boy, grabbing the doctor's arm.

"Hush, Tyrone. They need to take a statement and check the gun that shot you. Let me guess. Bernie's?"

Tyrone was clearly terrified but nodded.

"Tell them you were kidding around, and it accidentally went off. But you must tell them whose gun it is, so they can match that bullet." He pointed to the tray. "If they don't, they'll keep the case open until they arrest someone. Your mom and Mrs. Smith can straighten it out between them. Stay off that leg for at least five days. Miz Abernathy out front will lend you a wheelchair. You can bring it back next week when we check your wound. Understand?"

With a shrug of resignation, Tyrone turned to the two officers waiting outside the door. Hilda recognized Walter Johnson, who winked at her over Tyrone's head. Soon the victim, his older brothers, and the police were gone, toting the bullet in an evidence bag.

Hilda finished cleaning up the ER and her hands, then joined Dr. Osborne in the kitchen/break room. She felt the let-down as she eased into a chair. He shoved a mug of coffee at her.

"Is that a typical day around here?" she asked as she blew on her coffee.

"No, but it's never dull."

"You know all your patients this well?"

"No, but the Michaels are regulars. Not a one of them gets through adolescence without scars."

"Were they really kidding around?"

"Probably less friendly than that. Bernie Smith has had it in for Tyrone for a half-dozen reasons and may have partaken of judgment-reducing substances this afternoon." Hilda arched an eyebrow. "I will be so glad when they start school next week. It corrals their hormones for most of the day."

She laughed at that. "Does anyone see a problem with your practice? There are two full-sized hospitals in this town."

"They're happy to have me here. They hate seeing my patients in their ER's. Half of them are uninsured, and the rest are noncompliant, repeat business."

"How do you run a practice under those conditions?"

"Most of our patients respect me. I delivered many of them. I made house calls until I bought this place, and I still call on the shut-ins. I forgot to mention that. We're closed Wednesday afternoons so I can make those rounds.

"Medicare and Medicaid pay for most of them to some extent. That's why Doris is so important to me. She taught math at CHS, and she's a whiz with numbers and red tape. The government short-changes us on every bill, but I keep my costs down."

"All this state-of-the-art equipment?"

"Much of it is second-hand, and we don't have much staff—as you saw this morning."

"This is my first private practice, Dr. Osborne, but I've never heard of a doctor getting by on so little."

"I don't need much. I live alone, in the house that my great grandfather built. We never had much, but our parents made sure that we got good educations. No mortgage, no car payments, no school loans, no credit card debt—I'd rather put the money back into the practice."

Hilda rode home that evening with a different perspective on her new employer. She had found her first hero outside the army.

Back in the apartment, Hilda and Jack exchanged impressions of their first day at work.

"So, Osborne was really looking for combat experience," said Jack.

"I guess so, and I can't believe that the whole community has been watching me since I arrived. It turns out that Suzie Bennett is his niece!"

"I feel kind of spied on too. Shelby Barnhardt said that my name came up at a staff meeting back in June, and she was the one who put Kathleen Richardson on my tail."

"You knew this Shelby Barnhardt?"

"That wasn't the name she was using when I knew her. She was undercover in Germany a long time ago."

"Were you close?" Jack nodded. "That must have been a shock." She grinned at him. "Well, if you survive being my lover, at least you'll always get my name right." She gave him a kiss on the cheek. "Let's fix something for dinner. I'm famished."

39

RUGBY ROAD

MARIANA SIGNALED A STOP at the overlook on the Blue Ridge Parkway and swung off her bike. Emily caught the move in her peripheral vision only because she was looking at the same thing. She did a U-turn and joined the group.

"I don't care what our training goals are for today's ride," said their team captain. "This is a mandatory stop."

Six cell phones came out and snapped panoramas of the view. Then the women sat on the guardrail and admired the variations of color that stretched into the distance. The sun was still lighting up the mountainsides as dark clouds gathered to the south and began creeping up the valley. In addition to the peak autumn colors, the play of blues, grays, and purple on the landscape swirled the length of the Shenandoah Valley.

"Let's not cool off." They went back to their bikes. "Stay together in the peloton until we get past Wintergreen. The tourists aren't looking at the road."

They sped along the Parkway, passing lines of cars as often as being passed.

About twenty kilometers later, they turned left onto Route 664 and spread out as they plummeted to the valley floor below. Emily took the lead on the flat stretch but slowed after making the turn toward Nellysford, so they could catch up. They reformed the peloton and streaked back to Charlottesville.

A little less than three hours later, they locked their bicycles inside the converted garage on Grounds where the team kept their racing machines. Emily rode her faithful Bianchi back to Lefevre House, carrying it inside and up the stairs. She pushed open the door to her room just as the rain started.

"You're the lucky one," said Cindy, getting up to close the window as the storm tried to blow in.

"Yeah, we rode like crazies to get here before that broke."

Emily laid her Bianchi next to Cindy's new Marin Fairfax under the window. Bicycles were not allowed in the rooms. However, after the string of bike thefts outside the halls last month, the RA's had been looking the other way—if the students kept the bikes out of the hallways and did not track dangerous levels of mud into the buildings.

Emily stretched while Cindy went back to whatever she was studying. When Emily got back from the shower, she pulled the orange juice from the micro-fridge and started downing the half gallon in quick glassfuls.

"You want some?" she asked Cindy.

"Thanks." Cindy rubbed her eyes and took the proffered glass of juice. Emily poured another for herself. "You still going to the frat party tonight?"

Emily waved at the storm outside. "If this blows over in time—and if you're going too."

"Absolutely. Preston invited me."

"But you don't need an invitation for an open house."

Cindy sighed and rolled her eyes. "But he's a member and lives in the house. That's different."

Emily did not know why, but she did not pursue it. Cindy's easy infatuation with upperclassmen sometimes grated on her, but her roommate had the good sense not to bring anyone to the room. In fact, she seemed to have an uncanny ability to find men who lived off Grounds, either in the fraternity houses or their own apartments. Emily did not envy her because so far, none of the "boys" at the university had caught her interest. Spending a summer with the likes of Jack, Frank, Pierre, Jerry, Jean-Paul, Jacques, and Jean-Pierre had skewed her taste in male companionship.

"Can we go together? I don't know anyone on Rugby Road, and I don't want to show up by myself."

"Sure. Preston has to help with the preparations and hosting. But don't expect me to stay with you all night."

"Of course not. But maybe you could introduce me around."

After supper at the Observatory Hill dining hall, they went back to their room to change. Emily might have skipped this party because it started so late, but she was curious. With all her training and studies, she had not been to a single party since Move-In Day.

Taniqua had been accepted into the Junior Development Program and had her own training schedule with the team. Emily could sleep in and truly recover on Fridays.

"Don't you have another dress?" asked Cindy as Emily slipped into her all-purpose black number. "I know it's a Michael Kors, but still."

"Yes, but this one was a gift from my friends in Canada, and it goes everywhere."

"But don't you want to wear something different?"

"Not particularly. I don't dress up often, and then always with a different group of people, so no one knows that I'm wearing the same dress."

"You're not on tour, Em."

"I know. I keep meaning to bring some things from the house, but then I forget." She put on a little mascara and some of the clear sun-blocking lip balm that she used instead of lipstick. She had her mother's lips, which were naturally pink without help. While Cindy finished her makeup, Emily checked her email and Facebook pages.

"Oh, wonderful!"

"What?"

"Sam Wallenborn found a full sponsorship for Tani! Bicycle, uniforms, travel expenses, and everything."

"Who's Sam Wallenborn?"

"The coach of the CRC Team."

"Good news, isn't it?"

"Fantastic! Mrs. Jackson couldn't buy her anything, and the team was trying hard to line up a sponsor because sponsoring Tani costs more. Most riders at least have their own bikes and clothes at the junior level."

"Who is it?"

"Anonymous. Can you believe that? Someone just called Sam and made the offer."

"I'll bet they come out of the closet when she starts winning races like you."

"I'm not winning anything yet, just trying to crawl back."

"You will. I'm sure." Cindy took another look in the mirror.

"You ready?"

"Let's go."

The storm had blown over, leaving the air cool and fresh. Emily was grateful for the jacket that came with the dress. They walked down McCormick Road to Rugby Road. It wasn't a "Greek Row," but the neighborhood happened to have a prevalence of houses owned or leased by fraternities and sororities.

Preston's fraternity owned a big house facing the street. The trees in the front yard hid the Greek letters on the porch. Out front, a dozen students of both sexes stood outside, drinking from red plastic cups, and smoking.

Emily marveled at the girls who wore stiletto heels to these affairs when their shoes would sink into the red Virginia mud under the wet grass. She was glad that Cindy stayed on the concrete and led them straight to the door.

Preston was standing by the door. He took possession of Emily's roommate with a hug and a kiss on the lips, then waved at Emily.

"Make yourself at home. There's punch on the table—it shouldn't be spiked. The stronger stuff is in the kitchen."

"Thanks," said Emily. Preston steered Cindy toward the punch bowl.

Emily paused as usual. She counted fifteen boys, a dozen girls and a man in his midtwenties leaning on the banister of the stairs to the next floor. After a quick glance at her, everyone turned back to their conversations except the man at the stairs, who smiled and raised his glass. She chose to walk around the other side of the room, heading for the punch table.

"Emily!" a male voice called out from behind the front door. She recognized Peter Hawthorne from the UVA Cycling Club. Not one of the faster riders, probably because he missed so many training rides. He looked perfectly in context in a fraternity blazer, blue and orange bow tie, and boat shoes with no socks.

"Hi, Pete. I didn't know you pledged here."

"Not a secret. I haven't seen you at all except on the training rides."

"Between those and classes, I don't go out much. Cindy talked me into coming."

"Preston's Cindy?" Emily bristled at the suggestion, but looking at the two of them by the door to the back room, she could hardly blame Pete.

"Yeah. She's my roommate."

"Cool. Let me show you around."

Pete led her through the rooms of the main floor, introducing her to his brothers and a few of their friends. The appetizer table was well-stocked, but the traffic coming out of the kitchen with red plastic cups made it clear that the food was not the feature of the night.

"I thought alcohol was not allowed on Rugby Road."

"What can they really do about it? This is a private residence. To enforce anything, someone must file a complaint unless they catch you on the street itself." He motioned across the room. "Preston and Julius are the designated dry-guys, which satisfies the rule for sober supervision. Want some punch?" Pete handed her a plastic cup that he had just filled. It tasted sticky and sweet, like a soda fountain drink with too much syrup.

"You think they have some soda water?" Emily pointed toward the kitchen. "I'd like to cut this."

"Of course." They went to the kitchen. Pete took a two-liter bottle of seltzer from the refrigerator and topped off her cup.

"Much better. Thanks."

"You're welcome. Uh-oh. No one's manning the door. Would you excuse me?"

Emily raised her cup affirmatively and walked to the large room in the back of the house. That was the source of the music that was making everyone shout. She scanned the crowd—a half-dozen boys and girls dancing, and two couples chatting to the side.

"Want to dance?" the speaker on her right stood about her height. Black, wavy hair, pale skin and watery blue eyes. He looked earnest, hopeful even.

"Let's." Emily put her drink on the sideboard, and they moved into the crowd.

After two numbers, Emily danced with another boy, this one taller, with sandy hair, olive skin, and brown eyes. When the DJ started to spin a new song, she excused herself to go for her drink. As she approached the sideboard, she met the man who had been at the stairs. Clearly older than the others, Emily guessed that he was a graduate student. Brown hair and eyes, clean-shaven. He picked up the red plastic cup and said, "Is this yours?"

"It should be. Thanks." She sipped it. It seemed almost the same. *How many drinks were thinned down with soda like that? The difference might be the melted ice.* She took a deep drink and smiled uneasily at him.

"Nice party," she said, sipping her drink to avoid saying more.

"It is, but I find it stuffy in here. Would you like to step out back? The air is fresher because the smokers are all out front."

"Okay."

They made their way around the dance floor, Emily carefully looking around her. She felt a little strange. *It might be the air or the noise,* she thought.

He held the door for her, and she stepped out on the porch. The veranda stretched the width of the house but was only about eight feet deep. Directly in front of them, stairs led to the lawn out back. Emily saw two couples making out on the sofas to either side of the door. Then—

She woke up in a dark place. Branches scratched her face, and her back was wet from the ground beneath her. Her head was spinning, so for a while, she lay there, breathing deliberately and trying to grasp her surroundings. It was deathly quiet. No party. No passers-by. No normal street noise.

The frat house. The back yard. Bushes. She tried to shake her head, but that gave her a headache, and she almost threw up. Trying to identify the pain in her quads, she lay still until her head settled down.

Finally, she managed to roll over and rise on all fours. She crawled out from the bushes and found herself behind the frat house. It was dark. The doors were closed.

She took some deep breaths and used a rain gutter pipe to help herself up. The dizziness returned, but she knew that she had to move to get her blood going. She shivered; she had lost her little jacket. Looking down, she pulled her dress up to see why her quads hurt. In the dark, she thought she saw bruises—big bruises—on her thighs.

Breathing with some effort, she made her way to the side and then the front of the house. The yard was littered with bottles, cans, and red plastic cups.

Fighting dizziness, cold, and a crushing desire to sleep, she forced herself to walk to the street. She held on to the stone wall that ran by the sidewalk, making her way unsteadily downhill, toward the Beta Bridge. Near the brightly lit bridge, she saw an Ambassador SUV parked at right angles to the road. The Ambassadors, a private security service hired by the university to help students on the Corner, sat in the vehicle.

As she wobbled down the sidewalk, the driver got out of the car and walked toward her. He said something and looked concerned, but she could not hear him. She thought the streetlights dimmed.

଼ ଼ ଼

She woke up again. Bright lights. Intense blue eyes. High cheekbones.

"Hilda."

Broad smile. "Me again, Emily."

"What happened? Is this the ER?"

"Afraid so, but I'm not your nurse this time. Suzie Bennett was on duty, and she called me when you came in." Suzie came around Hilda, who stepped aside.

"It appears that you took in a dose of Ambien."

"Ambien's a tranquilizer. Why?"

"That's what we need to find out. You have some bruising on your legs, and your dress was torn. How do you feel now?"

"Not as dizzy as when I woke up before."

"Do you think you could talk to the detective? We think you may have been assaulted while unconscious."

"Like date rape?"

"Like that." Suddenly, Emily felt a surge of anger like she had never experienced in her life. She clenched her fists and struggled not to reach out and hit someone.

"I haven't even had a date yet and I get raped?!" The monitor by her bed started beeping. Suzie moved to the bed, but Hilda took Emily's hand on one hand and held her face close with the other hand.

"Easy, Em, the rape kit was negative," she said. "This is already serious enough. Let's not make it any worse. Can you talk to the police?"

Emily took a deep breath and forced herself to calm down. Her head did not hurt when she moved it.

"Can I see Mom and Dad first?"

"Let me see," said Suzie. She went outside. She came back with Katherine and Mark, and a man in a tweed jacket and a turtleneck, who stood back. Emily gave her mother's hand a squeeze and looked at Mark.

"Hi, Dad."

She asked Suzie, "How long have I been here?"

"About six hours. We checked you in at six thirty."

"Not the way I meant to sleep in on my recovery day." Hilda chuckled. Katherine smiled, but her eyes were still wet. Emily squeezed Katherine's hand again. "I'll be okay, Mom. Hilda's here." She lifted her head. "Is that the detective?"

He stepped up. "Lieutenant Hillsdale, Emily. May I ask you a few questions?"

"Yes. Let's do this." She still felt deep anger, moving darkly under her other feelings. The rage gave her purpose, a secret strength.

Suzie gently led Katherine and Mark out.

Hilda started to leave, but Emily called out, "Hilda, you're the expert on handling policemen." She winked. "Could you stay? And can we pull up some chairs? I have questions too."

Forty-five minutes later, they knew that someone had put Ambien in Emily's drink. She might have not passed out so deeply if she had not ridden so hard on training. The police lab found the drug in several other cups, but not in any of the punch bowls. A neighbor had called the police when the crowd out front started a loud drinking game.

The police broke up the party. By then, Emily must have been in the bushes because no one spotted her. When the police arrived, there was no one matching

Emily's description of the man who escorted her out back. Her would-be rapist had fled—or been apprehended in the confusion if he was not the man Emily described.

The hospital discharged Emily the next day. The news was full of the story of the bust, and the fraternity was suspended pending a university and police investigation. There was no mention of Emily or the attempted rape in the media, for which Emily was grateful.

Katherine wanted her to stay home, but Emily asked to return to her room at least at first. She hoped that focusing on midterm exams the following week would help her get back to normal.

Cindy was sitting cross-legged on her bed with her computer when Emily pushed through the door.

"Hi. I bet you had a good time, staying out the whole next day," she said. "Did you hear what happened after you left?"

Emily paused, confused, then slowly shook her head.

"The party got busted by the cops. It's in all the papers and on TV. There was even a picture of Preston being escorted by the police. I spent hours in the police station with the others, and only got back here at three in the morning."

"I'm sorry, Cindy. Are you okay?"

"No, I'm not okay!" Her eyes started welling. "Preston was an animal. He tore my dress before we even got cozy in his room. Then he ran when the police showed up. I thought he was in charge. I hadn't even gotten dressed completely when policemen came into the room! I've never been so embarrassed in my life!"

Emily stared at her roommate in amazement. Cindy noticed her silence.

"So, did you meet someone, after all? Where's your black dress?"

After a pause, Emily said, "Yes, I did, but I got in an accident and it was ruined. These are some things from home."

"Omigod! What happened?"

"I fell off a motorbike and bruised my legs. They'll heal. I can ask for a new dress for Christmas. What are you working on?"

"Chemistry. I should have saved that for second semester."

"Well, I'm worried about all my subjects. I don't feel like the A student I was."

"I hear that a lot around here. Most of us were top of our class, weren't we?"

"And now we're just a bunch of stupid first-years," Emily said.

She put the small bag she brought from home into her closet and booted up her computer. There would be time to tell Cindy the truth later.

40

GARRETT STREET

"Remember, tomorrow's a half day," Dr. Osborne said as he and Hilda tidied up their respective offices. "Doris stays behind to do paperwork, which she could never keep up with unless we leave her alone."

"You're going to visit your shut-ins, right?"

Reginald came out of his office, shrugging on his coat. "That's right."

"Why don't I come along?"

"No need. These patients never come here."

"You're paying me for a full workweek, and I'm curious. Would there be a problem?"

The doctor stopped and turned toward his nurse coming out. He did not answer right away.

"No. I don't think so. If you insist."

"I do. Thanks."

"Remember your walking shoes." He smiled and held the door for her. Hilda walked home, going left toward Cherry Avenue. It was a little longer than West Main Street, but she tried to be unpredictable about her commute.

A half-dozen men of various ages were drinking beer on the steps of the gas station on the corner of Cherry Avenue and Roosevelt Brown Boulevard. As she turned toward West Main Street, they hooted some catcalls and chanted "Oreo, Oreo, oh, so sweet-oh!"

She tried to ignore them, but her anger was building as she forced herself not to speed up. No one came any closer—she would have welcomed that—and slowly, the chant died off. She had been called that before, and she understood where it came from, but she still bristled at the insult.

When she opened the door to the apartment, she heard Bedřich Smetana's *The Moldau* on the stereo. Jack came out with a smile but halted.

"You look ready to take someone down." He backed up a little. Hilda let out a breath and her pent-up fury. She hugged him and gave him a kiss.

"I'm not taking you down that way. I didn't realize that I was still wearing my rage."

"What happened?"

"Nothing serious. A bunch of guys drinking beer on the corner shouted catcalls and insults as I walked by. No one came close."

"But you're still in your proactive striking mode."

"Something like that." She kissed him again. "Have you drunk all the beer yet?"

They each took a bottle of pilsner to the living room. There was only a bit of the pink behind the Blue Ridge Mountains. It was gone by the time they got comfortable.

"So why did this gang get to you?"

"Maybe because I'm more aware of how closely the local community has been watching me. It's disconcerting sometimes. I've been called 'Oreo' before Charlottesville, but I heard it twice in the last week."

"Does this have to do with me?"

"No. You don't call someone 'Oreo' just for having a white boyfriend. It means that I'm not one of them. I'm only black on the outside."

They watched the Pegasus helicopter come low over the neighboring houses, making its approach to the helipad at the UVA Medical Center. When it dropped out of sight, Jack looked at her.

"The problem is that you *are* white on the inside. You're the spitting image of your mother, even her eyes and the long, fine hair. You just got a special paint job at the factory."

"But it's what they see, and they judge me."

"I get more bad vibes about us from my white acquaintances than from blacks."

Hilda sighed. "I've never felt so foreign in my life as I have in my own country."

"Only one of your countries, *meine Geliebte*."

"I would feel more at home in Kaiserslautern, but I don't want to move back. I love this country, dammit!"

"I wish people could see you the way I do when we kiss."

"You can't see me. You close your eyes."

"True."

Hilda thought about that for a while. Then she leaned over and gave him a long, lingering kiss. "Thanks."

"For what?"

"For seeing me as I am. I love that."

The next day, Jack rode off to Rivanna Station. Hilda walked to work.

She was looking forward to the afternoon rounds. She remembered fondly the German grandmothers (and occasional grandfathers) who had seen so much and had such incredible tales to tell. She wondered if this would be like that.

Of course, here, there had been Jim Crow; there, it was the struggle to recover from the Nazi era. Here, she had to pay attention to detect the signs of systemic racism; there, reminders of the Allied bombing were evident in the ruins and in the shiny new cities rising from the ashes. The division of East and West Germany through the Cold War never let them forget.

She realized that while the army had taught her the rudiments of being black in America, it had also shielded her from the realities. She had learned code-switching between languages, but not between cultures. Her language, attitudes, and bearing matched the army's expectations but were essentially mainstream European-American—as Jack had told her.

With thoughts like these, she reached the porch of the house on Ridge Street to find the door still locked. She almost walked around to the garage, when she spotted Dr. Osborne's familiar figure walking up the sidewalk.

"Good morning, Hilda." He dug into his coat pocket and extracted a ring of keys. "Anxious today?"

"I was thinking of the rounds this afternoon and walked faster than I meant to." He held the door for her again. "These old people must have some incredible stories to tell."

"They're not all old, but many do have stories. Some will share. Some won't."

"I'll follow your lead." They hung up their coats in their respective rooms. "Want me to start the coffee?"

"Would you, please? I need to make a few calls and double-check the appointments. There's one I'm worried about."

Hilda went to the kitchen/break room and turned on the coffee maker. As she came back, he called out from the reception area. "The Pfizer and Novartis reps are coming this morning. They'll be bringing us samples. One has a new drug that has just been approved for Alzheimer's. I talked to Dr. Hogan at Martha Jefferson about it. It might work for Louisa Jackson's mother."

"Taniqua's grandmother?"

"Yes. You know her?"

"No. I know Tani through Emily. I met Louisa, but no one mentioned a grandmother."

"For some, that is part of why I make these rounds."

At eight thirty, Doris arrived and took over the reception desk.

The Pfizer representative arrived at eight forty-five, toting two Samsonite suitcases full of samples. She rolled them into the doctor's office while Hilda disarmed the alarm and unlocked the pharmacy closet. The rep was a stunning woman in a blue business suit, her blonde hair in a ponytail and her feet in conservative, but stylish pumps. Her good looks were an asset in a field where most buyers were still men, but Ms. Everett's knowledge of pharmacology matched her appearance.

As the doctor and the sales rep ran through the inventory, the woman had in-depth quantitative data to answer Osborne's many questions. Hilda knew that he kept up with the research, but she was always impressed by how broad a scope a general practitioner had to cover; this man read it all and in depth.

It took a half hour to discuss the new drugs, only a small portion of the load. It took another ten minutes for Hilda and Dr. Osborne to stow the contents of the two suitcases in the closet. Most were samples of ordinary drugs in production. Ms. Everett took charge of her empty suitcases and thanked Dr. Osborne.

At nine forty-five, the Novartis rep appeared, an equally smart Puerto Rican named Manuela Sanchez with two suitcases. The routine was almost identical to the ritual with Pfizer, but Ms. Sanchez had the new Alzheimer's drug, which extended the conversation by five minutes.

When she left at ten twenty-five, the closet was completely full. Hilda locked it and set the alarm. She put another pot of coffee on and came back to the doctor's office.

"I'm amazed at the amount of product they left you."

Osborne smiled. "Can you imagine having to stock that cabinet out of my business account?"

"How do they get away with it?"

"They don't 'get away' with anything, Hilda. They must distribute a quota of samples every month. Most of the doctors they visit only want the latest, hard-to-find drugs. Their patients have prescription insurance—like your Tricare for Life. The whole idea is to write prescriptions. Most of our patients would never have the prescriptions filled."

Hilda said, "Let me guess. They're delighted to have someplace to leave the quota each month."

He smiled and pointed to the kitchen. They walked down for refills before the first patients arrived.

With only four patients, they had everyone out, and the office closed by noon. The three of them had lunch in the kitchen, the first time they had been able to sit together all week.

"First off, Hilda," said the doctor, "when we're alone, I'm Reginald or Reggie. We only use titles in public. Many of the patients expect it."

"Do you see much of each other outside the office? I haven't seen either of you."

They explained that they had gone to school together and grown up in the neighborhood. As two of the few kids who went to college, they stayed in touch, with Doris teaching Reggie's two boys and he delivering her son and daughter. The children had grown up and lived all over the country. His wife died ten years earlier.

Reginald and Doris both went to Zion First African Baptist Church, where Doris was one of the soloists. They were surprised that Hilda attended Saint Paul's Memorial.

"We have a close relationship with Saint Paul's," said the doctor. "We worship together on Wednesdays in Lent and join for musical events at other times."

"How did you end up there?" asked Doris.

"I grew up Episcopalian. My father was Church of England before he emigrated to the US. My mother is *altkatholische*, which is a German church in the Anglican Communion. That and the music made Saint Paul's a perfect match for me."

Doris and Reginald exchanged glances.

"The music is beautiful, I agree," he said, "and the space has wonderful acoustics." The conversation shifted to the afternoon rounds.

"We have about two dozen shut-ins," Reggie said. "If I can see a half dozen every week, I can visit everyone once a month."

"They'd love you to come by more than that," said Doris. She got up and washed out her lunch container. The others put leftovers away and cleaned up too.

Reginald set a brisk pace as they walked the block to Garrett Street and began visiting homes in the multifamily row houses on either side.

"First stop is Jesse Benson." He pointed to the next house on the right. "Mr. Benson is only seventy-four, but arthritis attacked his hips and knees together. That and a heart attack two months ago have left him unable to walk even with a walker—until his heart gets better."

"Was he healthy before?"

"Depends on who you ask. He got cancer from Agent Orange exposure in Vietnam and recovered. I think it took more out of his system than even he admits. The Veterans Administration disability benefits on top of his Social Security leave him better off than some—at least the VA buys his meds and follows up on his health care when he can get out there. But the VA doesn't make house calls."

"So, he isn't actually a patient of yours."

"His family brings him to us for everything. Taking him to the VA clinic is a hardship for them. His daughter and son-in-law both work, and their little ones don't drive yet. Still, the VA will take care of the major problems, which would break them financially."

"Was he army?"

"Sergeant in the 101st Airborne when he was wounded and brought out."

A woman of indeterminate age with gray hair and a tired expression opened the door. The smile she gave the doctor took ten years off her appearance.

"Hello, Rachel. This is Nurse Paisley. Hilda, Rachel Madison."

"I live next door. When everyone is out, I stay with Mr. Benson."

"Is he awake?"

She nodded and motioned them inside.

Hilda scanned the room. The house was tidy and clean, though the furniture was well-worn. A shadow box with army decorations and patches occupied a conspicuous place on the sideboard, surrounded by framed photos of family.

The bed on the far wall held a thin man sitting propped up on pillows. His skin was drawn tight over his face and the blood vessels and sinews of his neck. His hair was snow-white, cut short. His smile showed a set of white teeth in excellent condition.

"Dr. Osborne! You're a sight for these eyes. Come in, come in!"

"How are you doing, Mr. Benson?"

"Same as last month, but I can make it to the latrine with a little help now." He looked up at Hilda. "What have you brought me today, Doc? This is an angel."

"This is Nurse Paisley, Mr. Benson. She started this week, and she asked to come around today."

Benson stuck out his hand. His grip was firm. His eyes peered deeply as if going for her soul. "Pleased to meet you, Nurse. You seem like a sturdy one. I wish you'd been around when I needed you."

"I understand you served with the 101st Airborne."

"That's right."

"Mind if we take your vital signs?" asked Dr. Osborne. He gestured to Hilda, who pulled a stethoscope out of her coat pocket. She rubbed it on her jacket to warm it up.

"Go ahead. The arm's sticking out already." Benson grinned at Hilda. "You're worth an extra twenty points on the blood pressure, you know."

Hilda smiled at him and stuck a thermometer in his mouth while she took his blood pressure.

"145/95, 98.6."

"Thank you, Nurse. Let me see if his heart sounds any different than last month." Dr. Osborne pulled his stethoscope from an inside pocket and checked the patient carefully.

"Mr. Benson, can you sit up on the edge of the bed?"

It was obviously painful, but he managed to sit up, then slide his legs to the edge of the bed. The effort left him breathing heavily for a minute. Dr. Osborne checked him while sitting upright. Then he had Hilda ease his legs back into bed. Benson clearly enjoyed her attention.

"Our medic was a skinny teenager and almost couldn't lift his own pack. That didn't even hurt this time." He winced as he shuffled back into a sitting position. "Where'd you get those eyes, Nurse? They're amazing."

"My mother, sir."

"Bring her around, Doc. I could fall in love again!"

Hilda smiled and tucked him in.

After checking on his supply of medicines and making sure that he was taking them, Dr. Osborne and Hilda made their excuses and left.

"Mrs. Dunleavy won't be so pleasant," said Reginald as they approached another home. "She's eighty-five, obese, diabetic, opinionated, and bossy. She's a hopeless gossip, which has its good and bad side because she invites neighbors in to trade dirt. Having company staves off depression, but also feeds her ugly side, which is the dislike of those on the nastier side of the gossip."

"Do I detect a warning about me?"

"Maybe. Let's find out."

He rang the bell. A young woman in a McDonald's uniform answered the door. "Dr. Osborne. Thank you for coming. Mom said she'd be here, but she's running late, and I gotta go to work."

"Will she be long?"

"She's on the bus, so I guess twenty minutes or so."

"You go to work, Becky. Nurse Paisley and I will stay with your grandmother until she arrives."

"Thanks! Nice to meet you, Nurse Paisley." Becky rushed out the door and walked quickly west.

"She works on Ridge-McIntire Street until ten o'clock. Becky's mother works seven to two. Becky's daughter gets home from school at four. So, the home care is usually covered if something doesn't go wrong with the buses in the afternoon. Fortunately, little Shiara is a bright, solid girl. She needs less minding than our patient."

"Any fathers around?"

"Nope. Four generations of single Dunleavy's."

"What about the gossipy friends?" she asked as they let themselves in the open door.

"Evenings sometimes, but mostly weekends. They work too."

Hilda paused in the entrance. The house was identical to the Benson home and just as tidy. Dr. Osborne walked to the stairs.

"Mrs. Dunleavy?" he shouted as he climbed. "Dr. Osborne for you."

"Reggie! Come on up!"

In the first bedroom at the head of the stairs, Mariah Dunleavy occupied most of a queen-sized bed. She seemed lively and well enough except for her enormous mass—skin smooth, hair gray, but cut neatly short. She had a TV remote in her pudgy hands, which she used to turn off the large-screen television on the wall opposite. She gave the doctor a broad smile and waved them into the room.

"Hello, Mrs. Dunleavy. I brought my new nurse with me. Mariah Dunleavy, this is Hilda Paisley."

The large woman scowled. She ignored Hilda's outstretched hand. Hilda withdrew it.

"I know about you." She looked at Dr. Osborne. "Why'd you bring her here?"

"She's my nurse." Reginald Osborne bristled and scowled back. Mariah Dunleavy seemed stunned. After a brief stare down, she lost her own scowl and dropped her gaze.

Hilda was shocked but kept her face expressionless. She moved back by the door to let the doctor examine the woman. Hilda's emotions ran in different directions beneath the surface as she occasionally caught Mariah frowning at her. She recognized the taming of a bully in her boss's subduing of his patient, but she also knew that most bullies hid insecurities and misunderstandings.

"We're going to check behind you," he said at one point. "Nurse, give me a hand, please."

"I don't want her touching me!"

"Can you do it by yourself, Mrs. Dunleavy? Your daughter isn't home yet."

Hilda touched the doctor on his arm. "Let me talk to her a moment." He stood back. Hilda walked up close to the woman and said, "Mrs. Dunleavy, just what is your problem with me?"

Mariah scowled at her. Hilda held her gaze, and the woman's expression shifted to fear.

"Don't like Oreos. The cookies or the other."

"Is that it?"

"Think you're too good for your kind. Living on the white side of town, hanging with white folk. You don't even know your own here."

Hilda smiled gently and said, "Mrs. Dunleavy, I *am* an Oreo, and I know it. Unlike most of the people you know, I was born an Oreo. Do you even know where I'm from?" Mariah shook her head. "Germany. I'm not even African-American. I'm African-German."

"But—"

"I saw the steins on the mantle downstairs. Have you ever met a German?"

"Yes. I worked in a Bavarian restaurant long ago."

"Try this, Mrs. Dunleavy. Close your eyes and listen."

Mariah looked at the doctor, who nodded. She shut her eyes. Reginald stared silently at his nurse.

"Before you open your eyes, imagine what I might look like if you had only heard me on the telephone, without ever seeing me. *Gut tag, meine Frau. Wie geht es ihnen heute? Ich bin eine Krankenschwester.* Now, with your eyes shut, describe the person on the other end of the phone."

Mariah Dunleavy squeezed her eyes. She was silent for a while, then let out a sigh.

"You sound like my first boss's daughter. Tall, straw-blonde, blue eyes, a little gawky, even clumsy."

"Skin color?"

"White, of course."

"Of course. Open your eyes." Mariah did and looked straight into Hilda's. "You pretty much described my mother."

"And your father?"

"Grew up in London. His family was from Rhodesia in Africa. My father was brought to the US as a teenager and became a citizen by enlisting in the US Army. We lived all over the world, but he retired to my mother's hometown, and I grew up there.

"I came back to the US to join the army myself. In many ways, it's an Oreo outfit, so I fit right in. I only just retired from the army."

Hilda and Mariah stared at each other for a long time. Hilda breathed steadily and quietly. Mariah opened her mouth twice, blinked, then shut it as if biting something. Reginald watched, immobile by the wall.

Finally, Mariah let out a long sigh, closed her eyes. She shook her head, then opened her eyes to look at Hilda.

"I'm sorry, Nurse Paisley. Please accept my apologies."

"Accepted. I'm still learning how to be black in America."

Hilda and Reggie got her turned over. Reggie verified that she was not developing bedsores and that her skin was healthy. Hilda noticed that the sheets were clean and wondered how the family got the linen changed. Just as they finished turning her back, the front door slammed.

"Hey, Mom, I'm home!" A strong voice from downstairs.

"Up here, sweetie. Dr. Osborne and Nurse Paisley are here."

In walked a middle-aged woman in a housekeeper's uniform from the University Housing Division. She was still out of breath. "I ran from the bus. Thank God you're here," she said to Dr. Osborne.

"It's okay, Marian. We had a most interesting visit with your mother, didn't we?"

"We sure did. You come back any time, Nurse Paisley."

Out on the street, Dr. Osborne let out a long breath.

"You had me worried there. That was brilliant. How did you think of that?"

"I didn't. My friend Jack did. Yesterday, some guys were chanting 'Oreo' at me. I knew what they meant, and it angered me. He pointed out how I really was white inside and helped me understand why."

"I could tell that your behavior and accent were natural, so I figured your family was Jamaican or something like that. Doris and I have been wondering."

They had time for three more patients, these on the other side of the street. They were in late stages of Alzheimer's. While Hilda checked their vitals and examined them physically, Reginald held their hands and told them fairy tales from their childhood.

"Will we visit Louisa Jackson's mother?"

"I saw her last week. Let's call it a day."

They walked back to the office. Hilda set up the coffee maker for the next day. They left their medical instruments in their offices.

"Good evening, Hilda. Thanks for coming today."

"Thank you for letting me come along, Reggie."

He smiled and held the door for her.

41

THANKSGIVING

ON MONDAY NIGHT, EMILY TOLD CINDY WHAT HAD HAPPENED on Rugby Road. To her surprise, Cindy took it calmly, apologizing for having been so selfish over the weekend when Emily first came back to the room.

Emily could not train after the attempted rape. *I need to study for midterms anyway*, she told herself.

In fact, she was hanging on by an emotional thread. During the day, she jumped at sudden sounds and found herself getting tense in crowds. At night, she tossed around, sleeping in fits. She struggled to appear normal.

"Is this like PTSD?" she asked Hilda, who stopped by after work each evening for the first two weeks.

"Some of it is your reaction to Ambien. The rest is PTSD. The *T* is for trauma. There are many kinds of trauma."

"How do I get over this?"

Hilda sat on her bed. Cindy had stopped studying to listen.

"You probably both need to hear this." She took a breath. "I never forget my first attempted rape. The drill instructor I told you about."

"There were more?" Emily gasped.

"Like I told you then, he was the last to get anywhere. The rest were attempted assaults. You watched me put down drunks and untrained would-be *jihadis* this summer. In the army, some fought back, and I took some hits."

Cindy's eyes were so wide, they almost looked crossed. Hilda went on.

"You won't forget this, either, Em. The question is how to go forward from here. Will it disable you? Leave you scarred?"

Emily's gazed went to her lap, then up. "You took martial arts right away. Became proactive."

"I did. I was still assaulted, as you saw in Atlantic City. In the army, I built a reputation for my 'look, don't touch' rule."

"Rule number one."

Hilda smiled. "The rule made it hard to score a date if I wanted one, but I didn't mind. When I did meet a guy I liked, it would be someone like Jack."

Emily chuckled. "Jack would be worth skipping the others for."

Hilda reached over and held Emily's wrist. "What are you going to do?"

"I'm not sure."

"How are exams going?"

"Not great. We're halfway through, and I got Bs in everything except French."

"You realize that you're coping already?"

"I am?"

"Yes. You're not exploding into tears. You're managing to study and take the tests, so those Bs are actually victories, this soon after the attack."

"She's awesome, I think," said Cindy. "If I hadn't seen her doing those breathing drills in the room after class, I'd never have known."

"Will it get better?" Emily asked.

"I can't say. We all react differently to our traumas. But judging from what I've seen, you should recover well. You kept your cool with Lieutenant Hillsdale. You don't seem to be focusing on anger or revenge. You're not having nightmares."

"What about this panicky feeling when there are lots of people around?"

"I felt something like that anytime one of the DI's was near, which in boot camp was all the time. I had to grit my teeth and focus until we graduated. Ever since, I try to avoid the middle of a crowd. I favor the edges of a room."

"I noticed."

"But I don't have that panicky reaction anymore. I just prefer to be where I can see better."

"And case the room before you step in."

"That helps."

"Thanks, Hilda. I can't believe how lucky I am to have you as a friend."

"It works both ways, Em. I wouldn't have survived the summer without you." She gave Emily a long, strong hug. "I'll stop by tomorrow." She nodded to Cindy with a smile and left them.

Emily let out a deep sigh and turned back to her computer. She clicked Spotify back on, and the strains of Berlioz's *Symphonie Pathétique* filled the silence. She brought up the Calculus text and found the place she was studying. She noticed that Cindy was still staring dumbfounded at her.

"What?"

"She 'wouldn't have survived the summer'? What was that?"

"We just looked after each other." Emily smiled. "Ask her tomorrow."

଼ ଼ ଼

Emily and Cindy survived midterm examinations. As they packed for fall break, Brianna came in.

"I thought you might like to know that the boy who tripped outside your room on Move-In night won't be back. Turns out the two sets of parents were not pleased. They decided that community college close to home would allow them to focus on their studies better." She paused in the doorway. "Enjoy yourselves. See you next week."

଼ ଼ ଼

On a dreary Wednesday in November, Hilda and Reginald walked back from the Jackson home. Taniqua's grandmother had improved, and she was able to join the family for special occasions downstairs.

It had stopped raining, but the wind was bitterly cold. Hilda carried the black bag with the instruments and medicines.

As they reached the corner near the office, two men in their late teens came the other way, eyes fixed on the black bag, hands deep in the pockets of their football jackets. They blocked the sidewalk.

Hilda recognized one of them from the crew that hung around the gas station, drinking beer in the afternoons.

"You got the goody bag today," he said, putting out his hand for her to pass him the bag. His other hand was gripping something in the pocket.

Reginald straightened up. Hilda passed the bag to the doctor and stepped forward.

"You're blocking the sidewalk."

"Just gimme the bag, bitch."

"It doesn't work that way." She saw him begin to pull his other hand out. She grabbed his extended arm, pulled him into her fist as she kneed him, then laid her fist to his temple. As he went limp, she shoved him into the other man. She had her foot on the younger one's arm before he could get up.

She dropped, pulled him over, and pinned him there.

"Call 911, please," she said to Reginald, reaching for the black bag.

While Reginald pulled out his cell phone and called, she took out some bandage tape from the bag and bound the younger one's wrists. Then she turned to the one she recognized and touched the outside of his pocket. He had a pistol. She left it there, and wrapped tape around him, binding him like a straitjacket. She checked his pulse and said to the doctor, "Pulse is strong. Breathing normal. He'll wake up soon."

A siren wailed up Water Street coming closer. Hilda motioned to the approaching cruiser. Reggie bent over to check the unconscious man. "Shakwan," he said, shaking his wrist. Shakwan woke up while the officers were getting out of their car.

Five minutes later, Shakwan was swearing loudly as the police took him in an ambulance to the ER at UVA. The other man got a free ride to the city jail in the police cruiser. Lieutenant Hillsdale showed up to take their statements.

"Oh, hell," said Hilda, looking out the window from the hallway. The Channel 4 news truck was pulling up. She turned to the detective, who was sitting in the reception area, taking notes. "Can I get away with a 'no comment'—or even slip out downstairs?"

Hillsdale looked at Osborne, who pointed to the door to the garage. "Can we limit this to 'Dr. Osborne and his nurse'?" asked the doctor. "Her name will trigger all kinds of stuff on the internet."

"We'll try," said the detective. He waved at Hilda. "Quick, get out of here."

Hilda ran downstairs. She put on her helmet and mounted the bike inside the garage. She rolled out under the rising door, took a right, and headed away from Ridge Street. She had to walk the bike behind a neighboring lot and along the right of way for the railroad, but she was able to make it home unobserved.

Of course, the neighborhood south of the tracks knew the full story before the six-o'clock news, but a quick word from Reginald to one of the basses in the choir kept Hilda's name out of the TV news that night.

The young reporter from the *Daily Progress* did not think to interview everyone or ask for the nurse's name. He made Reginald appear to be the hero. Shakwan did not have a concussion, so he was released to the police the next day.

ೞ ೞ ೞ

For Thanksgiving, Hilda and Jack joined Emily and the Dempseys on Brandywine Drive.

"I'm afraid to ask how you two are doing," said Mark as he poured a Barboursville Pinot Grigio. "It's almost too exciting when you're around."

"The robbers were cousins of the Monroes," said Emily. "Fran was seriously pissed, but not surprised. Did you and Dr. Osborne know them?"

"He did, and I recognized Shakwan, though I didn't know his name at the time."

Jack asked, "One of the Oreo chorus?" Hilda nodded.

"At least this time, your face didn't go viral on the internet."

"Thank goodness for that," said Hilda. "Everyone in town seems to know, but the media and the police kept my name out of it, so this won't bring up Chicago again on Google searches."

"That's twice you've managed to dodge the spotlight," Mark said. "I hope your luck continues." He took a moment to refill glasses. "Are you enjoying NGIC, Major?" he asked with a humorous emphasis on the rank.

"Actually, yes, so I don't regret flunking Retirement 101. Ask me again at Christmas."

"What's up, or is that classified?"

"It is, but I can tell you that I will be out of town some. I love to travel, but these won't be Disney cruises."

"Are you going to be okay?" asked Katherine.

"Probably. We'll find out if the medical board at Walter Reed was right."

"You'll be fine, dear," said Hilda. "On the other hand, how are you doing, Em?"

"After your talk in my room, I got better. Thinking before I step into a crowd has helped. Casing the room was a habit. I slept all through the night last week. That Ambien was powerful stuff, but I think it's finally worn off."

"Have you started training?"

"Tuesday, I went on the group ride. I got my rhythm back almost right away. Next week, I'll join Mariana and the team."

"Looks like we've a lot to be thankful for," said Katherine, "including that I didn't burn the roast. Shall we?"

They adjourned to the dining room. The feast lasted late into the night, including a walk in the bracing evening air before returning to the house. The five friends relived the adventures of the last year and filled in the stories from the time before Emily and Hilda met again in Charlottesville. They basked in the warmth of good friendship, keenly grateful for each other's presence in their lives.

They slept deeply and peacefully that night, knowing that whatever the future held, they would be there for each other.

THE END

Author's Note

Dear Reader,

Emily, Hilda, and Jack have more adventures ahead. In addition to the usual reminders that all the characters are fictional and any resemblance to real persons is coincidental, let me accept full responsibility for any errors you may have uncovered.

Reviews, both good and bad, are the lifeblood of a book after it is published. Please take a moment to comment on the book with the retailer you bought it from, or on any book sites or social media that you follow.

Feel free to send me feedback directly, especially to point out errors that I can address in the future books: jt@jthine.com. Thanks in advance.

Smooth roads & tailwinds,
JT Hine